Rika's Rooms

Gail Louw

First published in 2022
By Waterloo Press (Hove)
95 Wick Hall
Furze Hill
BN3 1NG

Text and associated E-Editions text © Gail Louw 2021 All rights remain with the author

Cover image, @Gail Louw

Gail Louw is hereby identified as author of this work in accordance with Section 77 of the Copyright, Designs and Patents Act 1988

This book is sold subject to the condition that it shall not, by way of trade or otherwise, be lent, resold, hired out or otherwise circulated without the author's prior consent in any form or binding or cover other than that in which it is published and without a similar condition being imposed on the subsequent purchaser

Copyright © 2022 Gail Louw

All rights reserved.

ISBN: 9798335252904

DEDICATION

This book is dedicated to my wonderful daughter Nicky,
reminiscent in all the best ways of her beloved grandmother.

Also by Gail Louw

Plays:
Blonde Poison
The Ice Cream Boys
The Good Dad (A Love Story)
The Only White

Gail Louw: Collected Plays:
Blonde Poison
Miss Dietrich Regrets
Shackelton's Carpenter
Two Sisters

Gail Louw: Plays Two:
Duwayne
The Mitfords
The Half-Life of Love
Joe Ho Ho

Gail Louw: Plays Three:
The Ice Cream Boys
Being Brahms
A Life Twice Given
Killing Faith

Praise for *Rika's Rooms*

'A Powerful and Compassionate Read. I loved this book and am still thinking about it nearly a year after I first read it. It appeals on so many levels as it melds together the history and politics of this extraordinary woman's experiences as she travels across continents with the personal: her descent into dementia and the impact on her family around her' *Lord Peter Hain*

'This is a 'must' read! A wonderful book written by a very talented and deeply charismatic author' *Fiona Why*

'A Tender Biographical Novel about Dementia' *Naomi Pitkeathly*

'A compelling read. It is a deeply touching story told with love and sensitivity. Highly recommended' *Brenda Gourley*

'Rika's Rooms is a fascinating and moving story that takes the reader to many places. I normally take ages to read a book - but I couldn't put this book down. I read the book in its entirety over a couple of days. It is a wonderful book and I would thoroughly recommend it as a good read' *Audrey Ardern-Jones*

'Gail has produced a real page turner' *Hayden Kendler*

'A must for the modern reader. It's hard to believe that Rika's Rooms is a debut novel. The structure, the plotting, the multi-layered story-telling, the detailed characterizations, the sense of history on the turn; all these come with the assurance of a practised novelist. In particular the way Louw navigates the tricky path of a hybrid fiction/non-fiction memoir, and gets a diverse web of connections to hang together, is most impressive' *RC*

Praise for *Rika's Rooms*

'I knew Gail Louw as a talented playwright, but am bowled over by her as a novelist' *Mrs R Mann*

'Very Insightful It is a story of 'oral' history presented in a unique and gripping way' *Monika L*

'A Compelling Story. A great read evoking pre- war Berlin, Palestine kibbutz life, Tel Aviv, South Africa and the south coast of England, where Rika lives in two worlds' *Jacquenetta Sherred*

'Fascinating story. Highly recommended. Having read the book and seen the play quite recently, I can highly recommend both' *Brad*

'Poignant and Personal. This is a warm and heartbreaking and extremely powerful read' *Natasha Warburton*

'Rika's Rooms is a truly remarkable book. The timespan it covers, the range of societies and politics it encompasses and, perhaps most of all, the heart-rending depiction of dementia, make it an unforgettable read' *Stras Mastoris*

'Beautifully crafted but tortuously tragic and desperately sad. A deeply personal story of love, hurt, courage and survival. Escape from Nazi persecution, a rollercoaster ride via kibbutz life in Israel/Palestine to the underground struggle against apartheid. There in South Africa marriage creaking, imprisonment, fleeing into exile and finally the cruelest of climaxes: the onset of dementia. 'Why did I carry on living beyond my life, into a living death?' - the bitter epitaph to a life well lived' *Lord Peter Hain*

ACKNOWLEDGMENTS

Thank you to my amazing family; husband Peter, son Peter and daughter-in-law Hortance, grandchildren Savannah, Sasha and Larichia. And to Nicky, Nick, Lily and Cleo. Also to my brother Brian and sister-in-law Helen and their children and grandchildren. And Peter's sons Andrew and Michael and family.

Thanks to Jill and John Harris for creating the artwork for the cover, and for all their support.

Thanks to Claire Dyer and to the Literacy Consultancy for early editorial work.

Thank you to my early readers; Peter Samuels, Peter Louw, Beverly Cohen, Helen Levy, Jacque Sherred, Jenny Priestman, Brenda Gourley, Sylvia Schwartzkopf, Tania Funston, Derek Louw, Louise Comb, Naomi Pitkeathly, Jenny Brown, Annie Feltham.

Rika's Rooms

Rika's Rooms

Prologue

I know this house. It is full of rooms. It's bright and the colours make me feel warm: maroon, red, orange, blue.

There are carpets on the walls and pictures I recognise. My pictures, pictures that belonged to me, that were mine once before in a time and place that isn't now.

Now is a time that doesn't belong to me either, but I'm here and these people are smiling because they're happy I'm here, in their time, in their place.

They don't know me. They think they do, they're sure they do. But they don't. They think I'm kind and loving, that I wouldn't hurt a fly and that I'm still me, because I laugh. They see me laugh and think everything must be alright in her strange, unfathomable, changeable world. They don't know my world is a jumble of sorrow and anger and regret.

They say, she's not herself, she's not the person she was. Well obviously she's not, they say, she wouldn't be, would she, not in her condition. But they don't know me, so how can they say?

She's had a wonderful life, they say, loving and loved. Though maybe they don't realise synchronicity might have been an issue here.

Images pass through my head, people and events, and words, words like, betrayal, infidelity, murder. Are they part of a wonderful life?

I don't know these rooms.

1

Vati and I are walking down the road hand in hand. I'm skipping to keep up with his long strides. It's a small street, not one of those big, long ones, majestic ones, like Unter den Linden.

He fetched me from school and we're walking and I'm skipping and telling him all about my day at school and telling him some words in English which we learnt today in our English lesson and we meet Herr Neumann coming the other way.

He stops and he and Vati have a little chat and I think, I'm in the middle of telling him things and they're interrupting, but I don't say anything because that would be rude and Mutti and Vati always tell me, to be rude is to be unpleasant and to be unpleasant is to be unlovable so I have to be pleasant if I want people to like me.

After a few moments, Herr Neumann moves on and we move on and I carry on telling Vati the English words I know, even the sentence we learnt and repeated to each other; I'm nine years old. How old are you?

Suddenly Vati slows down and he stops and I look at his face and he has become ashen. I look where he's looking and I see a group of boys wearing brown uniforms and laughing and jostling each other. And I see them stop and look at us and point and start to run towards us.

Vati pushes me into the wall and stands in front of me and we stand and we wait and I can feel Vati pushing against me so hard that I put my hands out on the wall to stop myself being squashed into it.

I hear the sound of the running boots and it gets closer and closer and suddenly, the boots carry on, they pass us and Vati moves away and I'm free of his body.

He looks at me and he laughs and says, 'My God, I thought they were,' but he stops because he's still watching them and he sees what's happening. They're hitting and pushing and beating poor Herr Neumann. I hear them shout 'Jewish vermin,' and they're kicking him as he falls on the floor and we stand, still.

We don't do anything but stand and watch as they kick and kick and kick.

Edith and I are sitting on our wall at our home, Dortmunder Strasse 3.

Some friends of Edith's from her youth movement come by and she tells me to 'Go away!'

Bloody cheek, I think. No, I also want to speak to them and hear what they say. I'm not a baby, I'm twelve and she's only fifteen. Or maybe sixteen because she's three and three-quarter years older than me.

'Just a moment while I get rid of the baby,' she says laughing to the others.

Look at her laughing, she's so, spiteful. It's fine and dandy when it's just me but as soon as others come, she gets all horrible.

Sylvie says, 'Leave her, Edith, she's fine.'

I smile at Sylvie. Sylvie's mother and my mother are best friends. So Edith lets me stay and I sit and listen to them talking about Palestine and where they plan to go and when and how they'll get there and how they're soon going to a farm near Berlin for a month to prepare and then they'll go start a kibbutz.

Vati comes by and says, 'Edith, Rika, come inside. There's something important. I have to talk to you.'

We're going to a new school, a Jewish one. Vati says we're not allowed to go to our old one anymore.

'But I haven't said goodbye to my friends,' I cry.

Mutti shakes her head and Vati just looks at me and sighs.

Edith says, 'Your non-Jewish friends weren't talking to you anymore anyway and your Jewish friends are going to the new school. So I don't know what you're worried about.' Edith is very angry and says she will go to Palestine now.

'Finish school first,' Vati says, 'then you'll go.'

'Will we even be allowed to finish school,' Edith says. It's not a question, it's a statement. Vati and Mutti don't answer. They don't know the answer.

So we go to the Theodor Herzl school and I like it there. Everyone is Jewish and nobody makes any nasty comments like some of the teachers and lots of the children did in my last school. I don't even think of my old friends who stopped being my friends.

We have lots of singing and sports and I'm a really good runner. In the last school, they didn't allow me to run in the races because I would've won. Well, that's what Edith said but she might have just been saying it to make me feel better, though I can run fast. My Hebrew is improving in this school.

I wake up in the night. My heart is pounding. I have an exam the next morning and I haven't been studying. They're so strict at the school and they're going to throw me out and say you Jews are just rubbish. It's a French exam and I can't remember anything in French, not even a single word. I try and think of a sentence, of a word, but nothing comes, it's Hebrew that comes into my head. I don't even know how to say French in French. What am I going to do?

'What's the matter, Granny?' I hear, 'can't you sleep?'

'I'm so worried about the exam tomorrow,' I say, trying not to cry.

'What exam?' Janine asks. I don't know.

'It's in English, and I can't remember any English,' I say.

'But Granny, you're speaking English now.'

'I mean French,' I say, doesn't she understand that I mean French.

'You haven't got exams tomorrow. You don't go to school anymore. Come, my Granny, let me take you back to bed. Try to sleep, ok.'

'Are you sure?'

She tucks me up and kisses my forehead, like Mutti does.

We learn about Palestine in the school and we learn about sewing and knitting and cooking and also French and English. We sing a lot, and we have dances, and races. And I'm in the school play. I'm so excited because I have a part and not everyone has a part.

'There are six hundred and nine children in the school, and not everyone can have a part,' the Headmistress says to everyone in assembly.

But I have a part. And I have some lines. I practice at home with Edith and with Mutti and when we perform the play and everyone comes to see it and they watch me, they all see that I say everything I have to say and I don't forget anything. I have a very good memory.

Edith's gone to Palestine. She writes a letter to us and says, 'It's so wonderful here. We have to get up at four in the morning to work and there's not much food. We also have to be careful because the Arabs have been shooting at us lately. But I love it!'

Mutti says, 'Thank God it's so wonderful! Can you imagine if it was terrible!'

Mutti and Vati read it together out loud so I can hear it too, any excuse to read it again and again. She says that Tante Leah is working very hard to get me a student's visa to come to Palestine.

'That's good, isn't it,' Mutti says.

'I don't want to go to smelly Palestine,' I say.

'Would you rather go to England?' Vati asks, seriously.

'I don't want to go to smelly England either. I want to stay here in Berlin with you.' Mutti tells me not to be so grumpy and to have an apple.

They put my name down for the Kindertransport.

I'm standing outside the door to their bedroom and I can hear Mutti crying and saying 'Who knows where she'll end up. Who knows who she'll stay with in England.'

And Vati says softly 'It'll be with someone who loves children.'

And Mutti says, 'How can we be sure?'

And he says, 'Shh, she's so pretty, she'll be alright.'

And I run in and I jump on their bed and I say, 'No, don't send me away, please don't send me away!'

Vati's outside the school gates.

'Vati,' I shout and rush into his arms.

I'm fourteen, I know that because I just turned fourteen five days ago on 4th November, 1938. Lots of fourteen year olds wouldn't run into their father's arms and I can see some people sniggering but I don't care.

Vati isn't his normal self and he says, 'Come quickly, Rika, let's get home, quick, quick.'

Mutti's surprised by his anxiety too and says, 'What's the matter?'

I hear him say quietly to Mutti, 'I was told there'll be trouble tonight.'

He pushes a heavy table against the front door, and I help him. He locks all the windows and closes the curtains so not a chink of light can be seen from outside. We eat a little meal for dinner and then I get into their bed with them. We all go to sleep, me between Mutti and Vati, and I feel safe.

We are woken to boots thumping on the stairs. They're coming up, and up. Will they pass our door. I can feel Mutti trembling, I can feel Vati holding his breath.

BANG! BANG! on our front door.

'Shh,' Vati says.

'OPEN UP! WE KNOW THERE ARE JEWS IN THERE!'

Not even air comes out from us, we are frozen. And then they start to bang, to crash, to smash the front door and any minute they're going to break through and that table won't stop them, not for a minute, not with their hammers and weapons they've brought with them and what's going to happen to us!

Suddenly, amidst all this noise, we hear a voice, stronger than all of them and it says, 'WHAT'S GOING ON HERE! THERE ARE NO JEWS HERE. GO AWAY AND LET US GOOD GERMANS GO TO SLEEP!'

We hear them stop and murmur something like, 'Sorry, we were told there were Jews here, sorry, goodnight.'

I feel Mutti and Vati trembling and I am too. We lie quietly, trying to calm down, and Mutti says, 'That was Frau Weber from upstairs. She knows we're here.'

Next morning, Vati goes upstairs and knocks on her door to thank her, but she doesn't answer it.

I'm walking in our neighbourhood.

'Don't go far,' Mutti had said, but I wanted to see what happened last night, so I walk and I meet my friend Sofie, and we decide to walk together.

There is glass near all the Jewish shops and buildings. We have to walk on the other side of the street where a synagogue is still smouldering. We wouldn't know it was once a synagogue.

There are so many people in the streets, sweeping up the glass and trying to tidy things. No-one is talking very much, but they just work and look very serious. From time to time we hear sirens going by from the police or the ambulance or firefighters. But it is all strangely quiet. It crunches beneath me as I walk because there is so much glass.

When I get home, I want to tell Mutti and Vati all about the glass, but only Mutti is there. She is standing like a statue.

I watch her for a second and say, 'Mutti?' But she doesn't answer me.

'Mutti!' I say louder and come right up to her and stand next to her and say 'Mutti!'

She sees me now and grabs me and holds me as tightly as a corset, and starts to cry and says, 'They've taken Vati!'

And I say, 'Who?'

And she says, 'Them.'

I sit on a chair and I hold the arms of the chair to stop from falling off it and crashing to the floor and plunging down into the earth and never being able to stop because I know that I need my Vati and without my Vati I'm lost. The phone rings and Mutti doesn't move.

'It might be Vati,' I say but she has grown roots into the floor, so I answer the phone and I say, 'Hello.'

'Rika.' It is Frau Weinstein, Sylvie's mother.

'Frau Weinstein,' I say, 'they've taken Vati' and I start to cry.

'Rika, let me speak to your mother.'

I look at Mutti and I say 'She can't come.'

'Rika,' Frau Weinstein continues, 'tell your mother that they have taken your father to a camp, to Sachsenhausen camp. Will you tell her that?'

I say 'Sachsenhausen' and that seems to cut Mutti's roots and she jumps onto the phone and says, 'Suzanna!' and then I just watch as she listens to her friend and the tears fall out her eyes.

I sleep with my Mutti and I stay with my Mutti and we sit and eat and bath and dress and sleep together. We don't talk and when the telephone rings we both jump as if firecrackers have been placed beneath us.

For four days we live like this until one day my Vati walks in the door and we jump and we run to him and we hug him and we cry and he starts to cough and sneeze and he's freezing but he feels hot all at the same time. Mutti puts him to bed and covers him with two feather beds and gives him lots of hot drinks and he shivers and he sleeps.

They explain to me why they are trying so hard to make me leave them.

'I don't understand why you can't come too, I say.'

Mutti loses her temper, 'How can anybody be so stupid,' she says and turns her face away.

Vati looks at me gently and says, 'If only.'

'What will happen if I stay? Lots of people stay. Why can't we just wait and see.'

'You saw what they did, what they're capable of doing,' Vati says.

'You didn't see the fires, you didn't see how many men and boys didn't come back from the camps, you didn't see how they tear out beards from old men, how they make old women clean the streets with toothbrushes? You haven't seen that! Yes, you've seen that, you stupid girl!' Mutti shouts.

And Vati says gently, 'Betti, please.'

'But why can't everything be as it was?' I ask.

I can't go to the cinema anymore. We aren't allowed to because we're Jewish.

And now I have a new name, Sara. It's been added to my name in my passport. And Mutti's. Vati has been given the name Israel. We are all either Sara or Israel depending on our gender.

Mutti has to take all her silver and gold to the police station. She cries as she collects it into a pile and puts it in a bag.

'My mother gave me these,' she says. Vati stands there and he can't do anything.

'You see,' she turns to me, 'they are taking everything from us. What's next? What's last? Our lives?'

'Don't be ridiculous, Betti,' Vati says 'you're just scaring the child.'

'She should be scared!' Mutti says and walks out with all her treasures.

I'm lying in my bed, I'm nearly asleep, almost, I'm not sure if I am or not and Mutti comes in and kneels beside my bed and kisses my forehead, a long kiss, and then says, 'Sleep well, my beautiful Rikalein.'

I come home from school and both Mutti and Vati are there sitting at the table and in between them is a piece of paper. What is it? I think. Is it our permit to go somewhere, like America maybe or China, even India. I know someone was able to go to India.

I smile and they smile, and I say, 'Permit?' And they nod.

'Where to,' I ask.

'Palestine,' they say.

'That's good,' I say, 'we'll be with Edith.' and they nod and smile and tears pop out of nowhere.

'Are you crying because you're happy?' and they nod.

'When do we go?' I ask.

And then they say, 'You're going, Rika.'

They pack a lift for me. 'I don't even know what a lift means,' I say.

'Everything you'll need we'll pack and send for you now in a big container and it will go by ship and be waiting for you when you get there,' Mutti answers.

She puts sheets with Katz embroidered on it because that was her family name before it became Wallach, and she puts in silver forks and knives and spoons with K embossed on it, and she puts in my feather bed.

'Will I need a feather bed in Palestine, Mutti, I thought it's hot there.'

'For when it's cold,' she says.

All I was left with was a little suitcase that I could carry easily because the trip to Palestine was going to take a few days.

And then I stood with my coat on and my hat on and my suitcase and another little bag and Mutti says, 'Remember that all your documents are safely in the side pocket of this little bag, and you have your leberwurst sandwiches in here, lots to keep you going until you have a hot meal, and some apples because you always need apples. And when you get to Trieste, they'll take all you children to the harbour and you'll get on your boat to Palestine.'

And the three of us are off to the railway station. We have to walk now because we're not allowed on a tram, but that's alright, we're used to it and the weather isn't bad because it's April, 1939.

We're here now, at the railway station and there are so many people and an official stops Mutti and Vati and says, 'Sorry, only the children can go now from this point.'

I look at my Mutti and my Vati and I say, 'Promise me you'll come soon.'

And they look at me and they both say together, 'We will.'

And then I hug them for so long that they have to pull me away from them and say, 'You have to go now, Rika, everyone's on the train.'

And I leave my parents. And when I search for them as the train is moving away, they are so small and far away, they look like dolls, or puppets.

2

'Ma,' Nina, my daughter says, 'we're going next door for dinner. That'll be nice, won't it.'

She talks to me like I'm a child. I don't even know where next door is. Next door is my room, next door is the bathroom. Next door? So many doors. It's all doors. Which is my door? I know my door. This one? No.

Where is she? There she is, walking into the room where he sits. Who is he, that man? I know him. What's his name? They talk in whispers. I look and watch. She sees me and tries to smile. She's been crying. Good.

We go next door. 'Hello Rika,' says the woman from next door. 'Sit down, Rika, how lovely to see you. How are you?' I shake her hand and everyone laughs. 'Oh, so formal, Rika,' next door woman says.

I sit, upright, in my chair, waiting for my food. What are all these people laughing about? They're laughing at me. I'll ignore them.

'Alright, ma?' she says. She. The bitch. 'Everything ok, ma?'

I'm waiting for my food. It comes. I eat. Everyone laughs.

'She must've been hungry,' next door says. 'Are you hungry, Rika?' I ignore her. I ignore them all.

'I want more bread,' I say. They give me more, quickly. Good.

I won't relax, I won't sit back, I will be straight, I will show them that I will sit straight. They all sit back in the chairs, in the sofas, they laugh, they talk.

'Are you alright, Rika dear?' next door says.

I don't answer. After a while, she, the bitch, says, 'I'm so sorry, I must take her home. I think the problem is that she's really tired. She hardly slept last night. To tell you the truth, I'm absolutely exhausted too. It's all quite difficult at the moment.'

I shake hands with next door and say, thank you very much.

'Oh my goodness,' next door says, 'she sounds so teutonic suddenly!'

I've always had good manners.

'Go to bed, ma, please.'

I stand.

'I'm going, ma. I've got to go to bed. Do you want me to help you?'

I don't answer.

'I just can't,' she says. 'Sorry, I just can't.'

She goes, disappears, where, which door, she's gone.

I stand.

'Good night, Rika,' he says, the other one, the man who lives here, I think he lives here, he's always here. 'Sleep well, alright. Are you off to bed now? I think you should. Good night.'

He disappears too. He goes upstairs. Their room must be that way, up those stairs.

I stand. It's not very dark because the light is on but not brightly. It changes, it goes brighter and it goes dimmer. But I can see. I can see doors. I stand between all the doors.

It's all quiet now. That's because it's night-time.

I walk through the doors. In and out the doors. They lead to rooms, different rooms, bigger ones and smaller ones. That's a toilet. No, no, it's not, that's not a toilet. I mustn't go to the toilet in that. That's what the bitch said, 'Don't use that, ma, it's not a toilet.' I must use that one, there. Or is it that one there? Which is the toilet? I don't know. I don't care. I think it's that one. Where's the paper to wipe ... oh well, I will just wash with water. I can wash with water.

There's no noise. I peek around the closed curtains and look outside. There's no-one. Is there someone? There is someone, there's more than one. They're hiding, they're waiting. What are they waiting for? For the right moment.

Mutti? Vati? Where are you? Are you hiding? They're in bed, they're waiting for me to come, to hide, to be safe.

I jump into bed. I cover myself with the feather bed, a big, soft feather bed. Ahh, here you are Mutti and Vati, that's nice, we can cuddle up, together, nice and safe together. Where were you, Mutti. Here? No, I was next door with, her, you know, I don't who she is.

But now we can all cuddle up. I love it with you, my Mutti, my Vati. Have you got nougat for me, Vati? Marzipan? Don't worry, tomorrow. Of course, not in the middle of the night, Mutti, I know that. I'd have to brush my teeth again. I'll go have a look, see if they're still outside. No, I will, Mutti. You wait here for me. I won't be long. Just a quick peep.

It's so dark outside. So cold. I need to put on my lovely fur coat that Vati gave me before I left. I take off my clothes and put on my coat. It's nice, cosy and warm and nice. Thank you, Vati, for giving me this coat, before I left, before I went to, where did I go?

What's that? It's a wolf. A wolf is running through the streets.

We're in the forest, it's so dense, so black. It's me and Edith, and Mutti and Vati, and we're walking. Vati has his walking stick, his pipe, oh I love that smell, I can smell it. Vati, let me smell your pipe, I like it so much. Thank you, Vati. Look Edith, Vati's given me some nougat. Do you want some? Well you can't have, because it's mine! Oh alright, here you are, just a little bite. Mutti! Edith's taken too much!

'Rika, don't be greedy,' Mutti says.

We walk through the woods, forest, it's forest not woods because it's so dense with trees. Vati swishes the leaves out the way and we walk behind him. It's winter and there is snow on the ground and I've got my lovely fur coat on and muffler and hat pulled deep down on my head almost covering my eyes.

'I can't see, Mutti,' I laugh. Mutti laughs and pulls it up a bit.

'That's better,' she says, 'that's better, isn't it my little Rikalein.'

Vati lifts me up. 'It's bed time, my little Rikalein. Go to bed now, you and Edith together. Off to bed. Tomorrow's school.'

The light goes on.

'Ma! I can't believe it. It's four o'clock in the morning. Why aren't you in bed? Why are you wearing your fur coat? Where are your pyjamas? What's the matter with you? You've got to sleep!'

I stand still. Get away you witch! Leave me. I know what you've done. I know what you plan to do.

'Why are you looking at me like that? What's the matter? I can't understand what the problem is. Oh for god's sake. I can't do this now. It's bloody four o'clock in the morning. I've got work tomorrow. I've got to go to bed. Please, please go to bed. Please!'

She leaves. Good riddance to bad rubbish.

Good riddance to bad rubbish! We walk straight so you'd better get out the way! I'm with my friends in the playground. We link arms, five of us, six, seven, we walk straight, laughing and shouting. 'We walk straight so you'd better get out the way!' Ones and twos get out the way, we laugh, we skip and run, we are friends, we are together.

'Girls!' the teacher shouts. 'Play nicely!'

We stop, we laugh, we feel so good.

Berlin, my home.

'Raus vom dem Bett!' Mutti shouts at me, pulling off the blankets. 'Up up. Off to school. It's breakfast time.'

I eat wonderful dark bread, almost black. I smear it with leberwurst, thick liver sausage. Leberwurst is my favourite, all of ours, we all love it, every morning, sometimes with tomato, but no, it's better alone.

What's that coming from the curtains, there in the middle, what? Careful, just pull, oh, that's all, it's light. That means it's morning. That's why I'm hungry.

It's morning. Listen. I can hear something. It's him, he always gets up early. Quickly, I'm going to run to the kitchen, get something to eat and then I'll come back here. No, it's too late, he's up too quickly, he mustn't see me, just stay here, hide. I've got to pack, I've got to escape. As soon as I can, I'll make a run, a dash, get out.

I must take this bag. This big black bag, yes, I'll put all my stuff in this bag. Here this stuff, I need all this stuff. Into the bag, and this stick, big strong stick, I'll tie the bag round the stick so I can carry it easily.

'Rika!'

It's him. He's seen me.

'Good morning. Are you up already? Did you sleep enough?'

Don't answer him. Look away. He goes back up.

She comes down with him. 'Ma! What's going on? Why are you dressed in your coat? What's in that bag?'

She tries to take it off me. I pull it away but she's seen inside. 'Ma! Why have you got those curtains? Why are they in the bag, and that stick. It's the one we got in South Africa. What are you doing with all of it?'

I don't say a word.

'My god,' I hear her say to him, 'her face is black. It's unbelievable, how black her face can get when she's like this.' They stand and look at me. I rush to the door.

'You haven't got shoes on, and there's nothing under your coat. What are you doing?'

I stand at the door. They stand at the other side of the room and they look. She looks worried. Good.

'Do you want to speak to Graham, ma? Here, I'll dial his number, and tell him you want to speak to him.'

'Graham, it's me, Nina. Ma's acting very strangely,' she says this in a whisper but I can hear.

I grab the phone off her and she moves back to her spot. 'Graham!' I say.

'Ma, what's the matter?' he says.

'I can't speak because they can hear,' I whisper to him. They move further out the room and close the door. 'Graham, it's happened. I'm in danger.'

'What do you mean?' he says pretending not to understand, 'what's happened?'

'What I told you would happen, when I saw you, yesterday,' I say, annoyed that he's even asking.

'I didn't see you yesterday,' he says.

I stand still and look at the phone. Why is he pretending. Is he in on it too?

'Ma, please,' he says, 'just relax, will you. There's nothing wrong. It's just you.'

I slam the phone down. There's nothing more to it, I have to go, I have to get out. The door's locked, it's bolted and there's a chain across it. They've locked me in. I'll pretend to go to the other room.

Yes, there he goes, he opens the door, now's the time! I dash out the door. It's raining, I don't care. I hear them shouting, calling me.

'Come back,' they shout.

I'm not a fool. There's my getaway car. I grab the door as the car's about to leave and it stops suddenly. Inside a little girl looks at me, why is she screaming? The driver gets out but he and she get to me first.

'What the hell is going on?' I hear the driver say.

'I'm so sorry,' I hear them say.

He, Sam, that's his name, he grabs me, he says, 'Come, Rika, come.'

He holds my arm and takes me, leads me, no, he pulls me into the house. She follows. They close the door. I sit in the chair.

I wait. She brings me breakfast and puts it down on the table in front of me. Ha! Does she really think I'll eat anything she gives me?

'There's some people coming, ma. They're going to take you away for a few days. Until you feel better.'

She leaves me. She beats a hasty retreat. Yes, she runs away from me. She's scared of me. Good.

Should I chance a bite? It's leberwurst and brown bread. Just a bite. And a sip. Just one. Just another.

There's a knock on the door. Who can it be? Is it someone to save me? I hear them talking to her. Two people come into the room where I am.

'Good morning, Rika. Is it alright to call you Rika?' She smiles.

I smile back. You see, I'm not a serpent, even though she, Nina, thinks I am.

'Would you like to come with us, Rika? We're going to take you to another home where you'll be looked after for a while until you feel better.'

I nod. This is exciting. There's a third person, I can hear him talking to her. The two sit with me.

'How are you feeling today, Rika?' they ask. They're making small talk.

'I'm really fine,' I say and I smile.

They smile back. I bet they think I'm sweet.

Nina hands the one a bag.

'It's just some clothes for you, Rika,' the woman says, 'and your toothbrush. Alright?'

She wants me to get dressed but I won't, though I put on socks and shoes. We walk out to the car and leave him and her standing together looking at us.

She's crying but pretending she isn't but I know she is.

We walk to a car, I'm free, I'm going, I'm getting out, and then I suddenly remember.

'I need my passport,' I say.

I sit in the car and I'm driven. It is like being in Bremen with Onkel Heinz and his chauffeur.

'Onkel Heinz,' I say, 'are we going to your work?'

They smile at me and I smile back because I like going to Onkel Heinz's work. They make a fuss of me and give me coffee in very smart cups and very good cake and those wonderful chocolates, those chocolates that are called, they are wrapped individually and they are called,

'What are those chocolates called? Onkel Heinz,' I ask.

They smile at me.

'Will Tante Marta be at work too,' I ask.

'Yes,' one of them says.

'Oh good. She's bringing the cakes, isn't she?'

'Yes,' the same one says.

'Vati always brings cake home and we sit and eat and have coffee or milk and eat the cake.'

They smile.

We arrive at a building. I don't know the building but as soon as we walk inside and see all those people sitting around, I know exactly where we are. We're in the dining room at the kibbutz.

'Hello everyone,' I say. 'I haven't seen you all for so long.'

I don't know why they don't smile or say hello. One comes and gives me a kiss but I don't know who she is.

Maybe it's Batya, Edith's friend, who I never liked very much.

Normally when I visit the kibbutz, they all come up and say hello and are really pleased to see me.

A woman comes to me and says, 'Welcome Rika, welcome to Lodge House.'

'Isn't it called Sdot Yam anymore?' I ask.

'Come along and I'll show you where you room is,' she says.

'Can't I sleep with Edith?' I ask. 'I don't really need my own room. I'll sleep on her sofa. It's very comfortable and it's where I always sleep when I come to the kibbutz.'

'Today you'll have your very own room,' she says.

I love being at the kibbutz. I walk around and speak to all the people in the dining room. Some aren't as friendly as usual, but I don't mind, I'm just so happy to be here. What a shame Nina isn't here with me. She loves being at the kibbutz.

The woman comes to me and says, 'Nina sends her love.'

'Oh, how funny,' I say, 'I was just thinking of her. Will she come to the kibbutz?'

'Not tonight,' the woman says, 'she'll come tomorrow.'

I'm in the little room. They made me bath and made put on my pyjamas and made me clean my teeth. I don't know who these people are. I don't know why Nina sent me away. Why did she give me to these people? I wouldn't eat. Or did I eat? Maybe I ate. I won't again. I don't trust them. I think they want to poison me. I have to be really careful.

Nina will try and get me out. I must stay awake so when I hear her I can call out and she'll know where to find me, because they won't tell her. They'll say there's no-one here by that name, no I don't know anyone called Rika, but I'll call her, Nina, Nina, I'm here. Save me! Save me!

I walk out the door. The big room is empty. Someone says, 'What's the matter, Rika? Do you want something? Why aren't you sleeping? It's the middle of the night.'

I go to the door and try to open it, but I can't because it's locked. Of course it's locked. They're not stupid. They keep it locked to make sure the prisoners can't get out. Nina, where are you, Nina!

The woman takes me back to the room and I hear the door being locked. They've locked me in. I can't get out! Agh, what's that? It's a rat, a rat! Help, help, there's a rat. I jump on the bed.

'Help me!'

The woman comes in. 'Rika! You mustn't make such a noise. You'll wake up all the residents. What's the matter?'

'Look, look,' I say pointing to the rat.

'It's just your shoe, Rika.'

Ahh, yes, I can see now. Just my shoe.

She goes and locks me in again. What are they going to do to me? Are they going to torture me? I mustn't tell them anything. I mustn't tell them the names. Don't tell them, forget the names, just keep your mouth shut, really tightly, don't even tell them your name. Once you start telling them anything, even one thing, you won't be able to stop.

They told me that, just don't say anything, they said. But I let them down. When they needed me, I didn't stick by them.

I'm a terrible person. I'm such a bad person, I killed someone, that's why Mutti and Vati sent me away, because they couldn't bear me, their little girl and I was only fourteen and they sent me away.

My pyjama top is wet. I take it off and put my face into it to stop the tears. I'm cold, naked and cold. I'm alone. No-one is here with me, to look after me, to comfort me. Why? Nina? Where are you? I always loved you so much, you're my daughter and I love you. Why have you abandoned me too?

'Good morning, Rika. Oh my goodness, you must be frozen. Come, put on these clothes. Do you want to have a hot bath? No? What's the matter, love? Did you have a good sleep? Oh no, the bed hasn't been slept in. Haven't you slept, Rika? Come love, let's get you dressed.'

'Don't touch me,' I shout.

She backs away. 'Rika, come darling. I'm not going to hurt you.'

Ha! That's it, isn't it. That's exactly what you're going to do. How they lie, these, these, vipers.

'Rika, come.'

I slash at her when she comes near.

'Rika! There's no need for that. Come and get dressed and you'll see there's a lovely surprise downstairs.'

They're tricking me, careful.

'Your daughter and granddaughter are downstairs, waiting to see you. That's Nina, isn't it? What's your granddaughter's name?'

'Janine,' I say, and then could kick myself. Don't give them any information!

We walk into the dining room, or lounge, or I don't what it is. There are people there and there, there is Nina and Janine. They come to me and hug me.

'Be careful,' I whisper in their ears, 'they're trying to poison me, they'll poison you too. Whatever happens, don't eat anything. Don't drink anything.'

'Ma,' Nina says.

'Granny,' Janine says and they hug me again.

'It's so wonderful to see you. How are you?' they both say, together.

'Just listen to me,' I say. 'Just be careful, be very careful. These are dangerous people.'

Nina and Janine try to soothe me, try to tell me I mustn't think like that.

They're not listening to me. Are they in cahoots with the others? They hug me again and I let them. They're on my side, not the others' side, they just don't understand.

'Ma,' Nina says, 'they said I could give you a hair wash. They have a little salon here in this home. What do you say? That'll be nice, won't it. A lovely hair wash.'

'I suppose it'll be alright as long as I don't drink the water,' I say.

They have a bunch of towels and wrap one around me. I won't bend over much, just a bit, to make sure no water slips into my mouth. They add more and more towels to stop the water going down into my clothes. It can't poison me if it goes onto my clothes just if it goes into my mouth. I keep my mouth shut very tightly.

'Would you like some tea, ladies,' a woman from the camp asks.

'That'll be lovely,' Nina says.

I send her daggers. 'Nina,' I say, 'don't drink anything, do you want to poison us all!'

She drinks it anyway.

'You must get me out of here, Nina. They'll kill me if you don't.'

She gets up and is talking to the camp commander, I can see her. What's she talking to her about? Doesn't she know those women guards, they're even worse than the men. I've seen pictures of them. She looks over at me, then turns back and speaks to the guard.

She comes back. I can see she makes eye contact with Janine, she's looking at her in a particular way. What does it mean? Is she hiding something from me? What's she playing at? She's planning something. Why would she be planning something against me? What have I ever done to her?

Janine gets up and Nina says, 'We're just going to the toilet, ma.'

'Ok, that's ok, but don't be long,' I say. 'Hurry back. Don't leave me with them for too long.'

I wait and wait but they don't come back. They've left me. They've gone and left me. They've deserted me. I'm all alone, again. I'm always alone. Here in this camp, alone, with no-one but murderers, and all those other prisoners, but they mean nothing to me. I don't care about them. I don't know them.

'Go away! Leave me alone!' I say to that woman who comes kissing me. She kisses everyone. 'Leave me alone.'

Yuck, she's smeared stuff on my mouth. Horrible, horrible. I rub my mouth till it's raw and sore.

'Are you alright, Rika?' the guard says. 'Come with me. I'll take you to bed.'

Again, those tricks. Who does she think I am. I won't go like a sheep, like our people did once. Not me. I'll show them what they should do, I'll show them what we can do. We're a proud people who won't die like sheep.

She tries to pull me up. This is my moment. I grab her by the throat and start squeezing with all the strength in my body. They think I'm a weak old woman. I'll show them who's weak. I'll show them we're not sheep!

They pull me off her, she's gasping. They grab me, two three four people, they pull me, they grab me, they lift me and carry me upstairs.

'Leave me!' I shout. 'I'm not a sheep,' I shout.

They put me on the bed and lock the door.

I lie on the bed. Don't close your eyes. Keep your eyes open. Do not sleep because if you sleep you won't wake up again. That's what they want, they want you to sleep. I jump up because if I lie down, I won't be able to stop myself from falling asleep and I must not sleep!

A different woman comes in. She's followed by others.

'Hello Rika. My name's Dr Johnson. This is Anna, she's a social worker. We've been asked to come and have a chat to you. How are you feeling now?'

I don't answer.

'Do you know why you're here?'

I don't answer.

'I understand from the manager in this home that you haven't been feeling very well and also that you haven't been sleeping. Is that right?'

I don't answer. Finally I've learnt to keep my mouth shut during interrogations. Thandi, Tembo, you'd be proud of me!

'Rika, we're going to take you to the hospital now, so that we can look after you better. I'm going to give you a little injection that will just help you sleep. Is that alright?'

Ha! That's it, the end, well, I won't give up so easily. I jump off the bed, I push her away, they grab me and hold me down.

'Ow, you're hurting me.'

I feel a scratch on my arm.

'Leave me alone you bullies, you Nazis, you.'

3

The bed is white and clean. I wake up and stretch. I feel good. A nurse comes in. I can tell she's a nurse because she's dressed like one.

She smiles and says, 'Good morning Rika. I see you've woken up. That's good. You've had such a lovely long sleep. Here's a sandwich and some tea. You must be really hungry.'

I open the sandwich but it's not leberwurst. It's egg and some green stuff. And the tea is white and sweet. I always have black tea, but I'm thirsty and drink it and oh yes, it's lovely, sweet.

I try to get up but she says, 'No, don't get up today, you might fall.'

So I lie in bed and look all round me at the lovely clean white room. A doctor comes in. He says, 'Ah, good, you're looking much better. Just stay in bed because we've given you some medication that'll make you relax, but it may make you unsteady, so just stay in bed today. Why not? You deserve it.'

Yes, I deserve it. I lie in my bed and close my eyes. I can feel the train chugging along. I can hear the noise of the rails.

Opposite me is a pretty girl and I smile weakly at her and she smiles back.

'Are you alright?' she asks.

I wipe my eyes and say 'I'm fine.'

'My name's Frieda,' she says, 'what's yours?'

'Rika.'

She's also a student at Theodore Herzl Schule, or was, I should say, but she's older than me, she's sixteen and I'm only fourteen. I think I've seen her before, but I'm not sure. She's blonde and tall and doesn't look archetypally Jewish. But when she smiles, it's broad and seems real, not as though she's pretending to smile.

There are so many young people in the train, all going to Palestine via Trieste. We all speak in quiet voices because we're still in Germany.

'Anything can still happen,' I whisper to her.

'Don't think like that,' she says.

It's dark now and the only lights I can see outside are the ones in the carriage. We've eaten our sandwiches and I shared my apples with Frieda, and she shares her cake with me which is much nicer than the apples. We are coming to the border soon and everyone is tense and quiet. We arrive and the train stops. The carriage doors open and they come in. There are about five of them but I can't look round, I can't look at them. I'd better get my documents out. Where did Mutti say they are? In the suitcase? It's so big and heavy.

'Can you help me get it down,' I say to Frieda.

'Are you sure they're in there? Aren't they in this little bag?'

Yes, of course they are, what an idiot I am. I open it and start looking throughout the bag and I can't find them. Where are they? Stay calm, I say to myself as I upend the whole lot onto my seat.

'They're not here! They're not here!' I whisper.

'Is there a pocket?' Frieda whispers back.

'Of course, of course,' I say as I push all the mess back into the bag and open the side pocket that Mutti had told me, 'Remember,' she had said. And there they are.

'Documents!' the guard shouts and I hand them to him and I don't look in his face.

I take them back with the stamp in them, the stamp that says, this Jew can leave.

The carriage doors slam, the train starts to move and it stops again.

Doors open, Italian border police move in, demand documents, we hand them over and doors slam again.

The train moves slowly at first and then faster and faster and as it goes the shouting starts and then the whooping and jumping and hugging and laughing and we all say, 'We're free! Thank God, we're free!'

We arrive at the station in Trieste. We all walk out and stand in a big throng. Opposite us is a little man.

'Welcome, welcome everyone, welcome to Trieste. My name is Maurizio Samueli and I'm the representative from the Jewish Agency. Aii, you all, you can always tell who are the Jewish migrants to Palestine. Overburdened with luggage, overdressed, and overcome with anxiety! Well, your time of anxiety is now over! So relax everyone. Enjoy the beautiful city of Trieste. You will be here for a week.'

'A week!' everyone cries. 'We only have ten marks, how can we live on that for a week!'

'Don't worry, everyone,' he says, 'the Jewish Agency will look after you. You will all be staying in penzione and there will be three meals a day. So you must lose that anxiety, yes!'

We are in a penzione overlooking a square in the old city. I'm sharing a room with Frieda.

'What's that smell,' I say and Frieda holds her nose. We can't identify it but get vaguely used to it. I jump on the bed that will be mine and ooh, I jump back off quickly. It's really hard. The mattress seems to be made of horse-hair or something.

'But look,' I say to Frieda, 'these sheets are so thick and bright white.'

We both laugh as we look around this room that is so contradictory. There are streak marks on the walls but the enormous mirror with a crack through its middle has a beautiful brass frame. And the floor boards are rough with splinters but there is a thick woollen rug in the middle between the beds. The wardrobe is enormous with beautifully sculptured patterns on it.

Outside is a balcony overlooking a square with trees and benches around an inner square of sand. There are narrow lanes leading into it and the whole place is full of wonderful colours of orange and red and yellow.

Some men in the square look up at us and shout, 'Signorina, scendi da noi!' Signorina, that's singular, so they're just calling Frieda. They're only interested in her! I'm prettier than she is.

We go down into that bright sunlight and walk past the men. I pretend not to glance at them but she is entirely unaware of them. I admire her cool and decide I must cultivate that same insouciance. Good word.

'We're still dressed too warmly,' Frieda says and takes off her cardigan.

We walk and see beautiful buildings and tiny streets and bigger streets filled with shops, and different piazzas. We arrive at a huge cathedral.

'That's the Cattedrale di San Giusto Martire,' Frieda says. 'Isn't it spectacular!'

I nod. 'Trieste is so different to Berlin,' I say. It's not like Potsdamer Platz or Gendarmenmarkt, I think, and it's certainly not as wonderful as Königsplatz, which is my favourite place in the world.

I'm walking in the Königsplatz with Mutti and Vati. We're licking ice creams and chatting and having a lovely time because it's Sunday and it's sunny and suddenly the police are there and they're pushing everyone to the side.

'Out of the way, out of the way, make space, make space, the Führer is coming!'

And everyone becomes so excited and they move back and they say, 'The Führer is coming, the Führer is coming,' and a woman faints and she's picked up quickly and revived and she says, 'The Führer is coming, the Führer is coming.'

Vati pushes us away from the crowds who are all coming closer and nearer to the point in the road at which no-one can now pass. But we can't go further back, we have to stay because of the crowd pushing us forward. So we stop and everyone stops and the atmosphere is so charged that if someone were to light a match at that moment the whole place would go up like a bomb.

And then from afar we can see a car, lots of cars in a line driving towards us and people say, 'It's him, he's coming, he's coming,' and as he gets closer everyone raises their right arm up, right up, like this, and they shout, 'Sieg Heil, Sieg Heil, Sieg Heil.'

People around us start noticing that we aren't doing it and they look at us. Vati quickly puts his arm up and shows us with his eyes that we must do the same, and we put up our right arm and we say 'Sieg Heil' but softer than the others. But now nobody notices because they are too excited and too busy trying to catch a glimpse of him.

And as he passes we see him, we all see him, and the sound of the Sieg Heils is so loud I fear my eardrums will burst. And the sounds continue as the line of cars pass further and further away from us.

I turn and look at Frieda. 'What's that noise,' I say suddenly hearing the same rhythmic roar.

We both stand still listening, it's coming closer and closer.

We can make it out now – 'Viva il Duce! Viva il Duce! Vive il Duce!'

The hard stamping of the boots on the ground as they march towards us is terrifying. We grab each other's hands and run as fast as we can and dive into a small street.

'Stop,' Frieda says and stands still. 'They're not coming to get us. Let's just watch.'

'No, I can't,' I say.

'Just for a minute,' she says and holds my hand tightly.

I snatch it away from her and throw myself against the wall, my head digging into it, my hands over my ears and my eyes tightly closed. Where is Vati to stand in front of me and protect me?

The roar is getting closer and closer, the vile harsh sound of thousands of human voices tear through the earth, bellowing in time to the beat of their boots, 'Viva il Duce! Viva il Duce!'

I'm screaming, 'Stop, stop!' and Frieda is holding me tightly and we're both sobbing.

And as the sounds die away, we stop crying and we stop shaking and we start to look around and the streets are empty but for a few people walking in the sun.

We're licking tutti frutti ice-cream. We've calmed down, the ice-cream is finished before we've had enough and we look at each other. Should we? We should, we do, this time, glorious chocolate.

In the evening we hear music from outside. The men who seem to sit there all day, are playing guitars at night and singing quietly. We sit on our balcony and listen and we talk about what the future holds.

'I'm going to live on a moshav in the north with my brother,' she says.

'I'm going to live with my Tante Leah and Onkel Bruno and their sons Dan and Moshe. But my sister Edith lives on a kibbutz in the middle of the country in Caesarea, and I think maybe I should live there with her.'

'You should live with your aunt, Rika,' Frieda says, 'you're still so young.'

'That's our boat, over there, look.'

We all look and there, quite majestic, is a white ship with Lloyd-Triestino Line on the side.

We all go on board and are told where our cabin is. I'm sharing with Frieda again. It's exciting running on board and finding our cabins and looking round and everything is so different and fun.

And then we run to the deck to watch as we leave Italy and Europe behind us and all I can see is a blur because I'm crying so hard and I can't understand what I'm crying for.

Alfredo is my own personal waiter. Well not really, but he always brings me things, chocolate drink and biscuits and wonderful cakes. He chats to me and asks me what it's like to be a Jew living in Germany.

I ask him if he's Jewish and he laughs and says, 'I don't think so.'

'Does that mean you may have been kidnapped from a Jewish family and given to a Catholic one?'

He laughs and says, 'I don't think so.'

We can't talk very much together because my English isn't very good, though his is better.

'Do you like Il Duce,' I ask.

He laughs, and says, 'We must.'

Frieda comes and sits next to me on my bed in the hospital. I have a strange feeling with Frieda. I think I once took something from her, I'm not sure what though, but I know I can't give it back.

She smiles at me, the smile I first noticed on the train to Trieste.

I hold her hand and say, 'You're so kind, Frieda. I'm so happy you're here with me.' She looks at me and smiles.

'My name's not Frieda.'

I laugh. Who is she then? I let go of her hand. I turn my head. Maybe it was Alfredo.

4

I lie in bed. It's all white around me. Bright. Sunny. I can feel bobbing and swaying and vibrating. What's the vibration? It's the big engine. It's a big ship. I'm on a ship. And it's sunny and there are lots and lots of people around me, people like me, my age.

There's excitement, there's running about and pointing and shouting, and hugging, they're hugging me, I'm hugging them.

'Look, look,' they shout, 'there it is, there's Tel Aviv.'

I can see it too. It's low and brown and white and yellow and red and sand, lots of sand, and it gets closer and closer and then it stops. Why has it stopped?

A voice: 'Everybody form an orderly queue, get in line, come on, order, order, everybody will get off, don't worry, no pushing please!'

I join the queue. 'What's happening?' I ask, everyone asks.

Someone says, 'We have to get on little boats. This big ship can't get closer. We have to get off this big ship, over the sides, and onto a little boat.'

How is that possible? I'll fall into the sea! I'm going to fall into the sea and I'm going to drown and Mutti and Vati will never know that I never got to Palestine because I only got to see it from afar and fell into the sea and drowned. I'm getting closer, it's almost my turn. Oh my god, it's my turn.

The sailors are waiting for me to be helped onto the rope ladder to step down and down and down until someone reaches for me and pulls me into the little boat.

'No, I say, I can't!'
'You must!' they say.

'No, I can't! I'll fall. Don't you understand, my Mutti and my Vati, they …'

'Go on, Rika! Move yourself. We can't wait all day. You'll be fine!' they shout.

I stand like a rock. 'I can't!'

'Rika.' I hear a soft voice near me, right by my ear. I recognise that soft voice.

'Alfredo?' I say, 'my Alfredo?'

'Yes, it's me. Don't worry, beautiful Rika. You'll be alright. If you fall, I promise you I'll jump in after you and save you,' he says.

'Will you?' I ask, looking into the blackness of his eyes.

'Yes,' he replies, 'and I'm a champion swimmer. Come on, you keep looking at me and just feel the ropes, like that, yes, that's it, well done, good girl, you're almost there, and you've done it. Bye bye beautiful young girl, have a wonderful life in Palestine.'

I am grabbed and set down on a hard wooden seat. I open my eyes and look towards the shore as it approaches us. There are so many people on it. There are the ones who live here, in their shorts and white shirts and their funny little hats, and then there are us, the refugees, the children with student visas for Palestine, the lucky ones, with our heavy coats and our bags, and our thick skirts and, it's hot, take off all these clothes, hot.

'Rika!' I hear.

And there she is, there's my Tante Leah. 'Your Tante Leah will fetch you,' Mutti had said, 'my little sister, your Tante Leah. Be good for your Tante Leah and Onkel Bruno. You will be good, won't you, my little Rikalein.'

'Rika, my god, Rika!' Tante Leah grabs me and hugs me and looks at me and smiles and cries. Onkel Bruno stands and then shakes my hand.

'Rika, your Mutti, your Vati,' Tante Leah cries.

Onkel Bruno puts one hand on her arm and his finger to his mouth and gives her a sort of sideways look. I know it says, not in front of the girl. She sniffs and stops and hugs me again. I look around, I want to see my sister.

'Where's Edith,' I ask.

'She couldn't come. They can't, from the kibbutz, it's too difficult, Rika. You must understand what's going on here. Things are very difficult,' Onkel Bruno says. He limps, this unfriendly man.

'He was wounded in the Great War,' Mutti had said to me. 'He is a good man, but, well, just don't worry too much if he appears...' But she didn't finish the sentence.

The bus is chock-a-block. Full, full, full.

We stand and bump into each other and try and hold on to the seats near us or a strap hanging from the top. Everyone smells, everyone stinks, everyone bumps into each other and says nothing, not sorry, not excuse me, nothing, but no-one expects a sorry. I say sorry but they ignore this unknown word.

Tante Leah and Onkel Bruno are quiet, they use all their energies to stay standing. No-one gets up for either of them to let them sit, even young people, even small boys.

Nobody says to the small boys, 'Get up for the elders.'

My suitcases are in between Onkel Bruno's and Tante Leah's legs. My big coat is on the floor between my legs.

'This is us,' says Onkel Bruno and we make our way off that hot bus and step onto the hot pavement and walk down the hot street until we come to Chissin Street, number 20 and walk into the hot flat.

Inside there are two boys, my cousins, Dan and Moshe. Moshe is my age and he smiles at me. Dan shakes hands with me and Moshe kisses my cheek. These are now my brothers. I don't have brothers. I have a sister.

'Where's Edith?' I say.

They ignore me because they have already told me that Edith can't come. She can't come and see me, her sister.

I think of when Edith left. I think of the last time I saw Edith. I think of standing at the station with my Mutti and my Vati, holding their hands and waving good-bye to my sister, to Edith as she got into the train with all her friends, going off to Palestine, a year before I left my Mutti and my Vati and got on the train to go to Palestine. A year I haven't seen her and I want to see her now. Where are you Edith!

Edith's room is my room now. She has gone to Palestine and now I have her room which is bigger than my little one. I move my pictures and put them on her walls, my walls now. Marlene Dietrich, Errol Flynn, Cary Grant. It's my room, my space, my walls, my door.

Mutti comes in, her eyes are red, she hugs me, she kisses me, she says, 'It'll be alright, Rika, she'll be fine.'

I only think of my room with my pictures on the walls, not of Edith.

'Where's Vati gone? Vati's not here. Where is he?' She doesn't know.

We wait and wait and at last Vati walks in, and his tie is on crooked and he smells like he never smells, and I know it is liquor, which is strange because Vati never drinks liquor, and his eyes are red and he's sniffing and sobbing and Mutti grabs him and hugs him and says 'It'll be alright, she'll be alright.'

And he says to her, 'It'll be alright, she'll be alright.'

My room in Tante Leah's flat in Tel Aviv is dark because the shutters are closed to keep out the sun. I stand in the shower and feel cool and five minutes later I feel hot again and I go into the shower. Onkel Bruno comes to me.

'Don't use too much water,' he says. 'You must treat it with respect, water. This is the Middle East and don't forget it. You are not in Europe now with its excess of water. It is scarce. A scarce resource and you must treat it with respect.'

Everything he says he repeats. I go back into the shower and try to stay just two minutes but it's so nice there so I stay two minutes longer.

When I come out, he says, 'You can have only one shower a day, Rika. You are using all the water. You must stop. And another thing, you must not use so much toilet paper. Two pieces are enough for anyone. One is enough if it is not kaka.'

I roll the toilet paper round my hand when I'm on my own toilet in Berlin.

I have to go to the toilet. I try to get up but I feel woozy and slide back into the hospital bed. I have to do peepee. Mutti, I have to do peepee. I pull something hanging above me and a nurse comes in.

'Is everything alright, Rika?'

'Peepee,' I say.

Afterwards she brings me tea and cake. I love cake.

'More,' I say, and she laughs and brings me more.

Nina and Janine come in to see me.

'Ahhh, my loves, my darlings.' I love them so much!

'Ma!' Nina says hugging me.

'Granny,' Janine says hugging me.

I hug them and I laugh and they laugh and I say, 'Do you want some cake.'

'We've brought you cake, Granny,' Janine says and we sit and eat and it's a picnic!

'Morris came,' I tell them, 'he came earlier and we went for a lovely drive.'

'That's good,' they say.

'It was so good to see him,' I say. 'I haven't seen him for so long. Why haven't I seen him for so long.'

'Morris is dead,' Janine says.

'Morris? Morris died? Oh my god, why didn't anyone tell me!' I cry and Nina holds me and says 'Don't worry, ma.'

'When did he die?' I ask. 'What happened, why didn't anyone tell me? I mustn't worry! I can't believe no-one said anything to me, I'm his wife. Surely I should know!'

'I'm so sorry.' I hear Janine whisper to Nina, 'That was so stupid of me.'

'It's ok,' I hear Nina whisper back.

They think there's something wrong with my hearing.

I'm sitting in Tante Leah's flat. We're in the dining room, all of us, all five of us: Moshe, Dan, Onkel Bruno and Tante Leah, and me, me, the fifth wheel, the wheel that doesn't belong, the redundant wheel. Everyone is served before me. Then I get my food and I look at it and I know I can't eat it.

'Eat your food!' Onkel Bruno says.

'Leave her,' Tante Leah says, 'if she doesn't want to eat, she doesn't have to.'

'Can I have hers?' say Moshe and Dan together.

They give it to them, half-half, and Onkel Bruno looks disgusted.

'Here Rika, have some halva,' says Tante Leah and I eat the delicious sweet crumbly thing that melts in my mouth.

'You can't just give her sweets, Leah!' Onkel Bruno says

'She has to eat something!' Tante Leah says throwing up her hands.

'Your teeth are going to rot in your head, Rika, and you'll be toothless,' Moshe laughs.

I lie on the floor in my room in Tante Leah's flat because it's cooler than on my bed. The sheet on my bed is like an iron. The floor has tiles and they are cool.

I can't have a shower because it's night-time and everyone is asleep and I mustn't disturb them because they have work to go to in the morning, or they have school.

I go to the kitchen and find a lemon and cut it in slices and suck them on the cooler tiles of the floor.

'What's the matter, Rika?' Tante Leah comes in squinting from sleep.

'I'm so hot,' I say.

'We're all hot,' she says.

In the morning Onkel Bruno makes a declaration.

'She has to go to school. She can't sit at home any longer, it's ridiculous. She must go to school,' he repeats.

Everything he says he always has to repeat! Just like me sometimes especially when I think of him.

'She's put it off long enough. Now's the time for her to start school,' he says.

The children run around the school yard. There's no grass in the school yard, not like my school yard at home, in Berlin. There's a tree and I sit in the shade. How can these children run in this heat? It's so hot. I'm so hot. I'm boiling, what can I do, how can I cool down?

The teacher says, 'We have a new pupil today children, Rika Wallach. Welcome Rika. Rika, although there are lots of children who come from Germany, you must now speak Hebrew with everyone.'

A girl sits next to me, she smiles, I smile back. 'I'm Gretchen,' she says, 'but I have a new name now, it's Tova, that means good.'

I smile. I bet she is good, a goody-goody. We're both fourteen, we sit, we don't run around in the playground. She's been here a year and comes from Berlin too, though far from where we live.

'Do you miss it?' I ask.

She came out with her family, they all got out.

'How did you get out?' I ask quietly.

'We escaped,' she says. I look away. I don't want to look at this girl who's living with her parents who escaped.

'I'm sure your parents will get out. At least you have your sister,' she says, then she offers me some bubble gum. I take it and we sit together blowing bubbles.

At long, long last I'm going to see Edith. I'm travelling in the bus to Kibbutz Sdot Yam, to Caesarea to see my sister in her new kibbutz, right on the sea.

'It's so beautiful here,' she had said on the phone. 'There are dunes and sand, and more sand. You'll love it! All that sand doesn't make it sound very inviting.

The bus arrives at the entrance to the kibbutz but Edith is nowhere to be seen. She's not here! I can't believe it, I've been looking forward to seeing my sister for five months since the minute I arrived in this bloody stupid country and she's never been able to come to see me, or so she says, and now I get here after travelling for so long in this horrible bumpy hot bus and – ah, is that her, there, behind the bush, oh my god, she's doing a wee! And the bus stops and Edith comes out from behind the bush pulling up her knickers and laughing like she's going to wet her pants again and I'm laughing, and I try to stop because I'm going to wet my pants, and we hug each other and laugh and laugh.

We walk into the kibbutz through a security barrier.

'Hello Rika,' says a young man I don't know.

'How does he know my name?' I ask Edith.

'Everyone knows everything in the kibbutz! There are no secrets, and of course they know you're here. Anyway, you'll see lots of people you know from the youth movement in Berlin,' she tells me.

And as we walk through the sand that is the kibbutz and the tents and the few buildings which are the dining room and the laundry, there are lots of people I know, like Sylvie, Edith's best friend from school, who I've always loved, and many others.

They all come up to me and hug me and say, 'Come and live with us, Rika, come and live on the kibbutz. We need people on the kibbutz.'

And they say, 'She's so pretty Edith, you're obviously the ugly sister!' And they all laugh and I feel shy, and look sideways at Edith to see if she is really laughing, and she is, she's changed. Anyway, we both know she's the clever one and I'm the pretty one. That hasn't changed.

She throws my bag on a little bed in the tent she shares with two other girls, who are both sleeping. It's after lunch and they all have a nap for two hours because they wake up so early to work before it gets too hot.

'But I'm not today because you're here and I'm too excited to sleep,' she says.

We rush out to the sea and jump into the waves and splash about and I feel so happy like I haven't since I arrived in this country.

We sit in the water, it's too hot to sit outside it, and start to talk. Our mood changes as we discuss what's happening in Germany and what it must be like for Mutti and Vati and will they ever get out.

We sit at tables in the dining room and people come by with trolleys and dish out food into communal bowls. Rice and vegetables in tomato sauce and oranges, lots of oranges.

Tonight, like many nights, there will be dancing outside. We are all in a large circle and outside is a man with an accordion and he plays and everyone moves and jumps and goes back and down and forward and it's such fun, I love it so much. And then it's for pairs, and someone grabs me and we step forward three steps, back two steps and twirl around. I love to twirl, I love to dance! And everyone is laughing and everyone is happy. I have never seen such happiness.

For so long it's been so dark and here there is so much light.

I sleep so well.

Suddenly I hear Edith get up and say to me, 'It's four o'clock sleepy-head. Time to get up for work.'

'I know I have to work and I will get up but just five more minutes, ok?' I say turning over.

'Just five,' she says and goes out.

I turn over and five minutes later I wake up and get up and get the work clothes on that she's left for me and I look at my watch and I see that it's eight o'clock. How did that happen, I think. Incredible.

I go to the dining room for breakfast because I know they come back at that time for their breakfast before they go back to the fields. I walk into the dining room and think, gosh, I'm hungry, and all of a sudden I hear this yell from the other side of the dining room, a yell from a voice I know and that everyone knows and everyone can hear and the yell says,

'WHO DO YOU THINK YOU ARE!'

I stop, everyone stops. They look at her, they look at me.

'YOU'RE NOT VATI'S LITTLE PRINCESS ANYMORE, YOU KNOW. IF YOU WANT TO EAT, YOU HAVE TO WORK. WE ALL WORK, YOU HAVE TO WORK TOO!'

'Stop it, Edith, don't be like that,' I hear people say around her, and Sylvie comes up to me.

'Don't worry, Rika. It's your first day. It's not a disaster.' The tears are falling, and I turn and run out the door, but Sylvie follows me and puts her arms around me.

'Don't worry about her, come with me now, or it will be hard for you later,' she says.

I walk back in with her and everything is normal again in the dining room, with people talking and eating and trollies moving around, and I sit with Sylvie and eat my breakfast and all I can think is, Edith hasn't changed at all.

5

Nina is taking me in her car. I like driving with her in her car. There is music and I hum along. I don't mind where we're going or how long we'll be in the car. We've come from, oh, where were we? Nina turns to me and smiles.

'Where've we come from?' I ask her.

'From the hospital, ma. You've been discharged, remember?'

I don't remember what hospital she's talking about, but I remember now where we're going. We're going home, back to Stanmore. She's taking me home to Morris.

'Why didn't Morris come and fetch me?' I ask.

'Uhm,' she says, 'he's busy.'

Strange. Morris likes to drive.

She stops the car and opens my door for me. She leads me to the front door of a house, a building, more than a house, less than a building.

'What is this?' I ask.

And Nina says, 'Come, ma.'

She knocks and someone answers, someone dressed in a blue dress who smiles and says, 'Hello Nina.'

I don't know who she is, but I don't know everyone Nina knows. She opens the door and Nina says, 'Come, ma.'

We go in and there are lots of old people standing around, sitting, walking, other people dressed in blue too, like this one.

'You must be Rika,' she says to me.

Must I? What if I don't want to be? I think, but I don't say because that might be strange.

'Come, let me show you your room.'

We all walk into a little room.

'Look ma,' Nina says, 'I've put your things in it, see, your bedspread, your vase, some of your pictures, so it feels like home.'

'Home?' I say.

'You'll be staying here, ma.'

'But,' I say.

'Yes,' the woman says, 'you must to stay with me now, dahling.'

'Who are you?' I ask. She sounds French.

'This is my home and I have all these people staying here with me. My name is Violetta. You will stay with me too and you will be very happy.'

I look at Nina. Who is this mad woman, I want to ask, but she is watching us with a crazy smile on her face. Is this a place for nutters? What am I doing here? I turn to leave.

'Ma,' Nina says, 'you're going to live here now.'

I look at her. 'Why?'

Her eyes brim over and I wonder what's the matter with Nina now. The French woman holds my hand. Am I a child? No. Leave me, I grab my hand away from her.

'Ma,' Nina says, 'please.'

Please what? Please what!

'I have to go now,' Nina says.

My daughter says. 'I have to go.'

I understand what that means, it means I'm going and you're staying. Me! Here!

'NO!' I shout at her, 'I can't stay here with all these mad people. What are you doing to me? Why do you hate me?'

And as she scrambles out and the woman grabs my arm, I start to scream, 'Leave me alone, go away, all of you!'

And then I stop and walk with her and as I walk I hear myself think; I'm taken away, my Mutti leaves me, my Vati leaves me, I'm on a train with people, lots of people who I don't know and I'm only fourteen, I'm not ready to leave my Mutti, to leave my Vati, I know I sound like a baby, but I don't care because I want to be with my Mutti and with my Vati.

She sits me down. 'Sit here, sexy bum,' she says.

Here on this sofa I sit and I wonder what she means by sexy bum. I look at all these people sitting around on other sofas, on chairs, at the table. And then I see him. I see a boy I know, a young boy. Who is he? I wonder. He looks so, I know him, oh yes, yes, he's Paulie, my grandson.

'Hello!' I say. 'How lovely that you've come here to be with me.'

I get up and hug him and kiss him. His lips are a bit strange, very wet and big and there's crumbs and things on his lips, but boys can be a bit strange, can't they, they don't know how to clean themselves very well when they're teenagers.

'Rika,' Violetta says, 'you mustn't to kiss Beryl.'

I smile at her and Paulie sits next to me and we hold hands and I feel better again. Why was I feeling bad? It doesn't matter because Paulie is with me.

'My schnookooks,' I say to him and he smiles at me.

But then he gets up and that woman says, 'Beryl, sit down, you will to fall,' and Paulie comes and sits down next to me again.

I seem to sit here all the time. I know I go to sleep, and I eat but I sit, here in this spot. Ah, here's someone I've seen before. She hugs me and kisses me and seems really pleased to see me. I'm pleased to see her too. I know her, I'm sure of it, but I actually know her mother better.

'How's your mother?' I ask.

She laughs. 'You should know because you're my mother.'

I laugh. 'No,' I say. 'I mean your other mother.'

'She's wonderful,' she says, 'she's the best.'

She's brought me chocolate. I love chocolate, how does she know I like chocolate so much?

'My father used to give me chocolate, you know,' I say.

'I know,' she says, but I don't know how she knows. She says to me, 'That's a nice pattern on your skirt, ma.'

I look at what she means, and I see the ring that goes round which protects me from getting pregnant. She laughs when I say that and says, 'Who's going to make you pregnant, ma?'

'Janine, of course,' I say.

And she looks a bit funny and says, 'Janine's your granddaughter, ma.'

I know that. Obviously.

Janine comes to visit me and plonks herself next to me on my spot.

'Granny,' she says, 'I want to speak to you.'

'Morris came last night,' I say.

'So, Granny, I want to ask you without mum being here, I want to go traveling. You travelled a lot when you were young,' she says, 'so you know all about it and you'll be able to advise me.'

'But I am young now,' I say.

'How old do you think you are, Granny?' she asks and I tell her that I'm twenty-one and she laughs and says, 'You're seventy-six.'

Strange girl.

'Morris came in his car,' I say. 'A nice car, very clean, he can take you if you like.'

'No,' she says, 'I want to go traveling for a year by myself, to India.'

'I've only ever lived here, in Israel,' I say.

'No Granny, you've lived in lots of places: Germany, Israel, South Africa and then here, England.'

England? What have I got to do with England!

I'm sleeping in my spot and it's nice to sleep because it's warm and cosy but in my dreams I hear a voice saying, 'Cuppa tea darling, give me a cuppa tea.'

I think, yes a cuppa tea would be nice, so I wake and I see no-one talking to me. But sitting there, in that seat there, is that woman and it's her and she's talking to her husband who isn't there. I can see he's not there, but she can't. She's always talking to him, but I don't know why she talks to him when he isn't there. She must be crazy.

Paulie is asleep next to me and he wakes up too and says, 'I'll have a cuppa.'

So I say, 'Me too,' and someone else does too and soon we are all saying, 'We want a cuppa,' except for someone else who says, 'I want coffee.'

Violetta comes in and says, 'What's all this racket going on here? It's not time for tea.'

Nina brings me chocolate. I like chocolate. I eat some and it's very nice and we sit and she talks to me and I eat some more, and more, and she looks at it and says, 'What's the difference, as long as it makes you happy, hey! You're not going to die from diabetes, are you?'

And now there is no more chocolate, and Nina laughs and says, 'Ma! You've finished all the chocolate, that whole entire slab.'

But my mouth is sweet, and the taste is there, and it doesn't go away, and I like it.

I'm in my bed now and it's night-time and I'm asleep and dreaming that a monster is sitting on my stomach and it won't move and all of a sudden it's gone because the pain is not there but I wake up and I see all this lovely paint stuff in my bed and I think I'll paint my walls and I take it in my hands and it feels warm and soft and squishy and lovely and I stand on my bed and take it round the walls in swirls and circles and long lines up and down and along the wall and it looks special because the walls were very bland before.

Someone comes in and says, 'Oh my god!' and rushes out and two more come in and say, 'Bloody hell,' and, 'For fuck's sake,' and they take me into the bathroom holding me by the elbows and one of them puts me in the bath and they shower me all over and then they put a nightie on me, and take me to a different room and put me into a different bed.

I'm sitting facing Mutti, and she is bouncing me on her knees:
Hoppe, hoppe, Reiter,
wenn du fällt, da schreit er,
fällt er in den Graben,
fressen ihn die Raben,
fällt er in den Sumpf,
macht der Reiter plumps!

And then she drops me, and I fall to the ground and we both laugh and laugh.

I put Paulie on my knees but not facing me, facing away from me and I go, 'Hoppe, hoppe, Reiter,' and drop him, but he doesn't laugh, though I laugh. 'Paulie, was that fun my schnookooks.'

'No,' he says and goes away.

'Hoppe, hoppe, Reiter,' Mutti goes, 'hoppe, hoppe, Reiter,' again and again.

Vati comes in. I run to him and feel in his pockets. He laughs. 'Leave him alone!' Mutti says, but Vati laughs and finally I find it and he says, 'What have I got for my Rikalein?' and it's nougat and marzipan.

'You're Vati's little princess,' Edith says to me. 'He always gives you nougat and marzipan.'

'He gives you things too,' I say. 'He gives you books.'

'What's the matter, sexy bum?' she asks me, 'why you look so glum? You don't like the food I make for you? I make it specially for you?'

I take a piece of mashed potato with my fingers and put it in my mouth.

'Don't use your fingers,' I hear someone at the table say.

I get up and walk away and she says, 'come eat sexy bum, you know I make the food specially for you.'

Look at that woman over there watching me. She just sits and stares. I look away and look back and she's still looking. She thinks I don't know why she's looking at me. She thinks she's clever, much too clever for me to understand what it's all about, what she knows. But I know what she knows. She knows my secret.

I always knew that one day someone would know about it. How does she know? How could she possibly know? Do I know her? Is she someone I've known before? I stand up and go to her.

'What are you looking at?' I say.

She just smiles, a snarky smile.

Violetta looks up from the table where she's doing something with her pen and a big book. 'What's the matter, Rika?' she asks.

I toss my head and go back to my spot. She's stopped smiling. 'I know you,' the woman says.

'What? What do you know?' I shout.

Violetta gets up and comes to me. 'What's the matter, sexy bum? Why are you so angry?'

'It's her,' I say pointing to the woman.

'But she's not doing anything. She hasn't even said anything.'

She'll tell people. She'll start with her, the woman who, that woman at the table with the pen, the one who gives the food, that one, sexy bum, that's the one. That woman will tell Violetta and then she'll tell the others in blue, those ones who, you know the ones who, they speak to people here, when we have to go to the toilet, that sort of thing.

Then they'll tell the police. They'll contact the police, and then they'll come for me.

They'll come and get me and say, 'It's you, we've been looking for you for a long time, because it's been such a long time.'

When was it? Long, long ago and what will Nina say because Nina doesn't know about it. And Janine, and Paulie. Where's Paulie, I'll tell him now.

'Paulie,' I call but Violetta comes and says, 'Shh, Rika, you're disturbing all the residents, you must to be quiet now.'

She's still looking at me, that woman sitting there. I have to get away from her.

I get up and move out the room. She follows me with her eyes.

I leave and pass a room and as I pass it, I hear it. I can't believe it. I hear a woman say from the room, 'You did it. It was you.'

I look inside and it's her, the one with the invisible husband.

I look at her and she mouths a word, she doesn't say it, she just mouths it, and the word is 'Murderer.'

I go in, she looks up at me and says, 'Get out of my room, you naughty boy! How dare you come into this room. I'll tell the headmaster. Darling, darling, look at that naughty boy coming into our room. Get rid of him now!'

I stand looking at her. What is she talking about? Why did she call me that? How does she know? If she knows, she will talk to the headmaster and then I'll be in real trouble. I have to stop her.

I go towards her and she shouts at me to 'Go away, you filthy little ragamuffin!'

I put my hands out and grab her round the throat and I start to squeeze. I must stop her! She's making a funny noise and her arms are trying to push me, moving all over the place, but I'm much too strong for her, she doesn't know how strong I am, and I squeeze and I squeeze.

Violetta comes running in, she grabs me and pulls me, but I'm not letting go and she yells something, and people rush in and grab my hands and prise them open and then I stop.

And I move away, and I go and sit in my spot and I close my eyes because suddenly I'm very tired.

6

I'm lying in my cold bed in this unfamiliar place. I'm listening to the sounds outside, people shuffling by, doors opening and closing, a woman's voice saying, 'Hey sexy bum, what you doing with that cushion.'

The curtains are closed and I know if I open them the sun will attack me with its heat and ferocity. Has Tante Leah gone to work yet? Is Onkel Bruno still at home?

I'd better get up because if they find me at home, they'll be angry and say, 'why have I missed school today.'

'Because it's too hot,' I'll say, but that isn't an acceptable excuse.

'Come on lazy bones,' someone says as they come in.

Who calls me lazy bones? I don't know anyone who does. Maybe it's Mutti, she often says different things. I open my eyes and look and see someone I don't even know. It's not Mutti.

'There's a surprise for you,' they say.

I say they because I can't work out if this is a man or a woman. I don't know who they are. I don't know where I am. What am I doing here? I don't know what they want from me. I turn away from them.

'Don't you want to see what the surprise is?'

I turn round and I see it's Moshe!

I jump up and run to the kitchen with him and there in the kitchen is a great big box. Tante Leah, Onkel Bruno and Dan are all standing around the box, and on the box it says for Rika Wallach, 20 Chissin Street, Tel Aviv.

I laugh. It's for me, a great big box, for me. And there, under sender, is my Vati's name and address.

They all help me open the parcel. I'd rather do it myself but everyone is so excited. Inside the parcel is a box and inside the box is a brand new, black bicycle.

'A bike!' everyone exclaims.

'I'll be able to use it to go to school,' Moshe says.

'I'll be able to use it to go on trips into the countryside,' Dan says.

'Have you forgotten whose bike this is?' Tante Leah exclaims.

And both boys say, 'Rika will let us use it, won't you Rika? Of course you will.'

Tante Leah and Onkel Bruno look at each other and say, 'I can't believe they managed to send this out, now! It's incredible!'

And I think, 'A bike! A bike! What am I going to do with a bike!'

But it's my bike, mine and no-one else's because this is a bike that my Vati sent to me, not to Dan, not to Moshe, but to me, Rika.

I cycle the bike up and down the streets of Tel Aviv, which is flat, it's not hilly, so I don't understand why it's so difficult but it's heavy and it's hot and I get sweaty and the cars pass by so close to me, and the horses and carts pass by so close to me and I can smell the horses as I pass and I think, I hate being on a bike, I'd much rather go by bus.

I'm walking with the bike in Dizengoff Square with cafes and shops all down the streets, and here in front of me is a shoe shop.

I stop and look at the shoes. Oh my goodness, just look at that pair of red shoes. How beautiful are they! How I'd love a pair of red shoes just like those. But of course they are far too expensive, I don't have any money at all.

The shopkeeper saunters outside. 'Hello young lady,' he says, 'is it that red pair you're looking at? Do you want to come inside and try them on?'

I try them on and I look in the mirror and I see a spectacle of beauty!

'They fit you like a glove,' the man says.

I start to take them off.

'Don't be in such a hurry, little lady. Why take them off? I can see you like them and they make you look very beautiful and grown up. Why don't you buy them?'

I laugh as I continue to take them off. 'I don't have any money,' I say.

'Well,' he says, 'money isn't everything. Sometimes there are other things you can give instead of money.'

'I don't have anything,' I say.

'Well, I tell you what I'll do for you, just because I like you and I can see that those shoes were meant to be yours. I have a little boy who would like that bike, so if I take that bike off you, you can have the shoes.'

When I get back to the flat, Tante Leah sees a new pair of red shoes on my feet.

Rika!' she says suspiciously, 'whose shoes are those?'

I smile and tell her the story of the kind shopkeeper.

'You what!' she says. 'How can anyone be so absolutely stupid! Come on, we're going back to that shop!'

But I won't.

'Dan and Moshe would have loved to have that bike, and you gave it away for a pair of shoes!' She spits out the words with contempt.

The atmosphere in the flat is really horrible. No-one is talking to me. I try to tell them I'm sorry, but they can see that I'm not really very sorry. I keep my new shoes on all the time. They can't even look at them. Or me.

Moshe comes into my room.

'Rika,' he says, 'come with me, but you've got to be fast.'

'Where are we going?' I ask, pleased that he's talking to me again.

'You'll see,' he says.

We get to the beach, it's night-time and there are hundreds of people on the beach. It's very dark and as we get closer I see that they are all young and they're dancing all over the beach, doing horas, round and round in big circles. Moshe and I push ourselves into a circle and dance and dance.

From far in the sea, people start pointing and I look and can see a ship.

'Carry on dancing, don't be obvious,' the call goes out and we carry on.

I can see lots of people breaking away and running down to the sea and getting into little boats that were waiting on the beach and now they're rowing out to the ship. They row back with a cargo of people who jump out the boats and are helped and taken away by others who have left the circle.

The numbers in the circle are getting smaller but I carry on dancing and watching what's going on.

'Who are those people,' I ask.

'Illegal immigrants,' I'm told.

'Come Rika,' Moshe says and we run down to the water's edge.

An elderly woman is being helped out but she's struggling. I wade in to help her but she's saying, 'No, no' and pointing back to the boat.

'Come on, come on,' I shout.

'Mein mann,' she keeps shouting, looking in the direction of the boat.

I look but the boat is too far to see anything and I don't know what she's going on about. To make matters worse, all of a sudden there's a terrifying sound of sirens screeching onto the beach and, from all over the place, police come rushing amongst the people, grabbing them and taking them back to their vans.

I hold onto the woman and pull her and drag her onto the beach and as we reach it a young British policeman puts his hands on both of us and says, 'You're coming with me.'

For an instance, he and I look at each other directly in the eyes.

'Please,' I say.

He hesitates and I think he's going to say, go, to both of us, but he says, 'Show me your documents.'

I show him and he says, 'Go,' but he keeps holding on tightly to the old woman who is crying and saying, 'Mein Mann, mein Mann.'

Moshe grabs me and says, 'Let's get out of here, that's all we can do for one night.' When we walk, he's jubilant. 'We got at least a hundred out,' he says.

'What will happen to the others,' I ask.

'A camp, probably in Cyprus, but only until we have our independence, our own land, and then they'll all be back!'

Moshe and I laugh as we walk up the stairs into the flat.

'Shh,' he says, 'they'll all be asleep.'

We walk in but the lights are unusually on. We look into the kitchen and there they sit, together, round the table, looking very sombre.

'Rika,' Tante Leah says and tears start to fall down her cheek. 'The war has started.' And I know my Mutti and Vati are not going to get out now.

I watch Tante Leah crying and I watch my own tears match hers. But I'm not making a noise. It's silent crying, and that shows I'm stronger, braver than her, doesn't it? Doesn't it?

Tomorrow's my birthday. I'll be fifteen and it's the first birthday ever that I won't be with my Mutti and Vati. Instead I'll be with Tante Leah and horrible Onkel Bruno.

I feel so alone and sad. I'm trying not to cry but then I think of what happened the other day when they asked me what present I wanted. I told them I wanted a ring. Maybe I should have lied and said I want a piece of paper, but I didn't know he was going to make such a silly fuss.

'What do you think this is!' he shouts. 'This is Palestine, and there isn't enough money for food, the world's at war, and you want a ring! Do you have any idea how difficult it is for me to get enough food on the table for five mouths and you want a ring!' and on and on and on.

And today is my birthday and I don't feel that excitement I always felt when I used to wake up and feel the presents at the bottom of my bed and get up, carrying them into the living room, and everyone would be there shouting happy birthday, and singing to me, and there'd be a cake and I'd cut it and share it and eat as much as I liked.

Today there are no presents at the bottom of my bed. It's just quiet and empty and I walk through to the kitchen. They are all there, sitting, smiling.

'Happy birthday, Rika!' they say.

Later they bring out a cake. It's a small cake without any cream. There was always so much cream on the cakes at home, but it's a nice cake and I cut into it.

'What's that?' I say, feeling the knife hit something hard.

I take the piece out and there, sitting there, in the middle of the cake, is a ring! And Onkel Bruno and Tante Leah are smiling so wide and they are so pleased that their little trick has worked because they hid a ring for me, for my birthday, in the cake, and it's a beautiful ring and I put it on.

'Thank you, thank you,' I say and hug them both very, very hard.

7

Nina is sitting with me and trying to make me excited that Santa's little helper is giving me a present.

'Isn't that lovely, ma,' she says, cooing at me.

What's lovely? That someone I don't know who is dressed in some strange clothes that I don't recognise is smiling at me and saying all sorts of things I don't understand and handing me a parcel of sorts. What are they expecting me to do? To jump up and down as if I were three. I can hardly get up, never mind jump up.

Yes, I understand this is supposed to be Christmas and I'm supposed to be delighted, but I've never celebrated Christmas in my life so why do they expect me to do so now.

Actually, the parcel is a really nice box of chocolates and that is quite exciting.

We sit and eat the chocolates and that Violetta comes over and says to Nina, 'Remember, Nina, chocolates,' and Nina takes them away and says, 'More later, ma, ok?'

'The thing is, Nina,' I say, 'Christmas doesn't mean anything to me. I mean, you married a goy so I can understand that it means a bit more to you.'

She says, sounding slightly irked, 'God, ma, some days you are certainly far more coherent than other days!'

And I continue, 'But to me, do you know what Christmas is to me?'

'What?' she says.

'Natan,' I say.

'Who's Natan? I've never heard of him before.'

I look at her and I think, how could she not know who her father is.

I look at the man dancing. He's happy and singing along with the music. Everyone is smiling with him.

He comes over to me after the dance has ended and says 'Hello. Who are you?'

'This is my sister, Rika,' Edith says before I can get a word in edgeways.

'Your sister?' he laughs, 'did she get all the brains as well as the looks?'

Edith gives him a play smack and he jumps away.

'How old are you, Rika? he asks.

'I've just turned sixteen,' I say.

'Oh, that's alright then,' he says and laughs and goes back to dance.

'Who was that?' I ask.

'That's Natan,' Edith says. 'He's new to the kibbutz.'

I can't keep my eyes off this new man and Edith laughs at me and says, 'You'd better get in line. Everybody in the kibbutz fancies him.'

There's another man dancing and he keeps looking at Edith and smiling at her. She vaguely smiles back, not as enthusiastically as he is smiling.

At the end of one of the dances, he comes to her and says, 'Edith, you haven't introduced me to your sister.'

'Do you need an introduction?' she asks.

I shake his hand and smile at him and he smiles warmly and I think, this is a nice man.

'I'm Joseph,' he says.

'Nu,' I say to Edith, bumping into her playfully when he's gone, 'what's the connection with Joseph?'

She flicks her hand as if to say nothing.

But I say, 'No, go on, tell me nu, come on already, stop being so secretive.'

'There's no secrets,' she says.

'Oh yes there are!'

Then she says, 'They came together, Joseph and Natan, well a bunch of them came and he is really nice.'

So, I say, 'Marriage in the air?

And she screws up her face as if there's a horrible smell and says, 'Don't be so bourgeois, Rika!'

Bourgeois. I'm telling you, bourgeois is like saying, fascist or even Nazi to those people in the kibbutz. It's the worst insult. Of course she thinks I'm very bourgeois because I'd once wanted to put on lipstick.

'Lipstick!' she'd shouted, 'there is no way a sister of mine will be seen alive with lipstick in this kibbutz!'

Honestly! They have nothing of their own in the kibbutz. All their clothes are shared, nobody can even have their own teapot in their room. Too bourgeois! Well, it's not for me, I can tell you. I want my own things, my own shoes, my own knickers, my own everything.

We argue about it.

'If you want to be a socialist, Rika,' she starts and I stop her from carrying on any further by saying simply, 'I don't.'

'But if you did,'

'But I don't.'

'It's impossible to talk to you!' she says and storms away from me.

In actual fact, I might want to be a socialist, if I understood what it meant, but I don't want to live on the kibbutz and not have my own stuff. I mean, I really don't want to wear big fat Yudit's knickers!

I go to the kibbutz for the wedding. It's a very kibbutz affair – not at all bourgeois! She is marrying Joseph.

'Why are you marrying him,' I ask and she looks at me strangely.

'Why shouldn't I? Do you think I shouldn't?'

'Of course you should, I really like Joseph.'

He's wearing a white shirt and black trousers and Edith's wearing a white dress down to her knees and she's holding some flowers in her hands. The ceremony is held outside in the little bit of green grass they have near the dining room. All of the kibbutz is there and a Rabbi is officiating.

When he says, 'I give this ring…' there is a mad scramble because nobody has thought of a ring.

But suddenly, Joseph pulls a ring out of his trouser pockets and says, 'It's ok chevra, it's Shimshon's ring from his wedding last month,' and everyone laughs.

I really think that if one is taking the trouble to get married, you should have your own ring and wedding clothes! Is Edith wearing fat Yudit's knickers too?

Natan comes up to me. It's quite hot suddenly, I fan myself with my hand.

'Are you hot,' he asks.

'No, it's just,' I start but don't finish and he laughs.

'You're looking very pretty today, Rika,' he says.

I fan myself even faster and then stop because I can see that I look ridiculous to him. I don't know how to answer him so I say, 'Isn't that very bourgeois?'

'Everyone must be able to appreciate a pretty girl,' he says, 'why should it be only for the bourgeoisie. We plebs should be allowed to as well!'

I'm not quite sure how to take it, but I think it's just a little joke so I laugh a little, not much, in case he's being serious.

There's a wonderful cake after the ceremony and we eat it and drink juice and there's

some alcohol, brandy I think or whisky. Edith throws back a little glass of liquor and I'm quite shocked but I suppose she is grown up and allowed to, especially as it's her wedding.

I'm not sure Mutti would approve because she hated alcohol, though I remember once when she drank some and became very giggly and silly and afterwards said, 'That wasn't very nice.'

Natan brings me a glass of yellow liquid.

'Ooh no thanks,' I say.

'Sure?' he asks with a raised eyebrow.

I feel so silly in his eyes so I take it and throw it back like Edith did and regret it because then I really look silly in everyone's eyes as I cough and splutter and make a real spectacle of myself.

'Come for a walk with me, pretty girl,' Natan says.

I feel slightly put out by being called a girl but then think, well that's what I am, I suppose. Besides, I want to go for a walk with him. He tells me he's from Munich, but he'd been at a moshav in the Gallilee before he got here. I know it's a bit of a long shot but they do say, all of Israel are friends, so I ask him.

'Do you know someone called Frieda Abramowitz?'

'Yes, I do,' he says surprised. 'We were,' and he stops.

'What?' I ask

'Nothing, it's alright,' he says.

We walk along but he suddenly stops and says, 'Actually, I need to do something, do you mind if we go back?' and of course I say no but I know it has something to do with Frieda.

'How is Frieda?' I ask Natan when I see him the next day.

'She's doing well. She's working on the moshav with her brother.'

'Why didn't you stay there?' I ask.

'I'm a socialist, I didn't want to be on a moshav, I wanted to live the dream on a kibbutz and build our land to be a socialist paradise.'

I never know if he is just laughing at me or being serious. Some people do talk like this, but I didn't think Natan did.

'Did Frieda not want to come here as well,' I ask.

'She didn't want to leave her brother,' he said, 'but she may.'

'What does it depend on,' I ask, but I'm a little frightened of the answer because I suddenly suspect it has something to do with them, him and her. But he just shrugs.

The phone rings. It must be for Tante Leah. No, I've moved, where am I living now because it's 1940, no, more, 1942, yes, 1942, the war started a few years ago and I'm, how old am I now, I'm, I was born in 1924, and it's now 1942 so I'm eighteen. Yes, I'm eighteen or maybe seventeen. And I'm living, I finished school, yes, I did that, I left a bit early but I went to school and now I'm living in, what's the name of that place, Jerusalem, yes of course, I'm living in Jerusalem. I'm working in a café with Shoshana.

Oh Shoshana, I love Shoshana. She makes me laugh so much and, she's my boss but she's just the manager not the owner, no the owner is, someone else, and Shoshana and I work together and we go out to the cinema and we have falafel in the street as we walk along and we sit and eat humous and pita and chips. And salad. And she is so rude about all the men who come into the café and we laugh. I really laugh with her, like I laugh with Edith, except when Edith's telling me off.

The phone is ringing at the café and Shoshana says, 'It's your sister.'

Why would my sister phone? Has something happened to someone?

'What's wrong,' I ask her.

'They're going into the British army, the new Jewish Brigade,' she says.

'Who?'

'Natan.'

'Natan's going into the army to fight?' I ask.

'Yes, and Joseph, and a few others.'

He might be killed, I think. He might be killed and he'll never know that I love him. And I think, I love him? And suddenly I know that Natan is the one that I have loved for this whole past year and I have to tell him now, because I might never get another chance.

'I'm sorry, Shoshana,' I say, 'I've got to go, I've got to go to Natan.'

It's not easy to travel from Jerusalem to Caesarea. A customer hears me say I have to get to Caesarea and he says, 'I'm driving to Tel Aviv after work, leaving at about six. You can have a lift if you can wait a few hours.'

So I do and I get to Tel Aviv at about eight and he drops me off on the Haifa road. I feel excited because I know that this is what love is. This strange feeling that I always get when I think of him, it's actually love. How odd. How wonderful.

I put my hand out to get someone to stop but there aren't many cars, and it is quite late already and there is a war on in the world.

But someone does stop, some British officer type and he says, 'Want a lift, love?'

What is it about this man that makes me think, uh uh. It may be his moustache that curls all the way round, or is it the way he calls me love, but then I know that British people use that word and it doesn't mean anything, or does it, what shall I do. And I look down the road and see not a single car coming and I think, it'll be alright, so I jump in and he sets off.

'Where do you come from, little lady,' he asks.

'From Jerusalem,' I say.

And then he starts. 'You Jews,' he starts and doesn't stop the whole fifty minutes I'm with him in the car. I needn't have worried for my safety, just for the anti-semitic boredom of his long unending diatribe. 'You Jews, you don't know what it's like for us here, trying to keep the peace between you Jews and the Arabs. You Jews don't realise what a job you've given us because you Jews just want everything your own way, typically, just like you Jews always have, because if it's not complaining about the Germans you Jews are complaining about the Arabs, or us Brits or anyone but you yourselves because it's never your fault, never the fault of you Jews.'

When we arrive at the turn off for the kibbutz, and I'm ready for my escape, he says, 'How are you going to get to the kibbutz from here?'

'I'll walk,' I say, 'it's only a few miles.'

'No, no, no little lady, I can't allow a young lady to walk by herself.' And he drives me all the way to the kibbutz gate. 'Look after yourself now, take care,' he says as he drives off.

The guard at the gate looks at me in real surprise.

'Rika,' he says, 'what are you doing here at this time. Nobody told me you were coming?'

'Nobody knows,' I say and wave him goodbye.

Shall I go to Edith's first? No, I'm going straight to Natan. He might even be expecting me to come, because he'd realise that Edith would have told me, and I bet he'd know that I was in love with him, because he's experienced in these sorts of things, so he might actually be waiting for me now, waiting for me to come to him.

I knock on his door and I hear him say, 'Yes.'

I walk in and see him lying in bed. He has a cup of tea with him and some biscuits on the little table next to the bed. He's surprised to see me, ah, so he didn't expect me.

'Rika,' he says, 'what on earth are you doing here?'

I haven't seen his room before, it's small and there's a piece of material covering the window, nothing as bourgeois as curtains. There's a chair and his clothes are on it.

He's lying on his bed with a sheet up to his middle and I suspect, yes I know, he's naked beneath that sheet. He sits up. I'm standing, looking at him. I don't know what I should do. I don't know why I came. I don't know what I was expecting. I don't know if he's pleased to see me or not.

'Come here,' he says. I stand still.

'Come on,' he says, 'come sit here, next to me.'

I'm shivering as I sit next to him on his bed. He puts his arm around me, 'Why are you shivering? Are you cold?'

'No,' I say.

'Why have you come?'

'I wanted to see you before you leave.'

'Ahh,' he says.

He turns me towards him and gently starts to kiss me. His mouth is so soft, so warm, oh my God, this is what it is to kiss a man, and his tongue, it comes out and it's, ahh, so good, and he pushes me down very gently and I lie on his bed and he's next to me and now he's lying on top of me and yes, he is naked and oh my god, I can feel, oh, he's pulling my skirt up, he's pulling my knickers down, oh yes, I want that, I really, and suddenly he's pushing into me and pushing and oh, my god, the pain, sharp, quick, ahh, and then from afar I hear a door open, this door opens and in comes, I look round, it's Edith! Edith, what's she doing, but he's out, he's away from me, he's sitting on the bed, and I'm lying here, alone with my knickers down by my feet and this feeling, this gooey, sticky, ugh. I put my hand there and bring it up and it's blood and I look at it and I look at Edith and she's standing leaning on the door post and Natan puts on his trousers, and leans over and takes two cigarettes out of his pack and lights them both. And then gets up and gives one to Edith.

They stand there, the two of them, not speaking, just smoking and I'm lying, still lying. I reach down and pull up my knickers and get up and walk past them and leave.

I can't believe what's just happened, what those two have done to me, how cruel they are.

I try and find my room because I need to lie down, but I think they must've moved it.

I go into another part where I don't normally go and I see someone I recognise, Paulie, I think it is, and I put my hand up and go, 'Paulie,' but suddenly I overbalance and fall, and I'm falling and I can't stop and I land on my side and 'Ahhhh,' I shout, 'ahhhh,' I cry and they rush towards me.

'Rika, Rika, are you alright, have you hurt yourself?'

And I say, 'My hip, my leg, my, ahhhhh.'

8

I'm lying on a very narrow bed and it's very hard. Nina is looking at me and every few minutes she says, 'Are you alright, ma? Are you ok?'

And all I can say is, 'Coave, coave.'

And Nina says, 'You're in pain. I know, I know, my darling.'

'Pochedet,' I say.

'Oh ma, I know you're frightened. I'm so sorry you're frightened, but they're going to come soon and fix you up and make you better.'

But they don't come, and all I am is hip and leg, nothing else exists of me only my aching hip and my throbbing leg. Someone is saying something and moving me around, pushing something up me.

'Ow, that hurts!'

'Sorry, sorry,' she says and then I hear her say, 'Oh your poor mum, I'm going to get someone more experienced than me to put this catheter up, it's really difficult for some reason.'

And then someone says, 'I'm going to give you some morphine, Mrs Levine. You'll feel much better in a minute.'

I look at Nina and she has tears in her eyes and then I'm gone.

I'm floating. How is that possible? I can see the sea. I'm flying, I can swoop down like an eagle, oh there's Edith swimming in the sea – Edith! Look up! Can you see me? Hellllooo!! She's looking up, she sees me, she's waving furiously, how funny! I'm flying round the kibbutz, it's built up so much, there's so much greenery now, and flowers all over the place, and big buildings, big homes, and there are cows and chickens and there's the orange orchard. I can fly anywhere, I'm Superman! I'll fly to Russia, why not! I've always wanted to see it. So much snow, it's too cold up here, it's affecting me this cold, I'm freezing and it's starting to hurt me, it's hurting, ahh, ahhh.

'Mrs Levine, can you hear me?'

Yes, I can hear someone calling me from far away.

'Mrs Levine, Mrs Levine. I know this is hurting but you'll feel better very soon. Try not to move.'

How can I move. I can't move. I'm still, as still as a baby is still in the extremes of pain.

'Ma?' I hear Nina's voice. 'Ma, can you hear me?'

'Yes,' I say.

'Oh good, she's responding now, she can hear me.'

I open my eyes and look straight ahead. All I can see is material, white material with light blue lines going down it. I look left and right and the material goes all around where I'm lying. Nina is there sitting on a chair looking at me anxiously. I smile.

She smiles back and says, 'She's smiling!'

A nurse comes in and smiles too. 'Ah, Mrs Levine, how nice to see you smiling. Are you feeling in less pain now?'

'What happened?' I ask.

'You broke your hip, ma,' Nina says, 'but they've fixed it all up and given you strong pain killers, morphine actually, so you should be feeling like you're'

'Flying,' I say. They laugh.

I can hear noises coming from the room. It's dark but there's also light. There are voices talking and someone's screaming and someone's calling, 'Nurse, nurse,' and I hear footsteps and I hear someone say, 'What's the matter?'

What's the matter?

I'm lying in my bed in Jerusalem, a small bed in a room that is cool even when it's hot.

I'm lying in my bed and it's the middle of the night and the light is coming from outside and travelling through my weak curtains.

I'm lying in my bed and I'm feeling so angry. I'm feeling so angry but I don't know who I'm angry with, who I'm angry at. I see a picture of two burning tips, what are the tips, cigarettes. Yes, that's it. That's who I'm angry with, the tips.

There's a knock at the door, a bang, and a shout.

'Rika! Let me in!'

It's Shoshana. I get up and open the door and go straight back to bed.

'What's going on here, Rika? This is impossible. You have to come to work. I really need you.'

'I'm ill,' I say.

'You're not! You're just heart-broken.'

'There is no such thing,' I say.

'True, so come back to work.'

I'm back at work in the café and I've forgotten my anger. What anger? I don't feel anything. Edith? Who is she? I've forgotten I have a sister. I speak to my aunt on the telephone when I can, which is not often. She tells me any news that is necessary and I tell her any news that is necessary but there's very little news. Nothing changes.

I go to the cinema with Shoshana and we laugh and she flirts with the soldiers in the street, or insults them and then we run away and laugh in little alleyways. We joke and chat and chuckle with our customers and it's all very pleasant, great fun.

Apart from when the war encroaches and people say, 'If they get here, we'll all go to Mount Carmel near Haifa. All of us, the whole nation of Israel, like the Maccabees.'

And someone else says, 'That's not going to help us much with planes and bombs.' We feel scared and anxious until there is a turn in events, like Al Alamein.

I'm walking in the old city. I buy a falafel from a little kiosk and I walk, eating it, enjoying it, looking at all the little shops in the old city. Here is my favourite shop, full of Jerusalem pottery. The intricate blue designs of flowers and swirls on the plates are so beautiful and I pick one up thinking, this time I'm not just going to look, I'm going to buy it.

'Tefadel, geverit,' the shopkeeper says inviting me in and I smile and look at the plate from all directions.

People pass all the time, it's so full of people, so many walking in the old city, so why do I suddenly notice one particular soldier passing in a group? But I do, and I look, is it really, it is, and I look away and hope I'm not noticed, and I move further into the shop, away from any chance of being seen, and peek out and look and watch him walk and get further and further away from me until I'm safe, until Natan has passed out of view, completely out of view.

I can't seem to stop crying.

'What's the matter with me,' I say out loud as I pinch myself and slap myself. 'Stop it, stop being so bloody childish,' I say as I hurt myself more and more.

But I can't stop crying. I lie in bed and this time I don't answer Shoshana's knocks.

Now there's a different knock. I look up. I wait. I hear my name. It's Edith's voice. Edith is at my door. Edith has come here. I open the door and there she stands, my sister.

'What are you doing here,' I ask at the door.

'Aren't you going to invite me in. I've just shlepped half-way across this country to get here.'

I step aside and she walks in.

'Mmm,' she says, 'so this is where you live.'

'This is where I've lived for six months. How did you get my address?'

'Your friend Shoshana phoned. She told me you're in a right mess. I thought I'd better come and sort you out.'

My god she knows how to infuriate me! I turn away from her and go to the window and open the curtains. It's sunny.

I put on the kettle and offer her a hot drink. I make the coffee and she sits in the only comfortable chair.

I'm not going to say anything to her. I'm just going to let her stew. She doesn't look uncomfortable, in fact she looks damned smug! After a while she opens her mouth.

'I suppose we'd better talk about it,' she says.

'Talk about what,' I say.

'Well I assume you're upset because of what happened.'

'What happened,' I say, nonchalantly.

'Oh for god's sake,' she says. 'Look, I'm sorry, ok.'

'What have you got to be sorry for?'

'Well, if nothing else, I'm sorry I busted in on your moment.'

'My moment!' I exclaim. 'My moment!'

'Yes, the moment you lost your virginity,' she says without a blush, without a semblance of hesitation, of sensitivity.

Jesus. 'What do you mean,' I say.

'Well it was a bit obvious,' she says.

I'm so outraged, so angry with her for being here now, sitting here now in my best, my only chair, sitting here being so self-righteous, so sanctimonious, so utterly Edith, that I pass beyond that extreme level of fury into an entirely different realm altogether. The result, the extraordinary result that I simply can't understand and neither can she, is that I burst out laughing.

Am I laughing? What am I laughing for? How can I be laughing when I'm so furious with her?

But when I laugh, she laughs, so now she's laughing too, and we both laugh and laugh and of course, what happens to us both when we laugh so much, when we lose control to such an extent, we have to run to the toilet and we both do it at the same time and we get stuck in the doorway and she says, 'Let me go first, I've come all this way, I was already desperate.'

And she runs off and I sit on the bed holding myself tightly down below and carry on laughing and when she comes back I run in and then we both sit down and we stop laughing and we drink our coffee.

'I know you slept with him too,' I say.

'Jesus, Rika, the whole kibbutz has slept with him,' she says.

'But you've got Joseph!'

'I know, I love Joseph,' she says.

'So how could you?'

And she says, 'I don't anymore.'

'Don't what? Natan or Joseph?'

'Natan.'

'I should hope not!' I say, taking the moral high ground. 'What would Mutti say if she knew you were such a..,

'Such a what?' she asks.

'Such a nymphomaniac,' I say.

She laughs. 'What a word,' she says.

'I'm not just a pretty face, you know.'

'It's actually a big problem,' she says.

'What? Your nymphomania?'

'Don't be so silly.' She's looking slightly, unusually, embarrassed. 'Him. The kibbutz has discussed it at a meeting and he's been told that he has to get married.'

'Really?'

'Yes, he has to look for a wife and get married and settle down. As soon as he finishes in the army.'

'Come on, Mrs Levine, today's the day we're going to get you up and walking. Right? Are you ready? Hold on to me tightly and Nina on the other side, and ready, one two three, go!'

It's too sore, it's too uncomfortable, my legs won't work, my legs won't…

'There's no reason for her not to walk,' I hear the nurse say to Mutti.

'Come on ma, try for me, please!'

Then the nurse whispers to her, 'Maybe if she wasn't so blocked up, she might be able to.'

And Mutti whispers back, 'Is there a connection?'

The nurse shrugs. 'It's been a week,' she says.

I have pains in my stomach, and cramps further down. I want to get rid of it but I can't. The nurse sits me on a chair with a hole in the middle.

Vati says, 'Do it for me, Rikalein,' and I try, I really try, I push and I push but nothing comes. 'Come on Rika,' he says, 'don't give up, push like you're pushing out your baby.'

I push and push and it's so big and so hard and so tight, but slowly, slowly it goes, it comes, it's here, it's out and there's a really big smell and the nurse puts her head round the material and I hear her say, 'Success!'

And I smile. Success!

But I can't walk. I don't remember how to.

9

'Help...... help...... help...... help...... help...... help......'

Who is it calling me? I hear it, it's the sound of a bird, but it's not a bird, it's a human, a woman's voice. She's asking me to help her. What can I do?

Janine walks by. I know it's her because of her long brown hair and big blue eyes. 'Janine,' I call, 'come here to me.'

It is her! 'Granny, there you are!' she says kissing and hugging me.

'Janine, there's someone in trouble, she's calling me to help her.'

Janine listens and hears it and says, 'That's so strange, I'll go find out.'

And I wait and she's gone and now I'm so worried that they've taken her as well, my little girl, my Nina, will I ever see her again, what if they've taken her into the woods.

Oh here's Janine and I say, 'Have you seen Nina?'

'Granny, mum's not here, it's only me, she's at work, but I went to find out who that was and it's alright, it's just a woman in a side ward, but she's fine, apparently she does it all the time, that's what the nurse said.'

And then I hear someone calling 'Help...... help......' and I say, 'Janine, someone's calling for help, I must go help her.'

'Granny, it's alright, I told you. I'm going to ask them to move you further down the ward so you can't hear her.'

I like being here. There are so many people and they walk about and chat and give me food. I watch them sit or talk to people, or get up, there's something to watch all the time. Here's someone singing with the person in the bed. Their heads are close together and they're singing a song and they both look so happy. I think the one in the bed is the little girl and the other one must be her Mutti.

Nina is here, she's sitting with me, but she doesn't look happy.

The boss comes to the bed and Nina says, 'Can I have a quick word.'

They move away but I can still hear them. The boss says, 'I know it's all a bit decrepit but we can't do anything about it. Of course it is terribly overcrowded, but the problem is there are a lot of Alzheimers' patients here, and they're all waiting for transfers to nursing homes, and it just takes time.'

'But how long do you think my mum will still have to stay here?'

And the boss says, 'Well, until you manage to find a nursing home.'

'But we were hoping to get her back to the residential home she was at before she fell. Nursing home sounds so next level, scary, you know what I mean,' Nina says.

And the boss says, 'She won't be able to. You'll have to accept that. If they don't walk, they have to have proper nursing care and you can only get that in a nursing home.'

She comes back to me and looks worried.

'Will you sing me a song, Mutti,' I say.

I'm lying in the bed, watching the people get up, walk past me, sit near me, come and go, and suddenly, out of the blue, (nobody would believe me, I'm telling you), who do I see walking down the aisle right ahead of me, but Natan. Of all people.

I call out, 'Natan,' but he just carries on. Maybe he just didn't hear me.

There's a knock at the door. It's quite late, who can it be? I open it and there in front of me stands Natan.

'Natan!' I say.

'It's me,' he says and I think, that's stating the obvious.

He's leaning against the doorpost and he's looking suntanned and handsome and strong in his uniform.

'What're you doing here?' I ask, incredulous that it is him standing in my doorpost. Did he notice me when I was hiding from him in the Old City. Is he going to ask why I didn't call out.

'We've got a few days off and I knew you were in Jerusalem.'

'How did you know?' Ah, he did see me. How the hell...

'Joseph told me.'

I don't want to invite him into my room. It's my room, my own place, I don't want the anguish that is Natan to contaminate it. I grab my bag and a coat because it's winter in Jerusalem and much colder than in Caesarea or Tel Aviv.

We walk the short way into the centre of town and we find a little place that sells good humous and pita warmed with black streaks on the charcoal grill.

'So Rika,' he starts, 'how've you been?'

'Oh you know,' I reply, 'not bad, pretty good really.'

I tell him about Shoshana and the café and how much I like Jerusalem.

'So, definitely not the kibbutz then, yes?'

'Ha,' I laugh, 'no thank you.'

'Did you know the kibbutz has given me an ultimatum? I have to find a wife or leave.'

I realise I'm holding my breath. What will I say? Oh my god, I know exactly what I'll say! I let my breath out halfway through his next sentence.

'Anyway, I'm not thinking about that now. I've got a mission.'

I'm still stuck on ultimatum but suddenly the rest catches up with me and I think oh my god, a mission, danger, trouble, killing, oh no.

'Anyway, I can't talk about it obviously. But, there you go. What can you do, hey. Our people are dying in Europe, Rika. We've got to do something about it, if we possibly can. Shall I walk you home?'

Is that a secret code for shall we try it again, seeing as it was prematurely terminated first time round.

'If you like,' I say.

He's much more gentle second time round. He kisses me and says things that make me feel good and clean. I experience this extraordinary thing I've never felt before where all these colours flood through my head and my whole body becomes unconnected from the rest of me and judders and shudders and I yell and he laughs and I cry and then I laugh.

'Goodness me,' I say after I've calmed down and all that emotion has drifted away. 'You were fantastic,' he says and I think, yes, true.

He stays with me, I stay with him, we stay together in bed for almost three days, and then he has to go.

I want to say I love you to him. I want to hear him say I love you too, but he doesn't and I don't. I think about saying it, I try to say it, but those bright tips come before my eyes and stop my tongue from moving.

I want to cling on to him and say, be safe, don't take risks, come back to me. But I don't because I think, am I his to come back to?

I want to mark this moment, to burn it onto me like a brand, but I feel it's effemeral, it'll just disintegrate like ash after a fire, and I realise he's going and I've got nothing left of him.

I cry when he's gone and I tell Shoshana that I love him and I miss him and I don't know how I'm going to manage without him and I'm going mad and I'm going to die and she says, 'How often have I heard silly young girls say that, I wonder!'

Edith phones me, 'Rika,' she says and I know this is not a good news phone call.

'What's happened to Natan,' I ask.

'Rika,' she says again, and I know she's going to say, he's dead, he's missing, he's dying and I'm waiting to hear those words and she says, 'Chanah Senesh has been killed.'

And I say, 'What's happened to Natan?'

'She was a member of our kibbutz, only twenty-three, all her life ahead of her and she was such a wonderful poet. You remember her, don't you, Rika? You met her when you were here. I read you one of her poems, Eli, Eli, don't you remember?

My God, My God,

May these things never end:

The sand and the sea,

The rustle of the water,

The lightning in the sky,

The prayer of Man.'

'Edith,' I shout, 'what happened to Natan?'

'They were betrayed, they were in Hungary, did I tell you, Rika, they went to Hungary to save Jews there, Chanah's mother was one of them and they were betrayed.'

'And Natan?' I ask coldly.

'Natan, Natan, all I hear is Natan. Can't you grieve with us, Rika, we've lost a friend, a comrade and a major poet in our country.'

'Tell me about Natan!' I scream.

'Natan was captured.'

I don't hear anything after that, it's all background noise to the word reverberating round my brain, captured, captured, captured.

'Did you hear what I said, ma, do you understand it?' Nina asks. I look at her wondering why she's so calm when Natan's been captured. 'You don't need to worry,' she says.

'Of course I'm worried,' I say.

'Well, honestly, you don't need to because it's a really nice place with very nice people.'

'No it isn't,' I say, 'it's a prison, don't you understand? They're not nice people at all!'

'Don't be so daft, ma,' she says, 'it's not, honestly, would I put you in a prison!'

'What? What are you saying, Nina. It's not me, it's him!' I say.

'Who's him?' she asks.

'Natan! Natan's been captured. Can't you understand!'

She's smiling now.

'I don't see what there's to smile about!' I say.

'Sorry ma, I wasn't smiling at that. I'm sure he'll be fine.'

'But how can you be sure? They killed Chanah Senesh.'

'The poet? Who killed Chanah Senesh, oh wait a moment, you mean in the war, when she went into Hungary and they were betrayed.'

'Yes,' I say, 'yes, and Natan's been captured too.'

'That was a long time ago, ma,' she says, 'you don't have to worry about that now.'

We're driving in Nina's car, Nina, Janine and me. We're going on holiday, look at the views, all those hills, that greenery, I love driving in the countryside.

'I love going on holiday,' I say looking at their smiling faces.

'Is that where we're going,' Nina says.

'Where are we going, Granny?' Janine asks.

I laugh, 'You should know, you're driving.'

'We're going to Berlin,' Janine laughs.

'No,' I shout. 'Stop the car, Nina, we can't go to Berlin.'

'No, ma, Janine was only joking, we're not in Germany, of course not, where do you think we are?'

'We're in Israel.'

'Yes, that's right,' Nina says.

'And we're going to Teveriyah,' I say thinking, I love Teveriyah, I remember eating ice cream in Teveriyah.

'Exactly,' Nina says and we all laugh.

'Who fancies an ice-cream?' I say looking at their smiley faces.

We stop when we get there. We're staying at a nice looking hotel. It's quite big and on the outside is a sign that says Oakwood Grove Nursing Home. I like hotels that are homely.

'Hold on a mo, ma,' Nina says and goes up the stairs and rings a bell.

The receptionist comes out wearing a blue uniform and says 'Hello, Mrs Levine, how lovely to meet you. Can I call you Rika? We've been looking forward to you coming.'

Isn't that nice. How welcoming. I smile and everyone smiles. This is happy, I think.

The receptionist has a wheelchair with her but I'm not sure who that's for, oh yes, of course, it's for me! I forgot that I don't walk anymore but I can't remember why I don't. Ooh, that's a bit uncomfortable, I think, as she struggles to lift me.

'Are you alright,' I hear Nina ask.

'Yes, yes, I do this all the time,' she replies.

Ah ha, I laugh as I fit into the chair but as she pushes me it feels like I'm going to fall out, she's going so fast. I grab Nina's hand and she says, 'It's ok, ma, don't worry, it's only for a minute.'

I'm not sure I like this hotel very much.

'Shall we try a different one,' I whisper to Nina. 'I don't want to be rude, but there's a bit of a wee smell, don't you think.'

'Shh ma,' she says.

But Janine, whispers to me, 'I'm sure it's just a bad day, I'm sure it's not like this all the time.'

Well, to my mind, wee smell in a hotel is a bad sign, even for an off day. Once we get into our hotel room the smell has gone and the room's quite nice, mainly because it overlooks the hotel gardens and there's an en-suite.

'I do like an en-suite,' I say to Janine.

The receptionist is very helpful and shows me a red string that hangs near the bed and says I can pull it if I need help. That's useful.

'I'll bring some tea while you settle in,' she says.

I'm not sure how long we're going to stay here. We can't be very long because we have to go get our ice creams.

'Do you want to have a look at your rooms,' I ask, but they don't seem to mind just being with me.

After tea, the receptionist, 'My name's Millie,' she says, takes us round the hotel and shows us two lounges. Oh, that's nice, having two lounges, though the dining room doesn't have very many tables.

'Not many of our residents are able to get themselves to the tables,' she says, talking to Nina and Janine (why not me?) 'so most get fed at the comfortable chairs in the lounge.'

As they push me back to the room, I hear the woman say, 'Can you write Rika's story so we know the person she really is.'

And Nina says, 'The person she really is isn't the person she really was.'

I'm looking forward to jumping in the sea and looking round the old town.

'Shall we go now,' I say.

'Go where, ma?' Nina asks.

'We can look around the town, the sights, or the sea. Besides, I promised you an ice cream.'

'Ma,' she says looking strangely uncomfortable, 'you do know that this is where you're staying now, right?'

'Yes, of course, we're on holiday.'

'Well, we're not really. This here, this place, this is going to be your new home?'

'What?' I say.

'I'm sorry, ma,' she says, 'but it's what you need now, because you can't walk, you see, since you fell, and broke your hip, remember. But, we have to go now, Janine and me, we're going but we'll be back tomorrow, promise, we'll see you tomorrow, ok, see how you are.'

They kiss me and walk away quickly and I watch them and think they look like ducks waddling away. I'm left with Millie. Millie, Mollie, Mandy. I'm left alone again. Abandoned, like always.

I look around at all the people sitting on chairs in the lounge, sitting quietly, looking at nothing, and I suddenly see what I just hadn't noticed before, that all the people around me are old and hopeless and helpless and miserable and broken, just like me.

10

There are lots of helpers here. I don't know their names, nobody's told me their names, so I call them Millie, Mollie and Mandy. I don't know why, it just came to me today. It was Janine's favourite book when I used to sit with her and hold her and read to her.

They laugh and say, 'Oh, I'm Mollie today, am I? Yesterday I was Mandy.'

I'm sitting in a chair, a big chair with cushions all around and Millie or whoever is sitting on the arm of the chair feeding me.

Nina comes in and says, 'She is able to feed herself.'

The other one says, 'But it takes forever, and we're actually worried she isn't getting enough nutrition when she feeds herself.'

So Nina takes over and after a while she says, 'Come on, ma, open already!'

'So what happened to Natan in the end, ma,' Nina asks.

'Who's Natan, I ask.'

'Ma!' she exclaims, 'you've been on and on about Natan recently and now you can't even remember.'

'I don't know who you're talking about. I've never known anyone called Natan.'

Natan is home. He was hurt but he survived. He hasn't come to see me.

The war is coming to an end, it's all anyone can talk about.

I'm walking around in a daze of anxiety and excitement because I know, soon I'll see my Mutti and my Vati again.

But what if I don't, I think, but I will, I say out loud, but if something goes wrong, nothing will go wrong, but, but – enough with the buts already, they're fine, you always knew they'd be fine, so relax ok! They'll be fine!

I talk to Edith on the phone, 'Any news?'

'Of course not, my god, do you think I wouldn't tell you if I heard anything!'

I phone Tante Leah and say, 'You don't know yet when we might know, do you?'

'Honestly Rika,' she says, 'do you think I wouldn't let you know the minute I heard anything.'

So I just have to wait. And not think. Just picture what it'll be like when I see them again, when I hug them again, kiss them, hear about all their, no, I almost said adventures, but that's just silly.

The phone rings, I pick it up.

'Rika,' Edith says, 'I've heard from them, from the Red Cross. They're alive! They're alive, do you hear me, alive. They're in America!'

'I always knew it, I always knew they'd be alive. You'd know if your parents were dead, you'd just know.' I'm falling in a whirl like Alice down the rabbit hole. 'But they might not find us?' I sit up, eyes wide open in terror.

'Of course they'll find us, the Red Cross know where we are and they'll tell them.' The terror dissipates, the excitement escalates.

'When will they be here?'

'Soon, soon! Oh Rika, they'll be here soon! I'll let you know the second I get anymore news.'

And the very next morning, the phone rings again and again it's Edith, and I say, 'So, when are they going to be here, tell me, tell me.'

I hear a noise.

'What,' I say, 'I can't hear you, what's the matter with the line,' I say.

But as soon as I say it I know there's nothing wrong with the line, it's her, she's crying and she's struggling to get something out, something about the Red Cross man and,

'What's that, what're you saying, mistake? Mistake, who made a mistake?'

'The Red Cross man made a mistake?'

'How's that possible? Red Cross men don't make mistakes. They're in America, we know that, they told us that, they'll be with us soon. They're what? They're, dead! They're dead?'

NOOOOOOO!

Tante Leah arrives in Jerusalem to see me. She seems even smaller than she was.

'Rika,' she cries, hugging me and crying on me.

I cry too. She is the closest I have now to my Mutti. We hug and hold each other and cry. My Mutti's sister. My Mutti's little sister, like me to Edith.

'We have to be strong,' she says, looking very weak. 'So many people have died, we just keep hearing more and more names, more and more numbers.'

We know they died in Minsk in 1942. It's now 1945 and they've been dead all those years. When we thought they were alive, they were actually dead.

I feel as though there is nothing inside me, the whole of me is just an empty room, an empty wardrobe, just shelves and space but nothing inside.

Edith comes to see me in Jerusalem. We hold each other and cry and sob. The tears are being pushed out because there are so few left.

'I feel like a dog,' I say to Edith, 'a dog that goes from post to post leaving bits of wee until there's nothing left but he still lifts his leg even though there's not even a drop left in him.'

'That's a strange thing to say,' she says.

We smile but it's a little smile, a half one, one that doesn't linger.

'What I don't understand,' Edith says, 'is how did we not know? We didn't know, did we Rika? Did we know but not recognise it, not realise that we knew? How could we not know?'

'I don't know,' I say.

I'm on my way to the kibbutz.

I need to be with Edith but I know there's another reason, a dirty reason, a reason I mustn't tell anyone, a secret. I have to see Natan. I need to see how he is with me. Do I really mean nothing to him and why do I feel so unclean when I say those words?

I'm planning to stay just for shabat. I can't put myself through it for longer. I really only need two minutes, two minutes to know my future. And if he rejects me, what will I do with that future?

Edith and I go into the dining room for lunch. It's full as always with people in their work clothes, sitting in groups, eating, talking very loudly, laughing, shouting to others, people pushing trolleys and ladling out food into bowls on the table.

We sit and I look surreptitiously around, and there he is, just like the others, in his blue work clothes and his kovah tembel, fool's hat that they all wear. I watch him with my head down and my eyes up, looking up so hard with my head so far down that my forehead begins to ache.

He doesn't see me, but people come to the table to say hello and to say how sorry they are about our parents and I look at them and quickly glance at him – he still hasn't seen me, but now, he looks, he sees, he looks down again, then up and our eyes meet.

He smiles, I look down and don't look at him again. I know that smile. It's a sorry smile. Sorry. He has a lot to say sorry for. But I know it was not just a sorry about your parents' smile, it was a sorry for everything smile.

I tell Edith I'm going home.

'You can't go home! How can you get home on shabat. Don't be ridiculous,' she says, kindly, I think not!

I walk out and go back to her room. I lie on her bed and close the curtains. She comes soon afterwards.

'Well that's one way of drawing attention to yourself!' she says. 'What on earth's the matter with you? Don't tell me you've still got a thing about Natan, have you? For God's sake, Rika, don't you know he's getting married next week?'

'Married? Who's he getting married to?'

'Some girl from his old moshav. A girl called Frieda Abromowitz.'

I hear the comments in the café.

'What can you expect,' the customers say, 'An orphan. All alone. There's lots alone. She's not the only one. Nobody is alone. Kol Yisrael chaverim. All Israel are friends. She must pull herself together. She has to think of others. Not just herself, so self-absorbed. It's not good for her. So pretty. Such a shame.'

'Rika, listen to me,' Shoshana says. 'I need to talk to you about something important. You need to get some meaning into your life, right? Of course right. Well, what's more meaningful than working towards getting our own homeland in Eretz Israel. Independence, independence from those bastard British. Right? Of course right! Well, you can help, you can do things, little things but important things to help. Will you? We need you, Rika. We need everyone to help. Will you help your country?'

'Why not?' I shrug. I need something to put in this empty room that I am, something to fill a shelf.

'Great. Right, go to the felafel stand in King George street tonight at exactly eight fifteen, and as you're putting techina on your felafel, a man will say to you, can I help you with that. You'll say, no thanks. He'll say, come on, let me help you princess. Ok? Let me help you princess. Then you put this parcel down next to you and he picks it up and goes off with the parcel, and you finish your felafel. Easy. Ok?'

'Ok.'

'Rika, you did well. We need someone now to come and keep watch on something we're doing. Will you do that?'

'Ok.'

'Rika. You were so cool, so calm when those policemen came. I was so proud of you. You've shown that you can keep your head when things get difficult. They want you to deliver some guns. It means going through the checkpoint into the Old City. They asked for you, specifically for you. Will you help?'

'Ok.'

'Rika. They want you to become friendly with someone.'

'With whom?'

'A man. A British Colonel.'

'What sort of friendly?'

'Very friendly.'

'Why?'

'Don't ask questions, Rika.'

'Why me?'

'You're so pretty, Rika. No-one would look at me.'

'Ok.'

I've never seen the King David Hotel before, not from the inside. It's so grand, so different from everything around me which is either modern and cheap or ancient and crumbling.

This hotel is British, the wood is polished, the silver cutlery is shining, the cups are dainty, everything that is the exact opposite of me. Rich, proud, patriotic, perfect.

I've come for tea at the King David Hotel, sitting grandly, sipping English breakfast tea (not tasteless Lipton tea), eating morsels of little cakes and scones and biscuits, all paid for by the local branch of the Irgun, aka terrorists.

The waiters are so polite to me, yes madam, no madam, three bags full madam. Oh ha ha ha madam. Madam is so funny, so clever.

Madam gets up and walks past the table and trips, how conveniently, just by the old Colonel.

'My dear lady,' he says, ever so gallantly, 'do let me help you up. How terrible. Won't you rest here at my table. Let me see how you are. Oh, your ankle is looking terribly swollen. You, boys, get me some cold water with ice and some cloths please.'

He dips the cloths in the cold water with ice and squeezes it out and wraps them round my unswollen ankle.

'Dear girl,' he says, 'how absolutely dreadful for you. May I ask what your name is?' 'Greta,' I say and flutter my eyelids. I did. How absurd, but I did.

There's an expression I've read in books, a man wines and dines a lady. Wines and dines, I love the rhythm of that phrase, and that's what he does to me. I'm the lady, and he's the man, old man, enemy man, but the man who's wining and dining me, moi, and it feels so good.

'You're so beautiful,' he says to me every few minutes.

I don't mind. I know some would be put off by so much, well fawning, but it fills my shelves. I'm being fawned on by a man old enough to be my father, (no don't say that, don't think that) but the Colonel knows how to make a gal feel good.

He's driving me around in his big black car with a chauffeur, travelling around the country, stopping off at restaurants, at sights, at views, at dear little cafes for a little spot of coffee and cake and maybe a drop of brandy while we're at it.

On the tenth day, (he takes his time this man unlike someone else I know), he invites me into his hotel room at the King David Hotel.

'It's divine,' I say, and laugh at this pretentious word that doesn't fit me.

'Absolutely stunning,' I say, smiling at this unknown me who's speaking.

The wood is mahogany and teak, he tells me, and there on a table is a basket full of fruit and a bowl of chocolates, British chocolates, delicious chocolates.

He pops one in my mouth and as I swallow it, he bends towards me and kisses me very gently. I kiss him back, this old man, this man who is as different to Natan as day is to night, as a cow is to a bird, as a man is to a rat.

And my body surprises my mind, because while my mind mocks this old man, my body thinks something else entirely, it thinks, oh yes, I want this. He lifts me and carries me to the bed and undresses me, not as if I'm a child but as if I'm a stunning, divine creature, as dainty as the most delicate porcelain, as exciting as the most marvellous adventure. And I respond to this adventure, I'm part of this adventure, I can't wait for this adventure to get going, to get moving, to get inside me and oh my god I come like I've never come before. And it's wonderful.

And while he sleeps, this kind, gentle, loving man, I slip out of the room, and David, the waiter, my co-terrorist, my co-freedom fighter, my comrade, slips in and closes the door while I walk down the lavish stairs and out of the King David Hotel forever.

'What have I done!'

'You've done well, Rika.' Shoshana says.

'What would my father say, my mother, if they knew what I've become?'

'You've done so well, Rika,' Shoshana says, 'stop crying.'

'Who've I done well for, certainly not for him.'

'You've done well for the Jewish people.'

'Do the Jewish people want more blood on their hands?'

'Rika, this struggle isn't one of equal strengths, you know. Think of all the blood on their hands. That bastard was an enemy of the Jewish people. By his hand your Jewish brothers were killed and more would've been killed.'

By my hand, his life came to an end. I feel as if I can't get clean. I wash my hands and scrub them until they are raw and broken. Out damned spot, out. Who would have thought the old man to have had so much blood in him.

The more they say well done to me, you're a heroine of the Jewish struggle, the more I know what I am, I'm a ...

They know. They're going to come and get me. I've tried to hide it all my life but now I know they're going to get me. What will I do? Who will help me? Nobody will want to know me when they're told what I really am.

When they are told the simple truth, Rika is a murderer.

11

'Are you Frieda?' I ask the woman walking past me.
She ignores me.
'Are you Frieda?' I ask another one who is sitting opposite me.

She smiles.

'Are you Frieda?' I ask the woman who is pushing food into my mouth.

'No darling, I'm not. Who's Frieda?' she asks.

'Frieda is the woman who took my man.'

'Ahhh, really?' she says, 'what a shame. What a horrible woman to take your man from you. When was that darling? A long time ago?'

'No, it was last week,' I say.

'Well, maybe he wasn't worth having, huh? What do you think?' she says.

I smile. Yes, he just wasn't worth having. I close my eyes to sleep but she says, 'Rika, open your eyes, open your mouth.'

We're walking near the airfield, Shoshana and me, and we pass three airmen standing around smoking and laughing. They whistle.

'Hmm,' says Shoshana to me and flounces away.

I follow her but the men shout, 'Hey, come and talk to us. We're really lonely here, far away from home. Don't be mean, come on girls, come and be friendly.'

There's something funny about the way they say it, the way they speak, like little boys trying to be grown-ups.

'Where are you from?' Shoshana shouts back to them.

'That's more like it, that's more friendly. Come and speak to us and we'll tell you.'

So we walk over, very casually, and they say, 'Come sit down here,' while two of them take off their jackets and throw them on the ground as if we were delicate little creatures.

We laugh and sit down.

'We're South Africans,' they say proudly.

'Is that something to be proud of?' Shoshana asks.

'Yes!' they all say. 'It's the land of milk and honey, the real one, didn't you know that?'

'What are you doing here then?' I ask.

'Oh good, she speaks too,' someone says, the smallest one, the best-looking one. 'I was wondering if you could speak English.'

'Why were you wondering,' I ask with a half-smile.

'Because I wanted to speak to you,' he says full-smiling back. 'Anyway,' he says, 'to answer your question, we're Mahal soldiers, all volunteers.'

'Oh yes?' says Shoshana, 'what are you volunteering to do? Steal our women?'

'And why not,' says my one, 'when there are such beauties on offer.'

'We're not on offer,' I say mock indignantly. 'You make it sound as though we're pieces of meat in the butcher shop waiting to be chosen for dinner.'

They laugh.

'Talking about dinner,' one of them says, 'what about us taking you out for dinner.'

'When?' Shoshana says.

'Tonight, now, let's go, what do you say?'

Shoshana looks at me. 'What do you say, Rika.'

'Well, if you're going to offer fish, then I'd say yes,' I say with a laugh.

We're at this really fancy restaurant in Jerusalem. Well, I say fancy, but everything's relative really. It's fancy enough for me.

I have this great big fish on my plate and I'm so enjoying it. I put my knife and fork down to prolong this state of ecstasy – well that might be a bit of an exaggeration but the way Shoshana is looking at me, I can see it's precisely that, and, oh my god, what are you doing! the waiter, he's taking my fish away, what should I do, I can't scream stop, shall I, too embarrassing, oh no, he's taken it away! I'm such a fool, I shouldn't've put my knife and fork together like that. I've lost my beautiful fish.

I hate Shoshana sometimes, look at her laughing her head off, trying to hide it behind her hands. The boys don't seem to have noticed anything.

There's dancing in this restaurant and my one, who has told me his name is Morris Levine, and I are dancing. Well, neither of us is very good at it, but it's fun. Shoshana and I are shared between the three of them and I'm always happy to get back to Morris Levine.

They have to be back by ten so we leave at nine thirty. All three ask for a kiss from both of us and we oblige with a quick peck on the cheek and laugh.

'Can I see you tomorrow,' Morris Levine asks me.

'We'll see,' I say, thinking I shouldn't be such a pushover.

'Let's make a time to meet otherwise I won't be able to contact you.'

'You can send me at note at the café,' I say.

And next day, there's a note at the café saying how much he liked being with me, and the day after that he appears.

'Aren't you supposed to be an airman,' I say.

'I asked for special dispensation to take my girl out,' he laughs.

'Oh yes,' I laugh back, 'who says that's what I am?'

The next day he appears again and this time he gives me a present.

'What's this,' I ask.

'Open it and look,' he says.

Inside is a handbag. It's brown leather, a nice deep brown with lots of pockets and studs and it looks expensive. I like it very much.

'Is that how much I cost?' I ask with a smile.

'This is just a down payment,' he smiles back.

It's just him and me now. We go to the cinema, we meet for humous, we go for walks. We're walking now, back to my flat, well my room really with its tiny kitchen and bathroom, and he suddenly stops and turns me towards him.

'Rika,' he says, 'I want to marry you.'

Well, that's a shock.

'But I hardly know you, I say.

'I know what I want. I always have, and I knew it the minute I saw you.'

'You're exaggerating now,' I say.

'Well, as soon as the waiter took your fish away'.

'What, you noticed!'

'I hope you miss me as much as you missed that fish!' he laughs.

And I laugh back and think, you know what, why not!

'You must be nuts,' Shoshana says. 'You don't know the man! What do you know about him? Do you know anything about his family, his background? He might be a mass murderer. How do you know!'

So when I see him next I ask him if he's a mass murderer and he says he can honestly assure me that he's not.

Well he would say that of course, he's not going to say, huh, got me in one. But I believe him. I may not have finished school but I have common sense, I have instinct and I have intuition. This is not a mass murderer. Is that a good enough reason to marry someone?

I see the way he is with his friends and they laugh at his jokes and clap him on the back and generally he's a very good fellow, according to them. They're thrilled that Morris is going to marry me.

'Why?' I ask them.

'Why are we thrilled? Because one of us has bagged a beauty!' they laugh. 'And besides, it's just what this wild creature needs, someone to tame him.'

I'm not sure I like either of those comments, wild creature or tame. I'm certainly not a lion tamer or any other tamer, and I don't want to be married to a wild creature. I know the sort of man I want, and I want someone like my Vati.

'He's not your Vati,' Shoshana says. 'You do realise this, don't you, Rika. He's about as far from your Vati as it's possible to be.'

'Why do you say that,' I ask.

'If you can't see that, I really worry for you,' she says looking directly at me.

I write to Edith to tell her I'm going to phone her. There is only one phone in the kibbutz secretariat and she has to be there waiting.

'What is it?' she says, 'you've made me nervous. Has something happened?'

'Well, something has or I wouldn't have phoned you.'

'Nu, come on, quick before I platz!'

'Ok,' I say, 'well, the thing is,' and I stop.

'Come on already,' she says.

'I'm getting married.'

'My god, I knew it! I knew as soon as I told you about Natan, the next thing I would hear from you is that you're getting married too. Bloody ridiculous!' she says with a lengthy rolled out ridiculous.

'Edith,' I say, 'shhh. Do you want everyone in the office to hear what you're saying! Just be quiet, will you, stop embarrassing me! Don't you want to know who I'm going to marry?'

'Yes of course I do!'

'His name's Morris Levine.'

'Well at least he's Jewish,' she says.

'Oh for god's sake,' I say.

'What! You think Mutti and Vati would want you to marry a goy?'

'Well, I'm not,' I say.

'So who is he, this Morris Levine?' she asks.

'You sound very negative and you don't know anything about him,' I say.

'Well, you hardly know him,' she says.

'How do you know?'

'Because two weeks ago you hadn't met him and now you're getting married to him!'

I don't say anything.

'It's a bit worrying that, isn't it? You think there's no connection with you-know-who?'

At least she doesn't say his name but I can just imagine all those people in the office listening to everything she says, and of course it'll go right back to Natan. Do I mind? Do I want it? Is that what it's really all about?

I'm sitting in the other lounge with Mutti who is holding me as I fall asleep and wake up, and sleep again. It's just Nina and me and outside it's raining and dark and inside there's us. And someone called Linda. She's half-sitting half-lying in a chair that goes far back.

'I want a chair like that,' I say to Mutti.

She says, 'Listen ma, listen to them, it's just like a play. It's her birthday today, she's seventy-five, and the man there, that's her husband Joe.'

I try to listen but I fall asleep and then wake.

'I love you, Joe,' I hear her say.

'I love you too,' he says, but he doesn't look at her.

'Are you going now?' she asks.

'No, not yet.'

'Are you coming back tomorrow?'

'No, not tomorrow. I don't come every day, do I? I'll come again. Soon.'

Suddenly she shouts, 'Ahhhhhh.'

'What you shouting for, Linda?' he asks.

'You don't love me,' she says.

'Course I do,' he says.

'I don't know what there's gonna be for supper,' she says. 'I'm gonna die.'

'No, you're not,' he says.

'You don't love me,' she shouts,

'I do,' he says, 'course I love you.'

'I hate you.'

'No you don't.'

'I don't want sandwiches for supper.'

Later, when I wake, there's another man there.

Nina whispers, 'Ahh, you're awake again, good, because you're missing it all. Look that man there, that's her brother, the husband's gone.'

Linda looks at her brother and says, 'Do you love me, Fred?'

'Course I do, Linda,' he says.

'I love you, Fred. I'm gonna die.'

'Well it's one thing we're all gonna do,' he says.

'It's getting dark out,' she says.

'Look at you Linda. You look just like Mum. Your hair's exactly the same colour as Mum's. I could be looking at Mum now. You saved my life when I was little. I had pneumonia and you nursed me. Mum always said you saved my life. Do you remember Linda? You saved my life.'

'I did, didn't I,' she says, 'you had pneumonia and I nursed you and I saved your life.'

When I wake up, I'm in my bed and Mutti's gone and Nina's gone and I'm alone. And I remember that Edith wants to talk to me about Morris.

'We haven't finished our discussion about Morris,' she says. 'You haven't told me anything about him. Or maybe, you don't know anything about him.'

'I know he's a good man,' I say.

'What makes a good man?' Edith asks.

Why does she always ask such difficult questions?

'You know Joseph's good, right,' I try to continue, 'and you know Natan's not, right?'

'Well, it's not that he's not a good man, it's just that,'

'Stop Edith,' I say interrupting her viciously, 'don't say another word, just be quiet and listen. Joseph's good, Natan's bad, right accept that. Well I can't say Morris is good or bad, I just can't put him in that sort of category. I think that he's warm and friendly, he doesn't seem to be loud, and I don't think he's argumentative, but he is funny, I mean others laugh with him a lot, and I sometimes see what's funny. But I think he's kind.'

'How do you know he's kind?' she asks.

'Because he gave me a handbag,' I say.

There is silence and all I hear then is a very quiet, under the breath sort of, 'Jesus Christ.' I'm going to ignore it, I think.

'And anyway,' I say, 'his eyes laugh.'

12

I'm lying in this bed. It's bright but not too bright, the light isn't coming in but maybe it's night-time and maybe I haven't even been to sleep yet.

I'm not tired but I have to wee. But I don't remember where the toilet is, I won't be able to find it. Maybe it's outside, even outside the house, an outdoor toilet.

Where am I? What room is this? I don't know this room. I don't know where the door is, where the window is.

Am I in Berlin, no I'm at Tante Leah's, in my little room there, or, maybe I'm at Edith's.

I'll get up now, I'll find the toilet, I'm sure I'll find it. I'm going to get up now, I'm trying to move but I can't seem to move my legs, my legs aren't moving, and, oh no, the wee's coming. I've just wet my bed, what will Mutti say. I wait to feel the warm wetness but there's nothing.

The door opens. It's Mutti, she'll say, why didn't you get up and go to the toilet, you're not a baby. I open my eyes and see someone else, she's smiling,

'Good morning darling,' she says, 'did you sleep well? You slept late. I'll open the curtains and let in some sunshine. Lots of sunshine today, Rika, you'll be happy. Now, let's get that soggy pad off you, hey.'

'I don't want to stay in Israel,' Morris says. 'I want us to go to South Africa. We'll have a much better life there. Here there's nothing for us, no flat, no job, no help, nothing. In Johannesburg there's my mother and four brothers and three sisters, and they're really good people. I'm a very good mechanic, you know Rika. I'll make sure you'll be ok. It might be a bit difficult till I get on my feet, but I'll have help to do that. I'm going to work with my brother and I'll make a good living. I'll have my own workshop and one day my own garage with lots of customers who'll come from far and wide because of my reputation. I'm going to call my workshop Efficiency Tune-Up Centre. And do you know why? Because I'm efficient! So what do you say, huh? Tell me you think it's a good idea. Tell me you'll give it a chance. South Africa's the land of milk and honey, you know. This is just the land of sand and fighting. There's nothing here. Life will be too hard for us here.'

'So what did you say,' Edith asked, 'tell me you said no! You know things will be good here, it might take a bit of time, but things will work out. Anyway, you could come live on the kibbutz, he'll fit in well on the kibbutz. We need mechanics. He'll always have work and besides, he's a sociable person, people like him. Tell me you'll come live on the kibbutz, or at least stay in Israel. Besides, you owe it to me, to Mutti and Vati, to all the Jewish people! We have our own Jewish state now, you have to be part of it, you can't not, Rika. You're my sister!'

Shoshana laughs.
'How can you laugh, it's so serious,' I say.
That makes her laugh even more.
'Ok, stop laughing now,' I say, 'and tell me what you think I should do.'
'Six little words,' she says.
'And they are?'
'What do you want to do?'
'I won't live on a kibbutz,' I say. 'And he's right, it is all so difficult here, where would we find a flat, unemployment is so high, costs of everything are high.'
'And besides,' she says, 'you don't like the heat, you don't like the sand, you hunger for green grass, and you're not

that mad about hard work. South Africa sounds just right!'

I'm going to be married in Tel Aviv. Morris will be discharged from the Airforce next Tuesday and we're getting married on the Wednesday and on the Sunday we leave for Johannesburg.

Edith says, 'Come and stay for shabat before your wedding. We'll have a special time, we'll go on bike rides and cycle all round the place. Just you and me. We'll talk about things, because you know what, Rika, nothing is set in stone yet. You might have made the decision to marry him, and you might have made the decision to go to South Africa, but neither of those have been done yet. So actually, you could change your mind!'

And as she says this, I know that she's right. I don't have to go along with this. I don't have to get married to this stranger who gave me a handbag. If I said no now, what would be the problem. We would just have to let the Rabbi know it's not going to happen, in fact, I could even give his bloody handbag back to him. I've still got a choice.

When I'm with Edith, she seems to me like Janus, two faces, one looking to a future with me beside her and one with me far away. The first is happy and loving and caring and the second is besides herself with anger and rage. She tries to hide the angry face, but it spills over and I see it peeping out from time to time, pushing aside the caring one. But she's canny and knows she has to keep the anger under control if she has any chance of making me change my mind. I don't want to get into an argument with her. It can't lead to anything other than both of us getting upset.

I already feel such an emptiness at the potential loss of her. Six thousand miles apart is so far. It's not possible to get on a bus, or hitch a lift or even pick up a phone if I need to see her. Phone calls are only for absolute emergencies. All that's available is to write on those thin blue Aerogramme letters with limited space and which take weeks to reach each other.

She is after all my only really close relative. She's my sister. We were born of the same parents and in the same womb. We love (hate) each other with an intensity I don't have for anyone else.

Will I ever feel anything like it for this stranger who could soon be my husband?

No, for god's sake, no, don't think of Natan, get him out, out, out of that head of yours, he has no place there or anywhere else in your body, I say to myself with such force it almost gets verbalised.

Focus on the important question, is it possible for me to leave Edith, can I leave everything I've known, everything that is me, for a future that is so unknown. Of course not. It seems crazy that I even thought I could!

'Rika!' Frieda runs to me and hugs me. 'Rika! Can you believe it!'

I'm frozen. I can't move, my arms are stuck to my sides, my legs are nailed into the ground, my smile is stuck in a grimace.

'Rika, Rika, it's me Frieda, have you forgotten me!'

And then fluidity comes back, my blood restarts, my lungs breathe in, my smile returns.

'Frieda, Frieda, Frieda.' Three times I say it, perhaps as compensation for the time lapse. She looks wonderful. She is wonderful. She's Natan's wife!

'I can't believe it,' I say. 'Who would've believed it, it's just unbelievable.'

Everything's in threes. I have to pause, I have to regain myself, I have to calm down.

'Come let's sit down,' she says pointing to a bench, 'just you and me, we have so much to catch up on.'

We sit, and she puts her arm through mine.

'Rika,' she says, 'who would've believed when we sat opposite each other on the train, when we spent that time in that funny pension in Trieste, when we slept in the same cabin in the boat', (she's also talking threes, I notice), 'that I would end up here on Kibbutz Sdot Yam with you.'

'Well I'm not strictly here,' I say quickly.

'I mean, your sister', she says, 'and of course you are an important part of here too,'

'Am I?'

'Of course! Everyone knows you, everyone likes you, and I know Natan's very fond of you.'

I gasp, inaudibly, she wouldn't notice it, only I notice it because I can't breathe for a moment.

'I know that you and Natan had a little thing for a short while, but he told me it was very little, meaningless, which is good because it might've been embarrassing for you, and for me, for both of us if it had been, you know, really significant.'

'Oh no, rest assured,' I say very quickly, 'it really was nothing, less than nothing, a second, that's all it lasted. Nothing.'

She tells me their story. I don't want to know their story. I really very much don't want to know how they noticed each other, how they became friendly, how it became more, how in fact, he was her first, how he took her so gently, how he stroked her and helped her through the pain, how he wiped her (I really don't want to know about that!) how beautiful their first time together was.

Oh Jesus, enough, enough, enough!

'I've got to go Frieda, you'll have to tell me more later, sorry, but so lovely how happy you both are. See you later, Bye!'

I have to marry Morris. I want to marry Morris. He's a wonderful man, nothing like Natan. Just like Vati.

'I'm sorry, Edith,' I say, 'but I really think I've made the right decision. Sorry. Sorry.'

Today's my wedding day. How very strange. I'm not the sort who used to dream of white weddings, or play wedding-wedding, or plan what I'd wear, or how I'd look or what I'd say.

The day feels so ordinary. We received some telegrams which is about as exciting as it gets, from his family, congratulations, mazal tov, we can't wait to meet you, to welcome you into our family. And me? I can wait.

Morris is dressed up, he's wearing a suit, how very strange. I'm wearing the dress I went to buy last week with Shoshana. It's a lovely dress, whitish, creamish, modern, sleek. She can't believe I weigh less than one hundred pounds.

'How can you be so skinny and work in a café?' she says.

'It's because you don't let me eat the cakes,' I say and smile.

Edith and Joseph are here with their sweet little daughter who is now two. Tante Leah of course and Onkel Bruno who is not at all well these days. Their sons and their wives and their babies. And Shoshana.

And from Morris' side there are five friends, all South African, all airmen like him, or like he used to be because he's now been discharged.

And me, and Morris. Us, the couple, Morris and Rika, or Rika and Morris. Who knows what people will say – we're off to see Morris and Rika. I think in South Africa it will always be M and R whereas here in Israel they'll be coming to visit R and M.

Oh, don't forget the Rabbi, he's here too.

It's not a religious wedding, god forbid, so don't expect the separate genders singing and dancing and holding the bride and groom high up on chairs, none of that, but of course there was the food. No Jewish wedding could happen without stamping on the glass and shouting mazal tov and eating lots of food.

It's at Tante Leah's house and she's prepared and bought in all the food I love.

They all give us presents of money. 'That's what you need and that's what you can shlep to South Africa,' they say.

We're spending the night at Tante Leah's, in my little room there. It's still quite a small room, 'But that shouldn't matter,' they all laugh.

Everyone leaves and Tante Leah and Onkel Bruno say, 'Well, off to bed. Exciting day!'

'Thank you Tante Leah,' I say, 'for everything.'

She cries but says, 'Happy tears, happy tears.'

My husband and I get into bed.

He says, 'Hello wife.'

I suppose that's sweet. Is he waiting for me to say, hello husband back. Somehow, I can't get it out of my mouth.

We lie together and kiss and get excited and make love and it was fine! Thank god that's over, I think, because what would I have done if it had been terrible, if he hadn't been able to, or if I'd screamed.

But I didn't and he could and it was all fine.

13

'When are we going to land?' I ask the woman giving me tea.

'To land?' she laughs, 'are we in an aeroplane, Rika?'

'Isn't that where we are?'

'We could be. Where are we flying to? I'd love to be in an aeroplane now. Oh my god, imagine, on a plane to a Greek island. How about that Rika? The sun, the sea, retsina, hmm. Where do you want to fly to?'

I don't answer her because I understand I'm not in an aeroplane, I'm in this place where I live, this room they move me to in the morning where I sit and watch people, but there's nothing much to watch because everyone else is just sitting.

There's a noise in the corner but it's just moving pictures and I don't know those people. I put my head back on the comfortable chair and I dream. But my eyes are open.

It's coming in to land. Morris is excited next to me. He's sitting with his head taking up the whole window, looking out, supplying me with a running commentary the whole time.

'It looks so brown already, the green of summer's gone, but the sun is shining. That's the thing Rika, middle of winter but the sun is shining. We've reached the beginning of houses, there's even a swimming pool in that one, lucky buggers.

Ah, I can see the runways, we're approaching, we're almost there. Rika, there's the airport. I bet they're all there, all of them, you'll meet them soon, Rika, I can't wait. Are you excited?'

I can't say to him, I'm dreading this actually Morris. How can I be cruel, so I smile, but he's not looking at me, and I say, 'Yes, of course.'

We cross the tarmac from the airport to customs and I can hear shouting, 'Morris, Morris.' Morris is waving like a lunatic and pointing to me and laughing.

I can see crowds of people and I follow his finger to where he's pointing and shouting.

'That's them, that's my brother Jonathan, that's Benji, Stevie, oh look all of them are there,'

I can make out some figures that must be The Family. As we walk through customs and into a big hall, we are accosted by hordes, or so it seems, all of them hugging me and smiling.

'Welcome to South Africa,' they're all saying, 'my god you weren't exaggerating Morris, she is a beauty, how was the flight, you must be starving, did you sleep, what was it like!'

I feel overwhelmed. I feel as if the air is being sucked away. I feel a black cloud threatening to engulf me and suddenly, 'She's going to faint, grab her,' and I'm grabbed and sat in a chair and water is brought and everyone is looking concerned and then they exclaim joyously when they see me open my eyes.

They laugh when I drink and say, 'She's going to be fine, just all the excitement, too many people, let's get her home.'

'Where's ma?' Morris asks.

'She's at home, she's waiting for you both at home,' they all say.

We drive through Johannesburg which is wide and flat. The centre of the city is full of tall grey and brown buildings and we pass a big flat yellow mountain.

'That's from the gold mines,' Morris explains.

We pass a lake. 'The Wemmer Pan, oh my God,' says his sister Chava who is in the car with us. 'Can you imagine that boy, aged ten mind you, swam all the way across the pan. He was such a naughty boy,' and they all laugh.

Was he? A naughty boy? That's interesting. That's a fact I can add to my very short list of things I know about my husband. I'm pretty sure it's going to grow massively being around his family.

'We live in the Southern Suburbs,' Chava explains, 'in a suburb called La Rochelle. Here it is, this is the street and this is the house and there's ma, standing outside.'

'What shall I call her?' I whisper to Morris.

'Either ma, or Shaina Raisa,' he replies, 'beautiful rose, because she's beautiful.'

I can't call her ma.

She's tiny and already grey with her hair held back in a bun, her legs are bandy and she has a big tum, but the biggest thing of all is her smile.

'Is this the Daytschke,' she says as soon as she sees me, 'aisch, she is a beauty,' and she comes and hugs me. And for a strange second I think, Mutti.

We're having tea, it's very dark brown and made with milk and sugar. It's horrible. I splutter and say, 'Sorry.'

'Don't worry,' they say, 'you don't like it like this? How do you like it, tell us and we'll make it how you like it.'

I say, weak and black and no sugar.

'Oy vay!' they all proclaim. 'Weak and black and no sugar. But there's no taste. You might as well have water.'

And they all laugh. They give me some biscuit things that are reddish brown with sesame seeds on it. I like sesame, I pick it up and it's incredibly sticky.

'What!' proclaims Shaina Raisa, 'you don't know taiglach! Don't they eat taiglach where you came from?'

'Ma,' says Morris, 'she's not a Litvak.'

'I know,' says Shaina Raisa, 'she's a Daytschke! So what do Daytschkes eat? Gefillte fish, kichel and herring, what?'

'Who knows!' says Morris.

Shaina Raisa says, 'A husband should know.'

'New husband,' they all say.

'She likes sweets,' he says.

'But she's such a skinny-melinks, how can she eat sweets!' and they laugh as though it's the funniest thing in the world.

'She'll eat what we eat, chicken, rice, potatoes, normal food,' Morris says and they nod. I watch them.

We have a room in Shaina Raisa's house. It's a small house and I wonder how they managed to have so many children living here when they were younger. There is a garden around the whole house.

The room we stay in was the one Morris shared with his brothers. Only the youngest brother Stevie still lives here but he's in a different room.

Morris has pushed two single beds together to make a double. I'm in bed and Morris takes a running jump and instead of landing in the bed, he lands half in and half out and hurts his leg badly. As he swears I burst out laughing.

'Is that the famous German sense of humour,' he says, 'laughing when someone falls.'

It's true, I recognise it, but it doesn't stop me. Nothing stops me other than the slow realisation that he is sulking and is sullen. I stop, like a car spluttering till it runs out of petrol.

'Sorry,' I say, but he doesn't reply.

This goes on the column that says, things I don't like about this new husband of mine.

It's morning and Morris is still sleeping. I'm feeling really hungry and I'm sure no-one will mind if I go and get something to eat. The whole house is quiet but I'll find where things are, it won't be a problem.

'Oh hullo, 'I say when I walk into the kitchen because there's a woman standing at the stove stirring porridge. 'Ahh porridge, good.'

'Morning ma'm,' she says.

I laugh and say, 'My name's Rika, what's yours?'

'Rebecca, ma'm.'

Why's she calling me that, I think, but maybe she hadn't heard me say my name, I'd better just leave it for the moment.

'Can I help?' I ask.

She laughs. 'No, ma'm, it's fine, you sit and I'll bring you your breakfast.'

'Oh gosh no, I say, I don't need to be served. I'll get us a couple of cups and what are you going to have, tea or coffee?'

She laughs again and covers her mouth with her hand, and shakes her head.

Just then, Shaina Raisa walks in and says, 'Good morning, Daytschke, did you sleep good?'

She asks me what I'd like for breakfast and I say, 'Rebecca and I are going to have some porridge. Do you like porridge?'

The two of them start laughing and Rebecca carries on shaking her head.

'Shall I take out three cups?' I ask

'There's only two of us,' Shaina Raisa retorts.

'But,' I start, and they laugh again, and I stop.

'Aii Daytschke, you don't know anything about South Africa, I see,' she says and leads me by the arm into the dining room. 'She's the girl,' she says to me as if that's an explanation. 'She doesn't eat with us.'

'Why not,' I ask.

'Because she's the girl, the shiksa,' and that explains it conclusively.

Morris arrives and says, 'Hey Rebecca, have you met my new wife? You have another missus now, an old missus and a young missus' and they all laugh.

Is this what my husband's like? Does he speak to all black people like this or just people who work for him. His manners might be off but there's nothing wrong with his appetite as he tucks into his breakfast.

Morris is talking to a man I don't know. They're smoking and laughing and they're so carefree together.

'Rika,' he calls, 'come meet my best friend, Philip. I told you about him. We grew up together and did everything, I mean everything, together,' they both laugh.

He shakes my hand and says, 'Jees man, I can't believe I'm finally meeting you. Yiss! It's really nice!'

I smile too, genuinely. I say genuinely and think, am I pretending the rest of the time?

We sit drinking tea and eating taiglach on the verandah, the sweet honey-laden hard biscuit that so many of the Lithuanian and Latvian born South African Jews make. We, just the women of the family. I'm now one of the women of the family.

'Morris was such a naughty boy,' his sister Chavah goes on as if continuing a conversation from five minutes ago. 'You wouldn't believe what he used to do when we were small. Well,' she says clasping her hands in glee with the others already smiling in anticipation, as if they'd never heard the story before, 'we never had enough money and every Friday afternoon, ma would give Morris a sixpence to go to the Rabbi to get a kosher chicken. Every Friday he came back with one. One day ma bumped into the Rabbi. Oy Mrs Levine, he says to her, I'm so sorry things are so difficult for you, I never realised it was so bad. What do you mean, ma says, what are you talking about! Well, that you can't afford a chicken, he says.'

They all burst out laughing.

'Oy ya yoy!' she continued, 'every week Morris was stealing a chicken, killing it himself, and pocketing the sixpence! Did he get a patz im tochis! Not only was he causing such shame to the family, but worst of all, we were having treif chicken every Shabbos!'

'He was such a naughty boy,' Hannah his sister takes up the mantle, (is she being competitive). 'One day, in the summer, he couldn't have been more than thirteen, he disappeared! His bike, gone, his friend Philip, gone. We put two and two together and realise they had both taken their bikes and gone off together. Can you guess where they went? You'll never guess! Never in a million years would you guess! They'd cycled to Durban! That's four hundred miles away. Can you imagine! Four hundred miles! They didn't have any money. They just stole food, picked fruit, slept wherever. Did he get a patz im tochis when he got home, I can tell you!'

His sister Naomi is not to be left out. 'He was such a naughty boy, he used to fight all the time. He was always sent home from school, for fighting or getting up to mischief. Him and Philip, they were so naughty.'

'Why did they fight?' I ask.

'Ach,' Naomi says, 'they didn't have to have a reason, but often it was because people said bloody Jew to him, or stupid Afrikaner to Philip.'

'They didn't have to have a reason,' Chavah concurred.

And now Shaina Raisa, who has been nodding her head throughout, suddenly joins in the fun and games. 'Oy, that Morris, was he a naughty boy, a real wilde chaye! So naughty, I'm telling you, you wouldn't believe it. What I went through! What I went through, you would not believe!'

'Why? I ask, what did he do?'

'What did he do? What didn't he do! You wouldn't believe how I suffered with that boy. And I didn't have a husband you know. He died when Morris was, he must have been nine, eight, nine. Something like that. I had to look after him, after all of them. But the others listened to me. Morris, do you think he listened to me? Ha! You can think again! Always he got sent home from school. Fighting. He could fight like, like a meshugenah, I'm telling you, like a goy! Thank God he's got you. You'll calm him. You'll make him stop fighting. Thank God for you, his skinny little Daytschke.'

I look at my husband. I watch him out of the corner of my eyes. I don't want him to think I'm studying him, but that's what I'm doing. I'm collating my list, my two columns on the paper.

On the left-hand side I note that he is good looking, short, but not that short, not for a short woman, so that's fine, lovely thick brown hair, a ready laugh, eager to make people laugh, though unfortunately for him and me, I suppose, he's realised I don't laugh easily at his jokes/antics/nonsense.

And his family love him. That's good, not everyone is loved even by their own family.

And on the right-hand side I note in big black capital letters, that he's got a temper, a temper which I don't understand. I can't work out what it is that he's actually so angry about. It all seems so mundane, so silly. So childish, I have to say.

I'm watching him storming through the house, shouting and swearing, he picks up a chair and slams it down, he goes out the house and shuts it with a bang. It's all so loud, so fierce, so violent. My leg is twitching and my arm is trembling. I feel the tears prick my eyelids.

'They shouldn't have taken my stuff,' Morris says.

'What does it matter,' I say, innocently, unaware of the importance of not having one's own stuff taken.

'It's my stuff,' he says, 'they shouldn't have taken it.'

'But what does it matter?' I ask.

I'm not getting at him, I'm not trying to make it worse, I just need to understand.

But he sniffs and gets up and walks away saying, 'People shouldn't take my stuff. It's my stuff. Not theirs. And they shouldn't take it.'

Shaina Raisa comes in and sits next to me. 'Ach, it's just Morris. You mustn't worry, that's just the way he is. He's got a temper. Nu, nobody's perfect!'

'Why is there so much noise,' I shout into the quiet.

Someone comes rushing up to me, 'Rika, darling, what's the matter? Why are you so upset?'

I look at her and I say, 'I'm sorry, I really can't bear so much swearing. You know my Vati never swore, never a loud word, never a swear word, never. I can't be expected to live with this now.'

'Don't worry, Rika,' the woman says, 'I'll tell them to be quieter.'

'Thank you,' I say, and close my eyes again.

14

I need to write to my sister.

'Miss, miss,' I say, calling someone, 'can you give me some paper please, I need to write to my sister. My sister is expecting a letter and I haven't written one yet.'

'Sure Rika, just one moment. I won't be a sec, just finishing this and then I'll get you some.'

She brings me a piece of paper and puts it on the little table that gets pulled in front of me and hands me a thing to write with, a pencil, yes. And I write to her, I write these words:

Dear Edith,

Hello. How are you? I'm fine. I'm happy here. It is warm but not so hot like in Israel. You remember how much I hated the heat. Everything is good. Morris is fine. He is starting his own garage next week. He will work in the same building as his brother Benji, the very short one. It is on the side of the building in the town, on the southern part of the town with lots of Indian people nearby. He will fix cars and his brother is a welder. It will be good when he starts his own business and we can buy a house for ourselves and not live anymore here with his mother. She's fine but it's better to be alone. You asked me in your letter if I am happy. Of course I am. Why would I not be? Do you think I am not? Why do you think that? One thing I don't understand in this country is the way it is with the black people – the schwarze, as the family say.

Please write soon. I am always waiting for letters from you.

Your sister, Rika.

'Here you are, I say to the woman, please post this for me.'

She takes it and says, 'What a lovely picture you have drawn, Rika. What is it? Some flowers, or, is it a dog?'

I'm feeling so sick, nauseous, I want to vomit, I rush to the toilet, get there just in time. Oh god, this is so horrible, I stagger back, exhausted, fall into the chair.

Shaina Raisa is looking at me oddly, every time I get up, she stops her knitting, her sewing, her crocheting and looks at me sideways.

'I don't know why I feel so tired,' I say eventually.

'Don't you know?' she says.

'No,' I say, 'I've never felt anything like this.'

'You're pregnant, mein Kind. You're going to have a baby.'

I stare at her, what is she saying. What! Pregnant, no, I'm not ready to be pregnant. I'm still hardly grown up. Am I grown up? I'm a bloody wife, I say, I must be bloody grown up. What am I doing swearing, I never swear, why have I started now? A child!

'Mazel tov,' she says, 'it's wonderful news. Aren't you thrilled?' She doesn't wait for an answer. 'Thrilled? Of course she's thrilled!'

She's going around telling everyone, the daughters, the daughters-in-law, the whole mishpocha is told while I'm still wondering why I feel so numb. Everyone is thrilled.

'You must be so thrilled!'

Morris is thrilled and grabs me and twirls me round,

'My God', he says, 'we're going to have a baby.'

Now that sounds a better idea, I think, you have it and I'll be thrilled for you.

'Ma', he shouts, 'we're going to have a baby!'

'I know, you nudnik!' Shaina Raisa says, 'I was the one who told her!'

They laugh and I watch them.

Mutti. Vati. Look at me. I'm not fourteen anymore. I'm a grown woman now. Can you see me? What do you think when you look at me? Do you wonder what I'm doing here? Do you understand that I have to be here now? I did have a choice but I couldn't decide.

Now the choice has gone. Has it gone? Do I still have a choice?

I'm having a baby. But actually, the baby can be born anywhere. I won't leave it behind if I go away. It'll come with me because it's still part of me.

Why am I staying here? I don't understand these people. I'm walking in a circle, I don't know what to do, I walk forwards and then backwards, go, stay, go, stay. This is the moment and every day the moment slips away, it has to be now. I have to decide. I write to my sister.

Edith, I have news. I'm pregnant and I'm going to have a baby. I think I should maybe leave him. What do you think I should do?

The moments drag. Two weeks I wait before the thin blue Aerogramme drops on the floor. I tear it open and read and sludge through news about the yield of oranges and bananas and what buildings have gone up on the kibbutz and gossip about members and a child for Natan and Frieda and finally at the bottom she writes:

You are not a child anymore Rika. You have made your bed, now you must lie in it. You must stay with your husband. He is not a terrible man and it is not a terrible family. You just have to get used to it. You know the kibbutz is not for you. You have always hated it here. Where would you go? Would you really want to go back to Tante Leah? They can't put you up and start again with a baby in their little flat. You don't have any more choices.

There is nowhere else for you to go. You must make the best of it.

'Edith is such a bitch,' I scream and then fear others in the house can hear me.

So Natan and I will have children at the same time, the same age. If I was at the kibbutz, they would be in the same class.

If I move, anything I've eaten since I was last sick will rise to the top and gush out like a volcano. Just don't move, not a single fibre, not a muscle or tendon, nothing, still, still.

'She doesn't move, that girl,' Shaina Raisa complains to Morris, and I hear her in my still, unmoving state. 'Honestly, you'd think she was the only woman ever to have been pregnant. She needs to move herself. What does she think! That the world revolves around her. That she's the only person in the world who's ever been pregnant!'

Morris comes to me. He looks at me lying, stock still, unmoving, dead. 'You need to move yourself,' he says, 'you're not the only person who's ever been pregnant. It's no good for you to just lie down all the time. The world doesn't revolve around you.'

Rebecca persuades me to sit outside at least, in the sunshine.

'Hau Madam,' she says, 'why don't you eat this in the garden. Then I can make your bed and you will feel much better.'

She brings me some bland lunch, boiled chicken and some white bread. Yes, that should be ok.

She stands over me. 'Please sit,' I say, 'why won't you sit with me.'

She looks around then sits, tentatively on the edge.

'Where is your family?' I ask.

'In Hammanskraal, ma'm,' she says.

'Is that far away?'

'Long, long way.'

'But you're always here.' I say, 'When do you see your family?'

'Only at Christmas.'

'Do you have children,' I ask.

'Yes, I have two girls.'

'How old are they?'

'They are still too small,' she says.

'Who looks after them?'

'My mother and my little sister.'

'That's not fair,' I say.

She laughs and hides her mouth behind her hand. 'Hau madam. You make me laugh!'

Morris and I are in bed. He starts kissing me.

'Why doesn't Rebecca live with her children?' I ask him.

He tries to ignore my question. 'Not now,' he says, inching closer and closer.

I push him away, gently, not get-away-from-me push, more like a, listen-to-me-for-goodness-sake push. He stops, looks at me as if to say, Jesus Christ, and then sits back with his head on the headboard.

'Where would they live? They can't live here. They're not allowed to.'

'But she's missing them,' I say.

'You don't know that.'

'But they're growing up without her. Imagine if that was us,' I say. Has he got a nicer side to appeal to?

'Well, that's true,' he says, 'but she has to work. She supports her whole family. Besides, they don't mind like we would.'

Oh my god, did he really say that! Please tell me I misheard.

'She's a mother,' I say, icily.

But he swats me away as if I were an irritating fly. 'You don't understand how things work here, Rika.'

'How much does she get paid,' I ask.

'She likes it here. She's got a good life with us. She's much better off living with us than she would be with almost anybody else.'

'Why do you say that?' I ask.

'Because we treat her well.'

And that's a full-stop it seems because he turns his back to me. But I'm not finished and I don't accept his full-stop.

'She works all the time,' I say.

'She has Sunday afternoons off. And sometimes she gets other times off too,' he says softly.

'She's always working,' I say.

'No she's not,' he says, forgetting that previous full-stop and sitting half up, leaning on his arm, facing me. 'She sits around in the front talking to her friends half the day. She's happy. You can see she's happy.'

I sit halfway up too. 'Well I wouldn't be happy if I was working all the time,' I say from my position of not working at all.

But he comes back with the definitive, 'You're not her, and she's not working all the time. As I just said, you don't understand. You're not South African. You don't understand us at all. South Africa is the land of milk and honey. Look how good we have it here. The weather's always good. Sunshine even in winter.'

Then he lies down on his back with his arm under his head, and he focuses on some misty cloud ahead of us. 'I'm starting to make money now, Rika. Very soon we'll be in our own flat, then things will be different, you'll see. Trust me. This is a great place to live. Give it time. You'll get used to it.'

'But how much does she earn?' I insist.

I'm standing in front of Shaina Raisa's mirror.

It's the only full-length mirror in the house. She's out so I stand naked, sideways, frontways, backways, and I look at this monstrosity that is me.

I know it's me because I recognise the face, but the body is unrecognisable, it's almost obscene. I've never seen anything quite so distorted, so ugly, a great big middle that isn't even round, it's oblong and changes shape with bits sticking out and moving.

As for the colour and texture, it's alien. And there are marks all over it, as if linen has been stretched so far that it's unable to hold itself together and becomes a mishmash of individual threads. It's getting worse, becoming more and more not me.

We're moving into a little flat of our own. Shaina Raisa asks me if I'm excited.

'I'll miss you and Rebecca,' I say.

'Pshh,' she spits out, 'nonsense, you'll get a girl of your own. And as for me, I'll see you all the time!'

I think, all the time?

Morris says, 'We'll get a girl to help with the flat and look after you.'

'I don't need a servant,' I say, 'it's just a little flat, it's not a problem for me to clean and look after it.'

'But you'll have a baby', he says 'and I don't want people thinking I can't afford to pay for a girl.'

'I don't want anyone doing my dirty work for me. I'm capable of doing it myself,' I state, metaphorically stamping my foot.

But that doesn't stop Morris asking his brothers and sisters if they can ask their servants if they know of a nice, clean, honest 'girl' who's looking for a job.

We're in our new flat. It's not very far from Shaina Raisa, in a little suburb full of flats and small houses. There's a park ten minutes walk away.

The flat's mine more than Morris' because I'm here alone all day while he's at work. I walk from one end to the next, it takes me at least twenty seconds if I walk slowly. But it's my twenty seconds worth of walk. I'm big and clumsy and tired a lot of the time but I can make that walk from one end to the next.

There's a knock on the door.

A pretty woman is standing at the door. She has a lovely smile, though she looks quite nervous.

'Hullo,' I say.

She calls me 'Ma'm.' I wish people wouldn't.

'Can I help you,' I ask.

'I'm the girl, ma'm,' she says.

'What girl is that,' I ask.

'The girl you asked for. Rebecca sent me. She said you need a good girl to work for you. My name's Dinah.'

But I don't need anyone, I think, it's my house, I think, I'll clean it myself, I think. I can't say that to her, not when she's looking at me like, like what, like a dog, that's a terrible thing to say, how can I say that, it's eagerness, hunger almost.

She sees my hesitation and quickly adds, 'Rebecca said the master said you need someone.'

Master! Hateful! I pause, she fills the silence.

'I've come from Sophiatown and I'm looking for a job.'

She needs a job. She probably has a family to support. What do I do? A door opens a few flats along and a woman I haven't seen before comes out. She smiles at both of us, unusual (not to me, but to a black person).

'Hello, I'm so sorry, you don't know me, but I couldn't help overhearing. My name's Jill, by the way, pleased to meet you.'

'And you,' I smile. She's small, petite is the right word, with fluffy, short blonde hair. Her face is taken up with her huge smile. She stands outside her door, one hand on the doorframe, as if she's rooting herself back there, showing she's not interfering, moving into my territory. Yet she is.

'So, it seems this woman here, Dinah, yes?' Dinah nods, 'she needs a job, and I'm sure you could do with some help now you're about to have a baby. It looks like you're about to. I don't want to be rude.'

We both laugh.

'Well, Dinah seems nice,' she continues, 'and you seem nice, so why don't you give her a job. I'm sure it will be helpful to both of you. You know, there's a lot of unemployment in this country.'

'You mean, she would come every day?' I ask horrified at the intrusion if nothing else.

Dinah looks me straight in the face. 'I would need to stay, m'am.'

'But there isn't any room in the flat for another person, we need the extra bedroom for the baby,' I say in alarm.

But Jill says, 'There's a room up at the top, the servants' quarters, that's where the servants sleep. A room for each flat.'

She arrives the next day with her things in a plastic bag and goes up to her flat. No, what a euphemism. I know it's not a flat, why am I pretending to myself, to make myself feel better that a woman is leaving her family to look after me as if I were an invalid, and I know I'm not, and to make matters worse she lives like a slave in a little room as far away as possible from the white people she serves.

I want to see it myself, I want to see how bad it is.

'Can I see your room,' I ask her.

She looks nonplussed. She can't say no to me because I'm the madam! The madam and the master, Jesus!

'Maybe I can give you something to make it nicer,' I say with a little smile.

We go up, it's a different world up there at the top of the building, almost slum-like, lots of little rooms, one shower, an open air sink, a toilet, one for them all.

The room is small and dark, the walls are gray, an uncleaned, unpainted, unloved gray. The single bed is high up on some bricks.

'We'll make it better,' I say to her. 'The bricks can certainly go straightaway and then I'll ask Morris to paint it nice and bright, yes? Is that good?'

I notice she's not responding as I expect.

'What's the matter?' I ask.

'We like the bed high, ma'am.'

'Really! Why?'

She smiles. 'It's what we believe'.

When I tell Morris he laughs at me and says, 'You really don't know anything, do you. It's the tokoloshe.'

I don't know what he's talking about.

'It's a little devil type thing that can get them in the middle of the night, so they have to be high to keep out of its clutches. You try to be nice, Rika, but you don't know what you're dealing with. These are ignorant people.'

'What's the matter, Rika? Why are you looking so worried?' asks MillieMollieMandy.

'Tokoloshe. Will come tonight to get me.'

'No darling, nothing's going to get you. You know you're very safe here. We're here to look after you'.

But not at night when the tokoloshe comes. They're not South African, they don't understand. It'll come, it's the devil, big eyes, long nails, will dig its nails into this arm, will pull the flesh off this arm.

'Bricks, I need bricks. Bricks,' I say.

'I don't know what Rika's on about today. Anybody have a clue what Rika's saying?' And they laugh.

'Don't worry, darling.'

They keep saying, don't worry, don't worry. The tokoloshe hears them and laughs.

Tokoloshe, it sounds so nice, I roll it round my mouth, tokoloshe.

I ask Jill, 'Do you know about tokoloshe.'

'It's an African thing. It's a way of making sense of what happened to them in the past. They used to sleep in huts on the floor around a fire which they kept burning at night to keep them warm during the winter. But of course, the fire just uses up the oxygen and people used to die in the night from carbon monoxide poisoning. They didn't know about carbon monoxide, all they saw was their family dying for no reason. They knew they had to be high up but not why. So they created something tangible to explain it, something supernatural. Makes sense, right?'

I put it to Morris, 'You know the tokoloshe thing, well there's an explanation.'

He listens and says, 'Ok.'

And that's that.

15

My waters have broken.
'Help,' I shout, 'help. I'm wet all over.' It's seeping out of me. The whole of my insides has gushed out. I will be left with nothing.

They come over, 'What is it now, Rika?'

'My waters have broken.'

'Darling, you just spilt some water. Who gave Rika an ordinary cup?' she shouts out to the others.

'What the hell...' Morris starts, and jumps out of the bed. 'Rika', he says and shakes me awake.

'What?'

I'm sleepy and know my dream, it's still in my head. I'm swimming in a beautiful warm lake near a waterfall.

The dream disappears as Morris says, 'Your waters must have broken.'

It's cold now, I'm wide awake, what does it mean?

'Let's go,' he says.

'Where to?'

'To the maternity hospital, where do you think!'

Nina is here with a baby. Has she got a new baby? I thought she was looking a bit fat lately.

'Is that your baby?' I ask, holding my hands out for it.

'It's yours, ma', she says handing me the baby.

Oh my my my, oh my my my my, look look at the little baby, look how sweet, oh I love this little baby, and she has such sweet clothes and she cries, but if I turn her upside down she stops, and she has such a sweet smile and her lips are painted red. Oh she's so lovely, my lovely little baby boy.

'Where's my baby? I've lost my baby. Baby,' I yell, 'I must find my baby, it's somewhere, it'll be worried, frightened, hungry, someone will take it, find my baby!'

'Rika, Rika, what's the matter?'

'My baby!'

'Hold on a moment, I know where she is, I'll get her for you.'

'Ahh, here's my baby, come to me babala, ahhh, that's it, that's my baby, ahhhh sweet sweet baby. Lalalala.' I sing a lullaby to him to help him sleep.

The woman smiles as she watches me look after my baby.

I look at my baby as they put him in my arms. Did I really believe I had some alien being in me, was that possible, I laugh. Look at this beautiful baby boy. How could anyone be so lovely. I hold my baby and put him to my breast. The midwives help to get him to take it, and eventually (after hours and hours) he does and it works, he sucks, he's happy, he sleeps.

The family come in and coo and murmur all sorts of encouraging things to him, which encourage me too. I look at them and smile, I look at Morris and smile, I look at the midwives and smile, everything makes me smile. I have become a different being.

'You're a mother now,' Shaina Raisa says.

That must be what's making me a better person.

I want to call him Willi, after my father, I tell Morris.

He laughs, 'Willi? Why not cut to the chase and call him Penis, or Pecker, or Dick, there's a real choice here, Rika.'

I don't think he's funny.

'Do you really want him to be mocked at by all the boys in his school?'

But why Graham?

'Such a goyish name,' Shaina Raisa says.

I don't know why Graham. Morris likes the name. His name is Graham. And Schnookooks, Grahamelushkela, motick sheli, my sweetie. Or 'Neshomelah' to Shaina Raisa.

The better person I am in the hospital disintegrates when we get home, when the night-time crying starts, the getting up seventeen times in the middle of the night, the attempts to get this mad ridiculous baby to take this breast that you took so easily before, when I had the help I then didn't need and now need, then you took the breast, you impossible dreadful monster of a baby.

Morris looks on, he is incompetent. Why is he so incompetent! Why doesn't he know what to do, how to help, how to take him off me and let me sleep. He knows he's incompetent and he doesn't like it, he's used to being able to do things, to achieve, to manage, to get things done, to be efficient. Efficiency Tune-Up Centre.

No-one's efficient with a baby, it's all in his time, when to sleep, when not to sleep, when to eat, when not to eat, when to wee, when to poo, he doesn't negotiate. He's the most selfish of all selfish beings because he's not even aware of your frustrations, your feelings, your climbing of any walls.

Dinah takes him off me. 'Go have a sleep,' she says and I don't argue, not for a moment do I argue.

I come back refreshed and see my beautiful gorgeous silent baby being rocked by the angel that is Dinah, and take him back into my arms and feel once again that I'm a better person.

And then suddenly, he starts to smile, this baby that was only ever inside himself suddenly reaches out to me with a smile, and the smile is the link with me, the smile is the acknowledgement that I'm a person too, an important person, a part of him, essential to him, loved by him.

And whereas at first he will go to anyone, later he won't, only me, and sometimes the father, but always me. Or

Dinah. Always me or Dinah. Yes, she is as important to him as I am, and she is as important to me. And I love her for it.

Shaina Raisa sits with me in the lounge. She is holding Graham and rocking him, and I can't keep my eyes open, but as soon as she sees them closing she speaks louder until I respond, 'Yes, of course, absolutely,' I say.

'This one's a crier. Some are, some aren't, but yours is. But he still is the sweetest thing in the world. But,' she pauses, loudly.

'Yes, yes I say,' eyes struggling to open.

'You mustn't spoil him. It's easy to spoil a baby but you mustn't. I bet you were spoilt as a child.'

I sit up, did I hear right? I was actually at the start of a dream, maybe I heard wrong. 'What was that?' I ask innocently.

'I'm sure you were spoilt as a child.'

'Why do you think that,' I ask, sweet as pie outside, bitter and poisonous as unripened rhubarb inside.

'Oh you know, just, I bet you were. No?'

How can this old yiddische woman insult my parents like this, my lovely Mutti who was never fortunate enough to be a grandmother like she is. My Vati, as kind as sweet as anyone in the entire world, who was never a grandfather, how can she impute that to them. I try to smile.

'They were wonderful parents,' I say between clenched teeth.

'Nu, I'm not saying not, I'm just saying, you know, the way you are.'

'How am I,' I say, trying not to say it in a tone that is too controlled, too quiet, too menacing, but knowing that's exactly how it's coming across.

'Don't get annoyed with me', she says, 'I'm not saying anything about you, just that you seem as if you were spoilt.'

'But why do you think that,' I say with a smile that would freeze jelly.

'Well, you always want things your way.'

As much as this is the last thing I want to happen, as much as I try to pull them back, to force them to act against gravity, I can't help it and the tears come pouring out and Shaina Raisa sees them. How can she not.

'Meyn kind, I didn't mean it to, oy, I'm an idiot, I should have thought. Though I don't know what I said, but it doesn't matter because I shouldn't've. But you don't have to,' and she stops.

I look at her and know she's an idiot, but she's also kind and she didn't mean to though she should've thought.

So I smile, and she says, 'I'm sorry.' And that's the end of that, for a while, because when Morris comes home, I intend to confront him.

It's a lot more difficult to confront him than could reasonably be assumed. He comes home late, he's tired and dirty, he sits down to eat because he's too hungry to bath first. We eat together, a good time to discuss burning issues like do you think I'm spoilt and do you tell your mother everything rather than discussing it with your wife. But, he's listening to the news.

'Shh Rika, the news.'

As if it's sacrosanct, as if he doesn't listen to it every few hours anyway while he's working, while he's under cars or inside their bonnets.

And after supper, he plays with Graham and pretends, to Graham's delight, that he's an aeroplane going round and round the dizzy heights above Morris' head.

And then I put Graham to bed and spend time feeding him, changing him, singing to him, patting him until eventually he's asleep and I can go and say to Morris, 'Do you,' but there he is, listening to a programme on the radio, deep in thought or deep in sleep, and then he has to have his bath and go to sleep because he can't keep awake a moment longer.

Those two columns of Morris I devised earlier have progressed to two sides of a coin. It's not too different, just a bit more developed. The smiling Morris, the laughing, jolly, jokey, everyone's best friend Morris is still in the same column. I see that side, it's not just for friends and family. It is the more usual Morris, the common one, the one people tend to mention when they speak of Morris.

'He's so funny, he's so much fun, he's funtastic.'

The other side is the screaming Morris, the temper, the shouting, the anger, the rage. I see more of that Morris. He reserves it for the closest family particularly me, and of course, his servants, his workers. I suspect his children, however many there will be, will see it too as they grow older.

It erupts this Morris, when things aren't exactly as he wants it, when he comes home from work and supper isn't ready, or is not to his liking, or is burnt. It erupts when the shirt he wanted to wear hasn't been washed or ironed or has been burnt.

These things happen.

I relate less and less to that funny Morris, I can't laugh at the jokes, to me they're not funny. I can relate to the screaming Morris though. I can relate to it because I'm there, it's in my face, it's directed at me. I can't miss it no matter how much I try. And I try. I read the newspaper, I pick up the phone, I start sewing or knitting so my gaze doesn't reach the perimeter of his screaming. It doesn't go near it. Which drives him nuts. He needs a wife that will come to him, touch him, speak softly to him, caress him as she brings him down from those heights to the gentleness that is her.

I'm not that wife. He needs me to be different. I'm as wrong for him as he is for me. I'm not his mother and he is not my Vati.

Or maybe he needs someone else entirely.

I'm sitting outside on the grass in the park. Shaina Raisa is sitting with me and Graham is lying on a blanket. He's able to roll onto his side and he's trying to start crawling.

'So tell me, Daytschke,' she says, 'what's it like for you to be a mother?'

I look at her and try to assess if this is a trick question. Is she trying to establish just how useless a mother I really am, so she can go back to Morris and tell him, or is she actually interested in me, does she want to know how I am, how I really am, how I'm feeling, how I'm getting on.

I don't trust her enough to be honest so I say, 'Fine.'

Fine is such a wonderfully obtuse word. It means nothing. It can be taken to mean nothing or she can dissect it further. She chooses the former and that conversation ends.

I might feel useless sometimes, and dependent on Dinah, but I know I'm a loving mother. This love that is so different to the love I felt (feel) for Vati, for Mutti, for Edith, the love (was/is it love?) for Natan, the love (really?) I feel for Morris, for Dinah, for Shaina Raisa (yes, I'm sure that's love). This love for this tiny, but getting bigger by the day, baby, toddler, little boy, has an intensity bound up with caring and protecting that I have never experienced before. I imagine I'm not the first to say this.

16

Jill is my South African Shoshana. She has filled the hole left by Shoshana's exit from my life. You can choose your friends, yes, I know, but not your relatives. Well, Jill and I have chosen each other. She has chosen lots of friends but I have chosen only her.

We drop into each other's flats just two doors along, two seconds walk, almost next door, we drink tea together and taste each other's baking.

'Oh my goodness that's good!'

We look after our babies together, we go to the park, the cinema, the café for tea and cake, we speak together. She is the only one I really speak to.

'Tell me about the kibbutz,' Jill says. 'I just love the fact that they seem to be experimenting so well with socialism. All those naysayers who constantly point to communism as an impossible ideal. Well, here you are, we can say. Look at Israel!'

I tell her that everything is communal.

'You know that lovely tea-set of yours, the one we both love so much, well, in the kibbutz it wouldn't be yours. You wouldn't have a tea-set in your room because that would be bourgeois.

And your clothes. Those lovely three-quarter trousers with the stripes. Uh uh. Someone else would pick it up from the communal laundry and you would be left with a dark brown, baggy pair that you have to hold up with a great big belt because it would be far too big for you.

And if you decide to wear make-up one day, everyone would laugh at you and mock you and ask what you think you're doing. And at the meeting of the whole kibbutz, it would be brought up as an issue. Jill is wearing make-up.

And, my Graham would be living in a different home from me with other babies and a housemother, and there would be only a few hours that I could go and see him in a day. I couldn't go more often than other mothers because it wouldn't be fair. And at the meeting of the whole kibbutz they would say, Rika went to her child more often than others and it's not fair, and everyone would look at me and tut, and complain and make sure I didn't do that again.

And I would be working in a job that I may hate, that I may be useless at, and I could only change if I made a fuss. But then people would complain that I was just thinking of myself and I was uncomradely and bourgeois. Which is the worst thing you could say of anyone!'

She listens to this long diatribe, this outpouring of feeling that I haven't verbalised before, and she says, 'But it's all for the greater good.'

'Not my good, that's for sure,' I say.

'Yes,' she says, 'I can see that kibbutz life would be totally unsuitable for you.'

'I hate the way everyone looks at me all the time,' I say.

'Everyone wants to look at a pretty woman, they're just appreciating you, Rika!'

I feel a stab of irritation. How dare I! I use my looks as a comfort blanket but then I feel annoyed when my closest friend states a fact.

But what I want to know is, if I'm so pretty, why is my life less good than unpretty Edith's? Surely the pretty inherit the world! Don't they!

I watch Dinah cook and learn from her.

'Hau ma'm,' she says, 'your mother didn't teach you to cook?'

'Please call me Rika, Dinah,' I say. 'I call you Dinah.'

She laughs and doesn't say anything.

'Why don't you call me Rika,' I ask her pointedly. Is she going to answer me.

'I can't ma'm.'

'Why not?'

'Because the master might hear me.'

'Well call me Rika when he's not here,' I say.

She laughs and shakes her head and says, 'You don't understand, ma'm.'

'I think I understand,' I say, 'but I don't accept it. I don't want it. It's wrong.'

She just smiles.

'Tell me about your home, Dinah.' I say.

'What must I say,' she asks.

'What's it like?'

'It's very pretty there,' she says 'but not where I live because it's very poor.'

'Why do black people accept this damn system here,' I explode.

She shakes her head and goes, 'Hai madam!' She shakes her head which says, I'm not going to answer that. I'm not going to talk about it with you because, because why? Because it's too painful, because I don't know the answer, because I don't trust you. Maybe it's all three.

'Dinah,' I say, 'did you know that my parents were killed in 1942?'

She shakes her head and says 'Hau!'

'They were just taken from their homes and put in a train with a whole lot of other people and sent to Minsk. There they were put into concentration camps. They weren't extermination camps like Auschwitz, they didn't gas them. In Minsk they killed them by making them build great big pits and then stand there at the edge and then they shot them, line by line. It was efficient that way because they would fall right into the pit and the Germans wouldn't have to waste their energy by having to drag them into it.'

'Hau madam, I'm sorry,' she says.

'But do you know why these people were killed,' I ask and don't wait for her to answer. 'Because they were Jews. So when I ask you why you people accept what is happening to you, why you don't fight, I really do understand how very difficult it is to fight against it. My parents walked to their death, and they knew they were doing it.'

'They couldn't do anything else,' she says softly.

'Why don't Jews help black people,' I ask Shaina Raisa.

We are sitting in her garden, Graham is asleep and the flow of tea is continuous. She doesn't flinch at my question.

'Of course we help them,' she says, 'we give them jobs, somewhere to live, food, everything.'

'But they are all so poor,' I say.

'Meyn kind,' she says (patronisingly?) 'they are poor because they are not clever like us. They are not developed. They need a few more generations to develop like we have.'

'But, Shaina Raisa,' I say, and don't get further before she interrupts me.

'No, meyn kind, you don't understand,' ha! 'because you're not South African'.

Of course, always the same thing, you're not South African, you can't possibly understand. I can understand poverty, I can understand unfairness, I can understand wrong, these things are universal, don't you understand.

But of course I don't say that and she continues, word for word what I know she'll say, I mouth it to myself as she speaks,

'You don't realise that for us this is a goldene medinah,' yes, land of milk and honey, I know. But then she carries on and I haven't anticipated what she says. 'Here we are safe, we must keep it like that. If we start wanting to change things, things could change for us. You understand more than my children what can happen when they start looking at you. For two thousand years they have looked at us. We lived with so much danger and so much worry. Everytime something happened we didn't know if we would be killed, or our families would be killed, or our neighbours. What sort of life is that? Do you want a life like that?'

I shake my head.

'So now you understand. Let them look at someone else for a change, not us. Keep schtum, close your mouth, close your eyes and enjoy the sunshine and the milk and the honey!'

'But,' I say,

And she says, 'No buts, keep schtum,'

And I say, 'but Shaina Raisa..'

And she says, 'Eishh! Shh! Let's have some more tea.'

MillieMollieMandy, I want to ask you a question. Come here my finger says. I smile so she knows I'm a friend. I smile to show I'm friendly. I smile so that she comes.

She comes. 'What is it, darling,' she asks, 'it's just that I've got a lot to do before dinner.'

I open my mouth to speak but I've forgotten the word. I try, it'll come, just speak and the word will find its place.

'Are you a,' but it doesn't come.

'Am I what, sweetheart? Am I a wonderful person? Yes, definitely. Am I what? What do you want to know?'

'Are you a,' I try again, 'mist,' I say.

'Mist, am I mist? No, I'm definitely not mist and certainly not fog!' she laughs. 'Commist,' I say.

'Rika darling, I'm so sorry but I must go. Think about it and you can ask me later, ok.'

Jill and I are sitting in the park and a white woman is walking by with a black woman, her nanny, pushing the pram. We can hear her as she passes, shouting and being angry and very rude. Jill and I look at each other.

'I hate that,' I say.

She turns to me and says softly, 'How much do you hate it?'

That's a strange question, what must I say, to the moon and back. 'It's very wrong and very horrible and I would like to do something to change it if I could,' I say.

She smiles and says, 'You can, you know.'

I laugh, but she isn't laughing now.

'There's a political party in this country that's doing a lot to change things. It's the Communist Party of South Africa and I'm a member of it,' she says. 'It's become an illegal organisation so it's banned, which means we can get into a lot of trouble just by being members. But it's the only organisation that's doing anything.'

I don't think of Morris, or Graham, I think only of my parents and I know I have to do something.

'I want to do something,' I say.

'That's good, Rika!' she says, smiling broadly and laughing.

Jill's husband is called Ivor. He's a gentle giant, kind and soft with glasses and a constant smile. He and Morris chat together sometimes and I decide to invite them for dinner. I'm going to make – ha! of course I'm not, but Dinah is, and she makes a lovely dinner of little soles and chips and peas and salad. And she makes a creamy melktert for pudding.

Afterwards we sit and listen to music and Ivor turns to Morris and says, 'What's your take on this new government, Morris?'

'No good,' Morris says and I look up in surprise but don't say anything.

'What can we do about it?' Ivor asks Morris and looks intently at him.

I look just as intently.

'I don't know. I really don't know. I have to make a living, I'm working hard. It's a bit touch and go at the moment, but I think it'll be alright. So, I don't want to go rocking any boats, so to speak. I mean, I know it's not right. You can't go around making slaves out of a whole people, but what can I as one man do?'

I use my hand to push my mouth back closed. What! How dare he lie like that, barefaced. I almost laugh out loud, almost say, he's lying, why are you lying.

Ivor takes him seriously and says, 'You're not just one man. There's a whole lot of us. Have you ever thought of joining the Communist Party?'

I expect Morris to say no straight out but he says, 'I don't like Stalin.'

'Well,' Ivor says, 'this is the Communist Party of South Africa, not Russia.'

And Morris says, 'It's something to think about, definitely.'

When we get ready for bed, I ask him the question, knowing it's pointless.

'Did you really mean you would think about joining the Communist Party?'

He says, 'What do you think?' And laughs.

'So you didn't think, you always knew,' I say and he shakes his head in disbelief.

'I'm not a bloody commie, Rika!' he says.

'What are you then,' I ask and he says simply,

'I'm a Jew.'

'But there are Jewish communists,' I say.

'I'm a Jew first and foremost. If it helps me as a Jew to be a member of the Communist Party, I will. If it helps me as a Jew to be a member of the Nationalist Party, I'll do that. At the moment, the Nats are the powerhouse, not the commies. And they're good to us. Dr Malan said just a few years ago that they don't discriminate between Jews and non-Jews. And they voted for the creation of the State of Israel.'

'So a Jew must only ever do what is right for other Jews, not other human beings?' I ask.

And he says, 'Go to sleep, Rika, do me a favour.'

17

I'm dreaming, no I'm awake. Am I awake? How can I tell? Pinch, Mutti said, pinch. I pinch, I can't tell, pinch hard.

I think I must be sleeping. How can I wake myself up?

I'm cleaning my house, hoovering all over, on the rugs, on the carpets, under the chairs, move the chairs, plump the cushions, wipe the surfaces, clean, clean, oh my goodness, I've been cleaning for hours.

I'll make some tea, lovely, where's the biscuits, yes, eat, eat, all the biscuits, eat them up, all gone, eat the ice cream, eat the chocolate, lovely, lovely.

No, I'm still sleeping, all that work and it hasn't even been done, I'll still have to do it when I wake up. But at least I won't put on weight from all the rubbish I've eaten.

Wake, wake, how can I wake myself, I can't wake up, I'm going to be asleep for ever! Help, help! Someone help me. I'm about to get into something that's really going to affect my life. I've got to be stopped. Stop me, someone, anyone, HELP!

'Are you alright sweetheart, you're looking very distressed.'

I wake up and fall straight back to sleep.

I'm walking in town, ambling along, looking in the shop windows, staring in the shop windows.

Graham's at home with Dinah and I'm dressed up for town, gloves on, hat on, dress with flowing skirt and belt on, high heels on, lipstick on.

No-one would think this elegant woman, so innocently spending her time shopping and window shopping, is really a spy! Ok, perhaps not a spy, but, I'm planning to be. Well, spy is probably wrong even so, but I will do something against this government and this is my first step.

Yes, being dressed smartly and window shopping is the way any self-respecting potential freedom fighter begins their new career.

I laugh at myself, I'm excited. I've forgotten how I felt after The Colonel in Palestine. Don't! But this is different because this one isn't about killing anyone.

Jill had said, 'We don't inflict damage on people, just things.'

'And for me,' I said, 'that has to be an absolute, a line, no killing.'

So I look in the window, stare, but I'm staring past the mannequins, past the theatricals, and into the images in the window from outside, particularly, is anyone watching me, anyone stopping when I stop, starting when I start, looking suspicious.

I walk with others across the street as the traffic light changes to red. Then I stop halfway, reconsider and turn back. Has anyone else done that? I stop and straighten my stockings and as I do so, look sideways, look backwards, anyone there, stopping, watching?

I pass the entrance to the building where I'm to meet the members of my cell, my co-revolutionaries, (ha! revolutionaries, wonderful, I love that word. You don't have to be pretty to be a revolutionary!) I walk past, round the corner, peek out, check for anything, anyone suspicious, cars stopping, looking, watching. Nothing. I walk back to the entrance and go in.

A young man and woman are sitting round a little table. They jump up when I enter and walk towards me, they smile broadly and shake my hand.

'I'm Tembo,' says the man.

'I'm Thandi,' says the woman.

'I'm Lily,' say I.

We were told to have pseudonyms, code names, nothing identifiable. We must not know who these people are, just that we are members of the same cell, linked together within the confines of a secretive membrane, like something biological, the mitochondria all working together for a single purpose, in this case, overthrowing the government. Freedom, justice, equality! God, I feel good!

'It's really good to meet you. We were told you aren't South African,' Tembo says.

'How long does it take to become South African?' I ask. 'Is this a good induction to becoming South African? '

'Not for white Nationalist South Africans, it's not,' Thandi laughs.

'If you're black, it's good!'

We all laugh and I feel the connective tissues growing.

'How long has this cell been going?' I ask.

Tembo immediately says, 'Don't ask any questions, Lily, for all our sakes. You never know when someone asks you questions you won't want to answer.'

'Of course,' I say, feeling stupid to have failed Test One.

'Have you been given any training?' Tembo asks.

'Yes,' I answer, 'I've had some, I was very careful when I came here.'

Thandi laughs. I look at her and she smiles behind her hand.

'I have to tell you, Lily,' she says, 'I followed you.'

What? Test Two failed. 'How did I not notice, I can't believe it,' I say feeling shocked.

'The reason you didn't notice her is that you weren't looking for black people following you,' Tembo says.

I see the film of myself in my mind's eye, travelling into town, walking around, looking at the shops, crossing the streets, and an appalling thought hits me like a filthy wet flannel; people for me equalled white people. What does that make me? A racist? Am I a racist? Do I really see black and white people differently? Yes I do because the black people I see are all poor, workers, servants, oh my lord, say it, be truthful – yes, inferior. Oh no, surely not, surely I don't think like that.

I look at Tembo and Thandi and know there is nothing inferior here, and I think of Dinah and Rebecca and know there is nothing inferior there. I must be careful, I must be aware of how living in South Africa, being around South Africans all the time, can have a very damaging effect on me. Achtung! Vorsicht!

I look at them and say, 'It seems like I've become more South African than I realised,' and they laugh.

'Well, at least your heart is in the right place,' Thandi says, 'but remember, there are lots of black informers and black people working for the government. Be careful of everyone!'

Tembo starts to talk and I listen, and see myself listening, part of a group of three, joining the good fight, and then realise I'm so busy being aware of myself that I'm not listening to what he's saying. I focus.

'The latest laws extending the pass laws to women has resulted in Sisulu and the executive calling for mass protests,' he says, 'They want people to be involved in the demonstrations from across the races. We have to get the message to people that are difficult to get to.'

'Like domestic workers,' Thandi says

I think, of course, I can help here and Tembo says, 'Lily this is obviously relevant for you.'

'Absolutely,' I reply, painfully enthusiastic?

'They are asking for our white members to get leaflets to their workers and for them to spread them around.'

'What else can I do?' I ask.

'You could secretly pass leaflets to people working in shops. But here you must be very careful that the boss doesn't see you or he may describe you to the police.'

'Of course,' I say.

'Thandi, if you can pass them round the factories, get small scale meetings going, that would be good. We're not alone. There are lots of other comrades working on this. But just to push the fact, comrades, secrecy is key. If you see someone passing leaflets, don't assume they're comrades, they may be spies, they may be government infiltrators. Keep vigilant. To reiterate, don't trust anyone, black or white. Remember your training at all times. Just answer workers' questions about the protests. Don't be fooled into trusting people who ask questions, seemingly innocent questions. They could get you or your colleagues caught.'

'When will the meeting take place,' Thandi asks, 'and is it just one or will there be a few at the same time.'

'There will be a few,' Tembo replies, 'the next big protest meetings have been arranged for two weeks on Saturday, starting at two in the afternoon. One will be in front of the Town Hall. There will be other meetings in Sofiatown, Moroko, Jabavu, Orlando and Alexandra Township. So we have two weeks to really push these leaflets.'

I want to go too, I want to be part of it, hear the speeches, be with the people.

'What about white protesters,' I ask.

'This is for all races,' Tembo replies. 'Will you be able to get the leaflets to whites, Lily?'

'Hmm, that won't be easy, my family are, not the sort,' I start.

Tembo says, 'Just be careful, that's the most important thing.'

I come home, and kiss and hug my little boy, happy to see him, happy to be with him, happy to see Dinah, happy to be me.

But I'm tired for some reason and wonder if it's because of the excitement of the day. In fact, I'm feeling slightly sick, and when I sit to eat my dinner, I have to run away and manage to get to the toilet just in time. I come back to the table and sit with Morris and Graham, and watch them eat, but all I can put in my mouth is some weak black tea.

Dinah is looking at me sideways, a concerned look on her face. Morris is eating, his food, smothered, flooded as always in Worcestershire sauce.

'Are you alright,' Morris asks and I nod. 'How was your day?'

Graham immediately replies to him, 'Mommy not home.'

'Really,' Morris says, 'where was Mommy, Graham?'

'Mommy out,' he says, 'I with Dinah. Dinah play with me.'

'I wasn't out for long.' I quickly jump in from my fog of returning nausea. 'I wasn't out for long, was I Grahamela? We had a lovely day together. What did we do? Did we play with the water?'

'Where did you go?' Morris asks again.

'I just wanted to look at the shops in town,' I reply.

'You went all the way into town,' he asks shocked.

'Yes,' I laugh, downplaying the journey as nothing major, nothing momentous, just a bus ride for god's sake.

'But why,' he asks.

'Sometimes I need a bit of, anyway I was looking for things in the shops. I wasn't gone for long, a couple of hours, nothing.'

'Dinah!' he calls and she comes in, 'was Graham with you the whole morning?'

'Not the whole morning, master,' Dinah replies.

Morris and I are sitting together listening to the radio. Graham's in bed and Dinah has gone to the slums upstairs.

Morris looks at me and says, 'Who did you see in town?'

'Nobody,' I reply with great innocence, 'just the shop windows.'

'You didn't even go into the shops?' he asks.

'A few,' I say.

'Which ones?'

'Why are you asking me all these questions,' I say to him with a quiet coldness. 'I don't ask you who you saw, who you spoke to during the day? Is that what you want? No trust?'

He looks surprised and says, 'Why are you acting as if you have something to hide?'

'I've got nothing to hide,' I say, 'other than sometimes I need to get out, by myself.'

He thinks for a moment, and turns the radio off. 'Why?' he asks.

'Sometimes I need to think,' I say softly.

'What do you need to think about? Do you think you wish you hadn't married me?'

'What?' I say.

'You do, don't you,' he says.

I can only say truthfully, 'It's not easy for me, Morris.'

'But it's getting better,' he says, a sort of pleading coming into his voice, 'my workshop's doing well, every day people say what an excellent mechanic I am, they're recommending me all the time. I have so many new people coming that I have to get another boy to work with me now. Soon we'll be able to move into a house. We might not be able to afford meat every night now but soon we will. You've got everything to look forward to.'

I look at him sadly, I see the boy in the man, the man people laugh with and like and I say, 'It's not all about money, Morris.'

That annoys him, and he says pointedly, 'You don't know how to recognise when you've got it good.'

'It's NOT all about money!' I say annoyed at that sudden turn from kindness and succour to accusation and impatience.

'Look, I'm sorry your parents died, alright?' he says.

I'm flabbergasted. I don't know where to look.

'I know it's a really horrible thing to happen. But you're a mother yourself now. You've got to get over it!'

Get over it! He did just say that. He said, get over it. How dare he! How dare this unknowable stranger say get over my parents' death to me! He's got a bloody mother! He's not an orphan, does he understand that from the age of fourteen I was without my, oh god, stop, just leave it, go, go.

I get no further with this barrage of venom in my head, my body rebels in two directions at once and I dash for the toilet once again, vomiting and sobbing simultaneously.

He is standing outside the door, apologising, begging me to come out, to forgive him, saying he understands how I feel. When I come out, he takes me in his arms and says one thing, 'Why didn't you tell me you're pregnant?'

18

'Wo ist mein Baby. Hullo, hullo, wo ist mein Baby?'
Why don't they answer?

'What's that you're saying, darling? You're speaking in German again, I think. Mary,' she shouts, 'Mary, you speak a bit of German don't you? Can you come see what Rika's on about. I think she's speaking German.'

'Baby. Baby. Mein Baby.'

'Oh, hold on, she wants her doll. Anyone seen Rika's doll anywhere? She hasn't used it for ages but she seems to want it now.'

They hand me my baby, did you miss me my little bubela? Ahh, how sweet you are, my little Ninale. Sweet little Nina, shall we play hoppa hoppa reiter? I put my baby on my foot and jiggle her up and down just like she likes it.

Hoppa, hoppa, Reiter,

wenn du fällt da schreit er,

fällt er in den Graben,

'Oh God, there goes the doll again,' someone says.

But Nina's laughing, she's laughing in that mad, wild, fun way she has of laughing, she laughs and laughs and says, again Mutti, again!

Shaina Raisa pops in for tea.

'Hello meyn kind,' she says to me and without waiting for a reply she adds, 'where's my boychik?'

'Graham's just sleeping,' I tell her, 'but he'll wake up soon.'

I don't have any cake to offer her, but luckily she's brought her own teiglach and enough for me too. I know why she's here. I wait until the inevitable comes out.

'So tell me, how're you feeling?'

'Fine, fine.'

I'm not planning to make it easy for her, besides, it's a bit of fun watching how she dances round and round before pouncing.

'Morris is doing so well, isn't he,' she says, 'he's such a good mechanic, you know, everybody recommends him. He's getting more and more people come to him. He has to get a new boy in to help, he's so busy.'

There's something déjà vu about this conversation so far.

'Really,' I murmur.

'What? He didn't tell you,' she asks.

'Yes, yes, he said something like that,' I say, non-committal.

'That's good, no? You must be pleased,' she says.

'Oh yes of course,' I say.

'So Rikale,' she says, 'how you feeling about the new baby. I'm telling you this is going to be another boy. I can see the way you look. It's always a boy when early pregnancy is like that.'

'As long as it's healthy,' I say.

She spits on her left side and says, 'Toi toi! And Grahamela, that he stays healthy too, what a neshomela! You must be very happy, no?'

I smile. But that's not quite enough for her, she hasn't got the confirmation she's seeking, not yet.

'I mean, you have so much more than you had before, right? Your own home, alright, it's a bit small, but this is just the beginning. And a girl to look after you and do everything you need, a child of course, that's the most important, and a new baby to come in a few months. What's not to be happy?'

And then I give it to her, she's an old woman after all, all she wants is everyone in her orbit to be happy, as long as they're still reliant on her that is.

'I'm happy, Shaina Raisa. I'm happy,' I say.

'Good. Good. That's settled then,' she says, 'I'm glad you're happy. I mean, chas ve'chalila you had Cyril Levy's problems, then you would have problems.' And she begins to tell me a raft of miserable tales befalling her neighbours and friends and friends' friends.

Once she's replete with tea, teiglach and gossip, Shaina Raisa gets up to go, but not before she passes on one last message.

'And, you know Rika. You have a good man in Morris. He doesn't drink, he doesn't gamble, he doesn't go with other women. Alright he has a bit of a temper, but his heart's in the right place. He makes people laugh and lots of people love him. You could have done a lot worse. And, and, he never hits you! Right? Of course right!'

I write to my sister.

Dear Edith.

How are you? I hope everything is fine with you. Everything is fine with me. Graham is a lovely little boy. He's so beautiful with lovely curly, black hair. Everyone says he's beautiful. And Shaina Raisa, she seems to love him more than any of her other grandchildren. You're probably laughing at me and saying, all mothers think exactly that. But I see how she is with him and with the others. It's not the same. So don't immediately jump to conclusions and assume you can't trust what I say. He's not two yet but he will be in September. The baby is due in mid October. Almost the same time as yours. What do you think you will have? Shaina Raisa is sure mine will be another boy, but who knows. As long as it's healthy.

Morris told me the other day it's time I got over Mutti and Vati's death. Have you got over it yet? What does it mean to get over it anyway? Does it mean to stop thinking about it, or to stop feeling sad when I think of it, or to stop feeling bad even if I'm not thinking of it. What will happen if we stop thinking of them? Will they just die again? Is that silly? Is it silly to keep them alive in us? Are you keeping them alive in you? I feel them. Is that the same as keeping them alive in me? I'm sure you're shaking your head and thinking, that stupid girl is talking such rubbish. Is it rubbish, Edith? I can't work it out.

I lie in bed, waiting to hear if Graham is going to call out, and as I lie, waiting and then slipping into half sleep, I dream Mutti is here. She climbs into bed with me and I can hear her breathing. It's ridiculous because she never used to get into bed with me, or you. Oh Edith, do you remember how she'd grab the blankets and pull them back with such force when we had to get up for school – raus aus dem Bett! And we sure got up quickly enough, do you remember? She was quite strict, wasn't she? She was, right? I sometimes wonder if I'm remembering correctly. Vati was so gentle. He'd gone to work already, hadn't he, by the time we had to get up for school. Is that right? Why can't I be sure that my memory is accurate? I can't rely on it. I don't seem to be able to rely on many things these days. Maybe it's pregnancy.

Love, your sister.

Today's the day I'm going to speak to Dinah about the leaflets. It's been half a week already, but pregnancy did rather get in the way. She's busy, but, this is a good time, Morris isn't here, he's at work, Graham is having a mid-morning nap, and Shaina Raisa came yesterday so probably won't pop in today.

Seize the moment! I think I'll lead up to it slowly, careful not to frighten her into total silence. I've got the ability to put my foot in it, just go slow, Rika.

'Dinah,' I say.

'Yes, ma'm.'

Oh Dinah, how I hate, anyway, forget that, focus, focus. 'Dinah,' I say, and pick up the dishtowel to dry the dishes that she's washing. 'Isn't it awful the way the government has changed the law about black people having sexual relations with white people.'

She looks horrified at me, 'Madam!' she says.

That damn foot of mine! 'I mean, you know, I just mean that as an example, of, of, all these laws that the government is passing, and now with women having to have passes, as well as men, well, it's terrible, isn't it? Don't you think so, Dinah?'

'I don't like to' Dinah starts.

I jump in, 'That's right, it's terrible!'

She continues, 'I don't like to think of politics.'

She doesn't trust me, of course she doesn't, what the hell did I think? I'm white, I'm her boss, her madam, how could she possibly trust me, but I can't stop now.

'Dinah,' I say, 'honestly, you can trust me, you know I'm not a South African. I come from a very different background, you know that. I hate what's happening here. I hate it for you and also for me. It's wrong. I want to do something about it. I'm trying to do something about it. Please trust me.'

She looks at me and looks down at her hands in the soapsuds.

Very quietly she says, 'I can't think about it.'

'But why?' I ask.

'It's too dangerous,' she says.

'Of course it is,' I say, 'but if we don't do something, at least try to do something, nothing will change. It can go on forever like this and it will get worse and worse. They're passing laws all the time. They're not going to stop. We all have to do something.' And then I appeal to her base instinct, 'Think of your children,' I say.

Me, the white madam with the child in his own room, looked after by three adults, loved, clean, fed, everything he wants, though perhaps not meat every night, but then again, who needs meat every night. Anyway, that's what I say to Dinah, think of your children.

She looks at me (with venom? distrust? anger?) 'That is what I'm thinking about,' she says very softly.

I don't know when to stop. 'Think of their future,' I say.

'I'm thinking of their now.'

'It's going to get worse,' I say. Will I stop at some point?

'Madam,' she says, 'you don't understand.'

'Well then tell me, help me to understand,' I say. 'I know my life is so much easier than yours, I have a husband living here with me who earns money to make my life easy, and I live with my child. So tell me, Dinah, please. Speak to me so that I can understand.'

She walks to the door. Is she going to leave me now, I think horrified, and she turns round as if she needs some distance from me.

'Do you know how many people are able to eat because I'm here working for you?' she asks but doesn't wait for a reply. 'I will tell you. Five people. My mother, my two children, and my little brother and sister. I'm the only one who sends them money so that they can buy food. They farm a little and grow some vegetables, but that is not enough for all of them. The land is very poor there. That is why they are allowed to live there. They have some goats and my brother and sister look after them. There is not money for them to go to school. You ask me where is my husband. I will tell you. My husband is in jail. Do you know why? Because he burnt his pass. He joined the protests and burnt his pass. Now he is in jail for two years. So, no madam. I won't do anything because I don't want my family to die of starvation. Just like I can't call you Rika. Because I don't trust that one day you will change your mind and not want me to call you Rika, and you will let me go. It is very easy to let your servant go. You just have to say, Go. I can't say to you, but you told me to call you Rika, because you can just say, Go. You don't understand how hard it is to get a job and it is impossible without a reference. Maybe you will give me a reference, but how do I know for sure? If you decide not to give me a reference, there is nothing I can do about it. And then I won't get a job.'

Dinah's shaking, fear, or rage, or emotion, I don't know. I open my mouth and close it again like a fish in water. I feel as if I'm in water, struggling not to drown. I want her to believe me, I can't bear that she doesn't believe me, I can't bear the pain she's showing. I don't know what to do or say and all I can do suddenly is to grab her by her shoulders and pull her towards me and hug her. She stands, stock still, her wet, sodden hands by her side and slowly she wipes her hands on her sides and puts her arms around me.

'What do you want me to do?' she asks very softly.

We move apart and I say to her, 'I can't ask it of you now,'

But she says, 'I can do something small.'

So I tell her about the leaflets and the protest meetings and ask her to just hand some out to her friends when she sits with them. That's all.

'I will,' she says, 'and I will come to the meeting, unless you need me to look after Graham'.

I need Morris to look after Graham on Saturday afternoon. How do I approach this without arguments, anger, suspicion? I can't tell him where I'm going. Bedtime, is that good?

I approach him and he thinks, 'Ahha, she's interested.'

I say, 'Just a moment Morris, I want to ask you something.'

'Must it be now,' he says, trying to kiss me.

'I need you to look after Graham next Saturday afternoon.'

'What?' he says, still believing this is a momentary intrusion.

'I'm giving you lots of warning,' I say.

'Why? Where will you be,' he asks, 'and why can't Dinah look after him?' He moves his head away slightly to look at me.

'Well,' I say, 'I'm going out and she needs the afternoon off so I said that's fine.'

This is the moment of course when he realises this isn't going the way he was anticipating.

'Where are you going?' he asks.

This is tricky, it can go either way. 'I'm meeting a friend, in town,' I say.

'Which friend,' he asks.

'You don't know her. I met her through Jill. Her name's Ruth.'

He considers this for a moment, sits back with his head on the headboard and reaches over for a cigarette. He lights it, breathes it in deeply, and blows out smoke rings.

'Why do you have to meet her then,' he asks.

'Because that's the only day she has off, she works during the week,' I say.

He responds quickly this time. 'Why can't she come here? Or why don't you take Graham with you?'

I can't think of anything to say.

He could have given me another moment to think but he replies very sharply, 'This is kak, Rika. What's going on? Do you really think I'm so stupid! What the hell's going on? Are you having an affair? Are you? Is that what it's all about? Tell me the truth for God's sake! I'm warning you! Just tell me the truth!'

Why didn't I expect this? Because it's so far from the truth? I look at him, I try not to sneer. Is he thinking I'm sneering, I'm not, I'm just looking.

'Jesus, you are, aren't you? You're fucking having an affair! I can't believe it! Is the baby even mine? Oh my God, you've been having an affair and sleeping with some fucking bloke and the baby isn't even mine! Is Graham mine? How long's this been going on?'

So many questions, so much swearing, I see red.

'I'm just meeting my friend Ruth,' I say as loudly as he, not even thinking that this might wake Graham. Why does he swear so much! I hate it! My anger acts like a sprinkler, dousing his flames.

He turns on his other side, away from me, and is quiet for a while.

I think this may be the end but then he says, and I think he's talking to himself, 'I'm working so hard for you, for Graham, for the new baby. I get to work at six in the morning. I get back at half past six at night. The whole day I work under cars, in cars, over fucking cars. And while I'm bloody working, my wife is fucking some fucking bloody fucking...'

It's strange to swear in such a quiet, sad way. One would think swearing comes with shouting. But it gets me, even with those words and I say, 'I'm not, Morris, honestly, I'm not.'

But he's not sure what I mean and he says, 'You're not meeting your friend Ruth?'

'I'm not having an affair. Graham is yours, of course he is. How can you think otherwise. And this baby's yours.'

'I can't believe you,' he says, infinitely sad.

I touch him, I put my arm around him as he lies on his side and I say, 'Well you must.'

Almost like a little boy he says, 'Why must I?'

All I can reply is 'Because I'm telling you. You can trust me.'

But it's not over yet for him. 'I can't trust you,' he says 'because there is no Ruth. I can tell you're lying. You think I don't know you, but I do.'

Perhaps because he's coming across so vulnerable, and he's feeling so desperate, I begin to cry. 'If you know me, how could you think I would go with someone else,' I say.

He turns round to me and looks me in my sodden eyes and says, 'Because I know you don't love me. I've always known it.'

I wipe my eyes and look deeply into his and ask him the question I've never asked before. 'Do you love me?

'Yes.'

'You never show it,' I say.

'I don't know how to show it.'

'You never say it.'

'You don't seem to want to hear it.'

'I'm so different from you,' I say.

'You are, but that shouldn't matter.'

'Why shouldn't it?'

'Because I love you.'

I'm close up to him and being close up often has a strange effect on vision, but all of a sudden, as I stare at him, the Morris in front of me transforms into Natan, for a moment, just a moment, but he's there, Natan, instead of Morris, Natan, what the hell are you doing, then he's gone, he's back to Morris and Morris is looking at me as if he can read what's just been going on in my face.

We stare at each other for a minute and it's broken by Graham starting to cry. We look at each other and get up and move together to his room. Morris picks him up and

Graham stops crying and puts his head on Morris' shoulder, sucking his thumb.

'You are both my life now. You must believe me. You say I don't show my love, but this is me. All I can do is tell you that I love you. I can't change into someone I'm not.'

I don't know what to say, so I say, 'You swear, my father never swore, never a loud word, never a swear word.'

And Morris says simply, 'I can't become your father, Rika.'

I take Graham off him and go into the lounge, leaving Morris standing by the cot. As I sit on the couch, holding my son, I feel a pain in my head, sharp and throbbing, and the thought appears like the ten commandments which suddenly appear on the tablets of stone in the film, and my commandment says simply, you will only ever love Natan.

No, I think, no, I won't, it's not true, just like those ten commandments aren't true, this too is just a stupid fairy story. I won't be told who I will and won't love. I won't love that stupid Natan. I will not!

Eventually Morris comes into the lounge and sits next to me.

'I'll look after Graham. I don't know what you're up to, Rika, but I'm pretty sure it's not another man. But you bloody better not be doing anything you shouldn't be doing.'

19

The baby comes from inside me. It comes out. Look everyone, here is my baby. I hold up my baby and show her to everyone, look, look, see how pretty. I made a pretty baby.

Can you do it, you, you there, can you make one? I can, I did it, I did it last night, out it came, and here she is, look, look everyone!

They just stare. They don't understand the strange words that come out of my mouth.

How wonderful it would be to say, I'm suddenly the mother of two. It just happened. I went to sleep pregnant and woke up with a baby.

Wishes and fairy tales.

But I wake up, only twenty minutes after I go to sleep, because I have those terrible pains, the pains I remember but don't remember from the first time. As soon as I experience them again, I remember, oh my gosh how I remember.

I believe myself to be a non-swearer, one may have heard me once or twice talk about my Vati. But my goodness, I didn't even know I knew these words, and here they come, every single one I've ever heard or imagined in the past, pouring out from my subconscious, and they are vicious, shocking even to these hardened women who have heard it all before, but maybe not in the variety of languages I bring to the table; English, German, Hebrew, Arabic. Do I really know Arabic swear words? Oh yes I do.

I look at this baby girl (girl, not boy, Shaina Raisa), and I don't forget the pain. What is this about forgetting the pain the minute you see your baby? But it's not long, it just takes a few deep looks, eye into eye, and sucks on the breast, and the oohs and aahs from the family who come and visit, and all is forgiven and forgotten until the next time, but my god there will never be a next time!

'I'm going to call her Nina,' I say, 'after nobody.'

'Why not Raisa or Rose, after my mother,' Morris says, 'or Rosalyn.'

'No, she will be called for herself alone. Her line starts here, others can call their children after her.

'Actually,' Morris says after a while, 'I like the name Nina, it makes her seem independent, like she's ready to say no, and do whatever she wants!'

We laugh, that is, Morris and I laugh together. How unusual, but it actually feels nice.

'She's a real Daytschke,' Shaina Raisa proclaims, 'not beautiful like Graham. Graham, ah Graham, he's such a beauty! She's just a Daytschke!'

Graham meanwhile looks round him at all the people and says, 'I know, let's play a game. You can be the mother (me), you can be the father (Morris), she can be the new baby (Nina), and I can be the big brother (himself).'

Dinah is gentle and loving with Nina. I watch them and feel so sad for Dinah. Can it be that this isn't real, that she's pretending in front of me. How can someone with her family history be so good with someone else's baby? Why would she pretend? Is that a bit of irritation she's showing? Well yes, it is a bit annoying hearing a baby cry like that.

'Here Dinah, let me take her,' I say quickly.

Nina is just happy to follow the food, whether from my breast or Dinah's bottle.

Graham has started wetting his bed and demands Nina's blanket.

'That's not your blanket,' Dinah says

'It's alright,' Morris says, 'let him have it for a bit.'

Morris seems content with his family of four.

His friend Philip comes to visit and they stand together on the balcony smoking cigarette after cigarette, talking and laughing. I watch how easy they are together. What does it take to achieve such ease, years of friendship versus years of sex and companionship. We have a bit of the one but little of the other. I watch them and long to go see Jill.

We sit with tea and biscuits and our two babies in our arms.

'I'm so pleased we became friends,' I say to her.

'I knew when I first met you that you weren't like the others,' she says.

'Was it the funny accent?' I ask.

'It was the way you looked at people. The way you spoke to Dinah when she first came to you. You know that strange behaviour many whites have of talking to black people as though they are five and short of hearing, and then speaking about them as if they don't have ears.'

She's talking of my family, actually my husband's family. I don't have to inherit them or take responsibility for them, they are his. Graham and Nina are mine. I'll make sure they don't behave like that.

'Morris is like that,' I say.

'Morris is a product of his upbringing,' she says, 'but there is something in him that makes him different.'

'Well he chose a Daytschke for one,' I say.

'But why would he go for someone so different from all the other girls and women he'd been surrounded by all his life. Look at the sisters-in-law. They're as different to you as black is to white!'

We start to talk about the party, THE party, not the party for new babies. But no names, never names, never any detail that might incriminate anyone. I ask her questions about policies and strategies and she gives me answers, teaches me, explains it all.

I feel as if I'm finally beginning to carry on my education, understand political systems, ideologies, power, activism.

'Why aren't we in the same cell,' I ask.

'Secrecy,' she says, 'it's bad enough that we both know we're members of the party and that we're friends. Imagine if one was arrested and tortured.'

'Tortured?' I interrupt.

'It's not a game, Rika,' she says. 'You know what these people are like. It's very difficult to withstand torture. How much easier to let out a name. Just one name, they'll say. Just one name and you can go back to your baby. And you'll think of your baby and you'll think of Graham, and your imagination will start playing tricks. Are they threatening them in some way? Was that an implied threat to my children? What would they do? What could they do? And you'll think, they could do anything. I wouldn't put it past them to do anything! And then a thought will come into your mind, just slink in unnoticed, and the thought will be an innocuous, well they know about Jill and Ivor anyway, so what does it matter. I could just mention them. It's not as if I'm betraying them.'

'Oh no,' I say, 'I would never!'

'Well,' Jill says, 'that's what we all hope, but none of us can put our head on a block and swear on our children's lives that we will not weaken. They're very clever. The thing to remember is never to give anything away, not the most innocent, banal fact. Just your name and date of birth. Nothing else. Once the mouth opens, it may never close.'

I find Nina's pram has become very useful for my 'activities.'

The Guardian is the Communist Party of South Africa's newspaper and many individual comrades distribute it, including, moi! Nina seems to find all the newsprint under her mattress in the pram particularly comfortable. It does make her a little high but no-one would notice.

Graham's started nursery school, so taking Nina for long walks in the pram is not suspicious, even for Morris, and I certainly wouldn't be having an affair shlepping the baby along with me in that huge pram.

At the end of the year Morris makes a proclamation. 'We're all going on a holiday for two weeks to Durban, he says.'

That word all is ominous and it turns out it is us, our family of four, together with all his seven brothers, sisters, their families and Shaina Raisa. The ganze mispocha!

'Two weeks is a long time,' I say.

'Rika,' he yells, 'nothing satisfies you! I thought you'd be really pleased! For fuck's sake, it's bloody Christmas and New Year.'

My stomach seems to grind when he screams like that. It makes me diminish into myself, become smaller, lesser. It's obviously the tensing of the muscles, but it makes me angry that he doesn't realise the physical effect it has on me.

I answer quickly, 'I'm not saying I don't want to!'

'Nothing's ever easy with you. For God's sake, everyone goes on holiday to Durbs and this year we can finally afford it too.'

'Yes, yes,' I say, 'that's nice, that's good.' Placate, placate.

'It'll be fun,' he says, softening, 'sun, sea, beach, fun.'

It's extraordinary how quickly the steam dissipates. Maybe I will be able to get used to this boom and quiet, boom and quiet.

'Where will we stay?' I ask.

'At the Rydal Mount Hotel, where we always stay,' he says.

Gosh, a hotel. Ooohh!

'When was the last time you stayed in a hotel?' he asks, and I shake my head to get rid of the image.

He misunderstands and says, 'Don't you want to go?'

'I do,' I say, and smile.

Dinah has two weeks holiday with her family and we go off to Durban. I cook a chicken and put it in an empty cake tin, and we wake at four in the morning and drive in our little car all the way to Durban.

The children sleep and we stop at the Valley of the Thousand Hills, 'Where we always stop,' says Morris and I feel I have just joined in the history of their holidays. It's so beautiful here with hill upon hill stretching into forever.

'I don't think I've ever seen anything so lovely,' I say to Morris and he puts his arm around me. It feels right somehow.

The rest of the family are already at the hotel, all in their family rooms but we meet downstairs in the hotel lounge. Hotel guests watch this 'reunion' of the eight families. They must think we are a long-lost group of people spread all over the world who never see each other. I laugh to myself, nobody would imagine we were all together just last Sunday. Everyone hugs and compares journey times and stopping times and how fast they managed to drive and what time they left home.

You can smell the glorious sea before you see it. When you do, all you see is an undulating mass of humanity bound by umbrellas, blankets, chairs and children running up and down. People are changing into and out of swimming costumes using towels to protect their modesty, mostly unsuccessfully, and there at the end of all that colour, is the blue and white sea. Oh the sea, the sea. It's wonderful, warm and safe and exciting.

All of us jump in, not Nina of course, as she is safely ensconced in Shaina Raisa's lap under an umbrella.

I love this sea. I swim and jump over the waves and dive into them. I float on my back and look up at the blue sky, no clouds, warm sun reaching onto my cool face. As I run out of the sea I'm confronted again with that mass of humanity, white humanity. The only black people are the ones selling ice cream and candy floss and cold drinks.

I run to the smaller group that constitute our family. They're all eating sandwiches, or ice creams, rubbing their children with towels, building sandcastles or letting their children bury them in the soft yellow sand. Some lie flat out in the sun getting burnt and wrinkled. Not the sisters-in-law of course, they sit under the umbrellas with Shaina Raisa protecting their skin and their perms.

Shaina Raisa sits in a little fold-up chair on the beach with her stockings rolled down to her feet and her dress pulled up so her knees can get some air.

'Nobody minds seeing an old woman's knees!' she proclaims.

She sits perched under her umbrella and only moves when she absolutely has to, which is twice daily to queue at the public toilets.

'Ma, why don't you just go use the toilets at the hotel? It's not far,' Morris insists.

'Ach Mann, tsu vas!'

She loves ice-cream and can happily eat three or four over the day if offered. I'm surprised by how much I'm enjoying being with the whole family. I bask in Shaina Raisa's effusive adoration of Graham,

'What a beauty that boykela is!' she exclaims daily.

The rest of the family don't seem jealous, they just laugh at her enthusiasm, besides, they can all see that Graham is the most beautiful of all the cousins, with his dark, curly hair and big, brown eyes. And because no-one is making a fuss of Nina, the unfairness is sort of balanced out.

When we're not at the beach we visit the Indian market, full of spices piled high on display, or the docks where a Castle liner's passengers are disembarking.

We go for the wonder that is a cream tea with thick fluffy scones covered in red jam and piled high with cream, the goyish version of taiglach. And once we go to a restaurant for lunch and have something delectable; chicken breast with mayonnaise and salad. I can't believe I've never eaten it before.

On Christmas day the hotel provides a traditional, though not particularly appropriate meal for the boiling weather, hot and heavy but quite delicious.

And on New Year's Eve, we all join the throngs on the pavements watching the 'Coon Carnival', a mass of brightly, in fact luridly, dressed Cape Coloured men and women, boys and girls, dancing around the streets of Durban, playing penny whistles and singing songs. Everyone laughs and dances along in their own little space, (dance might be an exaggeration, there's no effusive movement of limbs as is seen amongst the small group of black revellers, but there was some twitching of muscles).

I look at the faces of these dancers and musicians, playing and dancing and yelling and for all the world having the time of their lives, and I can't stop the image of their reality adulterating this happy, crazy scene. I look round at the people with me and near me; they are all laughing at what they see as childish behaviour and silliness, albeit good-humoured and funny and enjoyable. No-one seems affected as I am.

But then I notice Sadie, my sister-in-law, Jonathan the eldest brother's wife, and the member of the family I like the most. She's looking uncomfortable, or is it my imagination. Perhaps it's just that she is physically uncomfortable, being pregnant with her third child. We catch each other's eye and make a sort of upturned mouth, implying, what? this isn't quite right? She smiles and I smile back.

We sit together at the lunch table and she asks me a simple question no-one in the family has before, 'How do you like living in South Africa?'

'It's the goldene medina isn't it, land of milk and honey, that's what everyone tells me, so I must be very happy.' I smile to lighten any perceived cynicism.

She laughs and says, 'Well for some!'

'What do you mean,' I ask, careful not to read too much into what may just be a throw away remark. 'There's not much milk and honey if you're not white,' she says softly. I stare at her. For the three years I've been here have I missed a fellow communist in the family.

'I didn't realise you felt like that,' I say in what I hope comes across as non-committal.

'It's not something the family would endorse,' she says.

'So Jonathan doesn't...' I ask

'No, he doesn't.'

And I say, with a sense of the importance of this coming statement, 'But can you...'

She jumps in, 'Can I what? Live with it, live with him, not make waves, not spend our whole time together arguing? Is that what you mean?'

'I suppose I do,' I say.

She looks directly at me and says simply, 'I do what I can. I give what I'm able to.'

'Do you mean money, I ask and she can tell my intent by the way I spit the word out.

'Don't pooh-pooh it,' she says, 'some people have absolutely nothing, and all they want, initially at least, is some food. You can't fight a revolution with an empty stomach.'

'Can't you,' I say, 'maybe desperation is exactly what is needed to get it going.'

She smiles at me. 'You haven't got an empty stomach, Rika.'

I feel foolish and I say, 'It's just that for the revolution…,'

Again she stops me and says, 'What revolution? If the people fought back, what would they use? Hands, stones, a few guns? Against what the government has? They would just be killed. Alleviate their hunger first, Rika.'

'But it's a drop in the ocean,' I say, 'what you give against what's needed.

'So, let's get lots of people to give. Let's put political pressure on the government through the ballot box.'

'But it's for whites only,' I say.

'If the blacks had the vote we would be swamped. Do you want that?'

And that's when I realise that Sadie, sweet, lovely Sadie and I are miles apart, that however much I like her, love her even, she would always be on the other side, on the side of the whites. And that is definitely not my side. But there is just one more thing I need to know.

'Does Jonathan know you help the blacks out,' I ask.

She laughs, a real old belly laugh. 'God, no. Of course not. They're all terribly reactionary, you know.'

20

I'm going to help Ivor run his business, that means, I'm going to be a volunteer once a week. It's all very legitimate, not only legit but a 'good thing'. It'll give me something to do, I say, something more than just look after the kids.

'But that's your job, Rika,' Morris says to my fury.

'It's not a job, Morris, don't pretend. And if it is I have a very good deputy, a Deputy Managing Director, a Head of Service Operations, all in one person by the name of Dinah. She can provide the service very well while I do something else, sometimes.'

He agrees, best to agree than start another argument. 'You've got such a schver kop!' Morris says quietly, hard head, true, no doubt this comes directly from his mother.

Ivor's business is a Christmas Club, an organisation where poor people (aka blacks) can pay a small amount of money every week or month towards receiving a huge hamper for Christmas containing all sorts of edible goodies they would not normally be able to afford. The hampers have to be sorted and packed in the months leading up to Christmas, and before that, orders have to be put in and the accounts have to be kept.

But the reality is that the club is really a front to provide funding for the South African Communist Party (it had recently had a change of name), particularly to be able to continue printing its newspaper, The Guardian, which has also had several name changes; after each banning it simply changes its name until the next one.

I love working with Ivor and being around him. Actually, I know what it is, there's something about him that reminds me so strongly about Vati. He never swears, never says a loud word, and he's so gentle and respectful with people.

Goodness, I stop with a start, I've just realised what it is. I've always wanted a Vati look-alike, or a Vati be-alike. Does that mean I'm going to use my womanly wiles to try and take Ivor away from Jill! I laugh out loud at the preposterous notion. Apart from anything else, why would anyone look at me when they have Jill, all her vigour and generosity and fun and beauty and intelligence.

Rika, I say to myself, be honest, look as objectively as possible, would you really want Ivor. The answer of course is no. Apart from anything else, I don't wish Jill any ill whatsoever, but I also don't want to be in her shoes. I'm fine in my own, which is a good thing, I think, a new thing. Besides, I can't even begin to think of Ivor with passion. He's sweet and lovely and I admire and respect him but any image of us together in bed is – well, a bit like thinking of me and Vati in bed. Oh god, horrible, horrible!

I look at this woman who is me and wonder if she is a woman lacking in passion, a cold fish. She certainly doesn't think much of sex, or seek it out particularly unless her husband initiates it. She's not desperate for it, no erotic night-time dreams and orgasms with various men in diverse situations, but then again, she gets sex, she has it, so there is no innate frustration, no climbing of the walls, no desperate desires.

Well, I think dismissing it all, at least that's not one of my problems.

Going to Ivor's office is fun and busy with office workers, distributors, agents coming in, going out, talking loudly, laughing, joking, and shouting across the room. They are mostly all black, only Ivor and I and one or two older women volunteers are white.

It feels like a community, and I feel part of that community, a community I would never normally have access to or be accepted in. I like it. It's so different from the community I'm normally part of, the Jewish family, with its Sunday morning teas and its Jewish holiday meals. It has its loud laughs and shouts too, but it's, well, I could say ordinary, I could say boring, I could say it's always the same. It is all of those but that's not to say I don't want them. I actually do, but Ivor's office is exciting.

It's also a good place for me to meet up with Thandi and Tembo. There has to be a ready excuse, or legend as the Party puts it, for us to be together, and ours is that they're prospective agents for the company and I'm interviewing them. Easy. And there we have our meeting.

'Comrades,' Tembo says, 'How are we going to make protests more effective? That's the burning question that the Party is asking all of us to consider. All very well to do the marches, the meetings, the leafleting, but the government just ends up passing more vicious, more extreme laws.'

'Effective protests are just getting more difficult,' Thandi says and I wonder, what else is there?

Tembo answers, 'The leadership has decided it's time to protest in a way that damages the government but doesn't hurt people.'

(They flash up again, can I ever get rid of these damn images, I don't want them anymore, how does one forget!)

'Bombs,' Tembo says, 'but far away from people. Giants, kill the giants.'

'What giants?' I ask.

'The ones that give power.'

'Pylons?' Thandi says?

Ah, bomb pylons in the countryside.

'They want us to bomb a pylon. What do you both say?' Tambo looks carefully at both of us.

Can I get involved? Can I do it? I know what getting caught would mean.

'I'm for it', Thandi says and blow me, she doesn't give it even a moment's hesitation.

I'm thinking of Graham and Nina. He's five and she's two. I don't want to spend years in isolation not being with my children as they grow up, not seeing the sun other than thirty minutes per day walking round and round in a circle. I'm not strong enough, I'd forget how to speak, I'd lose my mind.

Thandi looks at me, 'It's alright, Lily, it's different for you. We don't have a family. It's only ourselves who would suffer if we were caught,' she says.

'You must understand that we will be extremely careful. We will make sure that all risks are limited, contained,' Tembo adds.

'How would it work?' I ask.

'You would have to reconnoitre first to find a suitable place, and then'

'Me?' I interrupt.

'Yes. We can't take a risk of us all going twice.'

'Whose car?' I ask.

'It must be yours. We don't have a car, or a licence. Can you borrow your husband's?'

Can I? What would I say? What would he say? I'd think of something. I'd work something out.

'If you can't get a car, we'll have to try borrow someone else's. I'm not sure whose, but we could try. It involves more people though. Containment is the thing though.'

'I'll have to speak to my husband,' I say, 'let's assume I'll be able to.'

'Right', he says, 'so you'll reconnoitre, and if you don't find a suitable place, or there's a problem, leave a message on this number – 457005. Just say, please tell John that Maria is busy next week. That's all. Remember the number, but don't write it down. 457005. Got it?'

'Yes, 457005.'

'In the meantime, I'll get hold of the sweets.'

'Sweets?' I ask.

'Sticks of dynamite,' he says.

Dynamite sounds serious, I show my alarm.

'Of course, Lily,' he says, 'how do you think we blow them up?'

What an idiot I am! 'But what if there's a problem with you,' I ask, 'how will you get a message to me?'

'I'll drop a little child's red sock on the pavement outside your building at exactly 10 am on Tuesday morning, but it will be to say it's on. If I don't come, it means stay away, something's gone wrong. Look out your window.'

'And if it's not on, what do we do then,' Thandi asks, 'how do we plan it again?'

'I'll get a message to both of you. I'll use the dead letter box we've used before in Joubert Park. The second tree behind the bushes near the bench Thandi and I sat on. Have a look the following Monday morning, but not before ten am. There will be two messages, one for each of you. Take yours with you and you will know whether the other has got their message. If it is not there, try again the following Monday, and the following Monday after that. If not, you will know something serious has happened.'

Thandi and I both look at him, we aren't able to conceal our concern.

He laughs, 'What? Anything could happen, we all know that. We just have to maintain our vigilance, and trust in God.'

He seems to throw this away as an afterthought.

'Or not,' I say quietly.

'Now, if it is on, you'll drive us near to the place, the nearest you can safely of course, and drop us off. After you drop us off, you drive somewhere safe and stop and then come back at a pre-arranged time. We'll go place the sweets and set a timer for a few hours later. We then get back to the meeting place and wait for you to turn up, hopefully very soon. And then we get the hell out of there. What do you think, Lily? Are you prepared to do it?'

He looks at me very intensely. I shift my glance from his eyes. 'I've got to think about it,' I say finally. 'I can't commit.'

No, that's not good enough, 'You've got to commit, either yes or no. You have to tell us now. We can't risk meeting again.'

'I, I really don't know,' I stammer.

'So then say no,' he says, 'we'll get someone else. I'm not messing about. Right Thandi, let's go.'

They start to walk out, I can't let them, not like this. I'm angry at this sudden turn of events, the fun, the laughter, the community, now this.

'Stop it, Tembo,' I say, 'why are you being so aggressive?'

'It's not a game, Lily,' he throws back at me, 'either you commit or you don't. I understand you have children and you're thinking of them. But I'm thinking of all the children who don't have a choice. They don't have a choice to have enough to eat, or a roof over their heads, or their parents at home to look after them. But, you know what, that's not really your problem!'

I can't believe he can dismiss me like this. Haven't I shown my commitment? How dare he!

He carries on, 'You've helped with hiding leaflets, delivering money. That's not blowing up the Apartheid structure.'

They begin to move out again and Thandi stops and moves towards me. She takes my hand.

'Lily,' she says quietly, 'you've told us before about what prompted you to join the struggle. It seems to me you're doing this for your parents, to rejoin the fight that they weren't able to be part of. It's all part of the same fight. Do you really want to leave it now?'

She's smiling a Mona Lisa smile at me. I look directly at her.

'No,' I say, 'I won't leave it now, I'm in.'

I've put it off long enough, I decide this is the moment to approach him. He's reading the paper, he should respond. It's not like when he's listening to the news on the radio and the parapet is up.

'Morris,' I say and he looks up. 'If I asked to borrow your car, would you agree?'

'When?' he asks.

'Uhm, not quite sure but it wouldn't be during the day.'

And of course he says, 'What for?'

'Well, the thing is,' I say,

He interrupts, sharply. 'Is this starting again, Rika? Is this, let's make Morris pretend I'm having an affair again.'

Oh god he annoys me this man!

'You know what, forget it,' I say.

'No, I'm not going to forget it! What the hell is this all about?'

'Stop swearing!' I say in the teacher voice I'm nurturing.

'Hell is not a swear word. If you want a swear word, I can give you much better than hell.'

Oh bugger off, I think. 'Forget it. I'm going next door,' I say.

'Sure,' he says in a spiteful way, 'run to Jill, run to the commie, leave me with the kids. What else could I possibly expect!'

As if! 'Dinah's looking after them,' I say, 'anyway, I was going to take them with me.'

'You weren't. You were going to leave them, like you always do.'

'That's not true,' I say, looking hurt.

'If you can go out without them you do,' he says, 'you only take them if you have to, like now, to prove a point.'

'That's not true,' I repeat and think, is it? 'I've, I've got other things on my mind as well as you, you know, you're not the only one who thinks about your business' (where am I going with this?).

'Oh, have you got a business now?' he says, 'what is it? Prostitution?'

Jesus. Did he just say that? I'm mute with shock.

He looks shocked himself. 'I didn't mean that,' he says and looks away. 'I'm sorry, I don't know why I said it.'

I go to the bathroom and look in the mirror. He doesn't really think that, it's just his immaturity, his inability to fight back fairly. It's probably because he's seventh of eight children, not the youngest but very young. I burble on to myself trying to find excuses, but the truth is, I'm dreadfully upset.

Is him saying that worse than knowing the truth?

I leave the bathroom and Morris accosts me.

'Rika, I'm sorry I said that. You know I don't believe it.' He sounds contrite, 'let's have a cup of tea.'

I'm not going to let him off so easily and I say nothing. Why? Is it a nasty streak in me or my anger, or not wanting to let the bully off. I walk out the door as if no-one is there and he shouts after me.

'For Christ's sake Rika, is that it? Are you not going to talk to me?'

Later, I hear him talking on the phone to his mommy.

'Rika's not talking to me… I didn't do anything… Of course I didn't do that! Are you crazy! I would never hit her. What do you think I am! … Well yes, I did swear… I know she doesn't like it. … No, I'm telling you. I did nothing!'

The next day he takes me by the shoulders.

'Rika,' he says, gently, 'I want to apologise to you for saying what I did. It was wrong and stupid and I only said it because I didn't know what else to say. Please stop torturing me like this. I'm honestly really sorry.'

I look directly in his eyes and say, 'Can I borrow your car next week in the evening?' He says, 'Yes,' and I smile at him and walk away.

When I speak to Tembo he says, 'We should leave at six pm.'

'That seems early, I thought it would be the middle of the night.'

'And what would our legend be,' he says, 'what reason would there be for you to have a black man and woman in your car at three in the morning?'

Yes, of course he's right. 'I can do seven,' I say, 'because Morris only gets back at about six thirty.'

We agree.

'Our legend,' Tembo says, 'is that we work for you and we're married. We are the garden boy and house girl and we've just had a message that our child is very sick and you have offered to drive us to our home.'

We agree to drive towards his real home, as this could be checked, which is in Sharpeville, on the way to Vereeniging, southwards.

First I have to reconnoitre the area, find the perfect pylon. I suggest to Morris that we all go for a family drive on Sunday.

'Let's go to Vereeniging,' I say.

'Why that dump?' he asks.

'I heard it's quite nice, nice countryside anyway. We can take a picnic.'

He seems pleased, and we agree to go after the sacrosanct Sunday morning family tea. 'I'd like to drive,' I say and he seems shocked.

'Why would you want to do that?' he says.

'Just to get used to it, to have some practice.'

'Strange', he says and shrugs. I know it affects his macho image, but anything that will put a dent in that can only be a good thing.

He squirms from time to time as I drive, putting his foot impotently on the non-existent brake on his side of the car. He tsk-tsks noisily, and breathes in sharply between his teeth.

When we get home he says, 'That wasn't that bad,' and I smile.

'I still don't know why you wanted to go down that little sand road though,' he says.

I respond innocently, 'Just to see what it's like to drive on that sort of road.'

I smile at him, almost seductively. I have found a perfect spot to drop Thandi and Tembo off.

It's Tuesday tonight, and Morris arrives home. I grab his keys and shout, 'See you all later.'

He says, 'What? Oh yes, Tuesday.'

'Bye!' I shout.

'What time will you be back?' he calls but I pretend not to hear.

I circle the block, then drive along several more, and then back again, a left, park, watch for other cars suddenly parking nearby, give it fifteen minutes to make sure surveillance vehicles are lost or not about, get out of the car and walk around the block, is anyone following, is anyone stopping, starting, looking at a newspaper, anything unusual, anything odd. I get in the car and drive around a few times, back on myself, stop, park, go. Right, should be fine, I'll go pick them up.

'Are you sure you weren't followed,' both ask when they get into the car.

'As sure as I can possibly be,' I say.

The traffic has calmed once we leave Johannesburg and drive towards Vereeniging. I feel calm too, I think, as I concentrate on driving. I don't talk, none of us talks. In the countryside I follow the quiet roads that veer nearer towards the pylons.

It's intensely dark now, no moon, the light of the stars are masked by clouds. We are here, the spot I identified as best to drop them off, with bushes and trees close to the road to provide cover. They get out, say nothing and I drive off.

They have to walk without light, I hope they don't fall, oh my god, imagine if they fell now, if someone broke their leg, what would we do. Don't think about it, just do what you have to do, it'll be fine. I look at the watch. We've agreed they need forty minutes to get to the pylons and plant the dynamite, and get back to our meeting place.

I drive further along and find a spot behind a thick clump of bushes to stop and wait for a while. No-one should notice me if they drive by. It's so dark and quiet and I'm entirely alone. I feel more alone in this expanse of empty blackness than I've ever felt in my life.

What are they doing now? Have they reached the pylons, what if the dynamite fails, or if it's unstable, who knows anything about dynamite for Chrissake. Just stop thinking, Rika, think of nothing. That's hard.

These hours of waiting are interminable. I've been here for, Jesus, it's only been ten minutes. Is that someone? No, for goodness sake, just calm down. Is that a light? Is it? My god, it is, it's a light. There's a car coming, oh Jesus, is it coming here, sit still, just watch, he can't see you, you're hidden. It's coming closer, it's so near, is he slowing, he's slowing, quick, duck down, further, I can't breathe, it's slowing. Life slows down, it takes hours for his lights to reach me, it's slowing, it's going to stop. No, he isn't slowing, he's going just as fast as before, he's passed me now, he's carrying on, look, it's going, you can hardly see it now, it's gone.

Ah, you see, silly, silly girl, that wasn't a problem, he came but he went, it's all ok.

I sit and tap my fingers on the steering wheel. I'm alright. I can do this. Not long now.

And I start to think. What'll I do if something goes wrong with them, if there's an explosion. Get out of the car, go look for them? But what if the police came before I even get to them, just as I get out of the car, when I could still leave. The police would come because they'll hear the explosion, they'll see the lights, the fire. I'd have to leave them. Just get out, save myself. But what if they're hurt, if they could be saved, or even if they're not hurt, just waiting like sitting ducks. I'd leave them to be picked up! My comrades, I'd just leave them? Is that the sort of person I am? What if it were me there with them and my trusted comrade just rushed off and left me with an arm dangling, bleeding to death.

Christ Rika, you've got to relax! Just think about something else, something safe.

No, don't think about the children, God, are you crazy, don't think about them, Graham, Nina, no, don't picture them, get them out of your head. Morris, yes, think of Morris, oh Jesus that just makes me feel guilty. I'm not going to feel guilty.

Think of, Edith, there she is in her kibbutz clothes, oh goodness Edith you look so awful, take off that ridiculous hat, put on some lipstick – as if she would! What would Edith say if she could see me now? Would she be proud or just think I was mad, you're crazy, what the hell do you think you're doing, she'd say. I'm doing it for Mutti and Vati.

No, she'd say, you're doing it for yourself because you're a fool and you don't know when you've got it good and to leave things alone. No, Edith, you're wrong. I'm right, you're wrong. Stop it. How stupid to get into a childish argument with my sister in my head.

Just don't think of her, don't think of, Natan? No, for God's sake, last person.

Dinah! Yes, think of Dinah, there in the kitchen, washing the dishes. Dinah's singing. She sings such a lot these days. I love listening to you singing, Dinah. I can hear you singing, I love listening to you and I love chatting to you and telling you about Germany and about what it was like when I was young, younger, before it all became, before it all, before everything...

I look at my watch, right, time to go. I turn on the engine. How lucky this car belongs to a motor mechanic, that it's reliable. I approach our meeting place and slow down and there are two shapes, they're approaching the road, they jump into the car.

'Go, go!' Tembo says and I speed away.

Tembo and Thandi start to laugh.

'When it slipped out of my hand,' Tembo starts.

'My God, my stomach just dropped straight down, straight out of me!' Thandi says.

'But we got it. We got it on. It's going to go off in eight hours. Six am. Shuw! Jesus my Lord! Thank you, thank you!' Tembo says.

I find a quiet, dark road and drop off first Thandi and then Tembo. They move away fast and I drive straight home.

My heart is racing and I sit in the car trying to calm down. It's almost ten thirty. Is Morris asleep or is he waiting for me? I creep inside and slide into bed next to him. I listen to his breathing to see if he really is asleep or just holding his breath. I try to sleep listening to his breathing but it's impossible.

I must've dropped off because when I wake, the room is quiet and Morris has gone.

I realise I haven't worked out my legend – what am I going to say to him when he asks where I was last night? Think, think, but Graham runs in and Nina after him, I pick her up and hold her tight, and put the radio on. There it is, right at the top. I'm amazed Nina doesn't react with shock to the pounding of my heart against her little body.

'Reports have come in of a bombing of a pylon on the road to Vereeniging. The banned South African Communist Party is suspected of being involved. Nobody has yet claimed responsibility for the bombing. There have been no injuries in this latest outrage.'

I don't get dressed. I sit listening to the radio. In the next hour's news broadcast, the Minister of Justice, Charles Roberts Swart has been asked to comment.

'We will continue to hunt these thugs and no stone will be left unturned till we find them, and believe me, their lives will not be worth living when we do. Because we will find them, that is for sure. We will hunt these people who think they can play willy-nilly with the security of this country, not caring about the inconvenience to thousands of people and the enormous costs that are incurred by their acts of tyranny.'

There is a knock at the front door. Who is it? I sit, forget to breathe and listen while Dinah opens the door.

'Hello,' says Jill, and I let out my breath.

She looks at me and mouths, 'Was that you?'

I nod my head and Jill gives me a broad smile and thumbs up sign. We don't say anything. Best assume they can hear everything!

'Did you hear the news?' Morris asks while we sit at the dinner table.

'What news?' I ask innocently.

'Tell us news, daddy,' Graham says.

'News Graham is that some very naughty people put a bomb by a pylon near where we drove on Sunday.'

'When we went in the car?' Graham asks.

'Yes,' Morris says, 'just the same place. Isn't that a funny coincidence?'

'What does coincidence mean, daddy?' asks Graham.

We're lying in bed. I'm breathing very smoothly, pretending to be asleep.

'I know you're awake,' he says, 'and I know you were involved.'

'I don't know what you're talking about,' I say turning to him, feigning sleepiness.

'Don't insult my intelligence, Rika!' he says sharply.

'It wasn't me,' I say unable now to pretend to be half asleep.

'We both know it was.'

'Why do you say that?' I ask.

'Because I know you. And you probably should have tried to clean the mess from under the car. You might not have noticed that I'd got a boy to hosepipe under the car after our Sunday charade. It's the same mess now.'

I stop and can't help but declare, 'I wish you wouldn't call grown men boys.'

'I think that's probably small fry compared to what you've done!' he says.

My anger levels shoot sky-high.

'Don't you understand,' I spit out, 'that I do that precisely because of things like this! Don't call grown men boys, and don't call grown women girls. Alright!'

'So you admit it then,' he says, almost gleefully, which is surprising under the circumstances, he's obviously jumped on this chance for a win.

'I'm talking generally,' I say.

'Look Rika,' he says seriously again, 'this can't go on. You're a mother, for Chrissake! I'm not even talking about me. I'm talking about the children! What would happen to them if anything happened to you? What's going to happen to them when you land up in jail? And what happens if you get sentenced to death!'

I don't even stop to consider what he's saying. 'They don't kill white women,' I say.

'Really? Have you got a guarantee on that?' he says.

'Well they haven't yet,' I answer, softly.

'Yet being the operative word!' he says.

I sit up and look him directly in the face. 'Morris,' I say, 'do you think I haven't thought of this? Do you think I haven't thought of the children? You've got to understand that I have to do something. I can't sit and have tea and cake and meet up with your mother and sisters and sisters-in-law and bake and knit and chat as if everything is alright in the world. It's not me. You should never have married me. You should have married a nice Jewish South African woman just like you who never thinks!'

I was getting loud. I repeat loudly in my whisper, 'Who never thinks!'

He lies back in bed. 'You're right. My God you're so bloody right. What the fuck was I thinking!'

'You don't have to swear!' I say, trying desperately to retrieve something, dignity or whatever it is.

'I will fucking well swear,' he says very loudly. 'You fucking well do what you want to do and I'll fucking well swear.'

I turn my back on him and say, 'Goodnight.'

'Don't you dare!' he says, 'don't you dare think this is the end of the conversation. Rika, listen to me, we have to talk. This can't go on. I have to tell you something.'

I turn slowly towards him. He's calmed down. He's looking straight ahead of him and seems to be talking to someone else entirely, someone standing politely in front of him.

'I need a wife to be a mother for my children. I refuse to let you get involved in these activities that can only result in terrible hardship for us as a family.'

'They're my children too,' I say.

'But they won't be if you land in jail,' he says. 'You can't mother them from jail and they're too young to be without one. If you go to jail I will divorce you and marry someone else, the Jewish South African you said I should. She will become their mother.'

'I won't agree to it, you can't divorce me without my agreement,' I say.

'I'll have a good lawyer who'll make the court see that it's my only option.'

I look at him and say, 'I don't believe you.'

'Right', he says, 'believe this then. I don't want that either. I want you to be my wife and their mother and to stay like that. But you've got to stop it.'

'They won't find out. I'm very careful,' I say.

'They will find out,' he says.

'How?' I ask. I suddenly feel very fearful of what he's about to say.

'I'll tell them.'

I knew he'd bloody say that! I look ahead. I'm sitting at the cinema and watching a film. The film is a kaleidoscope of my future life, shards of activities, events, prison cells, children's parties, a wedding with Nina as bridesmaid, a smiling stepmother, torture, pain, loneliness.

'It's your choice, Rika,' he says and it feels as though it comes from far away.

I turn and stare at him. It reminds me of the moment he asked me to marry him. I didn't know what to say then and I don't know what to say now. Edith's voice blurts into my head, you don't know when you've got it good.

What would Natan say, I think. Natan's married. What will I have when I come out of jail? Nothing. Where will I go? Where could I go? To the kibbutz? And never see my children?

What will happen to Thandi and Tembo if he tells the police. I have a responsibility to them too. I don't know their real names but they'll soon find them. I'll be quiet. I won't say anything. They'll torture me. Can I resist?

I suddenly know, I really know with a truthfulness that cannot be denied, that I would not be able to resist torture. When they keep me standing, hour after hour, refusing to let me sleep, refusing to let me sit, refusing to let me remain unconscious, I know I would tell them everything. I know I'm not strong enough. I know I'm not extraordinary.

'Alright Morris, I'll stop,' I murmur.

'Do you promise, Rika? Because I'll know if you're lying.'

'I promise.'

I lie back. I hear a sound. Is there a kitten, it's a meeawing, where is it? I look at Morris to see if he's heard it too and I see the noise is coming from him. He's sobbing, tears are falling from his eyes, not just resting on his cheeks, but gushing down. I've never seen him cry before.

His sadness seems to hit me like a wave. I put my arms out and he moves into them. I pull him towards me and hold him while he cries.

My face is wet either from his tears or mine. After a while the sobs subside. He holds me tight.

'I love you, Rika. I always will.'

21

I sit in this chair, useless, irrelevant. Nobody comes to me, nobody speaks to me, nobody wants me. I let everyone down. They wanted to help me but I was too weak, too greedy.

All I want is cake. Cake made me leave them when they needed me. I could have gone with them but I chose to go with cake. I don't even know my name.

Look at Jill, she's trying to conceal her disappointment in me but I see it so clearly as if it's written in bold in her eyes - you too Rika, I thought you were different, I believed you had it in you.

But she still smiles and she laughs and offers tea and is very sympathetic.

She doesn't tell me anything anymore about the movement. There is no talk of policies, and plans, and strategies. I'm out of it, I'm not part of that longed for community. I don't belong anymore.

All I belong to is the community of my family and other friends who fit into this narrow Jewish, almost middle class, getting there, tea-drinking, cake-eating, South African cluster, wanting things, cars, more, more. I'm now an ordinary white wife and mother, nothing special, nothing outstanding, nothing exceptional, just typical, normal, like everyone else.

Other than Jill.

I haven't said goodbye to anyone in the movement. No farewell party or drinks, no special cake brought through with everyone clapping, no medal for services rendered, for services to the people of South Africa in their time of trouble. Nothing.

Obviously.

I sent a message to Tembo and said my husband says I'm not allowed to play anymore, well, not quite, but not that far off. I didn't say he'd tell on me, on us, if I carried on, so I'm actually just protecting you, you know, you should really be grateful.

I didn't say, I'll miss this, I'll miss you, I'm not sure what I'm going to do with my life now, I'm not sure how I'm going to survive. I just said, I can't any longer, sorry.

I didn't get a reply. Tembo and Thandi have certainly changed their aliases, to protect themselves from me. I'm a danger to them now, being out of it, being on the other side - if you aren't with us, you're against us.

I hope they don't say, it just shows you, you can never trust whitey. That would be an insult to the many strong whites in the movement who are so extraordinary. I'm just not one of them.

Ivor asks me if I will still help with the Christmas Club. He asks Morris if that would be ok, and Morris says, 'Yes if it's only for one morning a week and she just helps pack the hampers, or sorts out all the goods. Nothing more. Promise?'

So every Wednesday morning the good little girl goes off into town to Joubert street where the offices are, and does what's needed.

I don't see many there, no comrades, very few blacks. They probably make sure no meetings are held on Wednesday mornings, that we must be very careful when Rika Levine is in the office helping out, because she can't be trusted anymore.

There are those few other white South African women helping too, those who sympathise with the cause but not enough to get involved, properly involved. So we work together and chat about our children and various meals that we make, and where we can find the cheapest but best cuts of meat.

I meet up with my sister-in-law Sadie several times a week. I go over with the children. Nina loves her cousin Helena who is a year younger and the two go off together to play with their blocks of wood, or build sandcastles in the little sandpit in Sadie's back yard. Sadie gets the servant to blow up a little plastic swimming pool when it's warm and fill it with water, and the girls splash about and have fun, and we watch. Graham's at nursery school so we walk round to fetch him and bring him back to play as well.

I'm starting to look like the others.

The hundred pound me when I married is not the me of now. Weekly, the weight goes up and up. It's the sitting, it's the taiglach, it's the delicious cakes.

Those are the symbols of our worth, the trophy we all compete for, and the prize is the request – can I please have the recipe! And we all write our recipes down and put them in a hardback booklet and the booklet gets fuller and fuller. It is all so pleasant, to sit, to drink coffee in the morning, tea in the afternoon, and all with that enormous variety of biscuits, cookies, slices of cakes. How good to sit and dunk the biscuit in the tea, to taste the cake and then swirl it down with a mouthful of coffee.

How easy, how lovely.

A part of me tells myself I should be doing more. A little whisper in the ear, this is all too easy, too pleasant, I wasn't born to this, my life must be more than this, surely?

'What on earth for?' Sadie asks incredulously when I say I should be doing something. 'You already do Wednesday mornings at that hamper place and Nina's so young. Graham too. You're a mother, that's the biggest job of all. And being a wife of course.'

If Sadie says it, and Sadie is such a good woman, I must accept it, so I sit back and take it as truth and smile and enjoy the sun and the laughter of the children, and have another bite of taiglach, and apply some sun lotion.

'We should move,' Morris says one day.
'You mean, move out of this flat?'
Morris laughs, 'Of course, into a house with a garden. What do you think?'
'Can we afford it?' I ask.
'If we're careful.'
So we move to a house in a street in Linmeyer in the southern suburbs of Johannesburg, a street just 100 yards away from a lovely big hill, with both front and back gardens and a driveway where we can park the car, and a path leading right up to the house from the front gate.

Dinah moves with us and has a room in the servants' quarters right at the back of the back garden. Out of the way, out of sight.

The rooms are far larger than the flat's, and both Nina and Graham have their own rooms. Nina has a big cardboard box in her room with all her toys in it, and Graham has started to play with Meccano and dinky cars.

Life with Morris has become easier. He swears less.

The children play happily, and Dinah continues to sing as she works.

I'm reading novels to keep myself busy and I've taken up sewing using a little sewing machine that Sadie passed on to me.

We go to the cinema on Saturday evenings with brothers and wives or sometimes friends. I love From Here to Eternity and Roman Holiday best of all, and anything with Audie Murphy in it – the singing cowboy. It's another world.

I'm sitting with Jill. Unusually it's just the two of us as the children are with their dads. We're talking, we're drinking tea, she asks for the recipe of the latest cake I made, and out of the blue, unexpectedly in this sunshine, in this pleasantness, in this life of ease, an avalanche of sadness suddenly engulfs me.

'What's the matter, Rika?' Jill asks looking concerned. 'You look so, far away, so, what is it? Sad? Are you sad suddenly? You seemed ok and then… were you thinking of your parents?'

'My parents,' I repeat. 'They're always with me, you know, somewhere there, a sense of looking over my shoulder, being around me, being present, making sure I'm ok. I do feel that quite strongly, I know it's ridiculous, but I suddenly felt this extraordinary wave of disappointment touching me. So peculiar. It's as if they're looking at me from the edge of their pit and they see me sitting here eating cake, just drinking tea and eating cake, and they think, is this it? Is this all you're doing? Is this your life?'

Jill is looking at me intently, she waits for more and when she sees no more is coming, she says, 'Well, you could've"

I stop her, 'No, don't say anymore, please.'

'Ok,' she says and keeps quiet.

I break the silence and say, 'It's a conundrum. I say stop because I don't want to hear you say I should've fought Morris, I should've never accepted his threat, I should've got him to change, I should've, should've, should've. I'm not strong enough, Jill. I should be part of the struggle, I know that, but I also know I would lose everything. But what is this everything that stops me from doing what I know I should do? Is it Morris? I don't even want him, yet I don't not want him. I don't want this life, yet I don't not want it. I don't want to risk suffering, not having enough, not having anything, so I accept second best, adequate, good enough. Is good enough enough? Should I be striving, and if I strive, what am I striving for? To become a revolutionary? I don't have it in me, it isn't me, I'm not that person.

But I'm also not the person who doesn't do anything. I don't want to be the sort of South African who spends her whole life shopping, or reorganising the house, or bossing the servants, or nagging, or gossiping. I know that if I go on like this, that's the sort of person I'll become, the life I'll have, because it's a slippery slope. It's easy to forget to be angry with the way things are, not to accept the way things are, to fight against the way things are. And if I'm going to stop this life that lies before me, I have to stop it now. But how do I do that?'

Jill looks directly at me, 'Do what you can, do what Sadie does, do as much as is possible within Morris' restrictions.'

'That's not enough,' I say.

'No,' agrees Jill, 'but it's a helluva lot more than most white South Africans do. Just speak respectfully, challenge bad behaviour, help wherever you can with money, with work, with clothes, anything.'

Is that enough? It has to be, at least for now, I think.

'But you do need to do something more with your life,' Jill says, 'I really think that's important for you. Why don't you get a job?'

'You mean, like a shopgirl? Working in a shop as a shopgirl? In a department store? You mean that? Can I help you, madam? That would look lovely on you. It would go so beautifully with this perfume, oh smell it, isn't it marvellous!'

Jill laughs, 'Well, look at you! You wouldn't even need training!' she says.

I laugh a little too, a chuckle, a snicker.

'Or you could become a secretary.'

'Can you imagine,' I say, 'I'd have to learn to do shorthand and typing. I'd be in competition with pretty young eighteen year olds who've just come out of school. Can you see me doing that?'

'You could study,' Jill says.

It is the last suggestion and the most obvious, but I'm not clever enough.

'I missed my chance of study,' I say, 'I had it, there's no doubt about that, but I…'

I stop there and Jill says 'You had things going on that were very difficult when you were at school in Israel. Don't be so hard on yourself, Rika. Give yourself a chance.'

But I can't give myself any leeway, I lash into myself, self-flagellation, it feels good.

'I'm so useless, Jill. That's the truth. I can't do anything properly, I can't even be a Jewish wife and mother properly.'

I can't get out of this pit of remorse even when Jill says I'm a good mother.

'What does it even mean, to be a good mother? To love them, to tell them they're wonderful. To kiss them when they fall, or rub them when they hurt. Yes, I make sure they go to bed on time, I look after their food, make sure they eat enough fruit and vegetables and not too many cakes and chocolate. Is that what it means, to be a good mother? Is that it?'

'It's all of those things,' Jill says.

'That's not enough for me,' I say.

After a while Jill looks at me and says, 'What about the wife side of things.'

I look self-pityingly and say, 'I'm a useless wife.'

I look so downcast, so morose and ridiculous that it becomes a joke, and we start to laugh again.

'I'm,' I say, 'I'm not interested in him, I don't find him funny, I don't want to talk to him particularly, I don't want to make love to him particularly, unless I need to physically, and that doesn't happen very often.'

Jill looks surprised. I suspect this is not something we have in common.

'Do you?' I ask.

She smiles and nods her head, 'I love it,' she says.

'God I'm jealous of you,' I say, and smile.

'I married the right man, Rika,' she says simply. 'That's your problem. You didn't.'

'Yes,' I agree.

'Have you ever been in love?' she asks.

I can't respond to this, I can't even look at her, I look away and there they are, the bloody tears welling up, idiot, once again you have to cry, control yourself, fool!

'Sorry,' I say.

'Don't be such a ... what's that word you always say?'

'Meshugenah! Schmendrick? Idiot!'

'Yes, all of those,' she says.

I toss the subject away with my hand and she says, 'No, don't do that, tell me, who was it?'

'Just another schmendrick in my life,' I say.

'And what was that schmendrick's name?'

'Natan,' I say.

'Where is he now?'

'Happily married with x number of children, who knows.'

'Ah ha,' she says with no smile.

'So it's now Rika and Morris,' I say. 'Morris and Rika. For ever and ever. How depressing!'

'That is a problem,' Jill says.

'Indeed.'

'Rika,' Jill says pointedly, 'you're young, you're beautiful, you could find someone else.'

'But I don't want someone else, not another South African. I need a good German, like my father, gentle, a man who never swore. Never a loud word, never a swear word, always kind and loving and sweet. And there aren't any around! Well, apart from Ivor, but you got him.'

Jill puts her head in her hands dramatically and says, 'Oy vay!'

The sadness doesn't leave me. It's hard to pretend even in front of people I love like Shaina Raisa.

She grabs my chin and holds it and says 'Rikale, are you not sleeping enough? If the children are too much for you and you need a break, I'll look after Grahamela for a little while. What do you say, huh?' She puts it down to lack of sleep.

'Thank you Shaina Reisa,' I say, 'but I'm fine, I sleep well enough.'

'Here,' she says, digging into the ubiquitous handbag she always carries in the crook of her arm, 'take these tonight. They're wonderful. You just drop off and there can be a fire and you wouldn't even know!'

'So that's a good thing?'

'I'm just saying, not a real fire, I mean, you sleep! You mustn't think too much. What are you thinking about? What are you worrying about? You don't have anything to worry about! You have a lovely husband, look how much better he is, alright he shouts but it's much less, isn't it? He never hits you, chas ve'chalila that he should hit you. But he doesn't. None of my children have trouble with people hitting them. It's not Jewish, you know. We Jews don't know thank God of such tzorres. I mean the goyim, alright, you can expect it, and the shvartse, they can hit. But it's not something we do. Thank God.

And you've got your two children, baruch ha'shem, thank God, they're healthy, they're lovely, especially that Grahamela, what a little bubela he is! Oy, I'm telling you, such a beauty! So what must you worry about? Nothing!'

I have a sudden need to write to Edith. I need to tell her everything is wonderful. If she believes me, it'll mean it's true.

Dear Edith

I'm missing you. I wish you could see the children. I know you said there is no way you could come for a visit, but it's been such a long time since I saw you last.

You asked me in your last letter to tell you honestly how I am. I wonder why you think I'm not alright. I told you I was. Why do you think I'm not fine? Can you tell me that? It's like you always say, appreciate what you've got. I do. I live in a country that is warm but not so hot that I can't breathe. I have water that I can use without worrying that if I use more than one cup I'm wasting it. I can use toilet paper without anyone telling me to use only two pieces at a time! There is enough food to eat, and I don't always have to worry that some Arab is going to burst in with a gun and shoot us down. Ok, so I'm exaggerating. But it's safe. It's the goldene medina as everyone is always telling me. I've shut my ears and eyes to what's going on here. Black people have ceased to exist for me other than my wonderful Dinah. So there you are. Stop worrying about me. I'm fine, as fine as a daisy. As perfect as a swallow. Oh god, I've never even seen a swallow. I don't know what I'm talking about. Tell me how you are. I'm sick and tired of feeling as though the only thing that comes out of my mouth is a complaint. I know I have nothing to complain about. How are you?

Love, Rika

Edith writes back and tells me she's happy for me, obviously everything's fine. Somehow, it doesn't make me feel better.

Like the canary in the mines, Dinah stops singing, and I know things are bad.

'Have you noticed that Dinah doesn't sing anymore?' I ask Morris.

'I never noticed her singing. Does she sing?' he asks.

'She was always singing,' I say.

'What songs? Shvartse songs?'

I approach her, I look at her, and I say, 'Dinah? Are you alright?'

'Yes m'am,' she says.

'Really?' I ask.

'Yebo,' she replies unsmiling.

So I say, 'What's wrong?'

And she says, 'Nothing m'am.'

'You can't tell me?' I ask.

And she says simply, 'It's alright.'

I can't walk away from her. I must persist, but is that fair, am I pushing her too far, I have all the power for Christsake, but she can just choose to close her mouth. I've got to try.

'Dinah, please, please tell me what's wrong. I know there is something. Is it something I've done? Or Morris? Is it the children? Don't you like it here in Linmeyer? Is it too far away from your friends? Have you not made friends here? Is it your children? Please tell me.'

I'm begging her. She looks at me, directly into my face and says nothing.

'Is it all of those things,' I ask and she shakes her head, but I notice tears appearing in her eyes. Just seeing them make my eyes well up too, and as soon as she sees that she begins to sob. I take her in my arms and we move to sit at the table.

'I'm going to have a baby,' she finally whispers.

'Isn't that good,' I ask.

'No, it's very bad.'

'Why?' I ask.

She says just two words, 'The father.'

'What about the father? Is it your husband?' I ask.

'Yes, when I went home.'

'You must be happy, Dinah, another baby,' I say optimistically, but she shakes her head again and the tears come faster and more furiously.

'We have no money. What will I do? I must work,' she says.

'But you will still be paid, Dinah. Do you think you won't be paid?' I'm appalled that she fears that.

'My mother can't look after so many children, she needs help, we need someone to help her,' she wails. 'My husband hasn't been out of prison for long and there's no work. He says now he's going to Johannesburg to get a job in the mines, but it's very dangerous for him to go there, to live in a hostel, his lungs are bad and there are so many accidents in the mines. The lives of the people are so cheap.'

Her despair seeps into me as if it by a process of osmosis. What can she do? What can they do? They have nothing, not even the barest of basics. We celebrate a new baby, they can't. For us it offers joy and wonderment, for them it augurs only disaster.

'How can I help you, Dinah, please tell me.'

'You can't do anything to help me.'

The children distract me and I move away from Dinah but as soon as Morris gets home I grab him.

'I told you she wasn't singing anymore.'

I explain the situation and he shrugs.

'Well, there you are,' he says, 'she shouldn't've got herself pregnant. They breed like rabbits, these people.'

I shake my head in disgust but he hardly notices it or doesn't care.

'We're going to pay her while she's off having the baby,' I say pointedly.

'I can't afford to pay for two girls,' he says while walking away from me. I watch him with deep loathing.

I have no money of my own, therefore I have no say, I have no clout, I have no power. I can do nothing to help Dinah. I go to Shaina Raisa, for support I hope, but suspect it might be just to let off some steam.

'Morris is right,' she says, 'do you have enough money to pay for her to be off while she has her baby and for you to have someone else. Two shiksas. It's a lot of money. It's a lot of tzorres for Morris. Look at all his expenses. A wife, two children, a new house.'

And then I realise, how simple, what on earth was I thinking!

'Morris,' I say, 'I don't need anyone else while she's away.'

He laughs in a sarcastic way. 'And what am I supposed to eat,' he says.

'I can cook!'

And then he adds, 'Anyway, what do you think it'll look like? Everyone will think I can't afford a girl.'

'For god's sake,' I shout, 'do you think I care what other people think!'

'Well I do!' he says.

I look him deep in his face and I say, for the first time in my life I think, (perhaps apart from when I was in labour), 'Well, you know what Morris? You can go fuck yourself!'

And I walk out, just after I see his mouth falling to his chest.

I drive over to Jill and knock on her door. She invites me in and puts the kettle on.

'I can't take this anymore,' I say. 'I was wrong. How can I live with someone who is so ungenerous, so uncaring, so reactionary, so racist, it's just not possible anymore.'

She looks at me and says the inevitable words, possibly the words I've been waiting to hear, the permission that someone dear to me is giving me, 'You can leave him.'

But, the questions immediately come rushing into my head. Am I prepared to do that? And then what?

'The family won't talk to me,' I say, 'what will I do, how will I live? How will I look after my children? Must I become a waitress again?'

She moves in close to me and whispers in my ear, 'The movement can try and help support you.'

'But that would be so unfair,' I say, 'there are people who need so much more than I do, I couldn't live with myself if I took money when people like Dinah and millions of others have nothing!'

And Jill has to admit I'm right. Of course I'm right.

I can't turn to my Mutti, and I can't turn to my Vati, so I turn to the next best thing.

Dear Tante Leah

I'm so sorry to write to you with my tzorres. You have always been such a help in my life that I feel turning to you now means that I have somehow failed. And I have failed. I must admit it and admitting it to you is much easier than to anyone else. I have failed as a wife and I'm not sure I'm a very good mother. I have also failed to do what is right in this country. I feel I'm going crazy. I just don't know what to do. Help me please Tante Leah.

Love, Rika

By return of post Tante Leah writes one line.

Come. Come for a break. Get away from it all, come here and think.

And the thought that goes over and over in my mind is, If I go there, I'll be able to see Natan.

'I need you to pay for me to go to Israel,' I say to him that night as we lie in bed.

He doesn't reply. I wait, my heart in my mouth (stupid expression), surely he'll agree. He always agrees when I say I need/want something. He's quiet. Bloody hell, he's fallen asleep.

'Who'll look after the children?' Morris demands when I tell him I'm leaving.

'I've spoken to Sadie, she's offered to have the whole family stay with her until I return.'

'When will you be back?' he asks.

'I don't know,' I say.

'Will you be back?' he asks.

'I don't know,' I say.

'You mean, you might not be back,' he says.

'I don't know.'

'You don't know much, do you! Well I know something. I know that you're a shit wife and an even shitter mother. If you can leave your children just like that, then I don't know who you are!'

I get up and walk away. I have to walk away or the trembling will erupt into palpitations.

'Yes, I'll pay,' he says quietly after me.

'Ma,' Graham says, 'are you going to bring me back a present?'

And Nina says, 'Ma, present for me.'

I hug them till they shriek with pain and I let them go.

'Just make sure you pay Dinah while she's off having her baby,' I say to Morris as we stand at the airport.

'I'll give you a month, Rika, and then I'm going to start divorce proceedings. I'll find a new wife to look after the children,' he says softly to me, out of the children's hearing.

'Promise me you'll pay Dinah!' I shriek in a loud whisper back to him.

'Alright. I promise, I promise, for Christ's sake!'

'Don't fire Dinah,' I plead, 'you'll need someone to look after the children.'

The children and I are all crying, we hug each other and Graham says, 'Come back soon, ma.'

'Mommy's only going for a little while,' Morris says, 'she'll be back soon. She just wants to see her aunt and sister and then she'll be back. And in the meantime we'll have a lovely time with Auntie Sadie and Uncle Jonathan, and you can play nicely with your cousins.'

I walk through the departure gate. I dare not look back. I can hear Graham crying, Nina screaming, Morris trying to soothe them. If I look back, I may forget why I have to leave. And I know I have to get away or I risk losing myself. And what will I have if I don't even have myself.

Nina arrives at Sadie's house after the airport wearing a little red and white checked dress. When it's time for bed, she refuses to take off the dress.

'I'll wash it for you, my little love,' kind Aunt Sadie says, 'and in the morning it'll be dry and clean and you'll be able to wear it again.'

The next night the same thing happens and once again Sadie tells her that she'll wash it and dry it and it'll be ready for her to wear again.

And so it went on, day after day after day. At least, that's what I was told.

22

The people all around me are my family.

We're all in Tel Aviv and look how happy we all are.

It's better than, than, the other place, where everyone sits and looks and dreams.

Here is Tante Leah. Tante Leah, I haven't seen you for so long. I'm fourteen, and I'm with my Tante Leah. She'll put me to bed, she'll tuck me up, she'll sing lullabies, she'll give me nougat and marzipan.

She'll love me until Mutti and Vati come and then they can take over.

I'm lying in the bed I used to sleep in when I first arrived in Tel Aviv. There's something comforting about that.

It's early morning and there's no noise. Tante Leah is alone in the flat now, she's been a widow for seven years already, and her sons are married with their own families and homes. She looks older, smaller, more round-shouldered and greyer.

'Rikalein,' she comes creeping into the room, 'come have a glass of tea. I've got some lovely bread for breakfast. Come eat and drink. You need to eat. Come liebchen. Come with me.'

We sit together on the little balcony overlooking the rooftops of Tel Aviv. The air is cool as it's almost winter. I swallow the tea and chew the bread and the effort and concentration it takes helps keep the tears down.

'What's the matter, liebchen, tell me.'

But how can I tell her my silly little nonsense when she has suffered so much in life. I go for walks with her and explore Tel Aviv again. It's been a while.

Four days later I go see my sister. I'm in the bus and it's approaching the kibbutz entrance, ahh, there she is, there's Edith standing there. At least she's not doing a wee behind some tiny bush, I think and laugh out loud.

It's so good to see her, we hug and don't let go and then start laughing until I sit down hard on the ground clutching myself to make sure the wee stays where it's supposed to stay. But she carries on laughing and I carry on laughing, holding myself harder and harder.

'Stop stop,' I shout, 'it's going to, oh no, no no, it's ok. I've controlled it!'

Joseph, Edith's husband, is wonderfully welcoming.

'We've missed you,' he says again and again. 'Come, let me take you to the children's house and you can see how big our children have grown.'

The three of us walk through the burgeoning kibbutz which even has a little patch of green lawn in one spot. Joseph points to it in wonder.

'It takes up water we don't have, but it's worth it for everyone to remember what green grass is and to know that's what we're aiming for.'

I exclaim in surprise at the number of buildings there are now, far more than tents, squat white buildings with four rooms to a building, each a couple's home, with a shower, toilet and basin at the end of the building serving the eight people living there. Single people sleep in smaller rooms either for one or two people to share. Basic, I think, but enough.

I wonder if I can see myself living here but even as I think it, I notice my head shaking forcibly left and right, no way.

The sea, the beautiful Mediterranean, is all around us with its deep blue water and gentle waves. A few Sycamore trees are dotted near the dunes leading down to the seashore. It's so clean and pure, I think as I breathe it all in and feel it entering deep into my lungs.

My antipathy to the communal dining room, the eyes, the gossip, the comments is still as strong as ever.

'Do we have to eat in the dining room,' I ask, 'can't we just bring food back to the room, or we can have a picnic and eat outside by the sea.' But Edith scoffs.

'Don't be ridiculous, everyone's dying to see you.'

The smell of the food hits me even before we walk in through the door of the bustling dining room, a good smell though my anxiety prevents me from feeling hungry.

'Rika!' I hear the shouts from several people simultaneously. There's a sudden quiet in the room as everyone looks up and there they are, all smiling, and waving and calling me over to say hello. I glance quickly over the whole crowd but he isn't there.

'She's still such a beauty, though she's put on a lot of weight, but she was so skinny before, she looks so lovely, such beautiful hair, mind you, she still wears lipstick, honestly!' I hear people speak as I walk past them.

And then directly to my face: 'Why didn't you bring the children? The whole family. Where's your husband? How long are you going to be here? What's happening there in South Africa? Do you like it? But what about the way they treat the blacks? What is your mishpocha like?'

More and more and more questions. I smile, I shrug, I laugh, I make inane comments. I can't understand how I can hate and love all of this as much as I do.

'Rika!' It's Frieda. I stand still and my smile disappears though it remembers immediately and reappears with great certainty. We hug and laugh and she says, 'Natan is so looking forward to seeing you, Rika. Come and have aruchat arba with us today. You and Edith, come.'

'Oh, I can't,' Edith says, 'we have the children.'

'I'll come another time,' I say, 'I want to see your children too.'

But Frieda insists and says, 'Come, Rika.'

It's four o'clock and I'm walking over to Natan and Frieda's room. They and their three children are waiting for me to come so they can eat their small four o'clock meal. This is it, this is their little room/flat. I knock and over the loud roar of my heart beating I hear his voice.

'Come'.

He's standing there looking at me and the three children pounce on the cake as soon as their guest, who has looked very briefly at their father, just the briefest of brief looks to see if it really is him, arrives.

'Hullo, hullo,' I say quickly trying to gather the mess that is me into one non-quivering whole.

'Oh my goodness,' I say, 'the children have grown, oh hello Natan, good to see you, Frieda, lovely to see you again,' (all of this in one breath). 'Look,' (I carry on quickly, why, no idea), 'I have a little thing here I brought with me from South Africa for you.'

I hand them a colourful little beaded African mat which Frieda takes and loves and immediately puts centre stage on the table.

'Rika, sit,' Frieda says, and as I sit I realise that Natan hasn't yet said a word.

'How are you keeping, Natan,' I say looking directly at him.

'Good, good,' he says still looking as if he's just woken up from a nightmare.

'Everything alright with you, with the kibbutz?'

'Yes, yes.'

Frieda laughs, 'I don't know what's the matter with him today. Natan, what's wrong with you? It's Rika, back here for a visit from South Africa. Have you got nothing to say to her!'

He jumps as if an electric cable's been attached to his battery. 'Of course, of course, I know, I know.'

'Why is he repeating himself all the time,' Frieda turns to me in mock incredulity. 'Do you need to go back to bed, Natan!'

'Sorry, I just,' Natan starts and sits down and cuts some cake.

'Cake, Rika?'

So we all sit and drink and eat and Frieda and I chat and Natan just sits.

The children are sweet and now that they've eaten they start to chat away.

'What's South Africa like? What's it like to live there?'

I tell them the summer is not as hot as Israel and the sand is red and the grass is strong and very green.

'Can you sing an African song,' the oldest says.

Quite shakily, I sing Tula Tula Baba, and explain it's an African lullaby I learnt from Dinah. I tell them about Dinah, about the lovely young African woman who works for our family and how she sings as she works.

They can't understand that someone would work for you, 'You mean, they do all your work and you give them money? What do they do with the money?' The concept of money is still quite unknown to them.

'Yes,' I say, but I don't say anything about how little she gets paid.

I'm leaving now, I say thank you for the cake and how lovely it's been to see them and meet their gorgeous children, and Natan suddenly seems to wake up.

'I'll walk you to Edith's,' he says.

The youngest shouts, 'Daddy, let me come too.'

But Frieda stops him and says, 'No, leave him, come and help me tidy up.'

We walk slowly down the path without talking. What shall I say, I think, I must say something.

He suddenly says, 'Why are you so unhappy?'

I can't believe he's just said that. I was effervescent in there, cheerful and wagging my tail like the happiest of golden retrievers.

'Why do you say that?' I ask.

'I know you,' he says.

I don't know how to answer his question. Do I say, you're right, I'm sad because I actually hate my husband and I still love you. Or, oh no, how wrong you are, it shows you, you don't know me at all. Or, I'm fine thanks, the ubiquitous, I'm fine thanks.

But instead I don't answer him and I start walking very fast away from him. He starts to keep up with me until he realises that I'm actually trying to get away from him, so he stops and watches me until I turn behind some trees and he then runs and catches up with me.

'Stop it' he says, 'we've got to talk, you know it.'

We both notice a kibbutznik walking down the path towards us.

'We can't talk now,' he says, 'meet me tonight at this tree, at ten o'clock. You must be there. You will come, right?'

I nod my head.

I slip out of Edith and Joseph's room at ten. They're listening to a concert but Edith looks up, of course she does, she misses nothing.

'I won't be long,' I say.

'Where are you going?' she says.

'I won't be long,' I repeat.

We walk together quickly towards the sea. Is it too quick, will we arouse suspicions if anyone in the kibbutz is looking. We have to be so careful, everyone is on the look out, for gossip, rather than anything more sinister. We slow our pace a little and here is a spot that's just right, secluded, private, cosy at the bottom of the dunes.

We sit close together and look out at the waves.

'It was so good to see you,' Natan says at last, the first thing either of us have said since we met.

I don't reply, what's to say.

He tries again. 'I really was happy to see you. And you?'

'What me?' I say after a while.

'Were you happy to see me?' he asks.

I say, 'Well, I didn't know how I'd feel.'

'And how did you feel?' he asks.

I say, circuitously, redundantly, 'You mean, when I saw you?'

'Yes.'

And I say, 'I could only see you as a husband and father. The man I knew had disappeared. His identity has changed.'

He looks surprised and says 'But I'm still me.'

'Inside somewhere, maybe,' I say.

'Rika, I'm still the man who',

I jump in, 'Took my virginity.'

He's startled. 'Is that important?' he says.

'Of course.'

'I was going to say, the man who loved you,' he says.

'You didn't love me when you took my virginity,' I say.

He laughs, scoffs almost, 'Took your virginity! Rika! That's such a mad thing to say. Such a bourgeois concept. You got into my bed. You knew what you wanted.'

'Did I?' I say.

'Is this the time to talk about it?'

'Yes, actually, it is!'

'Why didn't we speak about it before?'

'I don't know.'

'So you tell me now when I tell you I loved you?'

'But you didn't love me then, when you raped me.'

He jumps up, 'I did not rape you! How can you say that? I can't believe that you can say such a thing! Do you know what you're saying? To accuse a man of rape! It's a very big word, Rika. It has enormous consequences, you know.'

'I do,' I say.

'So if you do understand it, then how could you have gone on to have a relationship with a man who you say raped you? It doesn't make sense!'

'No, you're right,' I say, 'it doesn't.'

'You're just a mass of contradictions, Rika,' he says.

'Yes, blame me.'

'I'm not blaming you. I just can't believe what you're saying!' He's staring out at the sea, then sits down again.

I face him. 'Oh Natan,' I say, 'do you have any idea what it was like for me? Do you have an inkling? You slept with so many women. It was so minimal for you. Just a non-event. I bet you never even thought about it afterwards. But for me, do you know what it was for me? It was pure…'

… and he interrupts me and says, 'Pleasure?'

'No! No, not pleasure. Humiliation. Utter devastating humiliation.'

He says, 'What?!' in such a way that I might be telling him grass is pink.

'You were entirely uninterested in me,' I say, 'and for me, it was the first time. That might be just a statement to you, but you have to understand what that means. A girl anticipates the first time. She lies in bed, aroused and imagines with a beautiful fantasy, what the first time will be like for her. He'll hold you, she says to herself, he'll be shivering with joy, with arousal, with expectancy, he'll kiss you gently, and touch you and, yes, the cliché, whisper sweet nothings, and slowly, slowly, he'll enter you and he'll be aware of hurting you and share the glorious moment of transition.'

'Jesus Christ Rika, what kind of romantic schoolgirl are you?' he says dismissing me.

'That's what I was, Natan,' I say, 'a young, innocent, naïve, lonely, desperate child wishing just to be held by another human being, just held with affection, warmth, with, support. But you never took a minute to realise that. And then, you ignored me and lit two cigarettes, not one for you and one for me, but one for my sister, your lover. And you looked at her while this girl who had just been with a man for her first time ever, was left to wonder what to do with the blood and the semen that was leaking from inside her, and which she ignored, and then, ignominiously, pulled her knickers up and left without anyone saying anything to her, noticing her, acknowledging her.'

He is quiet. Eventually he says, 'When you say it like that...'

'I should hate you and should always have hated you. How is it possible for someone to love someone who did that to her? It's mad. It's perverse. It's actually so pathetic, it speaks of insanity,' I say.

He puts his arms around me, gently, and says, 'You're not insane.'

'No, just crazy,' I say and lean into him.

'I did love you, Rika,' he says.

'I think for a very short time you did in as much as you can. But you stopped loving me. You stopped loving me long before I stopped loving you.'

'Did you stop loving me?' he asks.

I reply, quickly, loudly, 'Of course I did. Do you think I'd love you and marry a different man?'

'So why are you so sad?' he asks.

'I'm not sad,' I say.

'No, not now, because now you're with me.'

Oh my god, he still has such an unbelievable grandiose opinion of himself. I tell him that.

He laughs and says, 'Yes, that's true, I'm a terrible person! And you're right to agree.'

My god, I almost laugh, I almost laugh from annoyance, anger, irritation.

'You've turned now from being honest with me and you, to putting on a charm offensive. You've just recognised a military opportunity and you've changed tactics like the good soldier you are.'

He takes me in his arms. 'Listen Rika, when two people have a connection, like we do, whether they're together or not, that connection never breaks. You have to recognise in life who those people are, the ones you are truly and inevitably connected to.'

'But if you recognise it, what can you do about it,' I ask. 'Nothing. It's best to break that connection. Which is what we've done. It doesn't exist anymore for me,' I say and believe I believe it, which is far more than he does.

'Really? Are you really telling me that you never think of me, never long for me? Because I know that's not true of me.'

I can't believe what he's saying. 'You long for me?'

'Yes,' he says.

'When? When you're having a fight with Frieda, or the children are difficult and you think of an alternative life, a parallel universe. Is that when you think of me? Or do you think of me when you look with adoration at your wife, at your children, and think, good god, imagine if I'd been more truthful, more loving to that woman Rika, I could have been living with her. What a nightmare!'

I get up to move away from him but at that moment he grabs me and kisses me on my mouth.

I kiss him back. My god, how I kiss him back.

This is Natan, Natan who I've longed for and desired for so many years, I'm actually here with Natan now, here and now. I feel such wild sexual desire for this man, that I'm shocked, I'm aware of the horror and wonder of these awful fantastic emotions. I'm going crazy, I'm going to erupt and we lie together and he goes into me and it is so extraordinary that I yell and he covers my mouth and I yell through his hand and eventually it finishes, it's gone, and I lie, unable to move.

He gets up and pulls up his trousers and says, 'I think I heard someone.'

I jump up and sort myself out and we say hurriedly, 'We must go, bye, bye, bye.'

Edith is watching me sobbing on the bed.

'I knew this was a bad idea. Right from the outset I thought, uh uh, not good. Go on, tell me, what happened? Did you earlier see a happy family, a loving husband, an adoring wife, and realise you don't have any of that, and then decide to have some of it? If only for as long as it takes to fuck?'

'Edith!' I say through my tears.

'So what happened? Tell me!' she says.

I just sob and say, 'I'm such a fool.'

Edith has so little sympathy, 'That's such a cliché,' she says.

'Why can't you be more helpful,' I say.

She looks at me with annoyance and says, 'Because I knew this would happen, and this is precisely why I didn't want you to come back. What do you want to do? Break up a happy couple, a couple with children, mess up the children's lives. Is that what you want? You've got your own husband. You've got your own children. Just accept that and stop crying.'

'You're so heartless,' I say.

'I'm not heartless,' she replies, 'I'm realistic and I've had enough of it. The world has just gone through a terrible time where there was far too much crying, justifiable crying.

Now we've past the time of crying, it's behind us, we've reached the time of hope. There's hope for this country, for the world, and for us as individuals. We're living in a kibbutz, Rika, a kibbutz, a socialist kibbutz living our ideals, bringing to fruition everything we fought for, a socialist kibbutz in a socialist country. We don't need people crying for something they messed up in the first place and, very stupidly as I'm sure you'll remember me saying at the time, chose someone for no good reason other than that he bought her a bloody handbag. And offered her another world. Well you might not want that world, but it's yours now. And do you know why? Because you've got children there. What are those poor children doing now without their mother? You should be home with them. Do you know that? It's just your stupid selfishness, your ridiculous inability to look beyond yourself that has made you reach this point, where you lie on the bed and cry like a fifteen year old. You're thirty, Rika. It's time to grow up!'

I finally fall asleep and the images of Morris and Natan intermingle in my dreams and I worry that I will call each one by the wrong name, calling out Natan as I'm making love with Morris, or the other way round. What will Morris think, will he realise there's someone else. And Frieda appears, standing and watching me making love, and I think, what's this doing to her, does she like it, is she getting excited by it, or is she just watching to see what happens, and anyway, why is she watching me making love to Morris. But when I see the children, a conglomeration of children, his, hers, mine, watching, I suddenly wake up with a start and feel very dirty.

Edith comes into the room. 'Coffee?' she says brightly.

'I hardly slept,' I say, morosely.

'It's your conscience,' she says with a smirk.

I really hate you sometimes, Edith, I think.

'Your conscience,' Edith says with another smirk.

'I really hate you sometimes, Edith, do you know that?' Only this time I actually say it.

'You sound ten again,' she says.

'I hate you with a passion!'

'Ahh, you're such a passionate girl!' she says.

'You're a bitch!' I say.

'When did you become a swearer? Can you tell me that?' she asks.

'Last night,' I say.

'Oy yay yoy!' she says, 'what would your mother say to that!' She's smiling.

'She would say that I always knew your sister could be a horrible person. But you Rika. You're such a lovely, darling girl!'

'No, I think you're wrong there,' she says, 'I think she'd say, your sister Edith is such a wonderful person, very clever, amazingly clever, it's just incredible how she understands right from wrong.'

We both giggle and she continues, 'And then Vati would come and say, come my darling little Rikalein, come and have some nougat. Don't worry about your mean sister.'

'You see!' I say, 'you're still a jealous little girl underneath all that big sisterly righteous indignation telling me I have to grow up.'

She pulls back my blanket and grabs my hands, 'Listen, let's go for a walk today to the orchard. I want to show you how beautiful our trees are.'

I start to get up, stop and turn to her.

'What am I going to do, Edith?'

'You're going to come for a walk!' she says.

'Seriously,' I say, 'help me. I feel so confused and useless.'

'Why useless?' she asks.

'What have I done in my life?' I ask pitifully.

'Listen Rika,' she says, 'you've had it tough. Your biggest problem is that you never had the strength that idealism can give someone. Zionism, Socialism, these provide a structure to one's life, a framework for someone to build their life, to plan where they're going and how they're going to get there. Your foundations in life were taken out at a very early age, at fourteen, just dropped from underneath you, and you've never found anything to dig your feet into, to give you a solid basis to stand on. You flounder in life. You thought marriage and a move to a new country would give you that grounding, but why would it unless you gave yourself fully to it. You never did, because part of you always longed for a man who was no longer yours. You can't base your life on someone like Natan. Do you know why? Because he can't give anyone security.'

'But Frieda,' I say.

'Frieda has so much more than just Natan. Why did Frieda 'allow' Natan to go off with you, stop her son from going with you, give him and you a chance. Because she knows that's who Natan is, and that Natan will always come back to her. And that Natan isn't her be all and end all, the basis to her life and identity. She has so much more. She has total commitment not only to the idealism that enfolds her, but to her children, and to her community. And that's why she's as strong as steel.'

'And I'm weak as cotton wool.'

'Well, you have to be quite strong to be involved in blowing up a pylon.'

I shouldn't have told her. She was the only one.

'But I stopped. I gave up. I gave in,' I say.

'You actually didn't have a choice.'

Hearing Edith say that, gives me the confirmation I think I need, that yes, I didn't have a choice.

'But you have choices now,' she says.

'That clearly don't involve Natan,' I say.

'Yes,' she says, 'and if you thought it did, you'd be very stupid.'

I'm on the phone to Morris.

'How are the children?'

'They miss you. I miss you. When are you coming home?'

'Is Nina speaking more,' I ask.

'She won't change the dress she wore on the day you left. Sadie washes it every night and every morning she puts it on.'

'She won't wear anything else?' I ask.

'But she's stopped asking about you. She's stopped saying when is mommy coming home.'

'She doesn't say that anymore?' I ask tears brimming over. 'And Graham?'

'He wet his bed.'

'Oh my god,' I say.'

What do you expect, Rika?'

Natan is near me in the dining room. We don't look at each other. Frieda sees me and we chat. She's very friendly but she doesn't invite me over again.

'It's like it never happened,' I say to Edith.

'No, it's like it absolutely happened,' she replies.

I dream different dreams of the children. I open the door and they come running, or I open a door, they look up, see me, and continue playing, or I open the door and they run to Sadie, or I open the door and they start to cry.

It's time to go home.

'What'll I do when I get back? How will I make my life worth living?' I ask my big sister.

'You've got to decide what you really want, Rika,' she says, 'you can't run away. You've got to decide what are the important things in your life. Then you have to list them in order of priority and see if they're compatible. If they are, fine. If not, you have to rethink. And if it still doesn't work, you have to just carry on and take each day as it comes.'

'And hope for the best?' I say.

'You can always hope. But hope can be as fragile as raindrops. However, the good news, Rika, is that hope can be fortified.'

'With love?' I ask.

'No. With idealism,' she says.

'You can't be an idealist and still do nothing,' I say.

'Well there you are,' she says, 'you've said it. You have to be an activist as well.'

We go up together to Tel Aviv to say goodbye to Tante Leah.

'Do you know what you want now, Rikalein?' she asks.

'No, not really,' I reply.

'But she's going to work it out,' Edith says. 'Isn't that so, Rikalein!'

I hug Edith and whisper in her ear, 'How can I hate you and love you so much, all at the same time?

'It's called sisters,' she says and we laugh.

23

Sick, vomit.

'Quickly, get a bowl for Rika, she's about to be.. ohoh too late. Don't worry darling, it's alright, it's all ok. Let me wipe you, here.'

Baby, baby no, no baby, no baby, no.

This nausea is far worse than the last two times. I really can't bear it. I'm going crazy with it. What can I do? I feel sick from morning to night. It just doesn't go away. Morris has a word with his brother-in-law, the doctor, and he gives Morris a box of pills that he says will work. I take them, religiously.

Nina says it's definitely a girl and gets upset when Graham announces with certainty that no, in fact, it's going to be a boy. Ah, this medicine is working, I feel so much better, I'm happy again. I might be hugely overweight and uncomfortable but I can live again.

What are you going to be like, little one?

I'm sitting in the sun, my feet are up and I'm communing with my bump. Are you going to be a beauty like Graham or a sweetie like Nina. You'll be the baby of the family. How will that affect Nina? She'll be the middle child, the one with problems, with identity crises. Her place in the family will be taken over by you, the new baby, the one they'll all love, the one they'll be jealous of.

How will Morris relate to you? Will you be interested in cars? Graham's interested in his little dinky cars but not real ones particularly. Will you become a mechanic like your dad? (A mechanic like your dad or a farmer like your... I make a quick calculation, yes, it should be fine!) Maybe you'll be a doctor. That'd be nice. A doctor in the family! Yes, I think that's a good idea.

It's ten o'clock at night. I've been in bed, exhausted and I wake swimming in water, once again. Morris goes and calls Dinah to come sleep in the house, (not, please could you, but I'm not going to think of that now) and off we go in the car to the maternity home.

It's as boring to talk of labour pains as it is to tell someone your dreams.

Yes, it was excruciating, but everyone knows that about giving birth. They talk to me, they tell me I'm a pro now, I know what to expect, but all I think is shut up, shut up, shut up, but I'm compos mentis enough not to voice it.

A baby boy is born.

'Nina will be disappointed,' I say to Morris and he moves the wet hair away from my face. The baby is rushed away, I don't even see him, it all seems so hectic somehow, so drastic.

'Where's my baby, Morris? Why aren't they letting me see my baby?' I say and he goes in search of someone clinical and sees a nurse.

She says, 'You'll have to speak to a doctor, sorry,' and she averts his gaze.

We're in the room, Morris and me. We're so tense and anxious that we are quiet, tight in ourselves, hyper-aware of any noise, any footstep outside, passing by, about to come in. The door opens and it's a doctor. We say nothing when we see his grave, harsh, sad face.

'We're trying our very best to save him,' he says.

'What's the matter with him?' The words seem to slip out unformed.

'He's, it's, it's actually very difficult. We don't know if he'll live through the night. But just know that we're doing our very best, we're doing everything in our power to save him.'

'But what's the matter with him?'

'We're trying everything we possibly can,' he says and walks out.

We look at each other, I turn over on my other side and face a wall, and Morris looks out the window. A nurse brings in food but I can't eat anything. We both drink tea and after a while I get out of bed and walk round the room holding onto Morris.

Nurses look in from time to time, but they don't say anything and they don't stay long.

'I can't believe those bastards are just leaving us here, not saying anything, not knowing anything. Why are they treating us like this! Those verkakte doctors! He could be dead now. Our little baby could be dead and we won't even know it,' Morris rages.

It doesn't help.

After a while Morris says quietly, 'Do you think we should pray, Rika?'

'To whom,' I ask.

'To God, of course.'

'We don't believe in God. Oh pray if it'll make you feel better,' I throw at him.

And he does, 'Baruch atah Adonai,' he starts.

'What the hell are you doing,' I say.

'You said pray if I want to!' he says.

'I didn't bloody mean it,' I say, but he turns away from me and closes his eyes and mouths some words silently.

'You don't even know what you're saying,' I grumble. 'You're probably saying a blessing over the wine!'

'It doesn't matter,' he says and we sit in silence again, unable to verbalise our nightmares to each other.

It's all my fault. It's because I slept with Natan. Who knows what he did to me. Maybe because I got so excited, it might have done something terrible to my insides and that's why he, or maybe I'm wrong with my calculations and it is actually his but it's, it's like a travesty, a travesty against nature and so he has to die, he has to suffer for his mother's terrible deeds. Oh my god, I should never have gone to Israel. I should never have gone with Natan. What have I done! Forgive me, you up there or anywhere, are you listening, please listen to me, please forgive me.

I sleep a little in the bed, Morris in the chair and at eight in the morning the doctor enters looking anxious, exhausted and downcast. Tears are streaming down both our faces as we wait for what we know he will say.

'We've saved him,' the doctor announces.

'What? Oh my god, thank you, thank you doctor!' Morris pumps the doctor's unwilling hand and our tears dry up like magic.

But the doctor takes his hand away from Morris and says, 'Look, it's not great. I have to tell you. He's very, very badly disabled.'

I can't see anything clearly, it's all misty, fog-like. I struggle to move my limbs, I sit, was I standing before? What does that word mean, English isn't my mother-tongue you know, I might not understand what he said. Is it not abled, not able to do something, to do what? To make a cup of tea, to sit up, to solve puzzles, to calculate the distance to the moon and back via Mars? It's just a continuum, able.

'What does that mean, doctor?' I hear Morris say.

'I'm afraid, he's utterly handicapped. He'll never be normal.'

What is normal? How not normal is not normal?

'Does he look normal?' Morris asks.

'No, I'm afraid he doesn't.'

What is that sound, a gasp, a sob? From whom, me, Morris, the doctor, the nurses?

'What does he look like?' I whisper.

'He's very small and,'

'Does he have all his features?' Morris interrupts.

'Yes. He does. But they are, not like normal babies,' the doctor says.

Again that damn word normal, 'What does normal mean,' I ask.

'Like others. He's not like others.' So that means he's special, that's what he is, he's special.

'When can we see him?' I ask.

'Well,' the doctor clears his throat, is he embarrassed? 'That's what I want to talk to you both about. We strongly recommend that you, that he goes into a home. A specialist home.'

'No! No way, of course not. He's our baby, he's our special baby. He's special, isn't he, Morris? He's not like other babies, he's special.' I look at Morris but he's staring at the doctor.

He puts his hand up, just a little, almost imperceptible. 'Rika, wait, let's listen to what the doctor says. He understands.'

'I understand,' I say, searching his face for understanding. 'Don't you understand? He's our baby. He must come home to us, to his family. We are his family, not some home!'

'You must understand, Mrs Levine,' the doctor says, 'he'll never walk, never talk, sit up, he is, I'm sorry but I have to say this, he's more like an animal, some might say unkindly, a vegetable, than a human.'

'No, no, no,' I shout, 'don't call him that!'

He stands aloof, he doesn't come near me, he moves towards the door and says, 'The best thing you can possibly do for both of you and your children, is to let him be looked after by people who know how to look after babies and children like him. There's a new home that's opened up in Sandringham. You're very lucky.'

'Lucky!'

'Lucky that it's open, I mean. It hasn't been opened for long. It's the Selwyn Segal home, and it's for the Jewish disabled. They have a couple of babies, similar to yours'

'Gary,' I say.

And he continues, 'to Gary. He'll have proper care from professionals. You wouldn't know how to look after someone…'

I interrupt him again, my voice cracking but loud, 'I would, of course I would, I'd know.'

'But you must also think of the other two children. They would be side-lined. Their entire futures could be put in jeopardy.'

I stare at him. What he's saying is true. Oh my god, it's true, it hits me smack between the eyes, I push my fingers into my eyes to stop that thought, to stop that vision, I don't want it to be true.

He recognises what's happening to me, he grasps the moment. 'You have to be really sensible,' he says and then refers to his ally. 'Mr Levine, you understand this, what this could mean to your whole family.'

'Yes,' Morris the traitor says, 'and what it could mean to Rika and me, to our relationship, to our relationship with the children, to the children's lives, their futures.'

I want him to fight, I want him to be even stronger than I can be, I want him to persuade me that we could do it together, that we could look after Gary together, that it wouldn't affect the other two. But he capitulates, abandons the fight before he even starts it.

'We have to listen to the doctor, Rika,' he says, stabbing the blade right through my spine.

When we get home, the children run up to us.

'Where's the baby, where's the baby?' they yell.

I pick up Nina and Morris picks up Graham and we all sit together and we tell them the lie.

'The baby died.'

'Where did he go?' Graham asks, 'did he go to heaven?' Graham asked.

We both nod.

'Where's heaven, Daddy?' he asks, and asks again when neither of us reply.

Shaina Raisa comes to see me at Morris' behest.

'Meyn kind,' she says, 'tell me why you're so sad.'

'It's alright. I'm fine,' I say, obviously, the normal response to leave me alone.

'Oy, you're fine like I'm fine, and I'm not fine,' she says.

I smile. 'I just didn't want it, Shania Raisa,' I say.

'Az me ken nit vi me vil, muz men vellen vi me ken. If you can't do what you like, you must like what you can do,' she replies.

'But was that the only thing we could do,' I say, looking away from her.

'It made sense. Didn't it?' she says.

'It just wasn't the plan, was it! It was never what we thought would happen,' I say beginning once again with the constant, never-ending crying.

'A mensch tracht un Got lacht. Man plans and God laughs,' she says.

'Oy, Shaina Raisa,' I find myself smiling, 'you're so full of Yiddish idioms today.'

'Sometimes, when things are really serious, they're the only things that help!' she says.

I hold Jill's hand and cry and cry and sob on her shoulder.

'He's living, Jill, he's not dead, he is actually alive and someone else is feeding him, and burping him, and putting him to sleep.'

She pats my back as if I need burping, which I probably do.

I go back home and say to Morris, maybe we should think again about the decision.

He stares at me, 'For Christ sake Rika! Are you ever going to get over this? It's finished! He's dead to us. We're never going to see him again and it's all over. We have two healthy, lovely, wonderful children. Can you not bloody think of them for a change and start living again. I'm sick to death of this crying and inability to just bloody forget!'

I stare at him, the disconcerting stare, the sort of stare that makes him avert his eyes and leave the room and go do something else, something less scary.

'We didn't fight for him,' I shout.

He storms back in, 'The real fighting that took place that night was by those bloody doctors who fought the whole night for his life. Why did they? That's what I want to know! Why the hell did they fight to keep him alive. Why didn't they let him die!'

I get in the car and drive to the Selwyn Segal Home. The building is white and brand new, the lawns haven't even grown properly yet and there are signs asking people not to walk on the grass.

At the reception, a woman is speaking into a telephone. I wait patiently with my heart beating like thunder.

'Can I help you?' she says.

'Rika Levine,' I say and stop.

'Yes,' she says kindly.

'I, I wonder if it might be possible for me to speak to someone.'

'Is it about Gary?' she asks and I stare at her.

'Yes.'

'Hold on one moment and I'll call his nanny,' she says and goes out.

I wait, eyes on the door, and soon an older black woman comes through wearing an overall, apron, and little cap to show her position as more than a maid but less than a nurse.

'Hello m'am,' she says with a friendly smile.

I start to cry.

'Come, come with me madam.'

We go into a little side room and sit down. I try to stop crying but she doesn't hurry me.

'How is he,' I ask.

'Have you seen him yet?' she asks and I shake my head.

'I can't even imagine how he looks,' I say.

'Would you like me to bring him here so you can see him.'

I nod my head and try to force myself to control the crying.

She brings in a tiny baby. He's very dark and seems skew, somehow, his features are not quite centred in his face. I look at him and reach for him and she places him delicately in my arms.

'Shall I leave you for ten minutes?'

I nod and hold this sleeping, skew, weird looking baby, and rock him from one foot to the other, just as I rocked my other two children. 'Gary,' I say, 'my Gary.'

When the nanny returns, I kiss him and hand him back.

'Thank you,' I murmur and leave quickly.

I sit in the car and slump onto the steering wheel. I start to howl, to yell, to screech and shriek. I surprise myself with the volume and the force of this noise emanating from somewhere so deep within me.

When Morris comes home he asks Dinah where I am.

'She's been in her room all day,' she says.

He comes to the bedroom and stops at the locked door. 'Are you alright?' he asks and I do not reply.

Next morning, after having slept on the sofa, he sees me and says, 'You went to see him, didn't you.'

The disgust is evident in my look.

'Stop looking at me like that, Rika! What do you want from me? To carry on suffering like you? There's nothing we can do about it! If I could, Jesus Christ I swear I would. What do you think? That I want our son to be a vegetable!'

'Don't you dare call him a vegetable,' I yell. 'He's a baby, a human baby, our baby.'

He sits, he puts his head in his hands, and from within the cavern of his body he says, 'I can't think of him as our baby. We've got to let him go, Rika, we have to forget about him, we have to go on living. Either we have him and devote our whole lives and our whole time to looking after him, or we forget about him, believe what we told the kids, that he died, and we carry on living. What do you want to do? Think about it really carefully and then tell me honestly if you want to have him. Just think of the consequences, the costs, will you. Just promise me that you'll think really carefully, and if you really want him to be with us, then I'll go along with it. But just remember, be careful for what you wish.'

I have to speak to Edith and to Sadie, to discuss it with them.

They both say the same thing, 'Leave him in the home and focus on the two you have and your husband.'

They speak, I nod. I tell Morris what I have decided.

'Baby, where baby?'

'Do you want your baby, Rika? You haven't been interested in your doll for ages. Wait, I'll go get him for you, he's in your room.'

My baby.

'Here you are darling, here's your baby.'

My baby. Gary, Gary. My baby.

24

I'm Shaina Raisa, she is me. I look like her, I'm her.

I'm getting fatter and fatter. It's all those morning coffees, afternoon teas, all with biscuits, scones, cakes, pastries.

I can't say no, apart from the days when I'm on a diet, and then I do say no, and I do feel self-satisfied. But those feelings soon pass and are replaced by resentment, covetousness even, the need for that creamy chocolaty bite of deliciousness to go into my mouth, not theirs.

So the diets don't last long, for which everyone around me is grateful, as Fat Rika is infinitely preferable to Hungry, Angry, Irritable Rika.

Graham is now twelve and Nina nine.

Morris is the grand owner of a garage with petrol pumps and workshop that employs around twenty staff (aka 'boys').

We plan to move to a nice Jewish suburb called Linksfield in the northern suburbs of Johannesburg. The southern suburbs have become strictly passé and no Jewish family of self-regard would deign to live there anymore; so early twentieth century, so old Litvak immigrants, so poor. Definitely not where we are now.

We buy a plot and employ an architect to build a house. No ordinary red-brick boring house for us. New, modern, unusual.

'Well it's certainly modern,' people say, but not always with a positive sheen. Equivocation, one might say.

Our architect has just one name, Filipec, which proves he's interesting and bohemian. He's Hungarian and walks about with a folkloric hat, colourful and strange for conservative South Africa. Morris is slightly put out by him but accepts it all – it is after all my project, I'm making the decisions, or agreeing Filipec's decisions.

Bold deep green walls with slits in them, white walls, a maroon one with bobbles, unusual, unusual. Very few walls partition one room from the other so there is a natural flow throughout the house. There are inside gardens with bamboo sticks in one little round garden in the lounge which reaches from the ground right up to the high ceiling. Another garden is in front of a wall made entirely of glass. People walk in and are able to look straight through to the garden, the inner and outer garden.

The ceiling of the dining room and lounge slope from low to very high. One wall of the lounge is just glass and overlooks the extensive garden.

I love it!

There are three bedrooms and a spare, which I use for my sewing machine, (yes, I've become a sewer, and a knitter, and a rug maker, no end to my useful pursuits.)

Another exciting addition to the house is a hidden room which is like a walk-in safe. We keep all our treasures in there, like my mink coat (yes, I have a mink coat, for the freezing Arctic weather we never get in Johannesburg - having a mink coat fits in with Morris' keeping right up there with those Jones'), and the family valuables of tinned fruit. You'd think with all the wonderful soft fruits that we get in this country, the children would prefer those to the sugary canned guavas and peaches that they nag for after dinner, (anything for N-E-X-T Morris asks, attempting to hide his request for pudding from the children before they finish their meal, resulting in the word for pudding in our house being N-E-X-T.)

The other thing that the safe room contains is Morris' gun, apart from when it's under his pillow at night!

The gardens outside are lavish and thick with strong green kikuyu grass and it's all tended by our gardener, Johannes, a relative of Dinah's from her home town. He's tall and middle aged and has a twinkle in his eye. He looks after the swimming pool. Of course we have a swimming pool – it wouldn't fit the image not to.

And thus I spend my days, a large part of which includes supervising the servants, as if they were unable to do things without my constant checking, or admonishing, or demanding more. Well, I have to have something to do.

I see Jill at least twice a week at her keep fit and exercise classes. I'm her oldest student, oldest in the sense of having been with her the longest. So I'm fit and flexible and the children delight in telling people who come to our house that I can sit with my legs right out and touch my head on the floor. They insist I demonstrate, which I mostly do.

From time to time, only when really needed, I go to Ivor's business and help with the books or packing hampers. It's just that I'm too busy to commit, you see.

We all go to Sadie's on Saturday afternoons to play Rummikub, or cards, or have our hair done by Sadie's eldest daughter who spends her afternoon curling all the aunties' hair while the children play.

During the activities we all eat a variety of wonderful sweet goodies. We all complain about our weight, it goes with the eating. The mouth opens, food goes in, and then we say, oy, I'm getting so fat! I'm not the only one.

On Saturday evenings now that the children are older, we tend to go to the cinema and buy a box of smarties and fruit pastilles and popcorn and watch the film while passing the boxes along between the four of us.

I've started laughing a bit at Morris' jokes and turn my ears off, as if I'm closing my eyes, when he shouts or screams or is ridiculous.

We have a great common interest now, it's called money, and he loves making it and giving it to me and I love spending it, not on fripperies but on art, or rugs, or ceramics. And I have good taste.

We've started making love more often, I couldn't after Gary and didn't for quite a long while.

We all eat dinner together, still in silence while Morris listens to the seven pm news.

And Dinah clears and washes, then dries up and sweeps up, and she and Johannes eat the food that she cooks for them, mielie meal with meat stews, meat that I buy from the butcher – it's called 'boys' meat', just one step up from dogs' meat.

After dinner we sit round the radio and listen to quizzes, drama series and fun-entertainment-for-the-whole-family. We sometimes listen to records and Morris is trying very hard to instil in the children an interest in Beethoven and Mozart, with a tiny semblance of success. It's an easy life.

And then there is Sharpeville.

It's on the one o'clock news and they speak of shooting in Sharpeville where several people have died after violent confrontations with the police.

I phone Jill, 'What do you know,' I ask.

'It seems about five thousand people walked to the police station to protest about the pass laws. They planned to burn their passes and give themselves up at the police station, on the basis that the whole system would collapse with so many people arrested. And the police just opened fire on them all, children, adults, running away from them, shot in the back.'

'My god, that's unbelievable, it's so terrible, so dreadful.'

'They're saying now there were knives and firearms, but you know what, the police are going round and sticking knives in dead men's hands. Sixty-nine people are dead, Rika! A hundred and ninety injured.'

'Why would they do that?' Morris says, 'It sounds like propaganda to me.'

'Because the world is condemning them, these bastards, these murderous barbarians,' I say, besides myself with fury that Morris is even questioning the need for anger.

'Hold on,' he goes on, 'just hold on before you get on your high horse. The police said they were frightened.'

'They're police,' I shout back, 'they should be disciplined, controlled, they should know how to control their fear.'

'That might be so,' Morris says quietly, 'but think, if you're confronted by five thousand native...'

The racism of the man drives me to distraction.

'Don't call me racist Rika! Legitimate or not, five thousand people facing you. Five thousand very angry people...'

'They were singing for christsake! How scary is people singing. For god's sake, Morris, don't you realise what this means? What this terrible government has done? What kind of a country do we live in that does this sort of thing? I can't bear it any longer, Morris. We have to leave. Let's get out. Take the children and leave. Now.'

'And go where? To Israel?' he says. 'I won't live in Israel. Can you imagine Graham going into the army. Is that what you want? For him to get killed in the next war. There's always going to be a next war there.'

And then I make a decision, and I say, if you won't leave, then you're going to have to accept that I'm not going to sit still and be part of this thing happening.

'Jesus, Rika, not bloody again,' he says, 'we had this out eight years ago. You saw sense then. Don't fucking start with that again!'

'First of all, I say, don't swear. Secondly, I'm warning you now Morris, either we leave or I get involved. I don't care what you say. I don't care what they do. I don't care how much they torture me. I will never speak. I'll cut my tongue out before I speak!'

'Drama queen!' he says and moves away.

I tell Jill I have to do something, anything to be involved, I can't sit around anymore doing nothing but getting fat. She tells me to do more exercise and then smiles.

She looks more serious and says, 'How can you get involved with Morris so antagonistic to it all?'

'He won't say anything,' I say.

'How can you be so sure?'

I look her straight in the face and say, 'Because I'll kill him if he does.'

Nina comes running up to me and says, 'Can I have an ice-cream ma?'

I say, 'No Nina, you don't want to be fat like mommy.'

She runs away with her chin quivering.

Jill turns to me, 'Not a good thing to say to her Rika, do you want to cause problems for her too?'

'What did I say, that I'm fat,' I say.

'Just avoid the f word when you talk to young girls and teenagers. Trust me,' she says.

I watch Dinah and Johannes talking animatedly, in their language of course so I don't know what they're saying. They stop, even though they know I don't understand.

I say, 'Isn't it terrible!'

But they don't respond. Dinah's stopped trusting me. I'm the madam well and truly now. Johannes didn't know me in the days I was Rika.

'Sharpeville's got this government worried, Rika, you heard the UK's Macmillan talking of the winds of change. Things have got to change, there's real pressure now from abroad,' Jill says.

We're watching the children swimming in the pool.

'Yes,' I say, 'calling on the South African government to abandon apartheid! Good message. Let's just not hold our breath waiting for them to heed it!'

Jill laughs at my cynicism. 'It's a start,' she says, 'and the US ambassador here told their government there'll be black rule in South Africa within eighteen months to five years!'

'Oh god,' I say, 'I can hear Morris and all those whites now. Can't you Jill?' I put on a whiny voice, 'Think what it'll be like, what they'll do to us! We'll have to run. I'm going to buy a gun now, I'll buy one for you!'

We laugh.

'Oy,' I say, 'a bittere gelechte! That's bitter joke to you goyim!'

Jill refuses to lose her upbeat moment.

'The thing is Rika, money is affected, and that's what really matters to these people. That's when they start worrying. Share prices are plummeting. There're boycotts all over the country, protests from abroad, international pressure. This is exactly what's needed, not only from inside the country but from outside. Black people themselves can see that the state isn't the granite wall it seemed to be. Things might change.'

A few weeks later, Morris comes to me, 'You see Rika, you and your friend Jill, you were so naïve. I knew it, I knew the state wouldn't give in. All the cards are in their hands. All the power is yours when you have the police, the military, the banks, the money, the laws. They knew what to do and they had the power to do it. Ban the ANC, ban the PAC, increase the budget for police and army, arrest all those insubordinates, all those terrorists, and it's finished. The threat is all over. We can breathe again.'

I sit with Jill, I feel inconsolable. Was it all for nothing? All those people killed, all those governments condemning South Africa. That sense that things must change, things will change, and now nothing. Only a stronger state than ever before? But once again Jill is less pessimistic than me.

'The change is deep, Rika.'

But I can't see that.

'So now we're back to being a pariah state,' I say, 'how's that going to change things? You know what happens when people feel their hopes are dashed to such an extent, when the leadership is wiped out, and people just feel desperate. They become impotent. They just accept they can't do anything about it.'

'No, that isn't what's happening,' she says. 'Desperation can lead to exactly the opposite of impotence. It can lead to real action. We still have great leaders and the change that was needed has come about from our leadership, the ANC leadership. They're no longer talking about passive resistance. The talk now is of armed struggle!'

I feel an excitement stir in me as she speaks, but I also feel it's perhaps less strong than I would expect. I push that thought aside, no, no, this is it, this is what we've been waiting for. I turn my head and watch the smiling, charming face of my colonel.

I'm sitting in the garden watching the children and their friends swimming in the pool. Shaina Raisa sits with me. Between us is the tea and taiglach, and cake, which I'm desperately trying to resist. So far so good. We gossip, the brothers, the sisters-in-law, brothers-in-law, friends, friends of friends, no-one is safe from our slanderous chit-chat. She falls asleep, hard work this calumny!

I sit enjoying her quiet snores and watch children swimming, screaming, laughing, play-fighting. This is the good life, I think, this is the goldene medina.

I'm strangely aware of how relaxed I feel, happy even. I think about my last discussion with Jill, and the idea that things have changed. It's no longer leaflets and protests, bombing pylons or empty buildings, it's now the armed struggle, Umkonte we Sizwe, the MK, the armed resistance. I see myself dressed in a camouflage uniform, holding a gun, somewhere in Africa.

Is that really me? Can I see myself as an armed soldier for the people, an MK soldier. Because, actually, where does it stop? If I commit, I have to take it all the way. It's not just driving people to bomb pylons where you know no-one will be hurt. It's bombing police stations, bridges, railway stations even. It's being arrested and tortured and being sent to jail. It's being put in isolation and tortured and, and isolation, yes, isolation. Nobody to see, to talk to, to touch, to, I look at Shaina Raisa, to listen to as they sleep, to care about in close proximity.

You're far away. You care, you continue to care but you are incommunicado. However much you want to speak to them, find out about, see, touch, anything, there is nothing because all there is, is you in your little cell, in your tiny space, with your hard bed and sliver of felt to lie on and your blankets to sleep with and your uncertainty and your reliance on the kindness of psychopaths whom you know are unable to show any kindness whatsoever.

I've heard what it's like in prison. I've heard about having nothing to read, just the Bible. I've heard how you sit in your tiny little cell, smaller than this verandah. Imagine, twenty-three hours a day you sit in this area with your cold hard floor, and your one hard chair and your toilet bowl in your room, bucket, not bowl. A bucket that is in your room, all the time. It has a cover but the smell is there all the time. This bucket of shit and wee sitting here in the corner.

And your food is brought to you, mielie meal for breakfast, a clump of bread for lunch, some gristle and old vegetables for supper. And you eat, by yourself, with the bucket of shit next to you. You have no freedom to decide for yourself, or to choose, or to argue. You have to accept, you have to acquiesce, you have to agree.

And before that? Before all of that.

What about the questioning, the demanding, the insisting on names, on dates, on who is who and where did this happen and where did that happen and what happened then and what did this one do and who did this one know and what are their names. And so and so has already told us so you might as well tell us too because they've already named you, they've dropped you in the shit, why do you have to be the one who takes the blame completely.

And they keep you standing in a small chalk-drawn circle that you can't move out of, move away from, sit, no you stand and you stand and the hours pass and still you stand in your little chalk-drawn circle.

And they hit you to stay awake, they throw water over you if you collapse and sleep, to wake up! Wake up! Word wakker!

And then finally they move you into the jail, and they give you a hard crude dress that makes you itch and you scratch but you can't escape the horrible material that is all over your body.

And they give you shoes that might or might not fit and you are given your felt for the bed and your blankets to cover you but you can't sleep until it's night-time, you can't lie down if it's day time, you have to obey all the rules, all the millions of rules that exist to make you into a non-person, into a prisoner, into a bandiet.

And what if something happened to the children, who would be there for them? Morris? Yes, Morris would, but can I rely on him to give them the love they need, to say the right things, to do what's needed? Morris loves the children, of course he does, but he's not the greatest father ever. He doesn't put them first. It's only if it suits him, if it doesn't put him out.

If Morris were different, if Morris were the kind of man that Ivor was, for example, or his brother Jonathan, a man who adores his children more than himself, then it would be different. Then I could do it, I could take it on, I could put myself in the front line, I could sacrifice myself.

But why am I sacrificing myself? Are these my people? Are they German Jews standing before the pits of Minsk? Are they the families waiting to be deported, waiting with their suitcases filled with their belongings from the list of allowed items to be taken with them, expecting to go to labour camps never realising for a minute that the rumours might be true. Waiting for the knock on the door, just thankful that your daughters are safe in Palestine, safe and not here with us, waiting for who knows what.

Stop! Stop it! Look at the children, swimming, having such fun. Look at Shaina Raisa, still fast asleep, murmuring in her sleep.

'What's the matter, Shaina Rasia. Don't worry, everything's alright. Just go back to sleep.'

No, these aren't my people.

Dinah and Johannes don't trust me. They're my servants. I'm their madam. They won't even call me by my name because they think I can turn. I can change. I'm untrustworthy.

Will I sacrifice my children for them? Why should I?

Why shouldn't I sit in the sun and eat that cake.

I've suffered enough in my life. I've got to be here for my children. I've got to protect them. Graham is twelve already. Nina is almost ten. If I went to jail, it would be for them just like it was for me.

Remember Rika, remember what it was like alone in Tante Leah's house, the fifth wheel, the motherless and fatherless child. Do you want that for Graham and Nina? Do you? Do you?

Something's been bothering me, these last few weeks. A little twitch, a little tingle. There's something I'm not thinking about, something I should be. And it suddenly hits me, Sharpeville, pylons, my god, of course, Sharpeville, that's where Tembo comes from. Was he there?

25

I remember this one here. She's a young girl. Why is she not young now? What happened to her? She must be very bad if she looks like this now.

'Hi ma, how are you?'

She's crying, I know she's crying. Someone sits with her. I look past them. I don't want to see them.

'Don't worry Nina, she's happy.'

'How can you know?' that one says. 'She's so vacant. It's as if there's nothing there, just a body. A skinny little body with nothing going on inside.'

She doesn't whisper anymore.

Nina is fifteen, she has long dark hair and blue/green eyes. She's pretty, not beautiful but definitely pretty and has a warm bubbly personality and intense social and political interests.

Graham is still beautiful but has his parents' growth insufficiencies so is not tall enough to be considered model handsome. Besides, his nose has also begun to grow, slightly out of proportion to his face – I should be blind to it. Does it make me a bad mother to admit it?

He has lots of friends in the neighbourhood and they've developed interesting fantasy games which intrigue Nina but exclude her entirely. She's not quite sure what she's missing out on, but nevertheless feels slightly disgruntled. But then again, she argues to herself, he's not interested in me, so he's missing out too.

The two haven't kept the closeness of their childhood, their interests are too diverse and their characters too different, but they are siblings with shared parents and that means something to both of them.

Nina tries to get closer to him and says, 'There's this boy I fancy,' but Graham is so horrified by this unwelcome disclosure he gets up and walks away.

Nina has two great interests in her life, Socialism and Zionism and both came with the passionate idealism of youth.

She and I love folk music and she particularly loves Pete Seeger. She sits in her room listening intently on her portable record player to the words of his songs. She feels so fiercely the anger, the disquiet, the rage, the fervour of the injustices depicted in his songs, it is quite disquieting.

I watch her or listen to her and see myself, the unrecognisable self from years back. Where did that idealist go? (Was I ever an idealist? Maybe not, though I did feel.) Did I teach her, was it my influence, it certainly wasn't Morris'. Or might she have turned out this way without me?

She certainly was aware of injustice from a very young age. I remember her pouncing viciously on a young boy who visited the house with his parents when she heard him call Johannes 'boy'. She bristled at the way a policeman spoke to Dinah when we took her to show her pass at the police station. I had to stamp on her foot to stop her opening her mouth.

'You just can't,' I said to her afterwards.

'Why not?' she said, 'what are you frightened of?'

And then she came home crying one day after fighting with a friend who made nasty comments about 'kaffirs'.

'I pulled her hair,' she said 'and had this incredibly overwhelming desire to hurt her really badly.'

She argues with friends who sprout their parents' Nationalist Party viewpoints. Nina's disappointment is unbounded when she finds out from Johannes that the words to Nkosi Sikelele Afrika are simply a plea to God.

'Can you believe it,' she says to me, 'I thought it was a freedom song.'

I laugh, she has my atheism, which I'm pleased about.

'How can you possibly believe in god when it's clearly the case that god was just a superior power invented by people for them to appeal to in times of crisis, like famine or drought. Surely you can see that makes sense!'

She and her friend Yaffa engage in lengthy debates about Socialism and Atheism and Zionism. They both agree entirely with each other which makes their discussions so enjoyable and worthwhile.

I have decided to engage more in 'good deeds', so I have become a volunteer with the African Children's Feeding Scheme. I drive to Alexandra Township to dish out great clumps of brown bread, peanut butter and bowls of milk to little children standing quietly in long, snaking queues. Nina comes with me when she's on holiday from school and helps hand out the bread, dying inside at what she sees as the horror and injustice of it all.

'It's so wrong,' she says to me as we drive home in our Mercedes-Benz. 'Can't you see that this is really not right?'

'What would you want instead,' I say,' that they go hungry, that they have nothing to eat until mealie meal for supper? You didn't go hungry this morning. Why should they?'

'Of course they shouldn't,' she proclaims vehemently, 'you can't possibly think I think…'

'Of course not,' I say, 'but just think, sometimes all you can do is what you can do.'

'But you can do more,' she says, 'why don't you do more? You sit at home like a great big fat white mama.'

What can I say, other than, 'Don't be rude!'

She says, 'Maybe people should be rude when someone is doing nothing to help others.'

'I'm not doing nothing,' I say, self-righteously. 'I'm volunteering to help feed hungry children!'

'Well that's not enough!' she says, 'you must protest, get involved.'

Oh god, I hate this.

'You just sit and visit friends and family when I'm at school. You sit around and drink tea and eat cake.'

I carry on driving and look straight ahead.

She won't let up. 'Why did you never do anything?' she asks.

'I was looking after you and Graham,' I say.

'So you chose two rich white kids over millions of people who could've benefitted,' she says.

'Those two kids are my kids. Would you have rather I'd been in jail than looking after you?'

And she looks at me directly, I can feel her eyes pounding the side of my face.

'At least I would've been proud of you!'

Nina tries to engage Morris, her father after all, in feeling her passion.

'Da,' she says, 'come and listen to the words of this song. It's so good.'

'Not now,' he says.

'Please. Please! I really want you to hear the words and you never do.'

He agrees and they sit in her room and listen to the song and then he gets up and leaves. She watches him leave and doesn't say anything.

She puts it on again and listens and tears fall. She decides to form a group to overthrow the government and arranges to meet her friend Yaffa and a boy from her class to discuss it in a field. She and Yaffa wait for the boy to come but he doesn't turn up. She sees him playing rugby in the school field and feels foolish. They try to think what they can do but can't find anything that might work. She phones the Black Sash, but they say she can only become a member when she turns sixteen.

Nina wants to join Magen David Adom, it's the Jewish Red Cross. And why not? A Friday evening among friends her own age, talking First Aid and Zionism. Could be worse. Actually, it soon becomes clear that it's more to do with the leader of the group than any interest in First Aid. Simon Mundy is twenty-four and 'incredibly dynamic' as she and Yaffa keep saying to each other.

Every Friday evening from seven to nine pm, he holds forth amongst the thirty or so eager young fourteen to sixteen year olds, and tells them stories with important moral lessons.

'Yesterday,' one goes, 'I went into the post office and said to the woman behind the desk, you've got such lovely hair. The woman was so pleased and couldn't stop smiling. I thought she had lovely hair and told her so. You see, it's always important to tell people good things.'

Another time he says, 'I went to the patient in the morning and she said, I had a baby last night. She was so happy. Every morning she says the same thing, I had a baby last night, and every morning, she's so happy. There was no point saying, no, you didn't. It wouldn't have helped. It would've just made her unhappy.'

The girls love the stories and discuss the ins and outs of them non-stop. They go home and say, 'I love him, he loves me!' and they laugh and roll around on the bed. 'Who does he love? He loves me!'

Nina finds a book in the library by Dale Carnegie entitled How to Win Friends and Influence People. She reads it and is more and more aghast as she realises every story Simon Mundy spoke of, every detail word for word, has been taken directly from the book.

She and Yaffa dissect the experience. 'How can we have been so naïve? I mean, my dad had told me that he was a masseur at his gym, so how could we believe that he was a psychiatrist treating patients in a mental institution. How can someone suspend disbelief without realising they're doing it! It's not like seeing a play and knowing they're really actors pretending to be someone else. We just accepted it all hook, line and sinker. The power of wanting to believe, of not wanting to question. It's exactly the same way this bloody government keeps control.'

She decides to go to a zionist, socialist youth movement, Hashomer Hatzair. The group there are made up of teenagers from much poorer Jewish families and the leader has been sent from a kibbutz in Israel. The discussions fit exactly into Nina's worldview.

'I have to emigrate to Israel,' she says.

She's sixteen and today she's having a party, an evening party at home. She was worried that Morris might be difficult but I've had a word with him, a finger in front of his face type of word, and he's promised to behave. After all, what could he do or say that would prove embarrassing to a sixteen year old. Ha!

The party is in full swing, all her friends from school and from the youth movement are here. They're dancing and eating and smooching in the corner. Morris decides it's time to go to bed. We've been in our bedroom most of the evening and things have gone smoothly. He goes into the bathroom to brush his teeth and lo and behold, his toothbrush is not where it's supposed to be.

'Who's taken my toothbrush?' he booms through the house. 'Someone's taken my toothbrush! Who's taken my toothbrush?'

The dancing stops, the eating stops and the smooching stops. They all stop and look up. What's going on? And there he comes, Morris, pre-bed, in pyjamas, hair mussed, fuzzy unshaven chin, angry and furious beyond belief, storming through the house, screaming and yelling; 'Who's taken my toothbrush!!'

They all stand quietly and watch. No one says anything.

'Right, get out, all of you! Out, out, all of you, out!'

The teenagers put on the shoes they've shoved off, jumpers that have been discarded, bags thrown wherever, and they troop out, heads down.

Nina stands there watching, and I hold onto Morris, trying to pour water on smouldering embers, trying desperately to exercise damage limitation, to salvage what I can from the disaster that is my poor daughter's birthday party.

Nina falls into my arms, sobbing from anger and embarrassment. 'I hate him. I swear, I really hate him.'

So do I, I think.

Niemals ein lautes Wort, niemals Schimpfwort.

'What's that darling? Mary! What did she say?'

'Never a loud word, never a swear word.'

'Oh that again. She's always on about that. Who's that then, darling? Your husband, Morris? Did he never shout or swear then? What a nice man. What a lucky girl you were, hey, to have such a lovely husband. Lucky lucky Rika.'

It's the Christmas holidays, two months after the disastrous party, and Nina and Graham are going to spend four weeks with Edith on the kibbutz. It's the holidays before Matric, her last year of school.

They're both excited, off alone, and why not, they're old enough, it's safe, off to stay with my sister. How will Edith be, I wonder? The exciting aunt, the idealistic (because she still is idealistic) aunt who will discuss Socialism and Zionism with Nina. She'll also be the strict aunt, wash dishes, there's no servants here, tidy your room, help with this or that, everyone must help, go to bed at a reasonable time. She's all of that and they love her, she's clearly so much more exciting than me.

I phone and speak to them and then in the last week, we've arranged that I go as well and then we come home together.

They're having a wonderful time. Nina dances folk dances every night, she loves them, she loves one of the dancers too, an older boy called Shalom. Graham reads and cycles around the kibbutz and the fields and loves to sit by the sea. They both go orange picking, and avocado picking.

Nina exclaims every day, 'I love living on the kibbutz!'

She sits in the kibbutz club house and eats wafer biscuits, drinks black tea and listens to people speaking and singing. She decides she's not coming home. Edith is in agreement.

'That's really wonderful. You can finish your education here in the kibbutz and eventually become a member. But I don't think you should think of Shalom as the right person for you.'

Nina asks why not and Edith says, 'He's a frank!'

'What's that?' Nina asks.

Edith simply says, 'Not for you.'

Nina asks Shalom what a frank is and he laughs, 'Your aunt is not that far removed from white South Africans. She also believes in apartheid.'

She asks her cousin who says, 'It's like a black, he's from Morocco originally.'

Nina cries to Graham that night and he looks at her and says, 'Well what do you expect. Would you want to marry a black man?'

Nina can't believe her ears and says, 'Yes, I would actually, I'd think it would be a real privilege to do that, if they would stoop to marrying a white person.'

She cries to me on the phone, 'They're so racist, ma, I can't believe it, even Edith is, and I really like her.'

I arrive for the last week and I'm so happy to see them both. They seem closer the two of them apart from that specific episode. Nina seems to have forgiven Edith.

About fifteen minutes after I get there, Nina blurts out to me, a sort of stage whisper, 'I'm not coming home, ma. I'm staying here.'

Goodness, talk about seeing red, black, all the colours of fury. I grab her by both shoulders and I say, no whisper here, loud enough for all to hear, 'There is no way in a million years that you are staying here. You're coming home and you'll finish your education!'

She cries, she tries to cajole me, she attempts explanations, 'I'll finish school here.'

'Their matric is worth nothing, you will always be uneducated if you stay here, you will go through life with nothing,' I say.

'But I'll be happy,' she says, 'I want to live a socialist life in Israel.'

'You can do that next year.' I say, 'Finish your matric and then go to university in Israel if you absolutely insist.'

'But I want to stay now,' she whines.

'You're a child,' I say, 'who will you turn to for mothering?'

Of course, she says Edith. And I lose it.

'My god, Nina, you have no idea. Don't you realise that that's what happened to me. I had an aunt who had to mother me instead of my own mother. But she had her own children. I was never anything more than just a niece. I'd never let you stay here now and have second-hand mothering. You have a real mother. Just realise your good luck that you actually have a mother!'

She cries in Shalom's arms and promises to love him forever, while he looks over her shoulders at another pretty girl dancing nearby.

We go home of course and she finishes her matric year, and arranges to study at the Hebrew University in Jerusalem.

It's the end of 1968 and we go first on a trip together to New York, to be together, to spend time just the two of us, alone, because who knows when we'll be alone again. Except of course, obviously I will be coming to visit, yes, you know I will, god how could I not! And indeed, how could I not! How could I not see my daughter for a year, two years. Ridiculous and impossible, and anyway Morris makes good money so there's not going to be any problem flying off to Israel, once or twice a year.

We spend time together walking the streets of New York, going up the Empire State Building, going into little cafés and bistros and sandwich joints, and dropping into tiny off-Broadway theatres and great big cinemas. We go to Washington DC for a few days.

'We won't book a hotel room,' I say assuredly, 'there's bound to be masses.'

Unfortunately our time coincides with Nixon's inauguration, though we manage to get a room only after promising to vacate it in time.

We sit in our hotel room one evening watching TV, a unique experience for us as we don't have TV in South Africa. We watch a programme where long lost adopted children finally found their birth parents, and the two of us cry as if we ourselves have been the ones lost. We cry and we laugh at ourselves crying and when we laugh, we laugh so hard at how ridiculous we both look and are, that we have to run to the toilet, one desperately waiting for the other to finish. Apart from Nina, I can only laugh this much with Edith, I think.

We go home and once again Nina packs her bags, big bags this time, winter and summer clothes, big heavy full bags. We take her to the airport and she goes. She's gone. She's left me behind. I'm bereft.

Alone, alone, alone.

'Ma,' Graham says. I look at him sitting in the car besides me. 'Don't worry, you'll see her soon. Da, just drop me off at the corner. See you later some time, ok.'

26

I love this time alone. It's six am and I'm swimming back and forth, one hundred lengths in our pool, naked. I feel the water in every crevice of my body, my leaner body, a bit leaner, what with all the swimming and exercises at Jill's, though still a long way to go to lean.

No-one can see me, thankfully, for them as well as me, as there is so much greenery sheltering us from our neighbours, or them from us.

I get out, shower and open the back door for the servants. Morris has already gone to work.

I sit on the veradah with my coffee and breakfast and wonder how I can possibly fill the day. Shaina Raisa is old and ill and I must visit her this afternoon. I will spend a few hours there and speak to her daughters, my sisters-in-law who will commiserate with me that my daughter is so far away.

I tell myself not to think of Nina, don't think of her, stop, but of course she is there in my head and I find myself overcome with gloom. So I call for the servants.

'Johannes! Come here!' I yell.

When he comes, I start. 'Why did you not plant those plants over there, those ones, why didn't you plant them like I told you to. No, no, this is no good. You must pull them out and do them again, just like I said. Ok? Good. Thank you.'

'Dinah, Dinah! Come here!' When she comes I start on her. 'This cup is really dirty. You must use bleach on it. I asked you to do that yesterday and you didn't. Can you do it now please. Thank you.'

They go off, doing their madam's bidding.

What now? Well, I might as well go for an extra exercise class at Jill's. And why not, that will use up the morning.

I arrive and the whole place is in disarray. Jill's children are there, both nearly grown up now but still living at home, and various other women whom I recognise as activists in the movement. They're all quiet and look distraught, in shock.

'My god,' I say, 'what's going on, why's the place in such a mess?'

Books, drawers, clothes, everything is all over the place. Jill and Ivor are nowhere to be seen.

Jill's son waves at me rather forlornly. 'They've both been arrested,' he says, 'they came this morning, made this mess. They left some letters. There's one for you.'

I open it and notice my hands are trembling. It's from Ivor.

Dear Rika

As you can see, Jill and I have both been arrested. This is just a quick note which they are allowing me to write to you, to ask if you can please look after the business for me. It won't involve an enormous amount of work, but we have commitments to get the hampers out to people who pay every month – as you know. I also need the books to be kept up to date, and the general running of the business. I know it is a big thing to ask of you.

I will ask for business visiting rights which they should allow, and hope that you will be able to come and visit me in prison from time to time when necessary to discuss the business.

Will you do this for us? I hope I can count on you.

Love

Ivor

For a moment I think only of myself, at long last, something to do! But then I look around, I stand, I'm impotent, dispossessed. I've lost my friend, the friend I depend on so much for her strength and wisdom.

I start to cry, god I'm stupid and so self-centred. I pull myself together and walk over to the other women. We start to pick things up, tidy, put away. We talk about who will look after the children. Both are at university and say they'll stay at home, with their belongings and their life.

'Who will care for you?' a woman asks.

They say, 'We'll care for each other.'

There's money in the bank to buy food and pay the servants and besides they say, 'Rika is going to look after the business.'

Yes I am, of course I am, I will do that for them (and for me).

I go home and sit thinking of my friend. I've heard such dreadful stories of life in prison, the same stories I played out to myself when I made my decision several years ago not to get involved. I could've been where you are now, Jill, but I wasn't strong enough, or, I have to admit, special enough. I'm glad not to be in prison, I wouldn't want to swap our lives now, so just accept your limitations Rika!

At one pm I phone my daughter in Jerusalem. It is a set time and I look forward so headily to hearing her voice.

'How are you, darling?' I say.

'Hi ma, oh my god, it's so good to hear your voice. It is so fantastic here, I just can't tell you! I love Jerusalem! I absolutely love Jerusalem! You can't imagine how beautiful it is. We're going for a walk on the wall in the Old City this afternoon.'

'Oy, be careful,' I say.

'There's nothing to be careful about. It's lovely. We're going as a group, our whole course. Oh my god, you just can't believe how amazing it is here. I love it so much!'

So, she likes it, I can hear.

'What about the studies,' I ask.

'Oh god, I don't know. I'm so not interested!'

'That's what you're there for,' I say.

'Well, sort of!' she says, 'I mean, it's a preparatory course but I have my matric so I will get into university next year even if I don't pass.'

Hm, not a great attitude!

'My Hebrew is so good,' she says, 'that's because all my friends are Israelis. Well, the boys are anyway, and of course we have our group from Jo'burg, so we're all friends. Shall I tell you what we did last night? We went to see the sun rise at the amphitheatre on Mount Scopus. Can you imagine that! It was so beautiful. And someone took a photo of me being held in one of the boy's arms and he was twirling me round with the sun coming up and in front of us were the hills of Judea and behind us was this ancient amphitheatre. It was so wonderful. By the way, Edith came to visit but I'd forgotten she was coming and I wasn't around. I think she's really cross, but I was having such a good time!'

I spend three days a week going into Ivor's office. I'm efficient, I never knew that about myself. I'm friendly and polite and I have a good relationship with all the workers and volunteers there. There aren't that many, maybe ten in all, but we get the work done between us.

I have to go to Ivor today to discuss the business. I go to the prison in Hillbrow which is called The Fort, no Apaches here, and walk through a small door within a much larger door and enter the prison compound. Doors don't close here, they clang and bang and each time I shudder involuntarily. They make me stand spread-eagled while a woman prison officer searches me, touching every part of my body, including inside my leg, quite far up, as I tell Morris that evening.

'I am shown into a little room with a small table and two chairs. He is sitting at one and I sit at the other. A prison guard stands on the side. He smiles weakly at me. He looks dreadful, so much older and so thin, and I can see faded signs of bruising and cuts on his face. I smile back to him weakly.

'Are you alright?' I ask but I'm shut up by the police guard.

'Only questions about business allowed.'

When we finish discussing business details I say goodbye and try to express, what, love, keep strong, stay safe if possible, oh my god I'm so sorry you're in bloody jail, everything but nothing.

I walk away from the clangs and the keys opening and locking and little doors in big doors and I start to sweat and shake. I walk over to the ice cream shop near the Fort and order a waffle with lots of ice cream and a chocolate milkshake. I need the sugar I think as I pour extra caramel sauce over the waffle.

I try to arrange a visit to see Jill on the pretext that I need it for the business but I'm not given permission. Besides, Jill needs all her allotted visits for her children.

She's released earlier than Ivor, but still serves twelve months. She walks out of prison and is immediately served a banning order forbidding her to see more than one person at a time, go to educational establishments (so she can't vote as voting takes place in school premises), can't publish, but can carry on her exercise business with a maximum of five participants at a time.

After the first class, I remain behind and we go into the garden, hopefully away from bugs which are planted throughout her house.

'The bloody Special Branch police are there day and night observing me,' she says, 'how long are they going to carry on wasting public resources on that, I wonder!'

'How are you, Jill? I've been so worried about you. I could hardly sleep some nights thinking about what you were going through,' I say, and clutch her hand.

'I'm sorry I put you out,' Jill says and takes her hand away.

I'm horrified by her words and actions.

'I didn't mean to make it sound as though it's about me,' I say.

'It always is though, isn't it, Rika,' she says.

I wince as though she's hit me and my stomach seems to crunch in pain.

'Oh Rika. Another rejection! How will you bear it?' she says.

I look at my beloved friend, who's been so important to me for so long. I don't understand why she's behaving like this.

'I'm so sorry, Jill,' I say.

She seems to soften slightly, 'It's been really tough, Rika. I don't mean to take it out on you.'

'I understand,' I say softly.

'No, you don't. You can't.'

'Of course, you're right,' I say. I gulp and then say, 'Do you want me to go?'

She smiles again and says, 'No, let's have this cup of tea, and, tell me about you.' Nothing to tell, of course. There never is.

'Normality,' Jill says, 'I wouldn't mind some of it.'

'You must be missing Ivor terribly,' I say and hold her hand.

Tears well up in her eyes and start to flow.

'I don't think I can bear it,' she says.

I hold her and she lets me and I feel a tremulous sense that this is better, you see, she needs me.

'I didn't say anything, you know Rika. I can hold my head up. I never said anything.' She has paid a heavy price to be able to say those words.

'I wish I had a tenth of your strength, Jill,' I say, and mean it.

Morris asks how Jill is and I say, 'She's changed, she's not herself any longer, they've destroyed part of her.'

Morris says, 'the bastards,' and I look at him differently. I look around me and think, I might be weak but I accept what I am and what I've got, and actually, I've got quite a lot.

The phone rings and it's Morris' brother Jonathan.

'Come quickly,' he says, 'she won't last long.'

We go to Shaina Raisa's deathbed. This is the first death of that generation that I actually witness, a death scene I'm part of. It's horrible.

We sit, listening to her shallow, rasping, sporadic breathing. We chat in between, but it's quiet, it's secondary to the main theatrical event - waiting for that last breath. We carry on talking because the breathing carries on, endlessly.

Yet there is an end and it comes, suddenly, which is strange after it took so long to get there. We all cry, and Morris and I hug each other and I actually feel some comfort from his hugs.

There's a big funeral the next day and all the brothers and sisters and their families are there as well as friends. People aren't too sad, not after she'd had such a good life, such a long life, as everyone says. We all wish each other long life, but a healthy one too, I think.

We go back to Jonathan and Sadie's and have an excellent tea with taiglach and delicious cakes. And that's it, she's gone from my life. My friend, really, Shaina Raisa. Beautiful rose.

Graham is sad about his grandmother's death but that sort of sadness is so momentary. And why not? He has so much in his life; friends, his work selling diamonds in the

Johannesburg Bourse, a girl he's interested in, golf, tennis, cars. So much more relevant to his life than an old woman.

Nina hasn't been affected by her grandmother's death too much either, though she does the obligatory crying, if not for long.

'How's everything going,' I ask her on the phone.

'Oh ma, you can't imagine how fantastic it is. We've been travelling all over Israel. It's so beautiful.'

Travelling, dancing, what about your studies, I ask, ever hopeful.

'Ach ma! That's not so important. I've been having such amazing discussions with people. That's what's important.'

Oh yes.

And then of course, she meets a boy.

'Oh my god, ma, I've met this boy. I mean I say met, but we've actually known each other for ages. He's part of this crowd and then we started,'

'Started what,' I say as I hear her stopping.

'You know,' she says.

I persist, 'No I don't.'

'Well anyway,' she says, ignoring me, 'it's been so amazing. I just love him so much.'

'Just be careful,' I say, 'please, do me a favour, just be careful!'

Morris buys me a ring. How odd, I think and say.

'Do you like it?' he asks.

'Are they all real diamonds?' I ask, looking it at closely.

'Yes,' he says, 'it's really expensive but I got a very good price through Graham, so just keep it on at all times. And Rika, if it falls off in the toilet, just put your hand down and take it out, right? No matter what!'

I look at him bemused.

Nina starts her first year at university. She didn't pass her preparatory course, well, there's news, but can still get in because of her matric.

'Don't worry,' she says, 'you're such a worrier. Just think what a great year I had learning all about life, and I've become such a good Israeli folk dancer.'

There's important and there's important.

I go see Gary, as I do every month. The receptionist smiles widely and says, 'He's outside with his carer today. Bit of fresh air on such a lovely day.

Gary's fourteen. He's very short but can stand, so go suck, I say in my mind to the 'vegetable' doctor. Of course his walking is very unsteady, and he doesn't talk or do anything else very much.

'Hello Gary,' I say and give him a little kiss which he seems oblivious to.

He doesn't like people to come too close so I stand away from him and talk to the carer.

'We're fine, thanks mommy,' she says. 'We're having a lovely day in the sunshine. And I ate up all my breakfast today because I'm a very good boy!' I smile.

'And how are you, Francine? You're looking well.'

'I'm fine, m'am, thank you. Gary has a new friend,' she says.

'A new friend!' Oh my god, my heart thumps, a friend, Gary has a friend. 'Who is he, I ask.

'It's a she, a young girl who came to join us, and they like each other very much. They look at each other and play with each other's hands.'

I can't stop the tears coming.

'That sounds so sweet,' I say.

'It's very sweet,' she says, 'you like your friend Jenny, don't you Gary?'

He looks up at her and down at his fingers.

Morris always knows when I've been to see Gary.

He asks, 'What's for supper?'

'Don't you want to know how he is,' I ask.

'No,' he says, I just want to know what's for supper.'

'The kids don't even know they have a brother who's alive,' I say.

'Just about,' he says.

'Well just about or not, he's alive,' I say.

'Let sleeping dogs lie, Rika,' he says.

'They should be told, Morris.'

'Well tell them then,' he says, 'tell them if you want to.'

We decide to tell them when Nina comes home for a short holiday. We think, best to just come out with it, not make a big announcement, we have something to tell you, sort of thing. Nina's home, today is Saturday when we all eat cold meats and rolls together on the verandah, and it comes out.

'So, kids, I start.

Morris continues, 'We've got something to tell you.'

'Really?' both children say, 'what is it?'

'Well, it is a bit strange, and you might wonder why we never told you before, but..' I stop.

Morris takes up this relay baton, 'You know when mom was pregnant that time, and we came back home from the maternity hospital,'

Graham pipes up, 'Yes, the baby died.'

'Yes, that's right. Well, in actual fact, he hadn't,' Morris says.

'What do you mean he hadn't,' Nina says, 'he hadn't died?'

'He didn't die,' Morris says and he's looking glummer and glummer. 'He was born, well, it doesn't sound very nice, but it's the sort of thing that was said at the time, he was a, a, a vegetable,'

Oh no you don't, don't you dare! 'Except he's not a vegetable,' I say, 'he's absolutely not a vegetable!'

'What is he then?' Graham asks.

'He's a boy, of course but he's, well, he's fourteen now, and he's very, well, very disabled,' I say.

'Oh my god,' Nina starts to cry, 'I can't believe it! Why didn't you tell us before? You never told us! Why?'

'We should've,' I say.

'We were trying to protect you,' Morris says. 'It was so horrible, such a tragedy. He was so,'

And I interrupt and say, 'He's not so. He's just a boy, he's very short, his face is a bit strange. He doesn't do much. He can walk a bit, sit, that sort of thing, but he can't...'

Nina interrupts me. 'Can he talk? Would he know us if we went? Does he know about us?'

'No,' I say, 'he doesn't know anything. He doesn't even know me, he doesn't recognise, he just...' I force myself to stay in control. 'He has a friend. A girl called Jenny and they like each other, and sit and play with each other's hands.'

'Can we go see him?' Nina asks quietly.

'Yes, yes, of course, if you want to,' I say, smiling for the first time.

'Does he know you, da? Does he relate to you differently from ma?' Graham asks.

I look at Morris and he looks across the family to the garden but doesn't reply.

'Don't you know?' Graham asks. 'Why don't you know? Don't you go see him? Have you never seen him?'

I want to protect Morris, why, I don't know. 'Come, enough, eat now, have some more,' I say.

But Graham won't stop there.

'No, it's not enough. It's not nearly enough. I can't believe you've left it so long to tell us, and then we hear that Dad doesn't even know him, that he hasn't ever seen him and,'

I stop him. 'Don't judge!' I say, 'You don't have any idea what we've been through. Different people react in different ways. Your father has suffered just as much as I have. Gary's in the best possible place. He has constant care by wonderful people who look after him incredibly well and love him. And I can tell you, that care doesn't come cheap. And your father is the one who works extremely hard and he's the one who's paying for it. So, just remember please, don't accuse anyone of anything too quickly.'

'But why did you give him away?' Nina asks.

We look at each other, Morris and me and we both look down.

'Why?' Nina repeats.

'We did it for you,' Morris says, and looks at me, silently apologising for the lie.

After far too short a time, Nina gets back on that plane and flies to Israel again. I miss her so much and think of her stories as I swim in the morning. I have a vicarious pleasure and excitement thinking of all the fun she's having and the people she's meeting.

I compare her life with mine and think, don't be such a jealous self-centred, and then I think a word that shows how far I've come from the non-swearing, non-shouting world of my father.

I worry about the little interest Nina shows in her studies but she insists she's learning masses, 'learning all about life'.

I'm busy at weekends with visits to and with friends and sisters-in-law, to each other's houses or the cinema or theatre, also art galleries and the shopping centres, so I haven't really paid attention to Morris' absence at weekends. It hits me suddenly, I wonder where Morris goes to, what he gets up to.

Do I care? Not massively, our lives are so separate, but has anything changed, I wonder. Well, I think, he hasn't been interested in making love since, god, when was it that we last did it, I actually can't remember.

I'm swimming and Morris appears, standing at the shallow end.

'Hullo,' I say, 'I didn't know you were home.'

'Rika, I need to speak to you,' he says.

I get out and stand with a towel around me.

'What's the matter,' I say, 'you look discombobulated. Good word, huh.'

'Rika,' he says, 'I'm really sorry, but I'm leaving you!'

'You're what,' I say and my head starts to reel.

I sit down and he says, 'I'm moving in with another woman.'

'I don't believe you,' I say, 'I don't believe what you're saying.'

'You never loved me. Hilda loves me,' he says.

'Hilda? Who's Hilda?'

'She's a South African and she loves me,' he says. 'She laughs at my jokes, she makes me feel good about myself.'

He doesn't normally talk about things like feeling good about himself, the words sound alien coming from his mouth.

'I'm really pleased for you!' I say.

'She's not sarcastic, and she wants to make love to me!'

'Well, there you are,' I say, 'you have it all, at long last!'

'I'm really sorry, Rika. I'm taking just some of my things but I'll come back for more.' And he goes.

'Don't you dare come back!' I scream after him, not caring an iota that the neighbours are in their gardens. 'Just take everything you want because believe me, anything you leave is going straight to Johannes!'

I sob on the phone to my sister.

'And can you believe it,' I cry, 'he'd only given me the ring two months ago. This really expensive diamond ring which, to tell you the truth, is as ugly as sin, but it's really expensive and he told me that if it falls into the toilet, to put my hand in and take it out. Can you imagine that, and now he tells me he's leaving me, and I can't believe it. I'm forty seven, Edith, forty seven, I'm not young, I'm overweight, oh my god I swear I'm on a serious diet now, I'll never find anyone else looking like this. Actually I don't even know what I'm talking about because I don't ever want another bloody man again in my life as long as I live, I swear to god!'

Edith murmurs all the right things, the supportive sisterly things interspersed with lots of vicious expletives directed at Morris. Just right, just what I need.

The family are all furious with Morris. They rally round me and say 'It's just not on, you just don't behave like that to your wife. Alright goyim do it, but not us Jews!'

I go swimming naked as always, then shower, dress and sit and have my coffee and bread on the verandah.

I look at the lovely garden and watch Johannes working outside and Dinah cleaning inside. I sit and carry on looking and staring until it's lunch and then till it's supper.

I sit outside in the dark and listen to the crickets. I hope a rat doesn't run past. You're always only a few feet away from a rat, I think mournfully.

What's it all about, Alfie, I say to myself. What's it all about?

Here I sit alone. All my life I've been alone. Even when I'm not alone, I'm alone. Oh my god, I think, that is such a ridiculous thing to say. There's nothing more pathetic than a fat yiddene sitting feeling sorry for herself.

I think of Natan and realise I haven't thought of him for a while. Would he still be interested in sleeping with me if he saw me now? Mind you, I'm not that fat and people often still say I'm beautiful. Ha! I think. Beautiful my tochis!

I think about Natan and Morris, and stick them up there in front of me, two models of manhood (I laugh) and I look at them.

I get them to turn around, pull down their underpants, take off their shirt, then put them all back on again. I shake my head. Natan is definitely the better looking, I think, well

Israelis are, aren't they. But Morris isn't too bad, really. He's good-looking, just a bit short. But he's getting a tum now, now that he's reaching middle-age. Natan must be getting a tum too. I put a tum on him and then the two don't look that dissimilar.

In terms of husband material, well, they both are pretty far down the league, both pretty unpromising, as a theoretical concept, as well as reality.

Who would I choose if I were starting again, starting from now, from here and now. Ha! I laugh. I wouldn't start from here. I'd start from somewhere else, somewhere far away from both of these two schmendricks.

I feel a bit better and I go to bed.

'Ma, I can't believe it,' Nina says crying on the phone from Israel. 'How could he do that to you, to us? I just feel so angry with him, I can't get over feeling such rage towards him. Who is this bloody woman, anyway?'

'Who knows,' I say, 'some Jewish woman who likes his sense of humour. Poor cow!'

Nina says. 'You're still really young, ma. I mean you're what, forty-seven? That's not old. You can find someone else.'

'Oy,' I laugh, 'from the frying pan into the fire.'

'Come to Israel, ma,' she says, 'come and stay here. You can live on the kibbutz with Edith. Or Tel Aviv. Come on, it's so lovely here. Please!'

'What have I got there, Nina?' I ask.

'Me. You've got me here,' she says.

'Let's wait and see what happens to you there. The studies aren't going so well, are they?'

'Life, ma. Life!' she says.

'Yes, as you always say, but you don't get a BA for life studies. Besides, Johannesburg is home for me now,' I say.

'I hate him,' she says, 'I just want you to know that if there were sides to pick, there is no question that I'm on your side 100%, not 60 or 80 or 99, but 100%.'

'Thank you, my babela,' I say, 'got to go darling,' as my eyes start overflowing again.

Jill has come into her own again when she realises how much I need a good friend.

We sit together day after day, swim together, eat and engage in long, intense, teenage-like discussions about ourselves, our experiences, where we (i.e. I) went wrong, where things went right, how much Jill is missing Ivor, how angry I've been with Morris, and what options I now have.

I decide to just sit where I am, not move, not make any decisions, just sit.

Life goes on, it actually doesn't seem very different. I feel hurt, rejected, but there is a sense of independence I didn't have before, which is strange, because I always could and did do what I wanted to do.

I'm sitting outside, it's about three weeks since the bombshell, or not, as the case may be, and who should open the door and come stand right in front of me but Morris, looking timid and diffident.

'What on earth,' I say.

'Rika,' he says and then stops, standing there, still, with his head hanging slightly down, his eyes not quite meeting mine.

'Rika,' he tries again, 'I've come back to you! I made a terrible mistake!'

I can't believe my ears. 'You made a terrible mistake? You mean she made a terrible mistake. She realised what a terrible mistake she made, what a terrible deal she entered into, what a pain in the bloody neck she's landed up with! Is that what you're saying?'

'No, Rika,' he says, 'not at all. I just realised I'd left you and…'

'You just realised!' I say. 'You just realised three weeks later that you left me? What were you asleep? Were you on some drugs or something? You've just woken up?'

'Stop it Rika,' he says, but gently, 'you're not the sarcastic type.'

'Aren't I?'

I'm shouting now, aware at the back of my mind somewhere that the neighbours might hear, once again, do they need to know all our business, and not caring a whit.

'You don't know what I'm like at all,' I say. 'Maybe in these three weeks I've changed beyond recognition. Maybe you'll realise very soon what a terrible mistake you made to leave her!'

'For goodness sake, Rika,' he says, 'I've known you for so many years. I've lived with you for so long. We have two children together.'

'Three!' I yell, 'We have three children, Morris!'

'I meant, you know what I mean,' he's whimpering now, 'for Christ's sake, Rika, give me another chance. Don't make me beg.'

'No? Why not?' I say, 'Go on, beg. Beg!' Am I bloody enjoying this too much.

'Alright, I'm begging you. I love you, Rika. Only you.'

'Till the next one comes along?' I say.

'You know I'm not like that.'

'I thought I knew,' I say, 'but you showed very clearly that you're exactly like that.'

'It's Amos' fault.'

'Who the bloody hell is Amos?'

'A friend, a customer who became a friend. He was such a womanizer, got me going out with him. He was a bad influence.'

Morris sounds pathetic, like a little boy who's got into trouble, it's his fault mommy, he's to blame, not me.

'I thought you were a grown up, Morris,' I say.

'We're all little boys sometimes.'

'And what? Is that supposed to make me feel sympathetic towards you?'

He is pathetic. 'Ach, Rika, please a bit of rachmonis, please!'

I think of Shaina Raisa, I see her looking at me, rachmonis, she is saying, have some compassion.

'You're a momzer!' I say.

'I'll give you that,' he says.

I answer, quick as a flash, 'You'll have to give me a lot more than that'.

'I'll give you whatever you want, Rika. What do you want? Just tell me. Anything.'

'I only want one thing from you,' I say.

'You want me to promise I'll never do anything like that again?'

'No,' I answer, 'because I don't trust such promises.'

'What then?' he asks.

'I want you to come with me to see Gary. And I want you to come every single month. With me. Together.'

I start to cry then and Morris takes me in his arms, and I let him and he holds me.

'I promise,' he says and smiles, tentatively.

I refuse to have sex with him for at least two months, but when I finally do, I have to admit it's better than I remembered. He laughs and smokes in bed and tells me of the disaster that was he and Hilda.

'Oy Rika, if anything made me appreciate you, it was living with Hilda. What a nudnik, what a pain, what a lot of complaints!'

'You're such an idiot,' I say and turn my back on him. But I do quite like to hear it.

'So,' Jill says, 'is he still going with you to see Gary?'

'He is,' I reply, 'but there's a problem.'

'What's the problem? Doesn't he get out of the car?' she asks.

'He comes in every time,' I say.

'So what? Is he rude, unpleasant, does he not speak to anyone, does he not relate to Gary? What is it?' she asks.

'He's charming, he's friendly, he speaks to everyone,' I say.

'And the problem is,' Jill says.

'Gary,' I say.

'Gary?' she asks.

'Yes, Gary's in love with Morris. He thinks he's the greatest ever. He looks at him, he smiles at him, he gets excited to see him. Me, he couldn't care less! Can you believe it!'

Jill smiles but I'm genuinely addled.

27

Nina's already been back home for a year. She's starting her second year at Wits University, studying English, 'Well so she says,' I say to whoever asks me, but in reality she's studying politics because all she does is get involved in politics.

You'd think she'd have learnt her lesson, I think but don't say, when she failed her first year of her BA at the Hebrew University in Jerusalem. You'd think she'd realise she has to study now, seriously, not life, not politics, just study.

But Nina doesn't mind terribly much. She passed the first year at Wits, just, but a pass is a pass, and she's having such a good time standing for office for various student committees, protesting, organising, what else could one possibly want!

I think of the trip home from Israel, just the two of us, me and Nina. Nina wasn't that upset about leaving Israel, though she'd cried about leaving the boyfriend, but I'm delighted to see the end of that unsuitable boy.

'He just makes her cry,' I say to Morris. 'What's the point of a boyfriend that just makes you cry!'

Nina says she'll go back to live in Israel after she finishes at Wits, and I think she may, but who knows who she'll meet or what will happen. She's determined never to live in South Africa.

'I'll just end up in jail if I stay there, and I don't want that,' she says to me, and I wince with the poignancy of it all.

The trip from Israel home includes a stop-over in Bremen to see my aunt and uncle. The family (aunt, uncle, cousin my age) were all in a concentration camp for the duration of the war, but they survived, and immediately afterwards, instead of doing what every other displaced person did, i.e. stay in a DP camp, emigrate to America or take one's chances in getting to Israel, they decided to go straight back to Bremen and pick up their lives once again, in Germany.

He was the head of the Jewish community there, the remnants of the Jews who stayed in Germany after the war, but it grew and expanded and prospered and now he is the pillar of a bustling community. They're kind and welcoming when we arrive, an embracing love so typical of the wider family on my mother's side.

Nina has pains in her legs and feels miserable beyond anything I've seen before and when we're alone together in our shared room, she blurts out;

'I think I'm pregnant.'

The words reverberate in my head as if a nail is being banged in by a steel hammer.

'Why do you think that?' I ask struggling very hard to control my voice.

'Well, I haven't had my period and I feel terrible,' she says.

I take her in my arms and hold her.

'If you are, we'll arrange for an abortion,' I say.

She smiles, miserably.

The differentiation between the controlled outer me and the inner wildly chaotic me is marked.

Oh my god, I think, where on earth does one go for an abortion? Who would I speak to? Would Jill know? Possibly. Don't think about it. We're tired. We have to sleep. Oh my god, this girl is still nineteen, what'll it mean for her? How will she react. She'll be alright.

Just don't tell anyone, none of the brothers and sisters-in-law, even Morris, I definitely won't tell Morris. I won't tell anyone!

Rika's Rooms

I barely sleep with all those thoughts dashing round my head, but when it's light, Nina wakes up and goes to the toilet.

She sees I'm awake and whispers, 'It's alright, ma, I've got it.'

Just to be absolutely sure, I say, 'Your period?'

And her broad smile says it all.

But as soon as we get home, I make sure she goes straight onto the pill.

Nina has a little car that Morris has given her, an ancient red VW Beetle. She loves it and drives it to university and back, as well as to friends, cinema, meetings, out out out. Sometimes in the evening, she drives back to the university to paint slogans on protest banners ready for the morning. The room's full of students all writing, laughing, drinking, singing.

'Ma, listen I don't want you to worry but there's going to be this big march into town. It's illegal, but there's lots of us so, don't worry, hey!'

Don't worry, she says, I think throughout the day, listening whenever the news comes on the radio. Ohh ohh, I think, when I hear about the progress of the march, and the storming by the police, and the mass arrests. I phone Morris.

'Let's just wait to hear from her. She'll let us know one way or the other. Don't worry,' he says.

Everyone's telling me not to worry, I think, worrying. It's six pm and I still haven't heard from her. Morris arrives home and we decide to phone the police station.

'After all,' I say, 'we're under the impression that the police will do the decent thing and let them phone. And if there's hundreds of them, then they won't, will they?'

So we try but we are just one of very many worried parents doing the same thing. After an hour of this constant phoning, we get in the car and drive into town to horrible, scary John Vorster Square.

'Ja, what do you want?' the policeman at the desk asks in a brusque vile way – did we expect friendliness? Politeness?

'My daughter,' Morris starts and is interrupted;

'Name?'

We tell him and he looks down a long list and says, 'Ja.'

'When will she be freed?' Morris asks.

'Who knows,' he says in the typical harsh superior manner of South African police. 'You should tell your children not to be so stupid and behave properly. I blame you parents. You don't know how to bring up your children properly.'

Morris answers, obsequiously I notice, 'Yes, officer.'

I stamp on his foot and march back to the seats. Eventually, from eleven pm, students are let out in dribs and drabs and they go off with their parents. At about midnight Nina comes out. She rushes to us and hugs us both.

'Oh my god,' she whispers, 'that was such fun!'

We're in the car and she tells us the whole story.

'I was right in the front,' she starts,

'Of course,' we both say.

'I was standing next to David.'

'Who's David?' I ask.

'Doesn't matter, let her go on,' Morris says.

'Anyway, we were marching and singing and we had all our banners. We knew the police were waiting for us. When we got to the top of the bridge, so we hadn't got far, it was all slow because there were so many of us. But when we got there, there was this line of police. One of the officers, I mean the senior ones, was using a megaphone and he said, you must disperse, if you don't disperse now we will arrest you. So some people broke away.'

'Obviously not you,' Morris says.

'Obviously!' she says with a smile, 'and we carried on walking, we were all holding hands, or arms or you know.

Anyway, all of a sudden, those bastards came running at us. We all turned around and ran. Oh my god, it was really scary. And then one of them just grabbed me and said, come on you.'

'Come on you? Do you think they were aiming for you?' I ask.

'Probably all of us in the front line.'

'How did you feel at the time?' I ask.

'She already said she was scared,' Morris says.

'But you know, the funny thing is, actually not really funny, but it doesn't reflect well on me I suppose, and I'm being honest,' she stops.

'Nu,' I say.

'I felt proud.'

'You've got nothing to be proud about, missy!' Morris says.

'Oh yes she has!' I say. 'I'm proud of you!'

'What are you proud of?' Morris says, 'that she got arrested for marching with a bunch of'

I interrupt, 'Of caring, young activists who are more concerned with the welfare of their fellow citizens than money!'

'They just want to be part of the group,' Morris says, 'look at her, in the front line. What does that say? That she's a big macha on campus. That she's part of the in-crowd. That she's popular. That she doesn't study and just plays politics. And I bet you one thing, ninety-nine percent of those caring young people you saw today will be earning good money in daddy's business next year!'

Nina and I look at each other and shake our heads and then start to laugh.

In between her laughter she says, 'God, daddy, you are so unbelievably negative and pessimistic.'

He responds, not laughing, serious, 'Realistic!'

But the mood of adventure has been spoilt, and it's late and we're all tired, and we carry on mostly in silence.

Nina has said she wants to meet Gary, the unknown one, the 'vegetable', the secret, mommy and daddy's secret. Graham wasn't keen and Nina says she wants to go alone.

At the reception she asks for Gary Levine's room, and is told to go to the third door on the left after the double doors. On the door was a name, Gary Levine. She walks in and on the bed is a young man who looks surprisingly 'normal', not really what she's expecting at all.

'Are you Gary Levine?' she asks.

'Yes,' he says, 'who are you?'

'I'm your, ahm, sister,' she says as he looks up, surprised.

But as she says it, something about the whole situation makes her suddenly feel very unsure.

'Is there, by any chance another Gary Levine living here?' she asks.

'Yes,' he says and smiles.

She burbles, 'Sorry' and dashes out.

The Gary Levine, who is her brother, is with his carer outside in the gardens. She looks at him from afar and knows immediately he is her relative. Although he looks so disabled, there is a definite family resemblance particularly to Graham and her mother. I don't look like any of them, she suddenly thinks.

'So who are you?' the carer asks.

'I'm Nina, Gary's older sister.'

This is the first time she has ever said those words.

'Ahh, that's lovely,' the kindly carer says, 'look Gary, here's your sister. Nina. You see. You have a sister.'

But Gary is not interested.

'He loves his father,' the carer says. 'Whenever he comes, he can't stop looking at him and wanting to hold his hand. His father is so good with him. They walk together. It's really an amazing sight. Of course he loves his mother too. And you, he will love you. Will you come again?'

'Of course,' she says, apparently meaning it and yes, meaning it at that moment, but as soon as she gets in the car she thinks, uh uh, can't, maybe one day, not soon. The truth is that boy means nothing to her. There is no connection, no bond. He's just somebody and nobody.

Nina manages to pass her BA.

'Just, but just is still a pass,' I say proudly.

On her graduation day, I walk so tall and I suddenly realise, this is the proudest day of my life, and I think, is that sad, that my proudest day should be about Nina and not about me? I shrug it away, something to think about maybe but not now.

Morris is at work but David comes to the graduation. I like him, he has lots to say about politics and other things and I find him interesting. Nina isn't sure what to do after her degree. She and David are talking about going to live in England, but he still has another year of his degree before they can leave.

Nina applies and gets a job in December working for the Bantu Administration Board, specifically in the Social Work department in Soweto. She's thrilled with the job.

The office is in town and the team is led by a Jewish man who is as passionate about the job and the people he is serving as he is tiny. It's a small team including a dynamic black woman called Princess who lives in Soweto and seems to embody her name; she is a princess, she knows everyone and everyone knows her. She drives through the streets of Soweto with her head through the window.

'Hey brother, hey sister, hello auntie,' she shouts at everyone.

'Mama hello' they all shout back. And they laugh and whoop and hoot and shriek and shout jokes.

It's an extraordinary experience for Nina, and she loves it! It reminds her of kibbutz life, that high octane, high level, high noise lifestyle. And when she leaves Soweto, when they drive back into the quiet, clean, empty streets of the white suburbs, they seem dead to her.

Everything outside Soweto seems like a second-class existence, a life she doesn't want. Her perception of 'normal' has changed.

Unfortunately for Nina, 'normal' returns far sooner than she would have wanted. Once the Bantu Administration Board returns from its three-week summer break over Christmas and the New Year, and they review all the appointments made over the holiday period, she is called into her manager's office and summarily dismissed.

'Pack your things and go. Yes. Now. We don't want radicals working for us.'

Nina and David move to England. The idea that my daughter has once again left, but this time with the prospect of any future grandchildren living far away from me, is unbearable. Morris too is upset. We speak about it a little, moan that it's unfair on us.

As if that matters. We both know South Africa's future is dire. At least Graham is still home. He's become very close with a woman, Jean, and they're now talking of getting married.

Friends and family are mostly still in Johannesburg so we will have to rely on them. It could be worse, we think, and we'll just have to travel to England to visit Nina as often as possible. Yes, it could be worse.

And then it is worse. Graham and Jean get married – a lovely wedding, modest really but I wear a new dress I bought, quite bohemian in a not-the-mother-of-the-groom, not-kitchy-fruh-fruh sort of way. And immediately afterwards, Graham and Jean tell us they're pregnant and by the way, 'We're moving to London.'

When? As soon as possible!

And Nina is pregnant!

We are alone in Johannesburg. Morris and me, just us, together, with Dinah and Johannes and the big house and swimming pool. We're grandparents without any grandchildren. We feel abandoned without the children.

We are not alone in our abandonment. Our friends and family suffer the same fate. So we meet together and empathise with each other and reminisce about the good old days. We listen to updates and stories of where the children are, what they're doing, how they're getting on, and how difficult it is for all of us, the parents, left alone in South Africa at this time of trouble and danger and violence and trauma.

Many start leaving too to join their children. They go to Israel, America, Australia, England. And one day, Morris comes home from work and finds me crying. He sits down next to me and looks at me for a long time, saying nothing.

'Shall we go too?' he finally says.

'Are you sure?' I ask. The crying stops instantaneously. It always seemed to me that he was the stumbling block. I would've gone like a shot. But his roots in the country were so far-reaching, so rooted, whereas mine were like a vine, clinging on to the walls around me, easily pulled away.

'I want to be a real grandfather. I want to be with them,' he says in a forlorn sort of way.

'And Gary?' I ask.

'I'll miss him,' he says, (Jesus Christ, I think). 'But we'll come visit.'

'What about your business? Won't you miss that?'

'I'll work with Graham.'

'What do you know about diamonds?'

'I'll learn. Besides, they're all nice yiddishe boche! We'll sit and drink coffee and talk.'

Will this work, I wonder. I have my life here. What will I have there? Is it right to just live for your children, live on top of them.

'Will the children want us all the time?' I ask Morris.

'We'll still have each other,' he says. 'Besides, we're not too old to make new friends. Are we?'

Are we?

I hug Jill. I'll never have a friend like her again. Not one I love. And I realise, I don't love people very easily actually.

'We'll write,' Jill says. 'I got used to writing letters in prison. We'll write. Every week!'

What will I have to say every week, I think. And she adds, 'But don't make it all about the grandchildren! News about you is what I want, right!'

And finally it is time to go say goodbye to Gary. He is oblivious, naturally. He's never really been mine, I think as we get back into the car and drive away.

28

We settle in North London, not too far from Graham's house. Graham is a diamond merchant at the London Bourse and Graham agrees that Morris should come and work with him.

'Seriously, Morris,' I say with a distinct element of patronisation. 'You know nothing about diamonds!'

He scoffs back at me and goes to work with Graham.

Extraordinarily, unbelievably to me, Morris is regarded by one and all as a real mensch, a good bloke, a really funny guy and such an interesting yid. They sit, they drink coffee, he runs some errands for Graham, they discuss politics, they tell jokes, they laugh. He never does get to know anything about diamonds, but he has found his milieu. Meanwhile I meet a few neighbours, play bridge, look after the grandchildren as and when required, and travel down to Brighton to help look after Nina's two.

We've moved into a very ordinary house in Stanmore, north London, nothing architecturally interesting or unique like Linksfield, no swimming pool, but the garden is pretty and big and there are four bedrooms for when Nina and family come and stay.

Nina and David divorce and I look after the children a lot more.

I adore those two children, (I adore all five of my grandchildren) and I sound like Shaina Raisa as she was with Graham, bubela, cookela, schnookela, and I kiss them non-stop and hug them and listen to all their stories.

I go down and stay with Nina and the children for two or more days every week, and I've became so close to the two little ones, Janine and Paulie.

'Say bye-bye to mummy,' I say, holding Janine and waving to Nina as she goes off to work.

One day I fall down a stair in Nina's flat, a sharp, horrible pain in my ankle and I sit on the bottom stair, unable to move. Janine, aged two, sits with me throughout the day, holding my hand, singing and talking.

Paulie comes to investigate from time to time, and eventually Nina arrives home and discovers me still sitting, still singing and laughing and playing games with both children but in worsening pain. I'm taken to the hospital for resetting and plaster of paris.

Nina meets and falls in love with Sam and very soon they move in together. I like him a lot and I'm relieved that Nina is so happy.

Life continues.

I travel to see my sister every year and Edith comes to visit me. We are growing older and it appears poor Tante Leah is developing Alzheimers. I hate to see her like this, confused, unsure, awkward. She deteriorates and her sons decide to put her in a home.

'Tante Leah sits in that home and just cries. It's horrible,' Edith says.

I go to Israel to see her and I am horrified. She knows nothing yet she is so uneasy, so sad. I feel my heart tear, but there is nothing I can do. It is all so desperate.

Nina tries to make things less awful by saying, 'But surely she doesn't know anything.'

'How do you know,' I say, 'how does anyone know.'

Edith phones and says, 'I look at her and know she isn't herself, but then again, she isn't anyone else either.'

I'm worried about my memory. Is it just because of Tante Leah, I wonder, but start to notice how often I forget things. I confide in Nina. She tells me not to worry!

'I have to worry. I'm really worried. I'm going to get Alzheimers, I just know it,' I say.

'Why should you?' she asks.

'It's in the family. Look at Tante Leah, and my grandmother Paulina. She dropped her knickers in the street and didn't even realise it!' But that just makes us laugh.

Oy, a bittere gelechte, I say thinking of dear old Shaina Raisa.

'Yes, but it wasn't your mother who got it. We're not talking about your mother,' Nina says.

'Well we don't know, do we,' I say, 'she might have got it. We don't know. She might've, if she hadn't been,' and I stop.

'But look, ma,' Nina says, 'just think, if you really do get it, you won't know about it. And if you don't get it, you would've wasted all this time worrying about it.'

'Yes,' I say, 'but the problem is you don't just get it one day, one day you're fine and the next you're not. It grows, it develops, and you see it growing and developing and you know that you're changing, your brain is dying, slowly but absolutely surely, and you're going to end up just like Tante Leah.'

'Ma, please, don't upset yourself. You might never get it!' Nina is exasperated.

'Nina,' I say, 'just do me a favour. If I get it, and I don't know anything, I don't know you and I don't know who you are, I want you to kill me. Will you? You know I believe in euthanasia, don't you?' I look deep in her eyes. I want her to understand that I am being serious, this is not hysteria, this is not just a funny joke.

'Ma, you know I can't do that,' she says looking intently back at me. 'It's against the law. I'd end up in prison.'

'But it's the right thing to do,' I say. 'I once stopped doing the right thing because I didn't want to end up in prison.'

Rika's Rooms

I look out the window, deep in thought and Nina asks me a question I find so hard to ponder.

'Do you regret it?'

Eventually I say, 'To some extent I do, but then I look at you and I think, your life would've been so different.'

She asks about Gary, 'Do you regret that you didn't keep him?'

'It's the same answer, you know. It would have affected you and Graham so much. Your life wouldn't have been the same. You wouldn't be the same.'

She says, 'Yes, it wouldn't have been the same. But maybe we would've'

I stop her. 'Don't.' I say. 'Just leave it like that. Please.'

Morris protects me from the growing loss of memory. He has the answers, he remembers everything and tells me, and he tells me in a way that makes me feel that I'm not stupid.

I begin to rely on him being around. We watch television together eating sweets and chocolates, and go for walks together. We chat but not all the time, and he tells me what people said at the Bourse and how they laugh at his jokes. He sometimes tells me the jokes, the ones he thinks I'll enjoy. And mostly he's right.

We seem at long last to have developed a way of being together.

I write to Jill every week in response to her letters. I can comment on the things she has told me. She tells me that things are going to get better there, that things will change, that it actually looks as though it might change peacefully. How is that possible, I still can't imagine it but I watch the news, and sometimes read the articles and hear from Jill and little by little, the unimaginable begins to seem probable, that there will be change without bloodshed. Incredible!

And then we watch Nelson Mandela walk out of prison. We watch, Morris and me, we sit together watching the television as Nelson Mandela walks out down a road surrounded by thousands of people and thousands of cameras from all over the world. Nelson Mandela is walking out to freedom. I can't believe those words.

'My god, he's looking old,' we both say, the whole world says, because all we've seen are photos from twenty-seven years ago.

I look at Morris and he looks at me, and we smile at each other. We smile and we laugh and we are happy to be watching Nelson Mandela walking out to freedom.

Then, one day, in 1998, as we sit at home, reading the paper, the radio on, Morris suddenly makes a strange noise, keels over, and dies.

I scream, I try and shake him to come back, to open his eyes, but I know he's gone.

I phone Graham, I phone 999, I wait for them both to come and they confirm, he's dead.

I look at him as they bundle him up and take him away.

I didn't have time to test my lack of belief. Would I have prayed to god if he'd taken longer to die?

How do I feel as his unliving body goes away from me? I've lived with this man for fifty years. So much of my life was taken up with him and now, it's not. I'm shuddering and shivering. I'm holding myself tightly. I recognise I'm in shock. I don't know how I feel.

The family surrounds me, they don't leave me, they talk about him, talk about the things people said about him at the Bourse, how well he's liked. Family from all over the world phone and say how funny he was. One of his nephews phones from America.

'What I liked most about him was how he listened to me. I could talk to him about anything,' he says.

I tell Nina what he said and she said, 'Are we talking about the same man?'

We have him cremated, much to the disappointment and anger of the religious faction at the Bourse who are dead against cremation for Jews. Bugger them, I think, it's what he wanted.

We scatter his ashes into a garden at the cemetery, and that's the end. There's nothing more to do, no more funeral to arrange or people to speak to, it's all over. Morris has left the building.

I walk through the rooms in our house in Stanmore. I am the only one there. I eat breakfast alone. In the evenings I eat with Graham and his family but I feel as if it's too much, so I begin to eat more and more in my home, alone.

I know I can rely on Graham and Jean, but of course they're not there all the time. They're not there to tell me what the word is that I've forgotten, what the thing is that I was going to do, what I need to buy.

I'm left to my own devices and I know I'm floundering.

Nina tells me I must come to live in Brighton.

'I know people shouldn't make drastic changes to their lives for at least a year after a bereavement,' she says, 'but I can't bear you being alone in that big house.'

Graham agrees and organises the sale of the house and the buying of a flat in sheltered accommodation near Nina.

'It's perfect,' Nina and all her family in Brighton say.

'How wonderful Granny!' Janine says, 'you're coming to live in Brighton.'

I smile, I'm grateful they want me, and why shouldn't they, a loving grandmother after all, but I feel surprisingly numb.

The flat in the sheltered accommodation is small but there are two bedrooms, one of which serves as a dining room so I can get my beautiful but large Spanish dining table and six chairs into it. It takes up the whole room.

The lounge is equally small and leads into a tiny kitchen, but it's big enough for me, I'm not such a cook, and my bedroom's fine too.

The building seems like a hotel from the inside, but it's fine.

Nina thinks I'll develop friendships and spend afternoons meeting people and having tea together and playing bridge. But I'm less interested in people than I used to be, they aren't Shaina Raisa or Sadie or Jill after all. I find it difficult to know what to say to these strangers, somehow.

I wake up in the morning and I work out where I am, where the door is, where the toilet is. I boil the kettle and pour hot water in a cup and take some bread and put something on it. I sit by the television and put it on. Sometimes I forget how to put it on and leave it off. I sit on the chair, and sit. I walk to the park and sit on a bench and watch the people go by. Sometimes someone will sit there too and they'll speak to me, my name, where I live, what my accent is. I know the answers.

I go to Nina in the evening, when she gets home from work and I eat my dinner there. She or Sam or Janine or Paulie walk me back to my flat after sitting and watching television with them for a while.

I make friends with a woman in my building and she invites me for lunch. We eat and chat a little but I have no idea what we talk about. Nina tells me I must invite her back to mine for lunch. I don't know what I would possibly offer her.

Nina says, 'I'll sort it out, it'll be fine,' and she gets cold meat and makes a salad and buys some rolls.

The woman comes and we eat and chat and I have no idea what we talk about. We don't arrange anything again.

The warden in the building is pleasant and friendly and asks me how I am and I always say I'm fine thanks and how are you.

Graham tells me I must eat mackerel because that's good for the brain, so every lunch I eat mackerel. He tells me I should have a glass of red wine every day as that's good for the brain too. So I buy a bottle and I pour a glass and drink it and think, if one glass is good, then two must be better. I sit on the floor and my head goes round and round. I can't focus, I can't think, I feel as if I want to vomit but I can't get up.

Nina walks in and sees me and I say, 'I feel so sick, I don't know what's wrong with me.'

She comes to me, concerned and looks at me and at the empty bottle and says, shocked, 'Ma, you're drunk!' and starts to laugh.

I don't see what's so funny.

The days are so long. But then Graham's eldest comes to stay. She's sleeping in the little room with the dining table and I love her being there. She's fast asleep and the door is closed.

Nina walks in and I say, 'Shh, Ella's sleeping.

'What do you mean?' she asks.

'She's asleep there in the room, with some friends.'

'No, she's not!' Nina says, angry.

Why's she angry? 'She is,' I say, even angrier, but quietly so I don't wake her.

Nina opens the door. Ella's not there. I don't know when she went, I didn't hear her leave. Was she ever there? Bloody Nina, always knows best!

We're sitting in my lounge, Nina and me, chatting, she's drinking tea and I tell her about the way I went out of the flat this morning, through the back way.

'There is no back way,' she says. I point to the window of my lounge.

'Through there,' I say.

Can't she see, it goes straight out, to the back. 'There, look, there.'

'We're on the first floor, ma,' she says, 'it's a window, there's no way out.'

It doesn't make sense to me. I don't know what she's talking about. 'God, Nina,' I say, 'honestly!'

She doesn't say anything but looks sad, or worried. I don't know, I don't care.

Nina and I are sitting on the bench in the park licking ice-cream cones. I watch the little children playing nearby with their toys. They throw the ball and it comes to us and they say 'Hello,' so sweetly.

I love watching them, we smile and laugh. One comes back, he's only little and he climbs onto my lap.

'Do you want some ice-cream,' I say and he nods his head and he licks and licks and I hold it for him and soon the ice cream is gone and Nina and me and everyone around us is laughing.

Nina takes me to see a doctor. On the way Nina tells me the name of the Prime Minister, and other things that don't seem interesting or relevant. She tells me and questions me afterwards and I try to remember. I don't realise she's preparing me for the visit with the doctor because he asks the same questions, but by then I've forgotten.

He sends me to a psychologist who does all sorts of tricks with me, like showing me items and then taking them away and asking what they were, or telling me a story and asking me to repeat it. How do I know! What does she expect from me! She suggests I go do something called a Memory Retraining Class. But I feel stupid there. Everyone knows everything and I know nothing.

I sit on a bench in the park. I am alone and I watch the people pass. A young woman comes and sits next to me.

'Hello,' she says, 'isn't it a lovely day.'

We chat and I like this woman so much and when she leaves she says, 'See you again.'

I tell Nina that evening that I have a new friend. She looks happy and when I tell her that she's a young woman, Janine's age, new to Hove, she just looks sad, and I never do see the young woman again.

I'm awoken by the sound of a key in the door and Nina comes in.

'Ma,' she says, 'why aren't you up? You're going to Israel today.'

'Am I? Why didn't you tell me,' I say.

'Of course you knew, I was with you last night when you were packing. Quick, get dressed.'

So I dress, and there in front of me is my bag, packed, oh yes, that's true, I remember now.

Nina says, 'Where's your passport?'

In my bag of course, except it's not and we start to search and look in every hiding place imaginable, in the fridge and the freezer, under the chair covers, amongst my knickers, and Nina's getting more and more agitated.

'That's it, we're not going to make it, bloody hell, Jesus Christ, I really could've done with a break,' she says quietly to herself though I hear her words.

I suddenly remember something and lift my mattress, and there it is. We make it to the airport and I fly to Israel.

Edith meets me at the airport and I tell her that I forgot my new coat on the plane. She goes to the officials and tells them and we hang about waiting for them to fetch it. They come back and say 'There's nothing there.'

'But it's my new coat,' I say. 'I left it on the plane.'

Nobody believes me. Edith is irritated, we're late and hungry and everyone will be waiting and there isn't a coat anyway! But there is, and now it's lost, and it's new. I don't speak to her. We drive all the way to the kibbutz and I don't say a word. When we get there she tells me she has to go out to the theatre as she has a ticket but I must be tired anyway so it doesn't really matter. She hasn't even made my bed and I have to make it while she goes out. I'm so angry with her, I remember how much I hate her.

In the morning I tell her she must phone the airport and tell them my coat is there, but she refuses. I can't even look at my sister, let alone talk to her. I'm so cross. I don't want to see anyone at the kibbutz. She persuades me to come for a walk and we walk along the beach. She points to an old man walking ahead of us.

'Look,' she says, 'there goes Natan.'

'Do I know him?' I ask.

She smiles. I seem to remember knowing him, but can't be quite sure. There are so many whose names I think I know.

We pull our skirts up and walk up to our knees in the water. It's cool and fresh and the water laps around us and threatens to go further up our legs. We laugh and I feel good again. We listen to music together and I close my eyes and see different colours whirling about and rushing around and I feel alive. She brings me cakes and I eat them, chocolatey, lemony, with strawberries, with raspberries. I'm happy.

I get back England and Nina fetches me and takes me back to my little flat. She asks me if I had a good time.

I say, 'No, I hate Edith, I don't want to see her again, I lost my coat and she wouldn't help me find it.'

'Your new coat?' Nina says.

'Yes, the new one,' I say.

I go for a walk. I don't understand why there are so few people around. Where are they all? Are they at work, at school? No-one is here. It's dark but then again it's winter and it gets dark so early in winter. I don't care. I walk and walk and it's good to walk and I feel good and there's a man there, and he comes towards me

'What are you doing out so late?' he asks.

I ignore him and walk past and he hurries up to me.

'Don't go away. Do you have some change? Just a few pounds and I can get a hostel place for the night.'

'What's the time,' I say.

'Gone midnight, two I think, got some change?'

'Leave me alone,' I say.

'I'm not doing anything to you, love,' he says, looking at me strangely.

I don't know this man, why does he call me love, he's going to hurt me, he's going to do something to me so I start to run away.

He stays behind and shouts, 'Just a few pounds. A hostel room. Please.'

But I run and run and then I don't know what happens but I'm on the ground and my arm is sore and I knock my head and I feel pains in my legs and head and all over my body. I get up and see there's my building. I'm not far away and I walk home.

In the morning the warden phones Nina.

'Ma,' she says, 'what the hell happened? Look at you. Black and blue. Ma, you can't stay here anymore, it's not safe, you're coming to live with us, with Sam and me and Janine. I'll look after you. I should've moved you in with me six months ago, Jesus I don't know what I was thinking. But you're coming now. You'll have a lovely room, our room, we'll move all your things in, you'll be really comfy. That'll be good, you'll like that, won't you, ma?'

I don't know what I'd like anymore.

It's night-time, I have to get out of here, quickly before they come. I gather the things I need and put them in my black bag. I move quietly to the door, but then she comes, she switches on the light.

'Ma! What you doing?' I hear her whisper.

'We've got to get out,' I say, 'they're coming and we haven't got passports.'

'Who's coming?' she asks.

Doesn't she understand anything, how can she be so calm.

'The Nazis,' I say, 'and we haven't got our passports.'

'But ma,' she says, 'listen to me. It's England. We're in England. There are no Nazis. This isn't Germany. This isn't the war. It's safe England. And it's 2001. November 2001.'

'Listen to me,' I say angry at her stupidity. 'The Nazis, dangerous,' and then I stop and I see her and I know who I am and where I am and I go back to bed.

I'm standing by the window, shivering, it's so cold, I don't know what to do, how I'm going to get through it.

'Granny? What are you doing' Janine says and touches my naked back. 'Where's your nightie? You must be cold. Let's put your nightie on. Have you been sleeping Granny? It's about one in the morning.'

'I'm so worried,' I say.

'What about?' Janine says, 'there's nothing to be worried about. What are you worried about?'

'I'm worried,' I say.

'What about, Granny?'

She hugs me and says, 'You've got nothing to worry about Granny, I promise you.'

I hug my little girl and I say to her, 'What would I do without you?'

She smiles and says, 'You don't have to do anything without me, Granny.'

She leads me to my room and helps me into bed and covers me with a soft duvet and kisses me on the forehead just as I used to do to her, and switches off the light.

'I have to go and see my sister,' I tell Nina.

She and Sam refuse to listen to me. I've been saying this for hours but they ignore me, they just keep their eyes fixed on that stupid television.

'Edith's expecting me,' I say, louder than before.

'But she's in Israel.' Nina says, exasperated.

'Well you keep saying that,' I say, 'but I have to go. I'm sorry Nina, honestly. She's going to be very worried. Don't be cross with me but she expected me already an hour ago. I can't keep talking to you. So, I'm off. I think I know the way. I'm sure I'll find it. I know where to go. So, don't worry and I'll see you later.'

I open the door and start to walk out and Nina comes to me.

'It's late and it's dark and it's bloody cold. You can't go off by yourself,' she shouts.

'Well I must,' I say looking back at her angry face, 'because I promised Edith I'd be there. And I'm late now so I have to go. So, I'm off. Bye.'

I walk up the road but I hear a door slam and a car pull up and it's Nina and she says, 'Get in, ma. I'll drive you.'

It's good to get out of the cold.

'Right,' Nina says stiffly, I can hear her irritation, honestly, she should be a bit nicer, 'you tell me where to go.'

So I tell her, 'Straight, now left, a bit further, right, to the end, left, ahhm, left here, ok, straight, yes, there it is.'

'That's just a building,' she says, 'we don't know anyone who lives here.'

'Yes, Edith lives here,' I say to her, politely I think, I don't want to be horrible like she is. 'I'll just go in and see. You can go.'

'I'll wait here!' she says.

I walk down the stairs and into the building and the door inside is locked so I look at the panel of bells on the side wall and look to see where Edith's name is and suddenly Nina comes running after me.

She grabs me by the sleeve and says, 'Come on, ma, let's go.'

'I can't quite remember which is Edith's,' I start to say.

She says, clenching her teeth, she barely opens her mouth, 'It's none of these. She bloody lives in Israel and this is England!'

I'm angry now because I promised Edith to come to her and Nina is stopping me from doing so. It's just plain rude.

'I'm NOT going with you because I promised her,' I shout.

She stops, it looks like she's breathing deeply, slowly and then she says, 'Look, I tell you what. Let's go home and you can phone her, phone Edith and tell her you'll be there later and that you're coming. Ask her exactly where she lives and then I'll take you there. How about that?'

'Yes, that's a good idea.' I smile at her, that's better, now she's being helpful.

After a while Edith answers the phone.

'Hello Edith,' I say,' I'm sorry I'm late but I'm coming now.'

Edith says, 'Rika! Why are you phoning so late, and what're you talking about?'

'Well I told you I was coming, I promised I would,' I say.

And she says, 'Rika, what's the matter. You live in England. Are you alright? Listen, go to bed and I'll speak to you in the morning, ok?'

And she puts down the phone.

Nina is sitting on the stairs looking at me.

'That bloody bitch,' I say to Nina and she walks me up to bed.

I don't know what to do. Nina tells me to sit and eat, she has to go to work.

'What will I do? I don't know what to do.'

'You won't be alone for long,' she says rushing off to work. 'The cleaner's coming at ten to be with you.'

'When?' I ask.

'At ten,' she says, 'she'll be here then, until about three, and then I'll be back at five, five thirty latest. So, you won't have to be alone for long.'

'Who's coming?' I ask.

'The cleaner. You know her. Her name's Lynn. She's really nice. You like her. I've got to go.'

'When's she coming?' I ask.

'At ten. It's eight now. Two hours.'

'And what must I do now?' I ask.

'Just eat. Eat your breakfast. Then you can watch telly until Lynn comes.'

'I don't know how to put it on,' I say.

'I'll put it on, just like I always do, and you can eat in front of the telly. Then it'll be on and you won't have to worry. Alright?'

'But', I say and she goes out the door. Gone. Alone.

I'm sitting in the lounge looking at that box and Nina comes in.

'Hello,' she shouts and sees me. 'What's the matter, ma? Why isn't the telly on?'

'I don't know how to switch it on,' I say.

'But it was on.'

'Yes, but then it wasn't.'

'Did you turn it off?'

'I don't know,' I say.

'Look,' she says, 'it's so easy to turn it on. I've shown you so often, can't you see' and she pushes buttons but I have no idea which ones they are and what she's doing, she's just pushing buttons.

'Bloody hell,' she says and walks out the room. 'This is so bloody, Jesus!'

I'm lying in the bath and Morris is sitting on the closed toilet, watching me. I'm not talking to him.

'What's the matter, ma?' he says, but I won't answer him.

I ruffle the water with my legs.

'Hmm?' he says again, 'what's wrong?'

I take no notice of him and splash water onto my stomach and flick the bubbles with my toes.

'Aren't you going to say?' he says. 'Well if you're not going to say, I'll go and wait outside.'

As he starts to go away, I say what's wrong. 'Why don't we live like husband and wife anymore,' I say.

'What!' he says.

'Why don't we have sexual intercourse anymore?' I say.

'Ma!' he says, 'I'm your daughter for Christ's sake!'

'Yes,' I say, 'that's what you always say.'

I'm so angry and upset.

I'm alone and abandoned. I've been abandoned by everyone in my life, first my mother and father, then my sister, then that man whose name I can't remember, then Morris when he died and now my own daughter.

No-one loves me.

I have lost everything and now I have nothing, nothing that is mine that belongs to me. I'm like a naked island in the middle of the deepest furthest ocean. There is nothing for me. It's all Nina's fault. It's because she, and then she, and she also... I won't talk to her!

'Ma,' she says, 'we're going next door, it's Burns night, come.'

I don't sleep.

'Ma, why are you so angry with me? What are you doing standing at that door with that bag and stick?'

I don't speak to her.

'Ma, don't run out there into the rain with only your coat on and no shoes. Come back!'

I don't listen to her.

'Ma, these people are going to take you away and help you.'

I leave her.

I lie as I have lain for so many years now, in this bed, in this room, unable to move any part of my body other than my fingers up to my mouth.

I lay as I have, unable to think, unable to hear, unable to make sense of anything happening to me or near me.

I'm the vegetable Gary was not, and have been for so many years now.

I'm not who I was, I'm another and yet I'm myself. Myself has changed over the years until I became unrecognisable and unknown.

In my state of sudden awareness, I know that I'm soon to die.

I see, though not with my eyes, I feel, though not with my fingers, I know, though not with this brain that gave up on me long before it was due.

I know that my children and grandchildren are around me, the people I have loved the most in my life. Even Edith is here. I look at her and watch her mourn for me. She is weak now, that strong one, but she is still alive. Always one better than me.

They are waiting for my last breath, just like I waited for Shaina Raisa's. They know it is time I stopped breathing, that it is long past time for me to stop breathing, that a dead brain that carries on living is not a good thing, it is far better simply to die.

Why did I carry on living beyond my life, into a living death?

Why would I not let go? Was it because I knew there is nothing after this? Mutti and Vati and Morris are not waiting for me. There is nothing beyond this. Perhaps I felt that something was better than nothing. But it was nothing anyway. Why didn't I realise this?

What was it like, this life of mine? It was just a life. Nothing more, nothing less.

It's time to go.

GLOSSARY

A mensch tracht un Got lacht - Man plans and God laughs (Yiddish)
Achturng! Vorsicht! – Beware (German)
Aruchat arba – 4 o'clock meal (small meal) Hebrew
Babala (or babela, bubela, cookela, schnookela) – all affectionate terms for a child (Yiddish)
Bandiet – prisoner (Afrikaans)
Baruch ha'shem – Blessed be God (Hebrew)
Bittere gelechte – sad joke (Yiddish)
Boychik – little boy (Yiddish)
Boykela – little boy (Yiddish)
Chas ve'chalila – God forbid (Yiddish)
Chevra – friends (Hebrew)
Cichel and herring – sweet flat biscuit and chopped herring (Yiddish)
Coave – hurts (Hebrew)
Daytschke – the German (Yiddish)
Felafel – chick pea ball (Hebrew)
Ganze mispocha – whole family (Yiddish)
Gefillte fish – minced fish made into a ball (Yiddish)
Geh weg – go away (German)
Goldene medinah – golden homeland (Yiddish)
Halva – sweet made of sesame seeds (Hebrew)
Hashomer Hatzair – Young Guard, a Jewish socialist youth movement (Hebrew)
Hau – Gosh, general exclamation (many African languages)
Hoppe hoppe Reiter, wenn du fällt da schreit er, fällt er in den Graben, fressen ihn die Raben, fällt er in den Sumpf, macht der Reiter plumps. – German song for children
Jees – gosh (Afrikaans)

Kak – shit (Afrikaans)
Kol Yisrael chaverim – all Israel are friends (Hebrew)
Kovah tembel – fool's hat (Hebrew)
Liebchen – darling (German)
Leberwurst – liver sausage (German)
Litvak – people from Lithuanian and Latvia (Yiddish)
Macha – important person (Yiddish)
Magen David Adom - Jewish Red Cross (Hebrew)
Matza kneidel – ball made out of matza meal usually put in chicken soup (Yiddish)
Mahal – international voluntary group that fought for Israeli independence (Hebrew)
Mein mann – my husband (German)
Melktert – milk tart (Afrikaans)
Mensch – good person (Yiddish)
Meshugenah – crazy person (Yiddish)
Meyn kind – my child (Yiddish)
Mishpocha – family (Yiddish)
Momzer – bastard (Yiddish)
Mutti – Mother (German)
Neshomela – soul (Yiddish)
Niemals ein lautes Wort, niemals ein schimpfwort – never a loud word, never a swear word (German)
Nudnik – pain in the neck (Yiddish)
Oy vay or oy yay yoy – oh dear, oh woe (Yiddish)
Patz im tochis - pain in the backside (Yiddish)
Penzione – small hotel (Italian)
Platz – square (German)
Pochedet – scared (Hebrew)
Rachmonis – pity (Yiddish)
Raus aus dem bett – get out of bed (German)
Schmendrick – idiot (Yiddish)
Schtum – quiet (Yiddish)
Schver kop – hard head (Yiddish)
Schwarze – blacks (Yiddish)

Schwimmen – swim (German)
Shabat – sabbath (Hebrew)
Shiksa – maid (Yiddish, derogatory)
Shlepped – trudged (Yiddish)
Shuw – Gosh (African sound)
Signorine, scendi da noi – girls, come to us (Italian)
Taiglach – sweet sticky biscuit from Lithuania and Latvia (Yiddish)Tchina – sesame seed paste (Hebrew)
Tefadel, geverit – enter, madame (Arabic, Hebrew)
Toi toi! – words after a wish (Yiddish)
Treif – not kosher (Yiddish)
Tzorres – trouble (Yiddish)
Vati – daddy (German)
Verkakte – bloody (Yiddish)
Wilde chaye – wild animal (Yiddish)
Wo ist mein Baby – Where is my baby (German)
Word wakker – wake up (Afrikaans)
Yebo – yes (Basuto)
Yid – Jew (Yiddish)
Yiddene - woman (Yiddish)
Yiddische – Jewish (Yiddish)
Yiddische Boche – Jewish boys (Yiddish)
Yiss – gosh (South African)

ABOUT THE AUTHOR

Gail Louw is a multi-award winning playwright and her plays have been performed throughout the world. In 2024, a Gail Louw Season of four plays was held at The Playground Theatre in London. In 2023, three plays were performed at the Edinburgh Fringe Festival.

Just a few examples of her plays: 'Blonde Poison' continues to be produced widely, with productions at The Sydney Opera House, Auckland, Berlin, South Africa and the USA. 'Duwayne' won Best New Play at Brighton Festival and Fringe 2014. 'Miss Dietrich Regrets' has been produced in Prague in Czech continually from 2017 to the present. 'And this is my friend Mr Laurel' began to tour in 2012 and continues to the present. 'Shackleton's Carpenter' is another play that has toured throughout the UK and Ireland and performed on the Queen Mary 11, together with playwriting workshops, during a crossing from New York in 2022.

Thirteen plays have been published in three collections and four standalone ones as well.

Before Gail became a full-time playwright and novelist, she was an academic at the Institute of Postgraduate Medicine in Brighton, where she has lived since moving to England from South Africa.

'Rika's Rooms' is Gail's debut novel.

***

Find out more information about Gail Louw at:
https://gaillouwbooks.com

Printed in Great Britain
by Amazon